RAGE FOR REVENGE

Alexandra's all-consuming passion for Darius Wentworth turned to all-enveloping anger when she discovered that this man of her dreams had, after the loss of his wife, taken a ravishing mistress, the incomparable and infamous Countess of Brentwood.

If Darius could play at love in that scandalous fashion, Alexandra would show him that she, too, did not lack for partners.

Waiting eagerly for her to say yes to marriage was the very wealthy if very boring Howard Ramsey. Waiting just as eagerly for her to say yes to a different proposal was Darius' own cousin Geoffrey, as handsome as he was notorious for his amorous exploits.

For an independent young lady like Alexandra, turnabout was fair play—but a most dangerous game. . . .

COME BE
MY LOVE

"Romantic in every sense of the word."

—*Seattle Times*

Current Regency Romances from SIGNET

(0451)

- [ ] **THE MARCHINGTON SCANDAL by Jane Ashford.**
  (116232—$2.25)*
- [ ] **A DEBT OF HONOR by Diana Brown.** (114175—$2.25)*
- [ ] **ST. MARTIN'S SUMMER by Diana Brown.** (116240—$2.25)*
- [ ] **LADY CHARLOTTE'S RUSE by Judith Harkness.**
  (117387—$2.25)*
- [ ] **THE SENSIBLE COURTSHIP by Megan Daniel.**
  (117395—$2.25)*
- [ ] **A SUITABLE MATCH by Joe Freeman.** (117735—$2.25)*
- [ ] **A SCANDALOUS BEQUEST by April Kihlstrom.**
  (117743—$2.25)*
- [ ] **FASHION'S LADY by Sandra Heath.** (118294—$2.25)*
- [ ] **A HIGHLY RESPECTABLE MARRIAGE by Sheila Walsh.**
  (118308—$2.25)*
- [ ] **A MARRIAGE OF INCONVENIENCE by Diana Campbell.**
  (118677—$2.25)*
- [ ] **THE DUKE'S MESSENGER by Vanessa Gray.**
  (118685—$2.25)*
- [ ] **THE AMERICAN DUCHESS by Joan Wolf.** (119185—$2.25)*
- [ ] **A VERY PROPER WIDOW by Laura Matthews.**
  (119193—$2.25)*
- [ ] **CAROLINE AND JULIA by Clare Darcy.** (120086—$2.50)*
- [ ] **THE CLERGYMAN'S DAUGHTER by Julia Jeffries.**
  (120094—$2.25)*

*Prices slightly higher in Canada

COME BE MY LOVE

DIANA BROWN

Ⓢ
A SIGNET BOOK
NEW AMERICAN LIBRARY
TIMES MIRROR

NAL BOOKS ARE AVAILABLE AT QUANTITY DISCOUNTS WHEN USED
TO PROMOTE PRODUCTS OR SERVICES. FOR INFORMATION PLEASE
WRITE TO PREMIUM MARKETING DIVISION, THE NEW AMERICAN
LIBRARY, INC., 1633 BROADWAY, NEW YORK, NEW YORK 10019.

SIGNET TRADEMARK REG. U.S. PAT. OFF. AND FOREIGN COUNTRIES
REGISTERED TRADEMARK—MARCA REGISTRADA
HECHO EN CHICAGO, U.S.A.

SIGNET, SIGNET CLASSICS, MENTOR, PLUME, MERIDIAN and NAL BOOKS
are published by The New American Library, Inc.,
1633 Broadway, New York, New York 10019

First Signet Printing, March, 1983

1 2 3 4 5 6 7 8 9

PRINTED IN THE UNITED STATES OF AMERICA

For my mother—
with love.

AUTHOR'S NOTE

Many of the remarks of the Reverend Sydney Smith (1771–1845) contained in *Come Be My Love* are his own, taken from his essays, letters and quotations, while diaries of others of the Holland House set have been used to create an accurate portrait of this illustrious Whig gathering.

Come live with me and be my Love,
And we will all the pleasures prove
That hills and valleys, dales and fields,
Or woods or steepy mountain yields.

CHRISTOPHER MARLOWE
The Passionate Shepherd to His Love

PART ONE

Wiltshire Moonraker

Good even, good fair moon, good even to thee;
I prithee, dear moon, now show to me
The form and the features, the speech and degree
Of the man that true lover of mine shall be.
—SIR WALTER SCOTT,
The Heart of Mid-Lothian

I

I FELL IN love with Darius Wentworth when I was twelve.

Even now I remember that day in late summer—unusually warm. Paul, my brother, and I had been playing by the stream that skirted the west boundary of my father's property, Seton Place, separating it from Charteris, the great estate of Lord Bladen, Darius Wentworth's father. The Wentworths, along with other powerful Whigs, had been raised to the peerage during the reign of William and Mary, at which time the head of that family had adopted the title Baron of Bladen. Charteris had, however, been in their hands long before it became a barony. It was the most extensive estate in our part of Wiltshire and was much renowned for the classical beauty of its Palladian mansion, which owed its design to Inigo Jones. It boasted a library unequalled in southern England, though on that summer day such a stuffy place was of little interest to me.

Paul and I had been playing French and English, and I had had to be Napoleon departing for Elba to Paul's victorious Wellington. Still I preferred Paul's company to that of my sisters even when at last I refused to be Napoleon anymore, the raft we had constructed for his exodus from Europe being decidedly flimsy, and Paul became absolutely repulsive with Sylvester, his pet frog, threatening to stuff him down the back of my dress. Finally I seized the poor creature from his grasp and threw him into the stream, thinking him better off there than left to Paul's uncertain devices. Paul, who was a year older than I and had a considerable advantage in size, caught hold of me and was about to throw me in after Sylvester when a voice called out, surprising both of us.

"Whoa there, young Cox-Neville, what are you about? Don't you think it's about time you started to treat a lady with some respect, even if she is your sister?"

Paul dropped his grip on my arms and flushed. I did also. I had never been called a lady before. In the uproar we had been making, we had neither of us heard Darius Wentworth ride up on the other side of the stream. We both knew him, of course,

3

though our families were not close because of what father always called the Bladens' damnable Whiggery, but I think it was the first time I really saw him.

He sat, reining his chestnut mare, his long, muscular legs encased in white buckskins and gleaming brown leather boots, a coat of nut-brown superfine enhancing the square set of his broad shoulders, his long face with its classic Wentworth nose and deepset grey eyes lit by a half-smile. I wondered for an instant if Sylvester had been changed into a prince, a most usual happening in fairy stories. I was suddenly aware of my own muddied exterior; my hands were covered with slime from the banks of the stream and my face, I suspected, was not much cleaner.

Paul recovered his composure somewhat, enough at least to reply, "But she threw Sylvester into the stream."

"Sylvester?"

"Yes, Sylvester. He's my pet frog, or was—now I'll never find him."

"I think it is for Sylvester to find you, and he will if he really wants to. Sit down quietly where you last saw him and perhaps he'll come back to you. There are times, though, when a loss may be a gain. I doubt very much that your mother would want Sylvester in her drawing room, and I've a strong suspicion that he may be much happier where he is."

With that he turned to me. How clear and direct was his gaze, yet I detected a trace of laughter in his eyes.

"As for you, Miss Cox-Neville, let's see, you're Henrietta, aren't you?"

"No," I answered quickly, annoyed at being mistaken for my younger sister, "I'm Alexandra."

"Alexandra, of course, how could I forget such a beautiful name. Perhaps you should go home and change that dress. You're awfully muddy and wet, and even though it's warm today, I don't doubt you could catch a chill."

I nodded silently, for no words I could think of seemed worthy of reply to such a paladin. He raised his riding crop in salute and spurred his horse to a trot, then a gallop. I stood transfixed watching his departing figure, imagining myself Queen Guinevere to his Launcelot.

"Come along," Paul ordered from the bank of the stream. "Come on, Alex, don't just stand there—help me find Sylvester."

"You heard what Mr. Wentworth said, Paul: you are to treat me like a lady and I am to go and change my dress."

"Oh, that stuff! Do hurry, Alex, you threw him in. He'll come to you. Please!"

"Well . . ." I hesitated. It was too fine a day to go home. "Since you said *please*." My haughty tones were reminiscent of my eldest sister, Eugenia, for whom I cared little but who had a triumphant way of putting people in their place with a word or sometimes just a glance.

I spent the next hour wading in the stream until I came upon a frog who looked remarkably like Sylvester, and I presented him to Paul.

"That's not Sylvester. I don't see that little brown spot Sylvester had behind his left ear," he complained.

"Frogs don't have ears," I decided, for I wanted to go home and think about my hero. Seeing Paul about to argue, an argument that might continue indefinitely, I hastened to add, "And even if they do, that spot was probably mud and it got washed off in the stream, just as you'd better wash off the mud behind your ears before mother sees it. I'm going home anyway, so if that's not Sylvester, you must find him yourself."

With that, I took off, holding my sopping skirts high above my ankles, bounded across the buttercups in the meadow and through the trees in our pear orchard until I came to our rambling greystone house, at which point I slowed to a more sedate pace in case anyone should be watching.

I went in through the kitchen, not wishing to run into mother, who would, I knew, appreciate the state of my dress even less than she would appreciate Paul's muddy ears, and asked Alice to bring me up some warm water.

"Been horseplaying in the stream again I see, Miss Alex," she sniffed.

"I have not." I lifted my head haughtily without looking at her. "I just sort of . . . fell in," and I ran upstairs before she could say anything else. Alice was my friend; Eugenia said I was far too familiar with her, but I liked Alice far more than I liked Eugenia. Of course, I liked almost everybody more than I liked Eugenia, even though she was my sister.

I washed and then I changed into my best white muslin dress, the one with the blue satin sash. Then I tied up my thick chestnut hair with a blue ribbon; as I did so I could not help wishing it were not quite so curly but resembled more Eugenia's sleek locks. I stood back and gazed critically at the results in the looking glass.

My eyes were almost exactly the same brown as my hair;

mother called them expressive, but I thought they were too far
apart for beauty. They were large; that I liked. But so, too, was
my mouth. There was nothing of the rosebud about that. I smiled
at myself and it became positively expansive, not at all what I
wanted even if it did make me look very happy. I wondered
whether repeating "true blue" over and over to myself would
help. I tried but I felt so silly I burst out laughing, my smile
broader than ever. Thank goodness my teeth were white and
even, since so many of them showed when I laughed. My
eyebrows were the next focus of my criticism. Why were they
not thin and arched instead of thick and straight. Oh, dear!

I turned to see as much of myself as I could in the oval mirror.
I was tall for my age, and my figure was just beginning to
develop. Yes, I decided, hands on slim waist, I would probably
have quite a nice shape, and perhaps that would offset my overly
wide smile and the fact that my nose tended to turn up ever so
slightly. I pushed the tip down to straighten it. I would be much
prettier if only my nose were as straight as Eugenia's. I sighed.
There was nothing I could do about it.

I sighed again, then I remembered *his* comment on my name—
Alexandra, such a beautiful name, he had said. It would have to
make up for my nose. I had always thought mother's choice of
names for us girls had been excellent: first Eugenia, then Cassandra
who was always Cassy for short, me, and then Henrietta, my
youngest sister whom we called Netty. But mother seemed not to
have taken the same pains in choosing names for the boys. I
thought them all most ordinary—Thomas, Paul and James, the
baby. I often wondered whether father had not chosen them,
boys being so much more important to him than girls. None of
them had the allure of Darius, a Persian king. I wasn't good at
history but I did know that Darius had been conquered by
Alexander, though the date I had been required to learn by heart
completely escaped me as dates always did. History always
repeats itself, our governess said, but she had managed to make
it so dull I had never wanted it to until now.

"Mrs. Darius Wentworth," I said aloud to myself in the
looking glass. One day, of course, Darius would be Lord Bladen.

I took up my journal and wrote in my best copperplate:

"Lord and Lady Bladen request the honour of your presence
at a reception in honour of the Prince Regent at 5 P.M. . . . ."

I paused, then added "sharp." It wouldn't do to be late for the
Prince Regent.

I leafed through my journal, looking over some of the stories I had written. The next one I wrote would be about Darius. I suspected that all the stories I wrote from then on would have only one hero.

I wandered over to my bookcase and took down a book of stories about King Arthur's court that Aunt Maud had given me on my last birthday. I had not been overly pleased with it then, for I had wanted the shiny, red top I had seen in Mrs. Stuckney's general shop in Linbury, but now I carried it over to the windowseat and turned to the picture of Sir Launcelot of the Lake, seated upon his horse, bedecked in full armour. Though I had not remarked it before, I now saw that he singularly resembled Darius Wentworth, though Darius was much better-looking. I turned next to the picture of Queen Guinevere, though I suppose I was closer in years to Elaine, the lily maid of Astolat, who had loved Sir Launcelot with a love that was her doom, for it was the queen who had won that knight's love. Unfortunately, Queen Guinevere looked nothing like me at all, having long, flaxen hair and pale blue eyes and a skin that had never been exposed to the sun as had mine. Nevertheless I started reading the story of their ill-fated love, but it was too sad. Tears streamed down my face at the thought of a love unfulfilled. Mine must never be so destined.

"There, now, you've gone and caught cold!"

Alice's accusing tones broke into my reverie and I jumped.

"Whatever makes you think so?"

"Your eyes—they're all watery."

"That's nothing," I wiped them hastily, "I was looking out towards Linbury and the sun got in my eyes, that's all."

And as if to prove my point, I scanned the outline of our village, nestling between the mysterious beauty of the Savernake Forest and the broad expanse of the Marlborough Downs. The most prominent point was the grey tower of St. Mary's, our parish church, which, as Mr. Linnell, our pastor, constantly reminded us, was the most beautiful proportioned in England, though all it brought to my mind was Mr. Linnell's interminable sermons, which I endured each Sunday with long-suffering forebearance, pinioned as I always was between father and Eugenia and as far away from Paul as was possible. The roofs of the village homes huddled around the church like grey lambs around an enormous ewe seeking to find warmth and comfort. There was little such solace in Mr. Linnell's exhortations.

Alice, standing behind me, pointed over towards the old Tudor house where our neighbours, the Fanshawes, lived.

"I know you wasn't out playing with Master Augustus or you'd never have got in such a state. He's a real little gentleman, he is."

"And a real sissy! Paul says even I have more daring, and I'm a girl."

Still I preferred Augustus to Howard Ramsey, who was older but so bossy and overbearing that I could not abide him. The Ramsey estate at Feltenham, some five miles from us, was still known as The Close though they had renamed it Ramsey Manor when they enlarged and remodelled the simple and elegant old house. The Ramseys had become wealthy in some kind of trade that was never discussed. Despite this defect—for father put a great store by lineage—they dined with us frequently, for their wealth, ill-gotten though it might be, coupled as it was with their staunch Toryism, made them acceptable social companions.

In the opposite direction, the towering outline of Charteris, with its classical Italianate facade, embellished by well-proportioned windows and surmounted by a balustraded roofline, bespoke harmony and perfect form even to my untutored eye. It was surrounded by a magnificently landscaped park with spacious, sloping lawns interspersed with giant Cedars of Lebanon. To approach it from Seton Place meant encircling its boundary of miles of sward and deeply wooded ridges, but Paul and I knew a shortcut through the woods behind our orchard, and it was by that route that we would raid their apple orchards when we had our fill of our own pears.

"Are you still friendly with the footman at Charteris, Alice?"

"You mean Miller?" Alice blushed slightly and busied herself pouring out the water in which I had washed and wiping the bowl.

"Yes, Miller—are you going to marry him?" I was suddenly avidly interested in their romance, as though a match between our parlour maid and the Bladens' footman would link our two houses.

"Goodness me, I don't know. A woman's got to be asked. What questions you do put, Miss Alex." Alice eyed me sharply. "Soon be dinnertime. Better get a move on and get out of that fancy frock or you're going to spoil it."

But when Alice left, I became so engrossed in gazing out towards Charteris and wondering what Darius might be doing there at that very moment that I did not hear the dinner bell and was startled when Eugenia burst into my room, calling for me to come down immediately. Eugenia, at sixteen, was the family beauty, tall and fair, with clear blue eyes. She resembled the Queen Guinevere of my book far more than I ever would.

"Mother will be furious when she sees you wearing your best frock! What on earth did you put that on for? It's not as though we have guests dining with us today. I suppose you got yourself filthy scrimmaging with Paul and had to change and now you've decked yourself up as though you're going to a party. Really, Alexandra, you have no sense of moderation," she railed as we descended the stairs together. Queen Guinevere would never have sounded so shrill, I decided, but I held my peace and made no reply, only apologizing for my tardiness to father and mother as I entered the dining room.

"If you are quite ready, Alexandra," my father's voice was edged with sarcasm as I took my place at the long table between Paul and Henrietta, "Thomas will proceed with grace."

Father, to me, was always larger than life, though he was, in reality, of moderate stature. My misconception may have stemmed from his alarming manner when rebuking us. At those not-infrequent times his bushy eyebrows, which formed a solid bridge across his nose, were raised high above his inordinately widened, dark, forceful eyes, and his already red complected face took on an even deeper hue, forcing attention on him to the exclusion of all else. He invariably filled me with a sense of guilt, possibly deserved since I was rarely entirely innocent of his charges. Little wonder, though, that I had a recurrent nightmare of being chased by a mad bull.

Thomas, my eldest brother, always placed at his right, promised to grow like father in every way, though he still had a full head of hair and his mouth was of a softer inclination than father's, which was usually drawn in a tight, straight line.

Eugenia sat to father's left and beside her was Cassandra, two years her junior. Cassy was not nearly as pretty as Eugenia; in fact most people said she was not pretty at all. She was short and rather plump, and her complexion lacked the lustre that made Eugenia so remarkable, but of my sisters she was my favourite. She was quiet and sympathetic, and she listened and never scolded.

A sidelong glance at Netty beside me showed that she was in her usual quandary of whether to admire or condemn an older sister who was constantly in trouble.

My mother occupied her usual place at the end of the table. I think she probably had been pretty in her youth, for she was still rather handsome, with her classical, oval face and her flawless skin. Despite the birth of thirteen children, only seven of whom had survived, her figure was still quite comely, but years of my father's dominance had aged her into a submissive posture which ill became her. I glanced up as her soft, sensitive eyes fixed questioningly on my white dress, and I breathed a silent sigh of relief when she made no mention of it as Thomas finished grace, merely passing the bread to James, whom she cherished as the baby of the family and who always sat beside her.

"And where, may I ask, have you been, Alexandra?" father enquired far too politely.

"In my room, reading," I replied dutifully.

"And what have you been reading?"

"The tales of King Arthur's court."

"Is that suitable for her?" he asked my mother. "Isn't there something undesirable in there, something about . . ."

"It's the book Aunt Maud gave me on my birthday," I interposed hastily.

"Very well, then, I suppose it is all right."

Aunt Maud was my father's sister, and I believe she was the only person of whom he stood in awe. "But remember, if you are late again this week, you will have to take your meals in your room for a period I will specify, and I can assure you that they won't be the same as those we have here in the dining room."

"Yes, father," I said, struggling with a piece of tough mutton and wondering whether bread and milk alone in my room might not be an improvement over both this food and this company.

Eugenia tossed her fair head and began to discuss the dinner we were to give the following week for the Ramseys. Since it was such a regular occurrence, I wondered at her interest, and then it occurred to me that she might have a mind to make a conquest of George, their eldest son. She had been flirting with Sebastian Fanshawe for some time, but I believed father had put a stop to that. The Fanshawes were not wealthy, and with eleven children to provide for, it was doubtful whether even Sebastian, the eldest, would inherit a great deal.

Even though Eugenia was not yet seventeen and would not have her London season for another year, she was allowed to attend many social functions. I thought she was lucky, but father was always more lenient with her than with the rest of us. It probably came of her being so pretty.

"I wish we could get in Bates to tune the piano," Eugenia said. "I'm sure it sounded quite odd last time I sang when the Harringtons were here."

"Are you sure it was the piano and not your voice?" Paul said, sotto voce, and I suppressed an appreciative giggle.

"Hush, Paul," mother cautioned, but all father said was, "Call him in if it is necessary," which surprised me, for father was usually against any expense not absolutely essential, and I'd never known him to be particularly fond of music. I suppose he was careful rather than parsimonious, for we had all of life's necessities but none of its frivolities. I never knew whether this was by constraint of circumstances or by father's design, but I suspected the latter, for though our estate was not large, he was a prudent manager, and mother had brought him a handsome settlement on their marriage. She had since been the recipient of a sizable bequest on the death of her mother, all of which had disappeared into the family coffers, along with the rents, to be ladled out by father in morsels and mites. I sometimes thought he found us as unworthy of receiving as did Mr. Linnell of the holy sacrament, which was begrudgingly offered thrice a year at Easter, Christmas, and Whit Sunday, those being the only occasions the communion table was decked with white linen and that pirivilege conferred on unworthy sinners.

It occurred to me that father's generosity in this instance might be occasioned by the thought of George Ramsey making a suitable husband for Eugenia. The Ramseys' wealth and politics were, I knew, to his liking, but my attention was drawn from this line of thought by father's next remark, addressed to my eldest brother.

"By the way, Thomas, Lord Bladen called this morning to offer you a seat in his coach when Wentworth returns to Oxford for Michaelmas term. I agreed, for it might not be a bad idea for you to get to know the ropes from him in your first year up there, though I know you'll be in Magdalen while he's at Christ Church, which may be just as well, for I don't want you to get mixed up with his political cronies. Apart from that I think Wentworth's quite a steady chap, and since this will be his last year up there, he can probably put you on the right path. I've no objection to Lord Bladen, either, for that matter, though why they are Whigs I'll never understand."

"Just so, father," Thomas agreed.

A long diatribe followed on the evils of Whig policies, which I did not follow partly because I have never followed father's harangues well but mainly because halfway through his monologue, I became aware that Paul had Sylvester, or the pseudo-Sylvester, in his pocket, or I should say Sylvester was in Paul's pocket until he popped out and looked around and then suddenly jumped to the floor. I felt him run across my feet, and a few moments later I saw an odd look on Eugenia's face and then she looked down and screamed and, jumping onto her chair, she overturned her plate.

"What on earth is the matter with you, my girl?" my father shouted, annoyed at the disruption of the meal but more so at the disruption of his discourse for he had just reached his favourite part, describing the methods of young Pitt in overthrowing the Whig aristocracy.

"It's . . . it's a frog," Eugenia shrieked.

"Don't be ridiculous and sit down," said father and turned to call the maid to clean up the mess when, unfortunately, Sylvester chose that moment to jump onto father's lap. At his muttered, "By God, you're right," the creature jumped from there onto father's plate and spluttered in among the green peas. Cassy screamed, as did Netty, and James chortled with delight. I never enjoyed anything so much in all my life and started to laugh too but I suddenly wondered whether that would not widen my mouth, so I reduced my laugh to a snigger, which brought down father's wrath upon my head.

"This is some of your doing, I have no doubt, Alexandra," he shouted, his face growing red. Infuriated at the mess Sylvester was making of his plate, he flicked at him with his table napkin, and Sylvester hopped from there across the table, upsetting a carafe of father's port before leaping across the room to make his escape through the service hatch. It was too much for me. Ladylike or not, I burst into laughter.

"You will go up to your room and stay there until I come to talk to you, do you understand?" father roared.

"Yes, father," I said meekly, and Paul, who throughout the fracas had assumed a distant expression of one unwilling to become involved, gave me a thankful glance.

"I'll bring you up something," he whispered as I left the table, but I shook my head. I would be only too glad to gain the quiet and solace of my own room, where I could dream of Darius.

II

EXCEPT FOR SUNDAY mattins I was confined to my room for a week, but I didn't mind. I caught a glimpse of Darius at the church service and again the following week when he came to call for Thomas to take him up to Oxford. We all gathered on the front steps to bid Thomas farewell. As Darius stood aside waiting for my brother, I found it difficult to believe that only three years separated them. Darius seemed so much older and so worldly. I wondered whether my brother would resemble him after the experience of Oxford, but I could not imagine Thomas with the same degree of self-assurance, the same debonair manner.

The Bladen coach with its four perfectly matched greys and the family crest upon the door—three white swans within an azure border—waited as mother tried not to cry and we all stood solemnly and one by one shook hands with Thomas. Darius caught sight of me and smiled.

"I see the frog saviour is here to bid you farewell, Cox-Neville. You may do well to take her as an example when you become bogged down in university precepts."

Thomas looked unhappy at being asked to consider me, whom he found completely beneath his contempt, as an example, and I was sure father saw in the remark confirmation of his judgement in punishing me for the incident in the dining room the previous week, but that was unimportant. I was elated that Darius had remembered me.

"Come now," Darius said to Thomas, wrongly attributing his long face to a reluctance to leave home, "don't look so glum. Remember, James the First said if he were not king he would like to be an Oxford man."

As they pulled away, all of us except father waving and Paul and James giving chase to the coach down the driveway, I envied Thomas the journey and the opportunity of enjoying for so many hours the company of my newfound love.

* * *

13

Paul was the first to notice a change in me.

"What's the matter with you?" he asked with asperity the third time I had refused to play outside with him.

"What do you mean?"

"Well, you won't play with me, and you're mooning around the house, and this morning I heard you tell Eugenia that you would like to go over to Charteris with her the next time she visits Margaret Wentworth. I know they won't let you listen to their talk, and you can't abide Patience, so why on earth would you want to go there?"

Paul was right. It was unusual that I should want to go to Charteris, for although Eugenia was friendly with Darius's seventeen-year-old sister, Margaret, I had never taken to his younger sister, Patience, who, although she was my age, was concerned only with feminine pursuits and wiles which theretofore had held little interest for me. However, in an effort to gain more frequent access to the home of my idol and to become better acquainted with his family, I had decided to cultivate her friendship. Eugenia had not been particularly pleased when I had suggested accompanying her, but she had begrudgingly acquiesced when I promised to behave with decorum. The morning we were to go I took such pains with my appearance, and during the visit I conducted myself in such a ladylike manner, that I believe she was surprised. I believe I had also surprised Patience, she of the carefully curled dark brown hair and immaculate garb, for I had agreed with all the views she expressed, though in truth scarcely any of them were my own, with the result that I received an invitation to return to see her doll collection.

It was because of my love for Darius that I learned the art of dissimulation as a means of achieving an end, that end being the ability to visit Charteris as often as I wished, to hear his name spoken, to become familiar with the rooms he graced, to be known by those he knew, to learn his likes and dislikes, to keep him with me even though he was far away, for to me at that time, Oxford represented the end of the earth. I soon discovered no prompting was necessary to hear his name, for he was idolized not only by all the members of his family but by the servants also. Once, on my way to examine Patience's doll collection, I had managed to slip away and peep into his bedroom. It was a large, airy room dominated by a four-poster canopied bed and a huge wardrobe. I studied the contents of his bookcase. Bentham's *Principles of Morals and Legislation* looked dull; preferable was Scott's *Waverly* and Byron's *Childe Harold,* next to which a slim volume, *Black Marigolds,* caught my eye. But Patience's petulant calling of my name prevented my opening it. I had time only to run my fingers lovingly across the monogram engraved on the silver-backed brushes on his dressing table before hurrying from the room and carefully closing the door behind me. How his sister would laugh and tease if she ever discovered my passion. Mine was a lonely love.

Lord Bladen I liked tremendously, and not simply because Darius resembled him, having the same deepset eyes and that straight Wentworth nose, haughty yet befitting his craggy face. There was dignity and grace in his bearing that no education could bestow, yet he was not a handsome man, and it was obvious that Darius had inherited his regularity of features from his mother, a comely woman, though when first I knew her I stood in awe, finding her cold and exacting.

I took pains to maintain my ladylike conduct not only at Charteris but also at home, much to Paul's disgust, so that it was remarked how much I had suddenly grown up. Would Darius also notice the change in me when he came home, I wondered. Patience certainly did. I had once heard her describe me as a tomboy who could never stay clean from one minute to the next, and my new mode of behaviour did not altogether please her, for she would often try to goad me into pranks or acts of caprice.

One day she had been particularly galling, wishing, I think, to force me into a dispute. I held my temper, knowing that if I quarrelled with her, my visits to Charteris might be at an end.

"Now you're such a little lady I suppose you've forgotten how to climb trees," she jeered.

"Of course I haven't. I just don't wish to anymore."

She stopped as we walked along the stone path that skirted their orchard.

"What a pity!" She pointed up into one of the apple trees. "I would so like to have an apple, but they are quite out of my reach."

"Goodness me, they're hardly out of reach at all. It would only mean getting into the fork of those main branches and reaching over. I could get them easily—if I wished," I retorted.

"But what if you fell? You might hurt yourself. I bet you're scared."

"Of course I wouldn't fall. I've climbed much more difficult trees than this one—when I used to climb trees, that is."

"I really would like one of those apples, but I wouldn't ask you to get it for me, since you're scared."

"I am not scared. Here, hold this."

I pushed into her arms a bunch of autumn foliage I had gathered and hoisted my skirts and was in among the branches in an instant. I leaned over to pick an apple, but Patience called up to me that the fruit was much larger and riper further out on the branch, and I crawled out in the dirction she was pointing. As I leaned forward to pick the biggest and reddest of them all, I heard a sickening creak and then a cracking as the limb broke. I reached for another branch, but it was too slight to bear my weight. The last thing I heard was a resounding snap as the branch gave way. For a moment I was aware of Patience's horrified face, then the crazy paving of the path rising inexorably towards me.

I regained consciousness in a bedroom that was not my own. At my bedside I recognized the anxious faces of Lady Bladen and my mother. Behind them stood Linbury's apothecary, Mr. Wilson.

"Thank goodness, she's opening her eyes at last." I heard Lady Bladen sigh with relief. "My dear Alexandra, you had us all so worried. How do you feel?"

I assured them I was all right, but when I went to move my head, it ached, and I flinched.

"You are not to move. Mr. Wilson says you should stay here until you feel completely well. Your mother and sisters can come to see you whenever they wish, but I refuse to send you home until I am quite satisfied that you are perfectly well. We shall take great care of you."

I was sure they would. I nodded and closed my eyes and went back to sleep, gratified by the realization that my accident, untoward as it was, had placed me where I most wished to be.

My stay at Charteris lasted well over a month, and it was then I became acquainted with its great library which, occupying as it did the whole west side of the house, was considered, with good reason, to be its most majestic room.

The walls, for the most part, were devoted to bookcases from floor to ceiling, and those that were free of books were covered with Cordova leather. The Bladen crest was carved over the great fireplace, before which was a large bearskin rug. The ceiling, comprising seven vaulted compartments, was of oak, each compartment decorated with a painting of a scene from Homer's *Odyssey*.

The library was a majestic room, yet it was one to which I became accustomed and which became a home for me. It was there I was carried from my room when Mr. Wilson pronounced me well enough to leave my bed. A chair was set for me at the fireside, and beside it a table with a selection of books especially chosen for my enjoyment by Lord Bladen. I think my interest in reading surprised him, his own daughters not caring to pass their time in like manner, and he came daily to discuss with me what I had read, asking me to question him on anything that needed explanation and suggesting further readings in which I might be interested. It was for this reason that I remained so long, for I was probably capable of returning home before two weeks of my stay at Charteris had been completed. But I so enjoyed the hours spent in the library and the interest Lord Bladen took in me that I preferred to remain there and continued to complain of head-aches long after they had ceased. This deception was not entirely fair to Patience, who felt responsible for my mishap and had been particularly kind to me during my stay in her home, insisting I accept her favourite hair comb as a present, but unscrupulously I did not enlighten her as to my bettered state of health. When at last I knew I must return home, my father having visited me twice to ascertain for himself my condition, I acknowledged to Lord Bladen how unhappy I was at the thought of leaving behind all the books and the hours of enjoyment I had spent in his library and in his company.

"But that is ridiculous," he said. "We are neighbours. Seton Place is only a stone's throw from Charteris. There is no reason you shouldn't come here as often as you wish. I'm sure no one except me uses this collection when Darius is away, and it is a great shame, for I and my father and his father before him have spent a great deal of time and effort in its accumulation. If you wish me to, I can set out a plan for your reading. I can assure you it would give me the greatest pleasure. I will, of course, ask your father's permission first. Then you may come here as often as you wish in order to read, or you may take the books home with you and read them there if you would prefer."

"Oh, no," I insisted, "I would much rather read here. It is so quiet and comfortable. Our home is not as large as Charteris, and there are so many people around that it is sometimes very difficult to find a quiet spot, especially when the weather is bad and I cannot go out of doors."

"Very well, then, that is settled," he asserted.

Lord Bladen was as good as his word. He put a great deal of time into a planned approach for me to read the books he considered essential to a humanistic education, and he must have used all his charm on father, for I was amazed when he gave his permission for me to visit Charteris to pursue my studies after my return home. Perhaps he thought that it was an inexpensive means for me to obtain an education, though since he did not believe in educating women, I doubt that that could have persuaded him. He was, of course, not insensible to the fact that it gave our governess more time to devote to the studies of my younger brother and sister. Whatever had occasioned his decision, I took care to behave with propriety in his presence, and my ladylike conduct pleased him. He may have thought my reading had improved my manners, though I cannot guarantee this to be a necessary corollary. Rather my good manners stemmed from a desire to continue my visits to Charteris, and I knew that to incur father's displeasure was a sure means of exscinding that pleasure.

I can vouch for the fact that the course of study planned for me by Lord Bladen completely changed my life. It produced a whole world for me that had never before existed, a world of ideas expounded by great minds throughout history but that became co-joined in my head, one complementing the other, and by my own absorption and rearrangement becoming to some extent my own. It was an exciting experience and one that I believe Lord Bladen enjoyed as much as I did. Whenever we discussed these ideas, he encouraged me always to give my own views. At first I was reluctant to do so, fearing ridicule at worst or to be discovered to be ignorant at best, but his patient, considerate attention at last overcame my fears until I was able to express myself freely, without qualm, to one who was an understanding teacher and who soon became my great friend.

My education was not solely confined to books on the library shelves, for when it was fine, Lord Bladen would take me walking with him across the sweeping lawns, over the Palladian bridge, to the oak woods beyond, and he would tell me about the Wentworths.

"My great-grandfather, like me, was a Septimus—Septimus and Darius have been Wentworth names for generations. Of course, he was very old when I knew him, but still a great wit. He helped form the Kit-Kat Club along with the Dukes of Marlborough, Richmond, Grafton, Devonshire and others in the time of Queen Anne."

"I've never heard of the Kit-Kat Club."

"It no longer exists, but then it was the gathering place for all the most powerful Whigs of the day. It was named for the

mutton pies of a most excellent baker called Christopher Kat.
The club was famed for its weekly dinners and its members'
toasts to renowned beauties of the day, whose portraits were
hung in the club room. Wait a minute. See that?'' He stopped
suddenly to lean down and examine the tracks of an animal. ''A
fox has been this way. Notice how the footprints form an almost
perfectly straight line.'' Then, as we started to walk again, he
resumed discussion of his great-grandfather Septimus, who had
known Steele and Addison. ''Addison favoured the Kit-Kat because it was founded around eating and drinking, possibly the
only points about which men can agree.''

As we rounded a bend in the path, Lord Bladen stopped again
with a cry of joy. ''There! I knew there was a reason we came
by this path this morning. What utter perfection!''

Before us in the hedge was a swarm of bell-shaped heads of
the deepest blue atop pale green lissom stalks, nodding in the
morning breeze—the spring's first bluebells.

''The bluebell stands for that which is most desirable—constancy
in love—even that old cynic Voltaire said, 'Change everything,
except your loves.' The bluebell's close cousin, the harebell, so
like it in every way except that it blooms later, means submission—
'O calm, dishonourable, vile submission!' to quote the Bard.
Perhaps that is the reason I love bluebells and give barely a
passing glance to the harebell!''

I thought over everything Lord Bladen told me. Constancy
was perfection. I would always be constant in my love for
Darius. As for submission, I had seen all I wished of that ignoble
posture in my mother and in others, too, married ladies for the
most part. Marriage to Darius would never be like that, yet as
my mind expanded, I longed for a purpose in life as well as
marriage. I saw and rejected the lot of others of my sex, decorative and bored, employing their hours at handcrafts or household
tasks that began again as soon as they were finished, filling their
days as inexorably as the waves had surrounded Canute's throne
despite all his commands to them to turn back. I wanted more
from life—more than Eugenia, pining for admirers and balls;
more than Cassy, wishing for beauty; more than Netty, playing
with dolls and dreaming of motherhood; more than mother,
distracted by a thousand little cares, none of which would have
any meaning in a year, a month or even a week. Would the
world ever offer me more? I made up stories in which it did,
stories I copied into my journal late at night when everyone
slept, stories with one hero, Darius, a hero who championed

right and justice and who always won the day, with me at his side, constant in love yet an active participant in life.

I was at Charteris when Darius came home for the holidays. Such preparations there were for his return as though he had been away a decade rather than a term. Hams were made and bacon cured and mock turtle soup liberally laced with Madeira wine and pigeon pies baked with the flakiest pastry imaginable.

Margaret embroidered handkerchiefs with his initials, and Patience bought him a frame for the miniature of Lady Bladen. I wrote him a poem of welcome in my very best hand yet would not have had the courage to give it to him had not Lady Bladen seen it, loved it and immediately rolled it up and tied it with a lavender ribbon and placed it with his other presents.

At the sound of his carriage on the driveway, everyone hurried to the doorway to see him spring down and bound up the steps, handsomer than ever, to greet his father and kiss his mother, then Margaret, then Patience. Turning to me, he tousled my hair before bending down to buss my cheek.

"I see I've acquired another sister, and a very pretty one. What a fortunate man I am!"

I found myself in heaven, to be with him daily, to have him as a companion on our walks, to hear him read aloud as we sat together after lunch when I found myself listening to and memorizing his voice rather than the content of the book he was reading. All too soon he returned to Oxford, but then I had his note of thanks for my poem, addressed "To the Most Amiable and Charming Poet of Seton Place." The envelope bore his seal; the note was signed with a flourished *D*. I slept with it under my pillow until, afraid it would crease, I put it between the leaves of my journal. Never a day passed without my rereading it, hardly a necessary act since I knew its contents by heart.

He returned briefly upon graduation, only to leave again for a tour of Europe that was to last almost a year. I heard of the places he visited through the letters he sent home, all of which were shared with me.

I dreamed I was with him in Paris and Versailles, at the site of the Battle of Waterloo near Brussels, in the Black Forest of Germany at Christmas and at last in Italy, where he stayed for so long that Lord Bladen began to fear he would join up with Byron and the exiles, never to return.

But return he did, his skin bronzed by the Italian sun, a bronze that turned the grey of his eyes to a startling, piercing intensity. Until then I had always thought of grey as nondescript. He had changed little, except there was an easier grace and charm about him, a greater readiness to laugh, to enjoy life.

"Is this really Alexandra, the frog saviour?" he had demanded when he saw me. "Such a handsome young lady. Why, you must be as tall as Margaret."

"I'm taller," I asserted.

"But not as contrary, I hope. Promise you won't tease me as she does, for I swear I can't stand it."

But of course he revelled in every minute of the love and affection with which he was held by his family. And he treated me just as one with his sisters, something I found difficult to bear, for my feeling for him was so far from sisterly. I wanted him to single me out, but not as he did.

"You've no idea what you mean to father, Alexandra. Do you know he talks of you more than he does of his daughters, he is so proud of you. He knows of no other young lady who would employ her mind as you do."

"Perhaps it is because so few have the opportunity to do so. Whatever I have learned I owe to his patience and kindness in teaching me. I am very fortunate."

"No more fortunate than is he in having your companionship. Everyone regards you as part of the family, myself also, and I must confess my delight at acquiring yet another sister—such a sweet, intelligent one at that."

He squeezed my hand affectionately.

"I know you are blessed with several brothers, but I should be honoured if you would consider me as one of them. If ever I can help you, you have but to ask."

It was said with such sincerity, such depth of feeling, yet not with the feeling I desired to arouse in him. He admired me, yes, yet nothing in his remarks could be construed, even in my wildest imagination, as loverlike. While I thought of no one else, I had no reason to believe that when I was out of sight, he thought of me at all.

He soon left for London and its pleasures, and I remained with his parents' speculations on his future. They were anxious he should not become an idler in the clubs or embroiled in gambling with his friends. He was expected to follow in his father's steps, in the steps of those who had gone before him, leading an easy yet examined life, above all providing an heir for Charteris. My heart sank at the thought. I could not bear to see him marry anyone but me. Surely he must one day view me in a different light: not as a sister, not as his father's protégée but as a woman, a desirable woman.

Margaret was presented at court that year, and the Bladens left to stay in their town house for her coming out. I continued going to Charteris in their absence, but I missed them. Constantly my thoughts wandered, even from my recreational reading of *Tristram Shandy* or Byron's *Giaour* or the poetry I myself had begun to write, wandered to life on Great Stanhope Street. What were they doing, I wondered, but more especially what was that one person doing around whom my imagination was constantly centred.

It was at tea one day that Mrs. Ramsey, Linbury's very own Lady Sneerwell, as Cassy and I secretly called her, told mother of Margaret's engagement.

"Mr. Ramsey was in town last week on busin . . . on a matter requiring his attention, and he ran into Lord Bladen. Overjoyed he was, for Margaret is to marry Sir Nigel Armbruster, son of a friend of Lord Bladen's, someone he was up at Oxford with or something of the sort."

I stopped in the midst of pouring tea. Marriage is like a flaming candlelight, we used to sing, placed in the window on a summer's night, inviting all the insects of the air to come in and singe their wings.

Mrs. Ramsey lowered her voice very slightly. "They do say that Darius Wentworth is besotted with this year's favourite. I must say for my own part I'm sick of the sight of her name. It's impossible for a single issue of *Lady's Magazine* or *Ackermann's* to come out without some mention of her."

"I know who you mean," mother nodded.

"But I don't. Who is it?" I cried out in agitation.

Mrs. Ramsey rarely wasted her gems of information on me—I was to be seen but neither heard nor spoken to—but in this instance, her news being of such import, she could not resist.

"Why, Philomena, the Earl of Flaxton's daughter, of course." She turned back hastily to mother, lowering her voice again though each word was sharp and clear as though addressed directly to my heart. "Of course Lord Bladen would say nothing on the matter, though Mr. Ramsey pressed him for details, but he didn't deny it, mind you. Mark my words, there'll be wedding bells twice in the Bladen family this year or my name's not Maud Ramsey."

The cup of tea I was at that moment passing to Mrs. Ramsey clattered precariously in its saucer.

"Do be careful, Alex," mother cautioned.

"You're looking quite peaked," Mrs. Ramsey enjoined. "That's funny, because when I came in I thought you quite the blooming rose."

"Roses fade," I said bitterly.

"Hardly, at fifteen. But have you noticed the Fanshawes' eldest girl," Mrs. Ramsey warmed to a new morsel. "I saw her in the village just yesterday. 'Dear me,' I said to myself, 'dear me, they're going to have a time with her, no colour at all, and no money to boot.' "

III

THE BLADENS RETURNED from London with Margaret and her affianced husband, Sir Nigel Armbruster, a likeable young man. Darius soon followed them, accompanying the Earl and Countess of Flaxton and their daughter, Philomena. She was all that the society columns had raved of: petite, perfectly proportioned, possessed of lustrous raven hair and imperious dark eyes. She was very, very beautiful and I hated her on first sight.

She flirted outrageously with Darius, looking deep into his eyes and tapping his arm with her fan to emphasize her words, spoken in so low a tone they were impossible to overhear. She seemed always to be chilled, for Darius was constantly placing her shawl around her shoulders; I observed how his fingers lingered there as he did so.

Her dress was as elegant as unlimited wealth, doting parents and impeccable taste could command. I don't believe I saw her twice in the same attire. I had to admit that she wore each creation with an air of elegance and distinction that came naturally to her but to which I knew, even were I not wearing Eugenia's hand-me-downs, I could never aspire. She did not deign to notice me as she did Margaret and Patience, or, if she did, she never acknowledged me. If she came into the library when I was there, she might smile in an abstract fashion in the general direction of the chair in which I was sitting, but she never spoke a word to me directly. I'm not sure she knew who I was; if she did she certainly considered me completely beneath her attention. I prayed that Darius would not marry her. I knew that prayer should not be used in such a manner and, as if to prove this to be so, mine went unanswered.

It was from Eugenia, who had been presented at court the previous spring on the same day as Philomena and who had had some slight acquaintance with her afterwards at balls and routs they had both attended, that I learned that Darius had proposed, had been accepted, and that a date had been set for the wedding. Eugenia told me in confidence the day before the announcement was officially made, proud, I am sure, of being privy to Philomena's confidence rather than of the grief she was unknowingly causing me. I cried so much that night that I was unable to go to Charteris the next day; I was relieved at least of having to toast the health of the happy pair. I could not dissemble, I could not pretend to rejoice at their happiness, but I knew I had no right to dampen the Bladens' joy.

The wedding was to take place in May at St. Mary's, our parish being situated more conveniently to London than the Flaxtons'. Eugenia was preening herself because Philomena had asked her to be a bridesmaid. I bitterly muttered that wantons marry in the month of May, but little good it did me; I knew I would have been only too willing to take Philomena's place in May or any other month. Particulars of their wedding tour to Europe were regaled to me with as much detail as could be discovered. I heard even more of the home they were to establish in Grosvenor Square, in a house given to them by the Earl as a wedding present. But at least I was grateful they were to settle in London; I could not have borne to see Darius in daily attendance on that frivolous creature, had they settled in our neighbourhood. As it was, I could not bear his all-too-obvious elation at his coming marriage. I avoided him whenever possible, leaving the room whenever he entered until at last he asked whether he had done something to offend me and whether he might make amends. It was said in such friendly, affectionate tones that I burst into tears and ran home. The next day I apologized, putting the blame on Descartes' *Discourse*, which I had been studying.

"Perhaps you are studying too hard," he suggested gently.

"Oh, no, no," I hastened to assure him, fearing that I might be separated from the books that had become my only solace. "It's not that, I assure you."

"Well, then, what is it? And don't say nothing, for I know there must be something. You don't talk to me as you used to; in fact you scarcely talk to me at all. You are downcast and wan.

Father has noticed it and is quite concerned. I am also. Are you sure you are quite well?''

"I am, I assure you I am.''

"Then leave this heavy stuff aside. Let me choose your reading for today, something a little light, a little frivolous. Frivolity becomes young ladies.''

"Frivolity is idle, empty. Why is it that men look for it in women?''

"Frivolity is also gay and imponderable and therefore to be treasured.'' He handed me a copy of Fanny Burney's *Evelina*. "She is, perhaps, a little vacuous, but nevertheless fun.''

"But this is a romance,'' I protested. "Your father has little time for such stories.''

"I have no wish to denigrate my father's opinions. Nevertheless, that heavy stuff he gives you needs some leavening. Today, as a favour to me, read *Evelina*. You may return to Descartes tomorrow if you wish. One romance will not mar your serious soul.''

And I did as I was bid, though I found the tale of that young lady's entrance into the world and her triumphant uniting with Lord Orville the more heartrending, reminding me as it did of my own shattered hopes.

I must resign myself. I consoled myself that at fifteen I was far too young to marry, yet even when I tried to be brave, I knew I would never love any man in my life as much as I loved Darius at that moment.

As the day of the wedding approached, I grew so thin and pale that mother threatened to dose me with Mr. Wilson's physic to bring the colour back to my cheeks; I would have willingly taken that horrid potion had it been a means of avoiding the ceremony.

Eugenia delighted in her role in a wedding that had been the highlight of all activity in our neighbourhood ever since its announcement. When, three days before it was to take place, she came down with chicken pox, she reacted as though it were the plague. Actually it was a mild case. The only apprehension mother had was that it might leave scars on her lovely complexion, but Eugenia wailed bitterly. It made her attendance on the bride impossible. Cassy tried on her gown to see whether she might serve in her stead, but not only was she shorter than Eugenia but she was also much plumper. It would require a new dress if she were to take Eugenia's place; being excessively shy, she protested vehemently at the very thought.

It was mother who suggested, over Eugenia's outward vociferations and my own equally vehement inner ones, that the dress might fit me. But mother insisted, and reluctantly I tried it. It was a perfect fit.

"Thank goodness! I was so worried, for I couldn't bear for us to be the cause of disturbing such a carefully planned event. Not one alteration required, and Eugenia will tell you exactly what you have to do."

"But I can't mother," I wailed.

"Of course you can."

"I can't. I can't."

"Why on earth not?" mother demanded. "You know how important it is, and I assure you that you will have a lovely time. Not many young ladies of your age have the opportunity to serve at such an elegant wedding. And we'll cover your hair with a floral garland, real spring flowers. You'll be very pretty, dear."

"I only hope she behaves herself," Eugenia glowered from her bed where she lay, her face whitened with calomine lotion and her fingers bound to prevent her from touching the itchy pustules.

"Don't be unfair, Eugenia," mother remonstrated, "You yourself have remarked what a perfect lady Alex has become."

"Then let's hope she keeps it up. I should hate anything to happen to Philomena's wedding on our account."

"Of course it won't," mother said sharply.

Philomena viewed the change with disdained resignation; I viewed it with horror. The fact that I not only had to be at the ceremony but now had to witness it, to be a part of it, was excruciating. The deepest circles of Dante's Inferno could have presented me with no greater penance, yet it became impossible for me to withdraw from the role thrust upon me. Miserably I listened to my instructions, while Netty acted out the role of the bride with a large tablecloth draped over her head under which James hid, insisting it was a tent. I rehearsed my duties in so perfunctory a manner that I was still being reminded of them up until the moment we set out for the church.

Thus it was I found myself bearing the antique lace train of Philomena's white figured-satin gown, trimmed with orange blossoms especially brought from Spain, down the candlelit aisle of St. Mary's, past pews filled to their capacity with friends and relatives of both families resplendent in their silks and satins, under the watchful gaze of the four evangelists who gazed dispassionately on the fashionable scene from their canopied niches high above the altar.

It was at the altar that Darius stood awaiting his bride, solemn yet eagerly impatient as he followed her progress towards him until at last they stood side by side, his tall, broad-shouldered figure clad in a dark blue velvet cutaway coat with pearl grey knee breeches, to the right of her slight figure with its tiny waist from which the satin curved, covered by the lace train which was in my miserable grasp.

"Dearly beloved, we are gathered together here in the sight of God and in the face of this congregation to join together this man and this woman in holy matrimony."

It was clearly Mr. Linnell's moment of triumph. His voice was nasal yet resonant as the words echoed through the nave, off the uneven crown glass of the windows, through which I could glimpse the yews and elms and the clouds drifting carelessly by. My hands shook; I tried to force them to be still but couldn't. I felt horribly sick. I had eaten nothing for several days, but that morning mother had insisted that I take several mouthfuls of cook's fresh hog's head pudding to provide me with stamina.

"Into which holy estate these two persons present come now to be joined. Therefore if any man can show any just cause why they may not lawfully be joined together, let him now speak or. . . ."

My stomach regurgitated violently I had an appalling desire to cry out. Instead I knew beyond a doubt that I was going to be sick, very sick. I turned and ran towards the church door clenching my teeth with all my might lest I desecrate that holy place.

Mr. Linnell had stopped speaking abruptly. I suppose he thought that for the first time since taking orders, a just impediment had been found. So, probably, did everybody else as all turned to mark my miserable progress.

I looked back briefly to catch Philomena's furious gaze at such an affront to her ceremony. I could not bring myself to look at Darius. Mother rushed up to lead me from the church and once outside I could no longer control my stomach and I wretched violently, spewing forth a mouthful of foul smelling, foul tasting phlegm.

The coachman was immediately instructed to drive me home and I lay back against the carriage cushions in silent relief at having escaped the ordeal of actually listening to those irrevocable vows.

"I knew she would do something awful. How too disgusting! If she had to feel ill, why couldn't she have fainted. It would have been a sight more ladylike. But to vomit—how could she do such a thing to me! Now Philomena will never speak to me again," Eugenia wailed. "Alexandra, surely you could have waited until the ceremony was over."

"I'm quite sure she wouldn't have done it if it could have been otherwise, for it was quite awful—the smell . . ." Mother shuddered faintly. "But she wouldn't do something like that on purpose. I don't doubt that she is coming down with the chicken pox also, and I suppose the little ones will get it too."

But I did not come down with the pox. The next day I was at Charteris apologizing to Lord and Lady Bladen for my unfortunate mishap. They were delighted to see me well. Their only sorrow was that I had missed the ceremony, for it had proceeded without a hitch after I had left. They had saved me wedding cake, which I promised to sleep on so I might dream of the man I would marry. Margaret and Patience regaled me with each detail of the wedding feast and everything that had been said and done, minutely describing Philomena's blue silk pelisse and bonnet of white crepe over satin, trimmed with Danish blue satin and parma violets, in which she had left with Darius on the first stage of their wedding trip. Despite my despair, I listened avidly to each detail, each striking me as surely as the asp had struck at Cleopatra's breast, like a lover's pinch that hurts yet is desired.

IV

LORD BLADEN WAS fond of telling me that books teach us to enjoy life or to endure it. It was the latter function they fulfilled for me during that long summer and autumn after Darius married. Though I had escaped actually hearing Mr. Linnell's words, "What God hath joined together let no man put asunder," still those words revolved in my head like the carp in the lake behind Charteris, which, even when they could not be seen, were inescapably there. My dreams died hard; in fact I cannot honestly say they died at all. Yet in continuing to love Darius, I knew I broke the tenth commandment, and each Sunday I prayed for forgiveness, only to begin each new week desiring him as much as ever.

Life at home continued uneventfully, though the atmosphere

had become more lugubrious since Eugenia's coming out. It was not that her London season had been unsuccessful. That is to say, she had been much admired and had received a multitude of invitations and had danced every dance whenever she went to a ball—by such criteria she could be said to have taken—but her season had not resulted in the hoped-for and anticipated goal of any young lady's season: a suitable proposal of marriage. Her admirable face and figure had been insufficient to overcome the size of her marriage portion, and no request for the bestowal of her hand had come from the more noble, the more wealthy of her admirers. She had returned to Linbury in a lamentably unpleasant frame of mind, and as time passed and no suitable prospects presented themselves, she became increasingly cantankerous. I was glad to have my daily escape to Charteris, to be free for a few hours from her critical eye and sharp tongue.

It was with some relief, therefore, that I heard her former admirer, George Ramsey, had returned. He had been in Yorkshire attending to business matters for his father. At one time it had been rumoured that he was to marry an heiress from the north, but the match had failed to come about because, I overheard Mrs. Fanshawe tell mother, her fortune had not been nearly as large as he had been led to believe, and since she was no beauty, he was not to be persuaded to cast his lot for her.

When next the Ramseys dined with us, George was with them. Eugenia took particular care with her toilet that day. I must admit she showed to great advantage in her London gown of yellow sarcenet surmounted by a white frilled bodice, the skirt just short enough to reveal her shapely ankles. She preserved just the right degree of amiability towards her former admirer without appearing overanxious to see him, and I, knowing full well the pains she had taken to please, could not help but marvel at her subterfuge. Her manner of talking on positive nothings as though they were the most fascinating subjects in the world, an art she had perfected during her London stay, was stifling yet oddly intriguing, and Netty took to copying her. Was that what Darius had meant by frivolity becoming young ladies, I wondered? No matter, I would never be able to charm a man as I saw she now charmed George Ramsey. His attentions did not escape my parents' notice or his own, though I fancy his were less happy with it than were mine. The Ramseys, wealth from trade notwithstanding, would want for their son and heir a wife with a fortune in addition to a pretty face and good name.

For my part I was having difficulties with Augustus Fanshawe.

For reasons I was unable to fathom, he became a constant visitor at Seton Place, waiting for me if I were not home, greeting me awkwardly when I came. I could not understand why he called so often or what he wanted. Perhaps he was simply lonely, for Sebastian had gone to London to study law, and even though his family was large, it was equally as easy to feel lonely within a large family as within a small one. I knew that from my own experience. So I spent my afternoons working on my embroidery while Augustus sat opposite me, talking sometimes of his ambitions to follow in his brother's footsteps and read law at Lincoln's Inn, more often saying nothing, forcing me to make conversation since I couldn't bear the weight of the silence. I didn't dislike Augustus; I had grown up with him, but he did bore me. Whenever he spoke, blinking his pale, myopic eyes behind his steel-rimmed spectacles, nodding his head at each word, he reminded me for all the world of a barn owl: kindly, pedantic and horribly dull.

I was quite pleased when George Ramsey joined us one day as he waited for Eugenia. Since she had not expected him, I knew it would take some time for her to change her gown and rearrange her hair, so I did my best to make him welcome.

He was a pleasant enough young man, a trifle heavy, perhaps, but of a build large enough to carry his corpulence though the future promised that he would become as rotund as his father. He had the florid complexion of all the Ramsey men, but at times his dark eyes twinkled in a way that made me believe he was not quite as stolid as he seemed. Thomas always described him as quite a card and winked in a way I did not entirely understand.

I made him talk of his travels in Yorkshire and found that he told amusing stories of the fierce independence of the people of the north, of their open hostility to officials who did not act according to their wishes. There was even one tale of a blanket-tossing.

"It is hardly surprising that you found them of a less even disposition than people in our southern climes—you've been in the home of the Cliffords, among people who openly support Mary Stuart."

"Nothing but a hotbed of primitive Methodists and Luddites if you ask me." George Ramsey was quite obviously happy to be able to voice his opinions, for he did little enough of that in the presence of his father or my own when he sat silently, nodding in unison with their every word. I suppose it was for that reason that father held him in such high esteem.

"Perhaps," I answered. "But I think you must admit that more often than not they exhibit a shrewd common sense."

"But how do you know so much of them? Have you been among them?"

"I've never been outside Wiltshire, but any reading of our country's history illustrates the rugged character of Yorkshire's people, a character that is only equalled by the terrain, from what I hear of it. But you must tell me about that, for you have seen it firsthand."

Thus it was that when Eugenia finally came down, George Ramsey was sitting next to me, regaling me with the tale of a West Riding squire and his gamekeeper, who had bested the squire's sly attempt to catch him sleeping by pretending to take his employer for a poacher and soundly thrashing him.

George was laughing so heartily at his own story that he had only a perfunctory greeting for Eugenia when she entered, wearing the new sprigged muslin she had trimmed only the day before with ribbons she had sent to London for specially, her hair carefully styled in bunches of curls at either ear. I could see she was furious, for she was left to entertain Augustus, who seemed as displeased with her company as she was with his. When I attempted to draw her into the conversation, she made no attempt to disguise her disinterest in Yorkshire, being more concerned with a ball to be given in Linbury the following month.

George Ramsey, however, refused to allow the conversation to be diverted, for he seldom got the opportunity to talk freely on topics of interest to himself. He resolutely turned his back on Eugenia and Augustus and began to discuss a family he had stayed with—I wondered if it could be the one with the heiress daughter—and their hospitality to him. Over his shoulder I caught a glimpse of Eugenia, her face pink with fury, and hurriedly suggested that since the weather was so fine, we should all take a walk.

Eugenia accepted my suggestion with an alacrity she did not usually exhibit for my ideas, and together we left the room to get our wraps. As we mounted the stairs, she hissed at me between clenched teeth, "Please stop pushing yourself. It is positively embarrassing to Mr. Ramsey."

I started to protest, but she held a finger to her lips and cast a sweet smile down to the hall, where our companions awaited us.

When we left the house, I determined not to walk with George Ramsey, but we had not been long gone before he took my arm to assist me over a fallen log and then made no attempt to release his hold. Eugenia, forced to walk behind with Augustus, would, I knew, be livid. At a bend in the path, I pretended to have twisted my ankle and begged Augustus to see me back to the house, a request with which he readily complied.

Mother came to my room that night, which was not her usual custom. She sat awkwardly on the edge of the stool to my dressing table and began to talk of commonplaces. I could see she felt uncomfortable.

"Is anything wrong, mother?" I asked at last.

"Eugenia is upset, Alex. She says you were trying to divert Mr. George Ramsey's attentions from her today. Is that so?"

"Of course not. I was interested in his stories of Yorkshire, that was all, and Eugenia wasn't. To say I tried to divert his attentions is absolutely unjust. Eugenia's attitude puzzles me. After all, Cassy sat next to him at dinner last week. I'm sure he talked to her, but Eugenia didn't take exception to that."

"That's quite different, Alex. Cassy, as you must be aware, is not—well, how should I put it—Cassy is not exactly beautiful and . . ."

"Am I beautiful, then?" I asked in surprise.

"You are growing into a fine young lady. You're almost seventeen and you're taller than Eugenia now, though I hope you stop growing, for while it is good to be tall, it is not good to be too tall."

"You don't think my mouth is too large for beauty, then?"

She laughed and came over and kissed my forehead, glad, I think that the interview had passed without rancour.

"Of course it isn't. You have a very attractive smile, but please keep it away from Mr. George Ramsey. You know how disappointed Eugenia has been since she returned from London. It is important for her to have an admirer, and it would be awful for her to be outdone by a younger sister—and a sister not yet out. You have plenty of time yet in which to find a husband."

I promised mother to be the model of decorum, and I was as good as my word and didn't speak two syllables together to George Ramsey the next time he called, so that he preferred Eugenia's commonplaces to my reticence and soon all was forgotten. Forgotten by Eugenia, that is, but not by me. It had amazed me that any man, even George Ramsey, had found me preferable to the family beauty. Perhaps, after all, men were not only attracted by frivolity. Perhaps, too, that was the reason that Augustus Fanshawe had begun to spend so much of his time at

Seton Place. Yet if his interest in me was more than that of an old friend, I was determined to discourage him; friend he was, but he was in no way the sort of man I could ever consider marrying. I knew of only one man whom I wanted, and since he was unattainable, I would never marry.

I could never tell my family of that resolve, for I knew it was considered the duty of every woman to marry. I wished I could have followed a career—law, or perhaps medicine—but that was only permissible for boys.

I was startled, however, when Paul accosted me one morning with, "Father says I'm for the church."

"Don't be silly," I laughed. "He must be joking. Imagine you preaching to people, telling them to mind their ps and qs, and all the time, like as not you'd have a frog in the sleeve of your surplice—remember Sylvester?"

"It's not funny, Alex, and father's deadly serious. James would do better," Paul went on morosely, "He's such a goody-goody, especially when mother's around. Thomas toes the line better than I do, but then he doesn't have to *do* anything; he'll inherit. Not that I'd want to run the estate—I'd rather have a profession, but not the church."

"Then talk to father; tell him."

"I tried, but he's set on it. He's not one to be disobeyed, but I won't take the cloth. I won't, I won't."

I agreed with Paul. It seemed as great a sin to go into the church without a calling as it would be to marry without love and respect.

Patience came out that spring, and the Bladens left for London. Lord Bladen had offered to present me along with his younger daughter, and father had been tempted by his offer, for it would have saved him considerable expense, but I overheard him telling mother he would not want to find himself with a Whig for a son-in-law. Though the thought of seeing London had excited me, I was not altogether sorry at father's refusal to let me go, for the visit would have brought me into contact with Darius and Philomena and I was not yet ready to face their married bliss with equanimity.

My relationship with Patience had been strained, perhaps because of the time her father devoted to me, though she had no wish to pursue studies herself. Since she rarely came to the library, being occupied with preparations for her presentation, our paths did not often cross except at the luncheon table, when others were always present.

The day before she left for town, she walked across the park with me as I was going home.

"And when will you come out, Alexandra?" she asked.

I had given the matter no thought. Father had made it clear that he refused to spend money on the rest of his daughters as he had on Eugenia's presentation, which, he said, had been money wasted. Cassy was to be presented in Salisbury, where Aunt Maud lived. She being willing to perform this office, it would make it an inexpensive endeavour for father. I presumed it would be same for me.

"But Salisbury—to be presented in the provinces is tantamount to not being presented at all!" Patience exclaimed. "How can you bear it! You can never meet anyone in the provinces—anyone at all worth knowing, that is."

"I don't know. I expect there are as good people in Wiltshire as there are in London," I protested. "After all, we live in Wiltshire."

"True," she said quickly. "It is quite proper to spend time in the provinces, essential, in fact, for England's landowners, but it is London that is the centre of society."

"Then it should provide you with much enjoyment. For my part, I am quite happy here."

When I paused to reflect, that was the truth. I was happy, or as happy as I could ever be without Darius. My mind was constantly employed, so that petty irritations that worried my mother and sisters had no chance to plant roots there. Some of my poetry was beginning to please me. To be sure, many might dismiss it as sentimental verse. I wrote of love—doomed love—but the writing, while cathartic, kept that love alive. It made me understand why poets throughout the ages had found the theme of love, particularly unrequited love, so consuming. Often I wished I could share my writing with Lord Bladen but I did not dare. He was too perceptive; he would read and then guess the source of my inspiration. It was a secret I could never confide.

News soon came of Patience's bethrothal to the son of Lord Brace; his second son, as Mrs. Ramsey carefully pointed out. Nevertheless, it was a desirable match which pleased her parents, though Lady Bladen, on her return, wept at the thought that both her daughters would be gone from home. She hoped I, too, would not soon be leaving them. It was the first indication I had of Lady Bladen's fondness for me, and I was unconscionably pleased by it.

If I had avoided Darius by not going to London, I was soon to see him, for he and Philomena were at Charteris for Patience's wedding. I think their return was the cause of as much celebration in the neighbourhood as was the wedding. Everyone wanted to see what Philomena wore, how she dressed her hair, for she was the acknowledged style-setter in London. She had, if anything, grown more beautiful. Marriage must agree with her, I thought bitterly, but was it my imagination or had Darius changed. He seemed to me more serious, more thoughtful, not the carefree young man who had come back from Italy. Gone were his gay, teasing tones, his easy affection. Marriage seemed to have made him serious, somehow older, though he was as forebearing as ever of his wife's whims.

I saw little of them, primarily because I could not bear to see Philomena at his side, but on the morning of the wedding I had promised to help Patience dress, and I met Darius as I arrived.

"I've seen nothing of you, Alex, but both mother and father have talked of you. Father showed me an excellent essay you wrote on Talleyrand's role at the Congress of Vienna. He is only sorry you cannot go on to Oxford to read history or philosophy under a tutor."

"There could never be a better teacher for me than your father, Darius. If I wish there were a university open to me, it is only because I wish that I could follow a career."

"How unusual you are for a young girl, Alexandra, to wish for such things. Yet I don't doubt that the next wedding I shall attend in Linbury will be yours, for you are quite grown now."

I shook my head. I did not tell him that I was resolved never to marry. Certainly if I were forced to marry, I could never do so under his eyes.

He came in to his sister to wish her well as I was adjusting the train of Honiton lace Lady Bladen had worn at her wedding. As he hugged her, I thought his eyes glistened—had he grown sentimental, or was it simply the reflection of the bright sunlight streaming in through the upper windows?

In the church it was Philomena, in an exquisite gown of appliquéd lavender silk with a new dropped waistline, who stole the limelight from the bride. Her brilliant smile and social grace were remarked upon by all, and Darius was pronounced to be the most fortunate of men. Quite selfishly, I was glad when they returned to London immediately after the ceremony.

V

IN DECEMBER OF 1819 the Tory government of Lord Liverpool fell under the repressive measures of the Six Acts enforced after the Peterloo massacre, in which six people had been killed and many others injured. The government's fears of social unrest caused by a combination of industrialization, unemployment and high wheat prices had manifested itself in the curtailment of public assemblies; that curtailment had been its undoing, and a general election was called for March. The Whigs, under the leadership of Lord Russell, banded together to campaign for reform, and Darius wrote to his father that he intended to run for our county seat held by Mr. Harrington, a prominent Tory and a friend of father's.

He arrived soon after, ready and enthusiastic to begin his campaign. Philomena was not with him, and I found myself unduly pleased because he was alone, but the reason for her absence was soon made known to me—she was with child.

"Why did you not tell us this as soon as you knew it?" Lord Bladen demanded. "It is the news your mother and I have been waiting for, and you young people keep it to yourselves. That's too sly by half. It is a time for celebration, not modesty. You should have spoken of this before you spoke of politics, by George! When is the baby due? How is Philomena? Who is your doctor? How long before the lying-in?"

Darius answered all his questions in a quiet, controlled voice.

"Well, my boy, you are taking it all very calmly, more so than I did when you were to come into the world, I can assure you. I must admit to a preference for a boy to secure the title for another generation at least."

That Darius was reticent in discussing Philomena's condition was hardly surprising, for even with the best of care, childbirth was not without great risk—even Princess Charlotte had not survived it, despite every precaution. A first confinement was difficult at best, and Darius remained uncommunicative despite his parents' jubilance. He refused to discuss baptism or education; he even balked at choosing names.

"Let the child be born first. There is plenty of time to decide," he repeated to the disappointment of excited, expectant grandparents.

Lord Bladen's attention was at last drawn from news of the birth by a gathering of Whig politicians to discuss election strategy; it was concluded that Darius would have difficulty wresting a seat from the Tories that had so long been theirs, but difficult or not, Darius went after it with unflagging zeal. Long hours were spent researching the blunders—and there were many—of Lord Liverpool's government over the past decade. He reread Harrington's speeches, noting his mistakes, yet noting, too, acts that had won voter approval. I watched the methodical way he approached his task, observing how his keen mind grasped issues, stripping away all extraneous material to reach the core. Seeing my interest, he began talking to me, using me as a first audience; he told me he could find no better to point out inconsistencies or misconceptions, and I glowed with pleasure. I became his amanuensis, copying speeches, finding references, keeping a diary of his engagements. We worked well together. He accepted all I did willingly; I, in turn, felt very happy and very close to him. I knew he was grateful for the help, though I cannot say that he thought of me personally, for he seemed thoroughly preoccupied with the political fray.

"You couldn't have a better aide than Alexandra," his father frequently reminded him

"No, indeed, though I hope her assistance to me does not upset her father."

My father had been apoplectic when he had learned that Darius was to challenge Mr. Harrington; if he had discovered that I had in any manner helped the Whig opponent of his close friend, Charteris would probably have been forbidden to me forever. Had he questioned me on the subject, I should have had to choose between lying or risking his wrath. As it was, I took a coward's course of avoiding him—his ill humour needed no further aggravation. In truth I suspect I need not have been concerned, for I doubt he would have conceived it possible that a woman could take any part in a man's political world.

The long hours I spent copying out Darius's notes, which he confessed even he found difficult to read though I deciphered his handwriting without difficulty, were hours that became as precious to me as life itself. As I wrote, I longed to hear him speak the words, just once, in the setting for which they were written—the political rally. Though it was unheard of for a woman to be seen at such an event, when the time came for him to address a meeting at the Red Lion in Linbury, I determined somehow to be there. I racked my brain devising schemes until I realized that though a woman might not be present, there was nothing to prevent a boy from attending. I was almost as tall as Paul, so I searched out some of his old clothes, a coat and some heavy breeches he wore when fishing. These I hid in a box in my room among my own things.

Fate favoured me, for the evening Darius was to speak in Linbury, the Ramseys were to dine with us. The family would be occupied, and I could make my escape. I pleaded a headache, and Eugenia was only too pleased when I said I wanted to retire early, though mother was concerned. Her attention, however, was captured by cook, who brought the disturbing news that the joint of mutton for the second course was most certainly spoiled and would not do, and something must be substituted immediately; mother sent word to Alice to bring me a tray to my room and hurried down to the kitchen to see what could be done.

I quickly disposed of the contents of the tray and gave it back to Alice, asking her to tell mother I would go to sleep immediately. As I closed the door of my room on her departing figure, I could hear the uproar in the kitchen and doubted that mother would come searching for me before the guests arrived. I stuffed my pillows under the covers to make it appear I was asleep should anyone glance in. Then I hastily dressed in the clothes I had hidden away and pushed my hair up to tuck it inside the cap. A glance in the mirror helped me decide that I would do as long as I was not under close scrutiny; with that I doused the candle and softly opened the window.

On my side of the house was a sturdy plane tree, and although it did not grow directly outside my window, one wide-spreading stout branch was within easy reach. Though I had not done any tree climbing since my fall at Charteris, dressed as I was in my brother's clothing, I felt free and limber. As I clambered up from that last short drop to the grass below, I realized how lucky boys were not to be encumbered by long skirts, but I had little time to waste in reflection, for I had no wish to encounter the arriving Ramsey party.

I ran most of the way into Linbury, a distance of some three miles. Even so, when I reached the large assembly room at the Red Lion, the rally had already started. The room was crowded, but I managed to squeeze into the back, taking care to choose an ill-lit corner but one from which I could observe the dais. I could clearly see Darius, who was being introduced by Mr. Sinclair, our local magistrate and an avid Whig. Several men surrounded him, not all of whom were known to me, but he stood out among them like the Persian king for whom he was named, despite the sombre hue of his dark brown coat and a cravat tied without a hint of dandyism.

Had I not already loved Darius, I am quite sure that I should have been unable to prevent it after listening to him that evening. Almost immediately I realized that the hours of preparation he had so painstakingly undertaken were without a doubt justified. His spontaneous replies to the many questions flung at him, at first by raucous hecklers, were of lightning speed, sharp, witty and always on the mark. He soon had the crowd with him, so that the hecklers lost all power to disrupt. In fact they gave up in fear for their own safety. His words on Peterloo pointed out the grievous conduct of the government without indulging in the radical oratory of Henry Hunt, which had done so much harm. He did not hide, however, that he favoured a greater voice in government by a larger majority of Englishmen, men who had fought for their country in the recent wars, men who were building her into a vast economic entity, men who were her life's blood.

"I'm a Wiltshireman. I'm a moonraker, just as you are," he concluded. "We may have earned that name in derision, for it was given by excisemen to Wiltshiremen found raking a pond in which the reflection of the moon appeared. When asked what they were doing, they said they were trying to rake in the great yellow cheese from the midst of the lake. It was only after the excisemen left in high glee at their stupidity that the moonrakers brought in their true prize, kegs of brandy." There were chortles of appreciative delight from the crowd. "Moonrakers stuck as a name for us, and I, for one, am proud of it. If others use it derisively, I consider it befitting; I consider it a matter of pride to outwit others. Tonight, however, I'm not after a keg of brandy, though I don't mind having a glass of that with you later—or a glass of our good local ale—but what I am after is your vote for me in this coming election. I have lived here all my life; I know you, I know what you want, I know what is good for Wiltshire and also what is good for England. Your representative in Parliament should be a man who thinks as you do, feels as you do—a fellow moonraker."

The applause as he finished was tumultuous. I was completely carried away, even though I knew most of his words by heart, yet it was not only the words but the ease and grace of his delivery. I only wished he had spoken for a voice in government by women, but I was learning political wisdom from him. I knew an election must be won with as much honesty as possible, yet with topics that could win; votes for women was not among them.

A brusque, burly man who had entered late (I recognized him as Ely Stuckney, who owned our village general shop though it was his wife who ran it), had complained throughout of being unable to reach his proper seat because of the crush, and at this pause in the proceedings, he began pushing his way through the crowd. In doing so he jostled against me, pushing me against a young farmer whom I had earlier heard say he was from nearby Netherton, who berated me soundly for encroaching upon him though it was none of my doing. He had, I was sure, imbibed already too much of the local ale Darius had mentioned, for though I made no reply—perhaps for that reason—he grew threatening and abusive.

"You'll look out, you little squirt, if you know what's good for you. Watch where you put your feet and elbows. Rascally little bugger, don't doubt you're trying to pick pockets. Better watch this one—count your change men, if you take my advice."

I was suddenly the centre of attention. I could make no answer; my voice would give me away, I was sure. I stepped away from the bleary-eyed fellow only to brush into the man behind, who lifted his fist as though to strike me. I dodged quickly and, in doing so, knocked off the obviously new hat of our blacksmith. The men's anger was aroused, yet also I was sure they got sport from abusing me. They pushed me from one to the other, elbowing, pinching and punching me. I was terrified. The commotion in our corner was attracting attention from the rest of the room. I saw Darius look in our direction, and not wishing to be seen, I made a run for the door in an effort to leave, to get away from my tormentors.

I heard the gavel pounding and an order for ale and refreshments to be brought in. It created a diversion, yet not enough of one for the Netherton farmer, whose perseverance in pursuing his quarry was only exceeded by his belligerence.

"He's off, and I'll bet our coins are to be found in his pockets," he bellowed. "Get him!"

I had reached the door, yet even as I did so, my arm was clutched in a vicelike grip and I was held to face my accuser.

"Let's search him," someone yelled, and hands began wrenching at my clothing.

"Let's get him outside, give him a thrashing while we're about it."

"His arms are soft enough. What do you do for a living, young 'un?"

"Let's take him out and see what he's made of."

They were laughing as they pushed and prodded me, yet there was no humour in their faces. I was petrified with fear as they began shoving me from the assembly room into the darkened corridor beyond where I would be at their mercy. A boy, I was sure, could expect rough treatment at their hands, yet how much worse it would be when they discovered I was a woman. I was in pain, yet my pain was oddly deadened by my fear. My only recourse was to declare myself. Perhaps my father's name, Tory though it was, might give them cause to consider. I would have to bear the consequences, even if they did let me go, from father and from village gossip, but I had no choice. I opened my mouth to speak when, as if by magic, I felt their hands releasing me and I slumped back against the wall.

"So it is you, Jack! I thought I caught sight of you in the back. Been up to some mischief, has he?"

"Beg pardon, Mr. Wentworth. Didn't know you knew the lad. He's been causing quite a commotion." The farmer reeled slightly as he spoke.

"I know," Darius said as he looked directly at the man. "I saw it all. He's the son of my manservant. I'd better see that he gets home or else his father will have something to say about it. Do go inside and get something to eat, all of you. I'll be back directly."

My arms and legs were throbbing painfully, yet my fear was replaced by distress at being discovered by the very one whom I would at all cost have avoided.

I could not look at Darius as he put his arm around my shoulders and led me down to his chaise. He helped me up without a word and took the reins from his groom. Without a word we started on the road to Seton Place.

When we had passed the last cottage, he reached over and took the cap from my head, allowing my hair to fall down around my face.

"What on earth possessed you to do such a thing, Alexandra? It was a foolish, ridiculous act. Why did you do it?" he demanded again when I did not speak.

My throat constricted. I could not have spoken even if I had wished to. He would dismiss me forever as a lamentable hoyden. Philomena would never behave in such a wanton fashion. I wanted to jump down, to run away from him. I wished the earth would swallow me up.

"Speak to me, Alexandra. Are you hurt? Have they harmed you?"

"No, I'm all right." My voice was muffled, but he seemed relieved to hear it.

"It was a foolish thing to do. I hope you realize that. There's no telling what may happen at times like these. Tempers are aroused; sometimes they lose all self-control. It's dangerous, certainly no place for a young girl. That fracas just now, for instance—anything could have happened to you." He paused before adding a softer voice, "Are you quite sure you're all right, Alexandra? Did they do anything—apart from frightening you?"

"No."

"Are you quite sure?" He reined the horses. "Look at me."

But I turned away. "What does it matter. You don't care anything for me. I only wanted . . ."

"It is quite wrong to say I don't care anything for what happens to you, quite wrong. But you only wanted what?"

"To hear you speak." I was crying, and that made me feel more gauche than ever.

"Alex, oh, Alex! Please don't! Here."

He handed me his handkerchief and I blew my nose, determined to say nothing more. That resolve was quite forgotten when he said softly, "If anything had happened to you, I could never have forgiven myself. Can't you understand that?"

I looked at him at last and managed a smile.

"That's better," he said and sighed in relief. "Now, what did you think of it, after all?"

"Oh, Darius, you were magnificent. Really you were! You had everyone applauding you. Even those who were against you in the beginning came around. You are a powerful persuader."

He laughed. "It was a Whig meeting, don't forget. It is often difficult, even treacherous, for those of contrary opinions to go against the majority. Besides, most of those present my family has known for years."

"But it wasn't that kind of applause, Darius, it was acclaim. They heard their views expressed, expressed forcefully, expressed beautifully. I was there amongst them; I could hear their comments. It was you they acclaimed—you, not just Lord Bladen's son.''

"It does help, though, you must admit."

"Of course it helps, but really, their praise was for you."

I couldn't see his face clearly, only the outline against the moonlit sky, yet I knew he was pleased.

"But the speech, what did *you* think of it? Is there anything that should be left unsaid, anything I omitted?"

I was eminently pleased at having my opinion asked.

"It was a good speech, Darius. There is nothing you said that should be omitted. However, you might put in a word for Queen Caroline."

"Why on earth . . ." he began.

"What I mean is, I heard a lot of discussion about it tonight, and they were on her side. The fact that the Prince Regent—I mean the King, I keep forgetting he's King now because he doesn't behave like one—the fact that he's trying to divorce her simply does not sit well with many people."

"I have little sympathy with the topic—or with the woman," he replied coldly.

"Perhaps not, but nevertheless, the Pr—the King is using all his power, and he certainly has the power, to defame her."

"He may be saying nothing but the truth. I can assure you she has not lived a pure life in Europe these past years; that I know from my own stay there. Her antics were spoken of everywhere."

"And the King—what of his conduct? Has that been any better?"

"But that's—"

"If you're going to say that's different, please don't. You were, weren't you?"

"I suppose I was." I could feel his eyes on my face. "But how do you know of such things?"

"I read a great deal—your father's newspapers and magazines as well as his books. Little secret has been made of the King's conduct. He has enjoyed himself and he hasn't cared who knew of it until now, when he wishes to dispose of his wife for doing much the same thing."

"You are awfully young to speak with such disillusionment. At your age I thought girls were still imagining princes in shining armour."

"Perhaps I still do," I said quietly, but I doubt he heard, for he was reflecting on the matter I had raised.

"I am loath to raise the issue, but it is true that the King's ministers are promoting the divorce, and it is a matter of great embarrassment to them.''

"Wiltshiremen—moonrakers—may be independent, yet they oppose infidelity, marital infidelity.'' I sounded like a prude, a hypocrite, too, I thought, feeling as I did for one married to another.

"That, I can assure you, is not the case in London.''

"You support the King in this matter, then?''

"I support neither of them. I find them ideally suited to one another. They are both thoroughly disagreeable, disreputable, disgusting people, entirely deserving of one another.'' He paused before adding slowly, "But I cannot help but wonder whether the course of history might not have been altered if each had found different mates.''

"I thought perhaps you supported the King on the assumption that the woman is always in the wrong. You were about to say it was different for a man before.''

"I was, perhaps, yet if the woman is not always in the wrong, that does not mean that she is not sometimes totally in the wrong.'' He was silent momentarily, and then he laughed. "Thank goodness you have the sagacity to save frogs that might, after all, prove to be Lycean shepherds or even princes in disguise, and the prescience to vomit at weddings, which, as in the case you pointed out this evening, do not always signify happiness ever after.''

The horses had grown restive at standing so long, and he set them to a walk and then a trot. We would soon be home, yet I wanted the evening never to end. Even as I thought this, the gates of my home loomed up before us.

"Do leave me here, Darius; don't come any further.''

"But I want to see you safely back. How on earth did you get out of the house dressed like that?''

"I climbed down the tree outside my window.''

"Then I must help you climb back up.''

"No, please don't,'' I insisted. "I know the way. I have used it often. It's almost as good as a staircase by this time with all the footholds I have made in the trunk. Besides, the Ramseys are dining with us. Two people are more likely to attract attention than one.''

"Are you sure you are quite all right after all that happened?''

"I am, except . . .''

"Except what?''

"Except I wonder if you are still annoyed with me for coming.''

"Of course I'm not. I wasn't annoyed with you at all, but very concerned for your safety. In truth, I am thoroughly flattered. I'm sure that no one has ever gone to such lengths just to hear me speak."

"I'm glad. I would never want to do anything to incur your displeasure."

I was turning to go when I remembered something he had said. "Darius, can girls be moonrakers too?"

"Only if they're born and bred in Wiltshire," he replied seriously. "On that score you certainly qualify."

He took both my hands in his, and instinctively I stepped towards him.

"Thank you for coming tonight, little moonraker." He bent down and kissed me, swiftly, lightly. "Promise me, though, you won't do such a thing again."

His kiss drove everything from my mind. I could only nod, afraid to speak, afraid of what was in my heart. Breaking from him, I ran and did not look back until I reached the house. He was still at the gate, still watching me. I waved, and he waved back before turning towards Linbury.

As I climbed my plane tree, I considered it unlikely that Philomena had ever done anything so unladylike, but somehow it no longer mattered. Yet when I regained my room I realized it was the second time that evening that I had compared myself to Darius's wife.

VI

"IT WAS SUGGESTED to me last night that a word in favour of Queen Caroline might be profitable," I heard Darius say to his father the next morning. "You know the government is very vulnerable over the issue of the King's divorce, and Harrington has supported him in other matters. If I come out for the Queen, he'll be forced to take the King's side, whether he favours it or not."

Lord Bladen eyed his son dubiously. "That awful woman. Do you think it wise? She's been in and out of so many beds all over Europe, and she's made no secret of her doings with Bergami or

Pergami or whatever his name is, that Italian lover of hers, sleeping out on the deck and—'' he broke off, looking in my direction, ''I don't know. Did Sinclair suggest it?''

''No, it wasn't Sinclair. The suggestion came from another moonraker at last night's meeting.'' Darius cast a conspiratorial smile at me. I had never felt so proud. It was all I could do not to openly acknowledge it. ''Brougham, you know, is undertaking the Queen's defence. I know he's not exactly a party stalwart, but he's a brilliant fellow, and it's my opinion he's going to win.''

''I'm not sure he will. You know what they say—if Brougham knew a little of the law he'd know everything.''

''He's a party radical, I know, and he's got enemies, but I'm willing to wager he'll give a good account of himself at the trial.''

''Well, if you feel strongly for it, try it and see what response you get.''

The first response that I heard was from Darius's opponent, Mr. Harrington, when he visited father later in the week.

''That young fool's come out for the Queen.'' He stood, fidgeting irascibly, moving from one foot to the other, with his back to the fire in our drawing room, his profusion of chins positively shaking with anger. ''Now I'm going to be forced into the King's corner, when I would just as soon have avoided the issue altogether. The whole thing's an embarrassment, but some damn fool is bound to raise it. If it's not one of our own, he'll send one of his Whigs to start haranguing me. I've got them spotted, though. I get them flung out whenever I can.''

''But surely you send hecklers to his meetings,'' father interposed.

''Of course I do, but that puppy is making inroads. The rascals he's sending are remarkably well-informed. They're asking some damned embarrassing questions.'' He looked towards the sofa, where Cassy and I sat at our needlework. ''Excuse me, young ladies. I fear that politics has a way of making a gentleman forget his manners on occasion.''

I smiled at him. ''I quite understand, Mr. Harrington. Think nothing of it.''

''It's a dirty business, best left to men.'' He bowed to us and turned back to father, who sat surveying his party's hope with a critical eye.

''I wish I could find something detrimental about him to spread abroad, but he seems clean as a new penny. You don't know anything, do you?'' Mr. Harrington looked hopefully at father. ''He is your neighbour.''

''And that's just why I couldn't tell you if I did know anything. I'll support the Tories right down the line—you know how earnestly I want you to hold your seat—but I have to live with the Bladens, much as I dislike their politics, and I wouldn't want any stories about them laid at my door. Alexandra's been at Charteris a good deal, and Thomas was up at Oxford with Wentworth.''

Mr. Harrington looked over at me pensively before crossing the room to examine my embroidery. ''You work a very fine stitch, Miss Alexandra. Next time I come to visit your father, I must bring my son, Arthur, with me. You are much of an age and should get along exceedingly well now. He is as much an admirer of beauty as is his father.''

I flushed at the heavy compliment and bent my head over my work; not before noticing father's awakened interest, however. Father was irked because George Ramsey had not yet come forth with an offer for Eugenia; I feared he saw in Mr. Harrington's remark a chance for another daughter, and I wanted none of that. I rose abruptly and made my excuses, saying I had to walk down to the village.

''I myself was just about to depart,'' Mr. Harrington proclaimed. ''Allow me to accompany you as far as the gate.'' Much though I would, I could scarcely refuse his offer.

''So you are at Charteris a great deal, your father says,'' he began as we set off together. ''You must know the family well.''

I nodded and commented quickly on the fine weather we were having, but he was not to be put off.

''And Mr. Darius Wentworth, undoubtedly you see a great deal of him?'' The question lingered on his protruding lips as though he savoured the words in anticipation of a fortuitous reply. What would he say, I wondered, if I told him I was desperately in love with his opponent, that I had attended a political rally, that he had brought me home, that he had kissed me. What political brouhaha would he make of that?

''I see him when he is there, but he comes only occasionally. He has lived in London since his marriage.''

''Ah, yes. He is fortunate indeed, a lovely lady, quite the *grande dame* of London society, I understand—but how does the beautiful Mrs. Wentworth take to the idea of her husband's entry into the political arena?''

If Mr. Harrington thought to ingratiate himself with me for

whatever reason, he could not have chosen a less desirable topic. "I really could not say. Mrs. Wentworth remains in London. She expects a child in the spring."

"Oh, I hadn't realized that." Mr. Harrington's face took on a deeper gloom, perhaps at the thought of the attraction that that blessing of his opponent's union might have upon Wiltshire's voting population, which was by no means universal since that privilege was confined to freeholders with an annual land revenue of at least forty shillings. "No doubt that gives Mr. Darius Wentworth much cause for jubilation."

"I am quite sure it does, but he says little. A first child can be a matter of some concern."

"To be sure; yet it will secure the title for another generation."

"Only if the child is a boy," I replied with some asperity.

"Quite naturally. Male heirs are essential. My own son, Arthur, is a source of continuing pride. He will, I know, be eager to solicit a dance with you at the election ball, and I hope you will so honour him."

"As I am not yet out, I doubt that I shall be there." My regret was sincere, though not for the reason Mr. Harrington presumed, for to attend Linbury's election ball would have provided an opportunity to dance with Darius.

"Then allow me to speak to your father on the matter, Miss Alexandra, for the occasion will not be a success without your lively smile." His obtrusive compliments, coupled as they were with his assessing look, were not at all to my liking. When I made no reply, he went on, "And how do you find Mr. Darius Wentworth?"

"Quite well."

"Does he have any—any, how shall I put it—any idiosyncrasies?"

"He took a first in the Greats at Oxford," I replied, deliberately misunderstanding him.

"No, no. I mean, have you observed any oddities about him?"

"Oddities?" I thought of Darius, of the crinkles at the corners of his eyes, those grey, expressive eyes, of the twitch of his mouth just when he was about to laugh, of the way he ran his hand through his hair when he wished to emphasize a point, of his manner of bending over his paper when writing as though ideas were coming so fast upon him he was afraid of losing them, of his habit of clasping his hands behind his back when walking, of—of—there were a million things I thought of when I thought of Darius.

"No oddities, exactly, although . . ."

"Although what?" Mr. Harrington prompted a trifle too hastily.

"Although he does tend to strive too hard when he means to attain something. He leaves no stone unturned, such as now, he studies so hard that I know it concerns his mother—"

Mr. Harrington's impatient snort did not allow me to complete my sentence. "Yes, yes, that is all very well. But I mean does he have any oddities, are there any peccadilloes of which you are aware? His affections, for instance, might they ever—ever—you know what I mean."

"You are possibly thinking about Belinda. I must say that she does rather lead him by the nose. It causes some comment.

"Belinda, yes, yes," Mr. Harrington urged.

"He wants her to be there, and she is fickle. She runs around so much and is never willing to simply wait. She must be off after every attraction. She is not faithful, I fear."

"And why should she be there simply when he chooses?"

"That is exactly what she thinks, but I can assure you it annoys him. Is that the sort of oddity you wished to know?"

"Yes, yes. And where does this Belinda live?"

"Why, at Charteris, of course."

"At Charteris! Under his own roof!"

"Well, not exactly under his own roof. She lives in the stables."

"In the stables." Mr. Harrington's voice grew faint.

"Why yes, that is where all of the hunting dogs are kept," I replied evenly, watching the indignation rise in his eyes. "Belinda is his own dog, but she is always after rabbits when she should—"

"I must confess it surprises me that your father allows you to spend so much of your time in a Whig household," Mr. Harrington snorted.

"It is perhaps not important, since I have no vote—"

Again he interrupted me in annoyance at my stupidity. "Members of the fair sex could never be publicly involved in such business. The government of the country must always be left in the hands of gentlemen. I need hardly point out to you that the hands of the ladies are fully occupied with government of the home." And, as if to make up for his sharpness, he patted my arm in a not entirely paternal manner. "But that does not mean that they cannot—indeed they should—always support their menfolk. For that reason your father's long association with the Tory party must make you a Tory in spirit, if not in fact. Therefore, since you have ready access to Charteris, should you hear of anything concerning Mr. Darius Wentworth, any—how should I put it—any misdoings, any imprudence, any inconstancy—and I do not refer to hunting dogs . . ."

I put my hand to my lips to smother a laugh which threatened to overcome me, a gesture which he took for one of agitation.

"I know, I know, it may seem distressing to a young lady, especially one of your tender years and family background, but as you get older you will realize that regrettable things do sometimes occur. Gentlemen do not always act as they should. Sometimes the vows of marriage are set aside, there are—eh— infidelities, that sort of thing."

His face reddened as he floundered on, and I made no effort to extricate him from his difficulties, only adding to them by saying softly, half to myself, perhaps reminding myself of what I must never forget. "The marriage vows state till death do us part."

"Of course, of course," Mr. Harrington made another effort to hide his irascibility. "But nevertheless, occasionally it is not always as it is with your father or with myself. Sometimes there is a tendency, particularly noticeable among the nobility, to stray from the straight and narrow way."

"You refer, no doubt, to the King and the matter you spoke of earlier. His conduct is indeed deplorable."

"I did not mean . . ." His annoyance became quite obvious, "Oh, well, never mind. You are becoming a very handsome young lady and must yourself draw many a gentleman's attention."

"I can assure you that I have not drawn Mr. Wentworth's attention, if that is what you infer." There was a trace of bitterness in my voice.

"No, no, of course not. I know you would never be a party to anything of the kind. Come, come, I assure you I meant nothing of the sort. I ask your forgiveness, Miss Alexandra, if my remarks were subject to any misconception." We had arrived at the gate and he took my hand. "I shall look forward to seeing you at the Linbury election ball next week. I know Arthur will delight in the company of such a pretty and principled young lady." With that he raised my hand to his lips in continental fashion and, though I had always heard that gentlemen on the continent did not actually kiss the hand but merely made the gesture, Mr. Harrington planted a firm and exceedingly wet kiss thereon, so that long after he had left I found myself rubbing it and thinking, for all the world like Lady Macbeth, that it would never again wash clean.

I had not for a moment supposed that I should be allowed to attend the election ball. I therefore forgave Mr. Harrington much when I discovered that I, together with Thomas, Eugenia and Cassy, was to accompany my parents there. Father allowed me to have a new dress for the occasion, yet another cause for rejoicing, for he was, as a rule, extremely careful with my allowance, saying often that I would cost him a pretty penny to bring out and, until then, Eugenia had plenty of clothes she did not need which should suffice.

It was to be my first ball dress, and I chose a soft green taffeta and had Mrs. Birdsock, our village seamstress, make it with the new lowered waistline I had seen on Philomena, and just short enough to set off my slim ankles. The result, despite Eugenia's denigrating comments on Mrs. Birdsock's abilities compared to those of London seamstresses, I found admirable.

The night of the ball I was ready long before anyone else and sat surveying myself critically in the looking glass. I had, with the assistance of mother's maid, parted my hair in the middle and wore it with soft curls on either side of my face, its chestnut colouring highlighted by the glow of the candlelight, warm against the cool green of my gown. I tried some green bows in my hair and, unable to decide whether they enhanced my appearance or not, I decided to ask Eugenia, who had always an eye for such things. But when she flounced into my room to announce it was time to leave, annoyed, perhaps, because I was to accompany them, I decided against it, and, looking back at myself, I resolved that the bows were superfluous and took them out.

At the Red Lion we were conducted to the same assembly room where the rally had been held, except it was no longer a plain meeting room but had an air of opulence in the mass of candlelight. On the dais, rather than speakers, the musicians were seated, tuning their instruments. Everywhere was gaiety and festivity, everyone dressed in their best. Even women I considered commonplace seemed suddenly transformed. I thought I would burst with enthusiasm when I saw Darius enter with his parents, but though they smiled at me they took their seats, much to my disappointment, on the opposite side of the room. Darius, clad in a claret velvet coat and silk knee breeches, cut a superbly dashing figure; I decided if women were to vote there could be no doubt as to the outcome of the election, watching as he moved from one to the other of the assembled company with just the appropriate degree of attention and civility. As the dancing commenced I saw that he remained always on that side of the room and danced only with those ladies, and I was aware of crushing disappointment as I realized that it was there that the Whig families were seated while father had, of course, arranged for our places with other Tories of the Linbury district. My hopes of dancing with Darius were dashed.

Mr. Harrington arrived, accompanied, as he had promised, by his son, a dispirited youth. Mr. Arthur Harrington, who was up at Oxford had come to Wiltshire for the election and was staying at Feltenham with the Ramseys. Thin and gangly, he had a complexion given to alarmingly active eruptions. He spoke not a word while his father was present, but at his father's urging, he asked me to dance, and once on the dance floor, some of his timidity dissipated. Though tall, he appeared of no great stature because of his stooped posture, which proposed to apologize to all and sundry for his height; thus his one advantage went for naught. I managed to elicit a few words from him and discovered that he had met Paul at Oxford, though he was in Merton, while Paul was in New College. I also discovered that he stuttered. When the silence became oppressive I asked whether he was excited about the coming election, at which his prominent Adam's apple bobbed convulsively.

"P . . . p . . . please don't let's talk of it."

"But why not?"

"Because n . . . n . . . nothing else has been d . . . d . . . discussed since D . . . December. When I'm with a pr . . . pretty girl I w . . . would rather talk of something else."

"Well, then," I thought for a moment, "would you like to talk of cricket? Paul is a fine player, you know, and he has taught me the game."

"Has he, b . . . by jove, and I don't doubt you make a capital p . . . p . . . pitcher. You have just the f . . . form for it." He suddenly blushed violently. "P . . . pardon me, I didn't mean anything p . . . p . . . personal, you know, I meant f . . . form in respect to the manner in which the ball is p . . . p . . . pitched. Though, of course, your other f . . . f . . . f . . . form is capital also."

He became quite overcome, and I was astounded that I could produce such convulsive feelings in a young man, albeit one as unattractive as Arthur Harrington.

"And what are you studying now?" I asked, trying to change

the subject, and the remainder of our time together in the set was spent in a minute if disjointed description of Euclid's *Elements*.

Though I did not dislike the younger Harrington as I did his father, nevertheless I found conversation with him tedious, and I was glad to dance next with Howard Ramsey, George's younger brother. He had recently been sent down from Oxford for some misdemeanour. I longed to ask what it was but did not dare. It lent him, however, a provocative air, of which he made the most. He was much like his elder brother in appearance, of medium height with a square jaw and dark eyes. I noticed he had a tendency to squeeze my hand whenever he had occasion to hold it in the set, and each squeeze was accompanied by a look I found difficult to understand till, at the end, he whispered, "You've grown to be absolutely adorable, Alex." I thought it improper for him to make such a comment, but I was unsure what to answer so I pretended not to have heard, though I suspect my flushed cheeks gave me away.

Between Arthur Harrington and Howard Ramsey I found my dances were taken, and since father had said we could not stay long after supper, any hope that might have lingered in my breast of dancing with Darius fled. I saw him on the dance floor with Mrs. Sinclair and later with Mr. Foster's daughter, and at supper he was with a large Whig party, while I was pinioned between Arthur Harrington and father. Father's interest in making sure that Arthur remained with us throughout the evening and always at my side reinforced my suspicions that he was the reason I had been allowed to attend the ball and to buy a new dress for the occasion, and I found the idea offensive. I had no wish for matchmaking, least of all with Arthur Harrington. He was innocuous, certainly, but the thought of him as a prospective husband was insupportable.

I was sitting with him after supper as he expounded on Christopher Marlow's *Dr. Faustus*, wondering how it was possible to make Marlowe's poem sound so prosy and boring, when I felt a light tap on my arm, and I looked around to see Darius.

I smiled with such relief that I fear young Mr. Harrington must have noticed, but I could think of nothing but the joy of speaking to Darius.

"Would you care for this dance if it is not already taken?" he asked.

Would I! My heart nearly burst with enthusiasm, but I managed a demure nod and walked out onto the floor, at once aware that everyone was looking at us and that all traditions had been broken by the Whig candidate dancing with the daughter of the neighbourhood's leading Tory. I don't believe Darius could have caused more comment had he already been elected to Parliament and crossed the floor to vote with the opposition.

"Do you suppose you should have asked me to dance?" I asked him, aware of the consternation.

"Of course I do, otherwise I should not have done so. It is a sad ball when a fellow can't have any fun, even if he is a candidate for Parliament. I can assure you it's been rather heavy going so far. You don't look overjoyed with your companion, so I thought I would do us both a favour."

"It was simply wonderful of you!"

"Don't be a silly goose, it's not wonderful at all—just rather selfish. I wanted to dance with the prettiest girl in the room. You know, Alex, I hardly recognized you when I came in. You look remarkably grown-up somehow. Perhaps it's your hair; you've done something different with it, haven't you? And now that I really look at you I realize for the first time that your eyes are exactly the same rich colour as your hair—altogether delectable."

"Are you teasing me?" I demanded, delighted yet unable to trust I had heard right.

"I'm trying to pay you a compliment, if you'll allow it, fellow moonraker."

My feet barely seemed to touch the ground as I danced. It was what I had wished for all evening. My happiness was perhaps all too evident, because as soon as Darius returned me to my seat, father announced that it was time for us to leave. Though he clearly disapproved he said not a word of my taking the floor with his party's opponent, but all the way home he sang the praises of Arthur Harrington. I said nothing, scarcely following what he said, busy with my own dreams. My silence must have satisifed him for I had no rebuke. Perhaps he thought that I found the ungainly young man acceptable.

Father's good humour increased when, at the end of February, the *Times* reported the discovery of the Cato Street conspiracy, in which a group of dissidents had planned to blow up the entire Cabinet while its members were dining with Lord Harrowby in Grosvenor Square.

"Let's see the Whigs win now," he chortled, disregarding that the conspirators were extreme radicals rather than Whigs.

The attempt cast a pall over an otherwise jubilant atmosphere at Charteris. Darius left immediately for London, Lord Harrowby's house being adjacent to his own, and did not return until he had vouchsafed that Philomena had not been unduly upset by the harrowing events.

Whig liberalism, though advocating reform, strongly opposed radicalism that sought reformation through violent means. Nevertheless, Darius, while disavowing the radicals, emphasized that it was the government's repressive actions that caused conspiracies such as the Cato Street affair.

Elections took place early in March, but it was almost a fortnight before the results were known. Overall the Tories were victorious once again, but Darius had gained our county seat for the Whigs with a respectable margin. Though he said little he was clearly elated at his victory.

At Charteris Lord Bladen toasted his son, " 'Tis an office of great work, and you an officer fit for the place." I joined in the champagne toast, the bubbles tickling my nose. Though I knew it meant that Darius would return to London—to Philomena—I felt light-headed, strangely satisfied.

"For all you've done for me," he said, handing me a small box. It held a gold signet ring engraved with the letter A. I put it on the little finger of my left hand, determined never to take it off, and in answer to father's enquiring glance that evening, I explained that it was an advance birthday present from Lady Bladen. My lie caused me no pangs, but the fact that it did not gave me cause to wonder.

Father's mood of deep gloom over the loss of the county seat cast a pall on Seton Place that threatened to engulf it indefinitely. Then it was miraculously lightened by George Ramsey, who could not have chosen a more propitious moment to solicit Eugenia's hand in marriage. To settle his eldest, his favourite daughter so handsomely immediately restored my father's spirits. Eugenia's humour also improved. Her husband captured, her trousseau now absorbed her entirely.

With Darius gone and the campaign over, I turned back to my studies in an effort to avoid thinking of his marital bliss, soon to be blessed by the birth of their child.

VII

Before Darius had been in the House a month, he had made his maiden speech on the abolition of slavery, the report of which I cut from the *Times* to put in my diary. It was the most impassioned yet thoroughly reasonable argument I had yet read of that iniquitous practice. His manner of delivery was praised as forthright yet unaffected; having been a firsthand witness to his oratory, I was able to endorse this praise.

The Bladens were clearly elated at his success, yet their attention was divided between that and their anticipation of the birth of their grandchild. Lady Bladen had wished to be with Philomena, but Darius had dissuaded her from returning to London with him, saying that Philomena's mother would be there and one mother would suffice. I knew Lady Bladen was disappointed, but she concentrated on preparing garments and making plans for the baptism while arranging, instead, to go to Margaret, who was to have her second child that summer.

The joy of anticipation was shattered three weeks before Philomena was due for confinement; an express arrived late one afternoon just as I was about to leave. I saw Lord Bladen's hand shake as he read it, and his face grew ashen.

"What is it? What has happened?" I cried.

I confess, with some shame—for I thought only of Darius—that when, speechlessly, he handed it to me, I felt a sense of relief that he was unharmed, followed immediately by guilt at that relief, for the express, written in obvious haste and affliction, conveyed the tragic news that Philomena had not survived the premature birth of a son.

The man who arrived shortly thereafter, bringing with him that son to be cared for at Charteris, was in no wise the same man who had only so recently celebrated his parliamentary victory. He was pale. His eyes, dark and brooding, were lifeless and heavily underlined with shadows bespeaking his lack of rest. He scarcely spoke and paid little heed to the tiny bundle carried by a nursemaid, which his mother took with such loving care.

John Frederick Wentworth had been baptised in London immediately after birth. I overheard Lord Bladen remonstrate with Darius for allowing Philomena's body to lie in London rather than at St. Mary's, to be entombed with the other Bladens.

"It was the parish in which we lived," Darius replied flatly. "I believe it is what she would have wished."

"But the child—why was he not baptised here, and why—why did you choose those names? They are so—so commonplace. He is your heir, yet he does not have a family name."

"It was imperative that the boy be christened at the earliest moment. It was believed that he would not survive, but he did." He spoke, as before, without any intonation.

"But the names," his father pressed. "Why not your own, or even mine?"

I knew he was hurt, yet I wished he would leave Darius alone in his grief.

"They are names for a male child. They seemed suitable at the time." His brevity clearly indicated that he would talk no further on the subject, and his father, grieving also, put his arm around his son's shoulders as I left the room, fearing to witness the sight of both men in tears. Water drops were women's weapons, not to stain a man's cheeks, King Lear had said, yet tears were a necessity not merely to wash the eye but to wash the soul, and my presence could only inhibit their freedom to express their grief openly.

Darius returned to London without a word, with barely a glance at his son. He seemed to place the burden of Philomena's loss upon the baby, and certainly the sight of him was an all-too-poignant reminder of his mother, for he had inherited her dark eyes and hair, yet he was of a paler complexion—so pale that at first his colour gave some cause for alarm at Charteris, though he was remarkably alert. He was, above all, an utterly lovable child.

I talked of him incessantly until Eugenia remarked, "To listen to you, Alexandra, one would think that child was your son rather than Philomena's." Stricken, I realized that somehow I felt he was.

Most of my days were spent with him, which pleased Lady Bladen, for it was long since she had had a child in the house, and though Darius had arranged for a nurse as well as a wet nurse, she would not have him left to the care of the domestics though she herself found such a tiny child tiring.

He grew in strength though he remained unduly pale and I took care to wrap him well when I took him for his daily airings in the park, there allowing him to sniff the roses while keeping his fingers from the thorns, holding bright yellow buttercups under his chin to show, by their reflection there, how much he liked butter, playing catch with the fluffy blue ball I had knitted for him. At tea he always licked my crumpets and cried out whenever I delayed bringing them over to him. In fact his liking for crumpets was so great that I gave him Crumpet for a nickname. It became a name generally adopted by everyone else, Lord Bladen particularly preferring it to John Frederick. Nothing in my life had ever delighted me as did those summer days.

Eugenia married in June. Against her better judgement she allowed me to serve as a bridesmaid at her wedding, though she did so with deepest foreboding, noting that she knew of no one better able to ruin a wedding. I could have assured her that her marriage delighted me and would in no way cause me to feel sick, and in truth, it was a delightful wedding. My father was extremely pleased and had allowed Eugenia a liberal sum to prepare her trousseau; she voiced her satisfaction with her new clothes and with her husband-to-be with such equality that it was difficult to tell which pleased her most. Cassy had been quieter than usual, but she was a shy person who had never emoted as did Eugenia. Mother, thinking perhaps that she felt left out, reminded her that she would be spending the spring at Aunt Maud's and attending many parties in her honour. That did nothing to cheer her, which hardly surprised me, for I knew she had never cared for Aunt Maud, who was noted for her brusque manner and sharp tongue so that even father stood in awe of her.

I puzzled over Cassy's despondency, and it occurred to me that perhaps she had developed a fondness for Eugenia's betrothed; I had noticed that whenever the Ramseys visited us she was more attentive than usual and paid greater heed to her appearance. Should that be the cause my heart went out to her. I knew only too well the anguish of seeing the one you loved married to another—how much worse it would be if that other were your sister, a relationship that would force you into constant contact with the happy pair, with the added burden of the freedom allowable between brother- and sister-in-law. If the sentiments Cassy entertained for George Ramsey were anything similar to those I held for Darius, her forlorn attitude was completely understandable.

On the day of the wedding, however, I was to discover—to my relief yet also to my embarrassment—that my suspicions were wrong, at least as far as Cassy's feelings towards *George*

Ramsey were concerned. The ceremony had gone well, the vows being repeated before an altar decked with white lilies and roses, Eugenia equally pristine in her gown of white lace. Mother cried, father tried to disguise his satisfaction and I remained perfectly healthy, so that all in all it was a great success. The party returned to Seton Place, where a wedding feast of cold ham, tongue, chicken, dried fruits, wines and cordials awaited us, after which we repaired to the front steps to see the newly married pair climb into the Ramsey coach for the first stage of their journey to Brighton. Mother was still crying despite the fact that they were to return in less than a month to set up their residence at Fern Hall, a property that adjoined Ramsey Manor.

As we turned to reenter the house, Howard Ramsey caught hold of my arm.

"Don't go in just yet, Alex. Let's walk down by the orchard and see whether that old oak is still there, the one we used to hide notes in, remember?"

I remembered those notes only too well; usually Howard's orders, which Paul and I had to carry out or bear the consequences. Still, it had been stuffy inside with so many people, and the long summer shadows and cooling afternoon breeze beckoned enticingly.

"I suppose you, like the rest of your sex, are busily planning another wedding now that this one has taken place," he said as we walked along the path beside the house. "I find there is nothing like a wedding to put women in a matrimonial frame of mind, not just for the bridal pair but for every other unmarried person present. One marriage is not made but another must grow out of it."

"Indeed, I hadn't thought of it at all," I assured him "*I* am not anxious to marry, and whether other people feel inclined to do so is their business. It does not concern me."

"You don't intend to marry?" he asked with incredulity.

"I didn't say I don't intend to marry," I replied, "only that I am not anxious to do so."

To myself I had to admit that since Philomena's death, untimely though it had been and certainly however much I loved Darius I had never wished for it, nevertheless I was acutely aware that he was free, and remembering his kiss and the election ball, hope had been rekindled that eventually he would look upon me with a more-than-brotherly affection. It was a remote hope, though, for he rarely visited Charteris except for brief sojourns on parliamentary business so that I saw little of him; when I did, his greetings were perfunctory. But I had waited so long for him, I was willing to wait indefinitely with nothing more to sustain me. And if he decided never to remarry, for his mourning of Philomena was so intense that he scarcely could bear the reminder of her in his child, so be it. I only hoped that he would cease to blame Crumpet for her death.

As we strolled towards the orchard, I became aware of Howard staring at me intensely; I had been so lost in my own thoughts that I was hardly pleasant company. I tried to make up for my incivility by asking his future plans.

"My father has it in mind for me to take a position with the East India Company, but I'm not sure it is what I wish to do. Many things could influence my decision, though."

He took my hand as we walked, a friendly gesture, I supposed, for we were, after all, now related through the marriage that had just taken place.

We entered the orchard and walked down the path between the pear trees towards the stream. I thought of the day that Darius had saved me from Paul's ducking—how long ago that seemed. So much had happened, so much had changed, except, that is, for the feelings he had awoken in me that day. They alone remained constant. I looked across the stream, imagining Darius as I had seen him then—young, carefree. He was older now, more responsible, but so, too, was I. One day he would see that. . .

My reverie was brutally interrupted by Howard pulling me close to him, holding me so that I could scarcely move and covering my mouth with his own so fiercely that I could scarcely breathe, either. It was a clumsy, ruthless kiss with nothing pleasant or romantic about it. His lips were hot and moist; he smelled strongly of the port he had been freely imbibing, and his grip upon me was vicelike; though I was strong, I was unable to free myself. I was about to kick his shins when, with great and utter relief, I heard Cassy calling my name. She was some distance away but she had certainly seen what had occurred. One look at her face convinced me that it was not George Ramsey whom she admired but Howard. As I broke from Howard's grasp to run towards her, I saw in her eyes embarrassment but also hurt and desolation.

"Mother asked me to find you, Alex," she said apologetically by way of explanation. "She wants to get up a table for loo." Howard did not look at either of us. He was busy paying great attention to his cravat, which had become distinctly disshevelled.

Without another glance at him, I ran back to the house, leaving them to return together.

That night I went in to Cassy to thank her for rescuing me from such an awkward predicament. "I can assure you I in no way wished for his attentions."

"But do you not find him attractive?"

"Not in the least," I said frankly. Cassy eyed me with an astonishment that bordered on incredulity. It is so when one loves; it is impossible to understand why all the world does not admire one's choice.

"But . . . but he is so handsome, so self-possessed, you must agree."

"It may be so," I hesitated, "but if you like him so, Cassy, why have you hidden it? He gives every indication of wanting a wife."

"Alex, oh Alex! You may be prejudiced by sisterly affection, but even you must admit me to be something less than a handsome, desirable woman. I have as much chance of attracting Howard Ramsey's attention as—as a fat June bug has of being swallowed whole by a gnat."

"But you are a great deal nicer than Eugenia; you are kind, compassionate, and sweet," I protested.

"I am also short and fat and my complexion is nearer to dun than dew. No man is attracted by kindness and compassion," Cassy rejoined.

"I'm sure you are wrong."

"Well, no man with the looks and bearing of Howard Ramsey, that is. He obviously prefers someone with your flair, and who is to blame him?"

"But I don't care for him in the least, Cassy; I assure you I don't. If he makes any further advances to me, I shall be obliged to . . ."

"To what?"

"To speak to him quite bluntly about his conduct."

"I dare say you may, but that will never secure him for me," she sighed. "You will never know what it is to be unattractive. The night we attended the election ball at the Red Lion, I saw you dance every dance. I don't suppose you noticed that I was only asked once and that was by Mrs. Baxter's son, and I think that was because his mama insisted he do so, for he said not two words to me the whole time. I am dreading going to Aunt Maud's because I know how it will be; she will insist on my going here and there and putting myself out to catch a husband.

And if I don't find someone—and I doubt much that I shall— then Aunt Maud will be upset and papa will be angry. You know how great a drain on his resources he considers all of us—especially us girls—he's always grumbling about how much we cost him. Well, at least he is happy about Eugenia, though I suspect he made her a better marriage settlement than he will be willing to make for the rest of us. She was always his favourite, and even though she is beautiful I don't suppose George Ramsey would have taken her without it. If I had a fortune I daresay Howard might look more often in my direction."

"Cassy!" I said, genuinely shocked. "Surely you wouldn't want him if he were interested in you for what you bring him rather than for yourself?"

"Your studies have made a romantic of you, Alex. That is all men look for in any of us—what we can bring them, monetarily at marriage and, of course, children, preferably boys, after it."

"I don't believe it is always so," I said stoutly. "Look at Darius Wentworth. He was certainly very much in love with Philomena when he married her."

"Undoubtedly he was, but he had the best of all possible worlds—an incredibly beautiful woman and a handsome fortune into the bargain. Now he has a son, so that despite the loss of his wife, the title is assured for another generation. And I don't doubt that he will soon marry another fortune and become even more wealthy and powerful. The world was made for men, Alex. If you don't know it now, you should. If all the reading you do doesn't tell you that, then look about you."

I had the uncomfortable feeling that Cassy was as right about Darius as she was about our own inferior position in the scheme of things. I was sure he had married Philomena for love, but it was true she had been very rich, and it had been described as a perfect match. I wondered, if another perfect match presented itself, whether he would put aside his grief in favour of it.

VIII

I MISSED CASSY far more than I had expected after her departure for Salisbury. Since our talk after Eugenia's wedding, a friendship greater than any sisterly affection had sprung up between us. I thought a great deal of her confidences to me and I empathized with her in her hopeless admiration for Howard Ramsey, though I would have wished her affections fixed on a more deserving object.

The object of Cassy's devotion visited Seton Place frequently. He was now received as a member of the family, but in observing him whenever Cassy was present, it was all too apparent that even had she behaved in some bizarre fashion, turning somersaults or dancing a jig, it was doubtful that Howard would have given her any special attention. I was not at all sure he was aware that she existed. I was convinced, much though I wished otherwise, that he had singled me out. I had been aloof, even cold towards him, since the incident in the orchard, yet he continued to pay me compliments I did not want, did not seek. Everything I did to discourage him, even, on occasion, being plainly rude and risking thereby my parents' disapproval, was without avail. His departure at last for Calcutta, where he had taken a position with the East India Company, was a cause of utter relief. I ignored his enigmatic farewell. "When I get back, I'll be a nabob, Alex. Then things will change. You'll see."

With Cassy gone and Paul up at Oxford, I found myself spending more time at Charteris. There I was always sure of a ready welcome. The soft English summer drifted on, lazy days and quiet, the stillness broken only by the fluttering marbled white butterfly or the daring green dragonfly. Despite the somnolence I found myself bursting with energy. I began to write again. Remembering my talk with Cassy, I was inspired to tell the plight of those of my sex possessing neither great beauty nor wealth, yet equally capable of falling under a man's spell as any other. Cassy would be the model for my heroine, but I refused to make the hero from Howard Ramsey's cloth. There could be only one hero of whom I could write and that was Darius. Yet how to make him sympathetic and yet break the heroine's heart? It was a task to which I applied myself with the omnipotence of the Almighty; even if life might deny happy endings, I could make it otherwise.

But my days were not spent wholly in writing, for there was Crumpet. In fact, as he grew, he consumed more and more of my time. Not that it was a sacrifice to give up writing for him, for he was the joy of my life. Eugenia had been right in surmising that I loved him as though he were my own. Yet look as I might, I could find no resemblance to Darius in him. He was Philomena's child totally. Poor little fellow! Had he resembled her less, perhaps Darius might have been able to look on him with less pain; as it was, to see him was to be reminded immediately of the woman who had died giving him birth.

If I thought of Crumpet as mine, equally I was his. He waited for me always, laughing and reaching out for me as soon as I arrived. It was with me that he took his first steps. I had taken him down beyond the south lawn, down where the foxgloves bloomed in such profusion. I spread out a blanket for him to crawl on while I opened my notebook and nibbled speculatively on the end of a pencil. Moments later my attention was attracted by a chortle of triumph. There was Crumpet, standing, quite on his own. He took one step, then another and still another.

"Ala! Ala!" he cried, which was as much as he could manage of my name, before toppling down first on one pudgy knee and then the other, in among the pink foxgloves.

"Oh, Crumpet! How very clever of you. Do it again for me."

And I took his hand and again he tottered, one foot before the other, four more steps. I was as proud as though he were the first of mankind ever to stand on two feet.

"Come along, Crumpet. You must do this for your grand-parents."

I scooped him up into my arms. Life was exciting and ever changing. One day this bundle in my arms would be a man, as tall and strong as his father, eventually to become the seventh baron of Bladen. His first step along that road had been taken.

Crumpet was closer to assuming that title than I, or anyone else, realized. The Bladens, as their rank demanded, had attended the coronation of George the Fourth—"that shameful affair," as Lord Bladen termed it, for Queen Caroline had been left pounding on the doors of the abbey, to be refused admittance. His wrath at the deplorable state of affairs into which the new King had plunged England caused a deeper depression in

Lord Bladen than I had ever known, yet no one foresaw the sudden and treacherous heart attack that overtook him on his return and that was to leave him paralysed for the short remainder of his life.

The efforts of everyone at Charteris were directed to his comfort. Lady Bladen scarcely left his side, and when she did so, it was to relinquish her place to me while I read to him or wrote letters for him. He was then, as he had been always, gracious and gentle, grateful for each small deed.

Darius came often. He it was who was with his father when he died. One look at his ashen face as he left his father's room told me all I needed to know. I ran home without a word to anyone. There I stayed, alone with my grief. I could scarcely believe that he was dead, that I would never see him again. I had never felt so lost, so alone. He had been my teacher and my friend. As I had learned from him in health, even more had I learned from him in those last weeks of his affliction. I loved him more than I would ever love my own father, and the tears I wept were those of a daughter, one bound by a bond closer than blood lines could bestow, for there was no duty in my tears, only unmitigated grief.

I could scarcely speak to Darius at the funeral, or to his mother, who leaned heavily on her son's arm, grown suddenly old. It was odd and strange to hear Darius addressed as Lord Bladen. It took a long time for me to think of him by that name. Darius was much concerned about his mother's health, and before he left for London he asked that I watch and comfort her as I could.

"She thinks of you as a daughter, you know."

"As your father was a father to me, so she is a mother. I shall do everything within my power to help her."

"I know you will, Alex. Sometimes I wonder where we would all be without you. My sisters, as you know, are wrapped up in their families, and my duties force me to return to London. Mother refuses to come there, though I believe the change would do her good. As matters stand, I would not return unless it were imperative."

Impulsively I reached out, and he clung to my hand for a moment.

"Give her time, Darius. This has been a terrible shock to all of us, but most particularly to your mother. She has to adjust to it in her own way, in her own time, and probably these familiar surroundings are the place to do it. Crumpet is here. She is so very fond of him . . . unless you were thinking of taking him back to London with you.''

"No, I had no thought of that.''

"Lady Bladen would never go to London if it meant leaving him behind.''

"Well, he could come with her if she wished it. I am giving up the Grosvenor Square house and moving back to Great Stanhope Street now. I doubt he would find it as comfortable there as at Charteris.''

"Crumpet feels comfortable wherever there is love.'' From the sharp look he directed at me, I knew I had said too much. Though he might think of me as a sister, even his own sisters never criticized him.

Lady Bladen drew a curtain of mourning around herself, one impossible to penetrate. She spoke little to me or to anyone else, yet if for any reason I delayed arriving at my usual time, she missed me. My presence alone, I suppose, supplied some comfort; that and the fact that Crumpet followed me whenever I came. He was a source of solace, yet mischievous as he was, he tired her. When I came she retired to the solitude of her room, not to be tempted, no matter how bright the sun, to join us on our rambles.

I buried my own grief in writing, rewriting and writing yet again until at last my novel assumed some measure and shape. There came a time, however, when I decided to change it no more. The last word written, I searched for a title and found it in Christopher Marlowe's *Conquests of Tamburlaine:* "Virtue solely is the sum of glory and fashions men with true nobility." *Sum of Glory* it should be, and I felt a thrill of excitement as I added that title to the first page. I then put it aside, feeling more bereft than ever.

Darius had been forced to relinquish his seat in the Commons on assuming his father's title, and he had moved over to the august body of the Lords, more powerful, perhaps, than the Commons, but on his frequent visits he told us how much he missed their lively debates. He had been promised a seat in the government when the Whigs regained power. As it was, he worked hard with their shadow cabinet. I would read aloud to Lady Bladen reports of his speeches in the *Times*. His was fast becoming a name of stature within Whig circles, and he worked hard at the bi-election for his vacated county seat to ensure that it was kept within his party.

Politics, though, were not his only concern. He was clearly worried about his mother. "She must get out of her room and out of this house, for some time at least. I've asked her again and again to come to London. I am sure the change would be beneficial to her. I believe she might agree if you were to come, too. She is fond of your company, Alexandra, I need hardly tell you that."

London! The very name excited me. What wouldn't I give to go. Yet father had refused before; he would never agree.

Darius, as if reading my mind, added, "I shall speak to your father if you would wish to go."

"Of course I wish to go, but father will never allow it."

"Don't give up before the battle has even been joined," he remonstrated. "Allow me to speak to him. I may be able to allay his fears."

"Don't be forceful or commanding," I warned. "He hates to be told what to do."

"I suspect that may run in the family," he smiled.

"Ask it as though you do him the favour by taking me," I continued, ignoring his comment. "Then he can't get you into a compromising position."

"My dear young lady," he assumed a mock oratorial stance, "I can assure you that I have not spent months on those hard benches in the House for nothing. My powers of persuasion have been much enhanced by that inconciliable body. Believe me, it is so."

It must have been. Father, after assuring himself that I cared nothing for the plan one way or another—for he hated to please any of us, excepting Eugenia—gave a grudging consent, emphasizing, however, that since I was not out I could attend no formal functions. He was anxious as ever that I not make my bow to society under Whig auspices, for I was certainly of age, having already passed my nineteenth birthday.

"Aunt Maud is to bring you out as she did Cassy, though with better results, I should hope." He directed an infuriated glare at Cassy, who, seated on the sofa, bent closer to her mending without looking up.

"I am so happy for you, Alex," she whispered when at last he left us alone. "I've so often wanted to see London. Now you can tell me all about it. Salisbury may have been a veritable metropolis compared with Linbury, but it was less than pleasant with Aunt Maud constantly admonishing me to bestir myself."

Cassy had already confided to me her humiliation at the hands of Aunt Maud. Much to our aunt's displeasure, Cassy had scarcely taken Salisbury society by storm. Miss Tabitha Bramble, Aunt Maud had designated her, a positive wallflower who should be at pains to please. But gentle Cassy had remained as she always was and would ever be, quiet and shy. Aunt Maud had packed her up and sent her home a month before she was due to return, with a sharp note to father telling him he must set to himself to find her a husband.

"To be treated with such incivility, as though I had no sensitivity, no feeling—it was hard to bear. I make no claim to be pretty, to be brilliant or witty, but that woman treated me as though I were some freak of nature. I hate her!"

I did also for her uncharitable behaviour to one least deserving of it. I resented my father even more for siding with her, for humiliating Cassy since her return by talking of the constant burden of her expense.

"One day we'll be free of all of them, Cassy; we'll break away, we'll be happy. We will!" I consoled.

"You will, Alex, for you will marry and be free of him."

"I don't wish to marry. There is no one . . . at least there is no one who will ask me whom I would accept."

"I think Howard Ramsey would. I expect he'll be back from India soon."

"Well, I would never take him if he did. I don't like him one bit. I'm sorry to say it, Cassy, but I wish you had fastened your attentions on someone more worthy of them. I positively detest him. He brags and he is as bossy now as when he was a boy. If he should ever ask me to marry him, I should certainly refuse."

"Oh, Alex, you wouldn't!" Her look of horrified astonishment made me giggle, and soon we were both thinking up the most improbable suitors whom it would be our duty to refuse: Mr. Wilson, the apothecary, who took greater care of his beaver hat than of his patients; Mr. Snodgrass, a friend of Mr. Harrington's, who imagined himself an orator and cleared his throat before each sentence he uttered, even if it were only, "Pass the butter, please"; Mr. Bunby, father's lawyer, who was stiff and dry and always dressed in sombre colours and gave the impression of having himself become the writing implement which he used so freely; or Mr. Flintwell, his partner, who was fat and round where Mr. Bunby was hard and thin, and who laughed constantly as though he had once been told that fat people laugh a lot and he was prepared to oblige on even the most melancholy occasions. Soon we were in such fits of giggles that we felt like little girls in short petticoats again.

As I bid her good-bye on the clear September day I left for London, I hugged Cassy and promised that the month would soon pass and then I would bring her back a surprise.

"A husband," she laughed.

"No, silly," I scoffed, "something much better and much more useful—a merino shawl, for instance, or a beaded reticule."

Everything about the journey was exciting to me—the road, the scenery, farm workers and cottagers waving as we passed, the Pelican at Speedhamland where we spent the night. Yet most exciting of all was the change as we entered London—crowded streets, houses squeezed one against another, cavernous alleys through which no light seemed to penetrate, horses, carriages, carts, vendors, people everywhere. The noise was deafening.

Footmen hurried to meet us as we pulled up at Great Stanhope Street. Darius's attention was immediately claimed by his secretary, who stood by in the hall, a sheaf of papers in his hand. Crumpet and his nursemaid were whisked upstairs, and Lady Bladen and I took off our travelling cloaks and settled down before a fire in the drawing room.

"I didn't realize how tiring that journey is," she said. "Septimus and I used to make it so often, and when we were together it seemed to pass so quickly, but I suppose I am getting old."

"No, it is a great distance, but I expect it passed quickly for me because I've never been away from home and everything was new to me."

I looked round the room at the Adam marble fireplace and white walls decorated with light pastel colours, which set off the beautiful mahogany of the doors and window frames.

"I see Darius has acquired some new paintings." Lady Bladen indicated two landscapes on either side of the fireplace. One was a rural scene at harvest time I judged to be a Constable, but the other was a hazy sunset in which colour had been used in a most exciting and voluptuous manner I could not place. I discovered it to be by Turner, who had adopted a standard quite his own.

"What a pity Darius did not get Lawrence to paint Philomena," she sighed. "But perhaps he would not wish to hang it here even had he done so. I have never seen a woman so mourned. It is out of all proportion. I see no inclination on his part to remarry, but I wish he would instead of frittering his time away on women like . . . well, I suppose it is not my concern. He is old enough to know his own mind. At least the succession has been assured, though I wish he had more than one son just in the event, heaven forbid, that anything should happen to Crumpet. I think that eventually Darius will forgive him for being the cause of his mother's death. I know I pray for it.''

She passed her hand across her brow, and I realized then how very tired she was and how she had changed since her husband's death. Never before had she confided in me her feelings about Darius, how concerned she was about his lack of parental affection. Apart from that, though, I was transfixed by her allusion to another woman in Darius's life, no matter that he was "frittering away time" with her. In my heart I had believed, quite selfishly, that his mourning must prevent entanglement with any other. Yet he was a man of consequence, a handsome man, an available man; judging by myself, I knew only too well the feelings he could arouse in the female breast. Yet if he sought such company, why could it not be mine? Who was she, this woman whom Lady Bladen mentioned?

Lady Bladen was gazing into the fire, lost in thought.

"I hope that Darius will soften in his feelings for the boy," she repeated.

"I am sure he will. No one can be with Crumpet long without succumbing to his charms, you know that. Darius has had a great deal on his mind, and, too, he has not spent time with his son. Now that they are under the same roof things will change. He may even resent us taking him back to Charteris with us at the end of the month."

But I was wrong. Though Crumpet was dressed in his smartest nankeen suits, though we made sure he repeated all the new words he was learning before his father, Darius remained indifferent towards him until one day Crumpet got into his study and attempted to make a sailboat from an official report.

I ran in when I heard Darius shout in exasperation, "Drat that child! At least keep him out of my rooms while he is here."

"Crumpet didn't mean to do anything wrong, Darius, he . . ."

"And I wish you and mother would stop calling him by that foolish name. He was baptized John."

Crumpet had broken into tears at our raised voices, and without another word I gathered him up and took him to the nursery. When I came down I offered, though none too politely, to iron out the crumpled pages.

"Never mind, I can get another copy."

"Then if you were able to obtain another copy, why did you scream at the child just now and upset him so?"

He looked up from his work. "I'm sorry. I'm simply not used to having a child at hand. Was I so harsh?"

"Indeed you were. And I think it is time you became used to having a child at hand, for he is your son."

My comment made him angry. Never before had I spoken to him in such a blunt manner; indeed, nobody had. His reply was stiff. "I suppose you are right."

"How can you not love him, Darius. Sometimes I can't understand you. You are a kind, reasoning, gentle man until it comes to Cr—to John. Just because . . ." But I had no right to speak to him of his wife's death. I broke off abruptly, breaking into tears, and I made to leave the room, but before I could do so, he came over and put his arm around my shoulders.

"I'm sorry, Alex. I realize I'm not a very good father, but I shall try."

The words were spoken unwillingly, as though he struggled to say them. Angrily I shrugged his arm away.

"Why try? Why don't you just feel, as any father should. He must not always have to pay for Philomena's death."

My outburst had injured him, and I was immediately ashamed and ran from the room. Yet that angry scene was not altogether without avail, for thereafter Darius's attitude toward his son changed to an odd formality which, while it was not the parental love I felt to be Crumpet's due, nevertheless was an improvement over his former indifference.

IX

LONDON, FOR ME, was both heaven and hell.

It was heaven because, despite our differences over Crumpet, I was with Darius, and for the first time I saw him in his own world, a world which until that time had only been a realm of conjecture for me, a world of political power and intrigue, a world of wit and intellect, a world of glittering, sometimes outrageous fashion.

I attended no formal gatherings—my father's edict forbade it—but I accompanied Lady Bladen on her round of calls and was present at the informal dinners given at Great Stanhope

Street. Lady Bladen's friends paid little heed to me, for I spoke little and my style of dress was plain and ordinary; nevertheless, I found stimulation in new faces, new conversation, new outlook.

But it was the contrast between the London of the society drawing room and the London I saw from the carriage window when we shopped at Spitalfields silk merchants or Clerkenwell drapers that pained me. The seething mass of people, their faces distorted in stupor caused by gin; children in rags, dirty and ill fed; street vendors vying raucously with one another for our trade as the Bladen coach passed regally and unheedingly on its way—these scenes, which refused to leave my mind, made of London a hell.

Lady Bladen seemed unaware of any incongruity between the crowded streets we passed through and the scenes of her own London of the West End. Once she remonstrated with me for throwing all the change I possessed in my reticule to a young child who pressed his face against the window when a crush of vehicles forced us to a standstill.

"That was a silly thing to do, Alexandra. Do you think that that child will keep those coins? Far from it. They are probably already spent on gin, the child sent off to beg or steal more. Far better that we do as we have always done: support our charities, do good where we know our help will be properly received and wisely spent. Casting wealth from carriage windows, I assure you, does no good at all."

I was chastised, yet I knew Lady Bladen meant it not unkindly. She was a generous benefactor, one to whom the needy of Linbury often turned; no beggar was ever sent empty-handed from the doors of Charteris. Yet seeing the squalor, the hand-to-mouth existence of London's poor, charities didn't seem enough.

"You mustn't blame mother or think her unfeeling," Darius said when I told him of the incident. "She does much in her own way, in the way she was taught, to redress the hardships of the poor. You are young and idealistic, but you must understand it is impossible for one person to save the world. The plight of the poor is more apparent to you here than in Wiltshire, though there are people around Linbury in just such straitened circumstances. There they are spread throughout the countryside, unlike London, where they are gathered together in enclaves. Throughout England many are in need; as many as the Poor Laws help, as many are left in worsened straits. It is impossible to ignore the poverty that exists; certainly anyone of any sensitivity must be aware of it."

"But who is to help them?" I asked. "Who speaks for them?"

"The Radicals say they do, but as often as not all they do is stir up malcontent with no positive plans for reform. I believe it is the Whigs who speak for them. It is one of the reasons I espouse their cause—I am not a Whig simply because I was born into a Whig family. So far our efforts have been thwarted—remember, apart from Lord Grenville's brief hold of the reins in 1806, our party has not held power for almost four decades—but never have Whigs ceased to advocate reform in our role as the loyal opposition. Reform is in the wind. Soon it will be impossible to ignore. I smell it coming, and though it may seem incredibly slow in your eyes, I asssure you their is steady progress. I expect there will be an expansion of voting privileges before long, and with greater representation, greater equality must result. In England we want no bloodbath such as they experienced in France. That is the reason I detest Radicals like the Hunts—they incite; they do nothing more. For England it is important that change be evolutionary, not revolutionary."

"Within this evolution you speak of, do you envision women ever being given the franchise?"

He smiled.

"No, don't smile. I am perfectly serious. Why should women not vote?"

"Indeed, there is no reason they should not, though I suspect should they do so they would vote as their husbands, which would only mean doubling the count, an onerous procedure even now."

"I am not at all sure that that would be the case. Besides, not all women marry. If I were allowed the means, the education so that I might make my own living, that is what I would prefer instead of relying on some man to support me for the rest of my life. I certainly think it would be unfair to grant the franchise only to married women."

"Alexandra, now you are funning me. It is ridiculous to say you won't marry. I shall take care to remind you of that when you follow your sister to the altar. You are young yet, but a very attractive young lady, and I don't doubt that the day is not far distant when I shall be wishing you happy."

His sincere interest, his speculations entirely those a partial family member might make, infuriated me.

"I shall never marry, " I vowed. "Unless . . ."

"Unless?" Darius prompted.

"Unless . . . unless I love. Few marriages are based on love, it seems."

"Perhaps," he replied slowly. "But one must be able to distinguish love from infatuation. They are totally different emotions, yet all too often they give every illusion of being the same. I sometimes think that few are privileged to experience love in their lives. In that case perhaps it is well that it is not the sole basis of marriage. But you, Alexandra, as I said earlier, you are an idealist. I wish you may find it."

I have, I longed to cry out, but his expression was so grave, so sad, I knew where his thoughts were.

"Love may come more than once into your life, Darius. Because Philomena died . . ."

"Philomena, as you insist upon reminding me, is dead. I would prefer not to discuss her," he interrupted me harshly.

"Forgive me."

An awkward silence ensued, a silence during which I reproached myself for my gaucherie. I was relieved when Lady Bladen entered, bringing with her Margaret and her husband, Sir Nigel Armbruster.

"Do look, Darius. I had not thought Margaret would be here before tomorrow, or that Patience was to come at all, but Margaret assures me she and Edward are to arrive within the week—it's going to be a real reunion."

Margaret kissed her brother and turned to me.

"And with Alex here, it *will* be a reunion. You've grown lovelier than ever. You must be turning the head of every young beau in town."

"Exactly what I should think." Darius was again at ease. "But she insists she will be an old maid."

"Oh, pooh, Alex. Wait until you've been besieged by admirers and then tell me that is so."

"Stop teasing Alexandra, you two. Her father gave us strict instructions before we left that she is not to attend any balls or formal functions here, since she is not out."

"What a shame!" Sir Nigel put in. "Damned hard on a pretty young lady, eh!"

"My feelings exactly," Lady Bladen nodded, "but there it is. Darius had to agree or she couldn't have come with us."

"It's a shame and unfair besides, because Alex is certainly old enough to be out," Margaret rejoined. "But still, to look on the bright side, that doesn't rule out the opera, and Lady Thurston told Nigel we were to use her box."

"And Grimaldi is at the Drury Lane," Sir Nigel reminded his wife. "You know how you enjoy him."

"Such a treat! We must go. He's really so funny, Alex, you'll adore him."

"What does he do?"

"What doesn't he do!"

Grimaldi did everything. His billing as the greatest clown of all time did not praise him too highly; in fact it hardly praised him enough. Agile and limber, he was a being set apart. Each limb of his body possessed a language all its own. He had the ability to make me laugh and cry at one and the same time.

"Here." Darius handed me his handkerchief, for my own proved quite useless in stemming the intermingled tears of laughter, of sympathy, of joy. He had suggested a stroll outside during the intermission, but Margaret and Patience had met with old friends in the foyer, so only the two of us set out.

"I'm always borrowing your handkerchiefs," I apologized, remembering as I did so the last one that still remained in my bureau drawer beneath my diary.

"Did you borrow one before? When was that? No, wait, don't tell me—it was the time you came to that rally at Linbury dressed up as a boy. You really are an extraordinary young lady, Alex—quiet, studious, most proper, yet you do and say things like no other of your years and your sex."

"Should I take that as a compliment?"

"You should. You're not an easy person to pay compliments to, though. You're far too serious and aloof. You really should take my arm or you'll be in danger of tripping on these rough cobblestones."

Contentedly I tucked my arm through his, and he caught hold of my hand and held it fast, smiling down at me.

"Now you look happy."

"I am, very happy."

"Do you realize, Alexandra, how much we all rely on you, every one of us? I often have the odd feeling that you know me better than anyone."

"I rely upon you, Darius. I can't ever imagine life without you . . ." I broke off, and then added awkwardly, "Without all of you."

He tightened his grip on my hand slightly. "Though you may deny it now, Alex, I've no doubt that one day you will be engrossed with a family of your own, yet I know you'll not forget us anymore than I—than we'll forget you." He stopped to look down into my face and began, "If ever I were to remarry . . ." but then broke off to conclude, "but I never shall."

"Never is a long time. I cannot believe that you are meant to go through life alone anymore than you believe I am."

It was the most intimate moment that had ever passed between us. We stood so close to one another that I could feel every breath he took, and he must have been able to hear ever beat of my pounding heart.

Later I conjectured what might have been had I said then what was in my heart, how much I loved him, how much I always would. But what he might have replied I would never know, for a cool voice shattered that moment.

"Well, coz, it is you, is it not? I thought I recognized the figure of our great lawmaker. Indeed, I should have expected to see you, for you have the unerring quality of always leading where I am bound to follow."

Darius immediately released his hold of me and stepped back. I looked upon an elegant young gentleman of medium height, dressed in the very height of fashion in a broad swallowtail coat of blue velvet with a high rolled collar and decorated with the largest crystal buttons I had ever seen. His face was narrow and pale, his form was slender; he wore his fair hair longer than most, and it waved slightly as it fell towards his collar. Had he not interrupted an intimate moment I had long awaited, I should have welcomed so fascinating a newcomer. As it was, I resented the intrusion, yet not as much as Darius.

"Poindexter," Darius acknowledged with no attempt at welcome.

"Are you not going to introduce me to your charming companion?" Poindexter smiled at me as though we already were acquainted, but my smile returned was suspended by Darius's brief, even hostile reply.

"You must excuse us but our party awaits us inside."

Without another word, another glance, Darius took my elbow and led me away.

"Was that really your cousin?" I could scarcely believe that it was, for it was totally unlike Darius to repulse anyone, least of all a member of his own family.

"Yes." It was clear he would allow no further discussion of that gentleman.

"There you are! We were about to send Nigel and Edward to search for you. Did you see Geoffrey? We told him you were here," Margaret greeted us as we entered. "Mother will be sorry when she hears of it, for she always says she sees nothing of him. I must say we see little enough of him ourselves, though we live so close to Maplethorpe and visit my aunt frequently. Geoffrey is a man about town, so I suppose one must come to London in order to see him. Philomena said that you used to entertain him when you were on Grosvenor Square."

"That's the signal that we should get back to our box," Darius interrupted. "Do come along, all of you."

"I never knew you to be so prompt for performances," Patience put in.

"Alexandra is enjoying it," Darius insisted.

"Then of course we should get back. We shouldn't want Alex to be disappointed." It was said sweetly enough, yet I always felt a trace of resentment in Patience. My curiosity was aroused by Geoffrey Poindexter, a curiosity that was to be assuaged soon after we had settled into our places by his arrival.

"Dear Geoffrey, I'm so glad you decided to join us." Patience made a place for her cousin at her side.

As he sat down he turned to me. "Is no one going to present me to the young lady whom Darius held in such earnest conversation outside? I appeal to you, Margaret, since Darius refused my request."

"Oh, Darius! You know what a tease he is, Geoffrey, though he may have thought you were already acquainted, with Alex, for she is one of the family by now, in practice if not in fact."

Geoffrey Poindexter looked quizzically from me to Darius and then back again. "Am I to take it that I owe my cousin and this charming young lady, to whom I have yet to be presented, joyous felicitations?"

Darius had half-turned from his cousin and was involved in conversation with Edward Brace, I was not sure that he had heard, though I blushed. Margaret, seeing my flushed face, interposed hastily, "No, no, Alexandra Cox-Neville is a dear friend and neighbour of ours from Wiltshire. Her father's estate, Seton Place, borders Charteris. Alexandra, allow me to present my fascinating but quite devastating cousin, Geoffrey Poindexter."

He smiled at me and bowed. I saw behind that smile a sharp scrutiny. His eyes, fixed on mine, were light and penetrating; there was about them a certain fervour in their intensity.

"Miss Cox-Neville must be allowed to draw her own conclusions on my character. For my part, though, I find myself delighted at making your acquaintance. Do you make your debut this season?"

"Miss Cox-Neville has accompanied my mother to town. She is not out," Darius interrupted sharply.

"A pity. But I shall surely see you again when I call on my aunt, Miss Cox-Neville. I had not realized that she was in town or I should surely have paid my respects before this—particularly," he bowed to me slightly, "had I known she had such a charming companion."

"You are such a flirt, Geoffrey," Patience complained. "And I do think it is too bad of you that you do not spend any of your time flirting with your cousins."

"But you are both married."

"Since when has that prevented you from flirting," she asserted. "From all I hear, it serves to encourage you, though I must say, you yourself seem to be terrified of the married state."

He looked over at me thoughtfully. "Oh, I don't know. Should the right set of circumstances present themselves, I should not be averse."

"You mean the right heiress." Patience smiled a trifle spitefully. "I'm afraid that lets you out, Alex."

"I am really finding this rather repetitious. I think Grimaldi has shown us the best of his act. Shall we go?"

Darius, rising abruptly, left little occasion for discussion. I was disappointed because we had all been enjoying the evening. I could only think that the arrival of Geoffrey Poindexter was responsible for its rupture. I saw a look pass between them as we left, hostile on one side, mocking on the other, a look that was to cause me much curiosity.

That curiosity was satisfied somewhat the following morning. I was sitting with Lady Bladen and wondering whether to mention Mr. Poindexter to her when his name was announced by the footman.

"My dear aunt!" He entered gracefully, holding out both hands as he advanced towards her. "Only yesterday did I learn of your presence in town, but I must apologize, for surely I should have made it my business to know of such an important arrival. Be assured, had I known I should have waited on you much earlier."

"Dear, dear Geoffrey." It was plain from Lady Bladen's greeting of her nephew that she held him in far higher esteem than did her son. "How lovely to see you. I asked Darius about you, but from what he said, I thought you were not in town at this time."

"But he knew I was here. I see him often at White's."

"I suppose it must somehow have slipped his mind. He is so occupied—politics, management of the estate, all of that is his now." She sighed in remembering.

"I understand he is in the way of becoming quite a statesman." I detected a caustic note in Poindexter's voice, but his comment caused Lady Bladen to put aside her remembrance of her loss for pride in her son.

"I am so very pleased with Darius, as was his father."

"People are always pleased with Darius. I know my mother constantly talks of him." Again I noticed bitterness, but he turned and smiled at me most civilly.

"And it is a great pleasure to see you again so soon, Miss Cox-Neville."

"So you two have met, and you didn't mention it, Alex."

I was about to explain when Crumpet, who had been playing quietly in the window seat with a set of lead soldiers his father had brought him, pushed one of the metal figures into his mouth.

"Don't do that, Crumpet," I admonished and rose to take it from him.

"Ah, so this is Darius's son." Poindexter followed me to the window and bent down to pick up Crumpet.

"How like Philomena he is!" he murmured.

"Isn't he though. Her eyes entirely, though he is paler in complexion. I was worried at first, but he seems healthy enough. In fact he is too lively for me by far. I don't know what I would do without dear Alexandra. She is goodness itself to the poor little motherless child."

"How very kind of her." There was an odd twitch at the corner of his mouth as he spoke, and the look he gave me made me flush in fear he would say more. But he carried Crumpet back with him and sat him on his knee.

"How sad that Philomena never saw the boy!"

That he seemed to have taken to Crumpet surprised me, for he did not appear to be the sort of man who would enjoy children, being so very much the beau. Yet he continued to dandle and play with the child as he chatted with Lady Bladen. He kept up a continuous flow of gossip, often witty, sometimes caustic, many of his remarks bordering on the malicious, but nevertheless keeping Lady Bladen entirely amused.

"You must tell your dear mother to come and see me at

Charteris," she said. "I don't know how long it is since she has been there, or you, either, for that matter."

"I can't say for mother, but I do promise that the next time I go down to Hampshire to see my dear friend Wilmott, I shall make a point of breaking my journey at Charteris."

"That would be splendid. It is indeed quite lonely there now." Her plaintive tones led Poindexter to express such sincere condolences on her loss that I wished Darius could have been there to hear him. Yet when he did enter some time later, it was to greet his cousin as coldly as he had done the night before and announce that he was quite decided to take us off to the Palace of Westminster to see the Upper House, something his mother had been trying to persuade him to do since our arrival.

Poindexter, in getting up to leave, was forced to disentangle Crumpet's hold from the tassels on his boots. He seemed not in the least to mind that those splendid boots had lost their gloss and were covered by a hoard of tiny fingerprints. I had taken him for a dandy, but his lack of concern bespoke less preoccupation with his appearance than I had thought.

"I shall take my leave of you then, aunt." Turning to me, he added, "I trust I may have another opportunity to meet you, Miss Cox-Neville. It is my hope that we should become much better acquainted."

It was said, I thought, to annoy Darius; perhaps he sought to disrupt an intimacy he imagined to exist between us.

Lady Bladen was particularly warm in her adieux, again encouraging her nephew to visit her.

"Such a lively young man Geoffrey has become," she remarked to Darius on his departure.

"Yes, quite the young blade." It was the most he had said about Geoffrey Poindexter, and it was certainly not said to compliment him.

X

THE ARRIVAL OF Margaret and her husband at Great Stanhope Street, with Patience and Edward staying nearby in Lord Brace's town house, caused an increased flurry of activity as friends of both daughters called, along with Lady Bladen's friends and Darius's political confidants.

I was outside these groups, yet every effort was made to make me feel a part of them, although Patience, while never excluding me, occasionally made me feel less than entirely welcome among her friends. Margaret, on the contrary, included me in everything.

As different as was the relationship of the sisters to me, so distinct was their relationship to their husbands. Margaret was so obviously content and serene in her marriage. She talked ceaselessly of her children and her daily activities in Hertfordshire, finding interest in the smallest tasks. It was clear that she held her husband in high esteem, as he did his wife. Sir Nigel Armbruster was a patient, undemanding, unprepossessing man who quite plainly believed that life had dealt fairly with him and he, in turn, intended to deal fairly with life. Patience and her husband, on the other hand, were never entirely satisfied with anything; perhaps for that reason if for no other, they were well suited.

Much as I tried I could not convince Margaret and Lady Bladen that observation of London life was sufficient amusement, and they vied with one another in seeking entertainment for me.

"Tonight we are going to take Lady Thurston up on her offer and use her box at Covent Garden," Margaret announced one morning, looking up from the paper. "I see Guiditta Pasta is again singing Bellini's *Norma*, and the *Chronicle* says it is not to be missed. You must come, mother, but I suppose Darius won't be able to, since he mentioned that the House would probably be in session late tonight and that we were not to expect him for dinner."

On the way to the theatre that evening, Lady Bladen explained how her husband had supported the rebuilding of the Covent

Garden only a few years earlier, after it had been burned to the ground. At that time it had rested with those members of the nobility and gentry who were patrons of the arts to rescue it from oblivion; they had done so admirably. The interior of green and gold was lit by a huge array of glass chandeliers, giving a dazzling light to the plush interior and the luxurious apparel of the audience, freely strolling and talking throughout the performance, a practice I found distracting, though I was to learn that people more often attended the opera to be observed than to observe.

Midway through the first act a party moving into the box directly across from the one in which we sat caused a flurry of comment. My attention was immediately drawn to the lady who occupied its centre and who seemed to draw all eyes, though she paid not the slightest heed to either the commotion she created or the performance on the stage. With an exquisite, oval face surrounded by silvery blond curls, large languid eyes and a half-smile playing on rose-petal lips, she was surrounded by a group of gentlemen who hung on her every word. When she removed her ermine wrap, her gown of silver-threaded muslin caressed her lustrous shoulders and curving breasts, against which, enticement among enticements, shone a dazzling array of diamonds.

"Who is she?" The question rose to my lips spontaneously. I was sure Lady Bladen must have been as aware of her entrance as anyone else, yet she asked coldly, "Who is who, Alexandra?"

"The lady in the box over there." I nodded my head in her direction; it was all I could do not to point.

"That is the Countess of Brentwood," she affirmed, and leaving me no chance to question her further, she turned to Margaret and took up in most animated converse the matter of little Nigel's proclivity for mud pies and Lucy's teething. These matters exhausted, she began a detailed discussion of the vaccination of non-fatal cow-pox as a vehicle to prevent smallpox—a method gaining widespread acceptance and the one Margaret had chosen for her own offspring—comparing it to the inoculation process brought to England by Lady Mary Wortley Montagu from Turkey, whereby a child received a small dose of the pox itself that she had used for her children. Her sudden, overwhelming preocupation with such matters seemed connected with her desire to keep her back turned on the box occupied by Lady Brentwood. Some moments later I knew the reason, for Darius entered that box to take the empty seat beside the lady, a seat that had undoubtedly been held in anticipation of his arrival. I could not doubt from the manner in which he greeted that lady and the manner in which she returned his greeting that they knew one another well, very well. My gasp as I saw him caused both Margaret and Lady Bladen to follow my gaze.

"Well," said Lady Bladen icily, "had I known *she* was to attend this evening, I should certainly never have agreed to accompany you."

"Oh, mother, don't fret so," Margaret placated. "After all, Darius has been mourning Philomena for more than a year. Surely you don't want him to mourn her forever. Is he to be denied all enjoyment of life?"

"I just wish he would have his enjoyment with someone less . . . less flamboyant, that is all. Why doesn't he remarry? He is much sought after. Why, Lady Babcock spoke to me of her niece, a nice young girl, just out and a handsome fortune, good lineage too, unlike this . . . this adventuress. I'm sure he could have his pick, but instead he dallies with this woman."

"I don't think he wants to remarry, mother; not yet, at least. I doubt anyone will replace Philomena."

"I know, I know. But this—this whatever it is—is beginning to cause talk. I don't like it. She may be rich, but she's nobody. I shall never forgive him if she forces him into marriage. She got the fortune of that doddering old Brentwood, and look at the way she flaunts it."

"She's a beauty, mother, you must admit it. And frankly, Darius is not hurting himself at all politically by being a friend of hers. She has great influence, you know."

"The Whigs' favourite hostess—and a good deal more, I've no doubt," Lady Bladen derided.

I saw the notorious lady had pointed us out to Darius and they rose and left the box, bound, no doubt for ours. I thought for one moment that Lady Bladen would bar her admittance or cut her, but Margaret laid a hand on her mother's arm with a warning glance, so that when the door of the box opened to admit the offending countess, Lady Bladen was composed if not entirely calm.

"Mother, I had no idea you planned to be here this evening," Darius began cheerfully.

"Of that I have no doubt."

If he noticed the hostility in his mother's reply he gave no sign, continuing with equanimity, "Well, I am delighted that you are here, for it gives me the opportunity to present to you the

Countess of Brentwood. She tells me that you have not met before.''

"I knew Lord Brentwood well—before he remarried."

The vision of beauty before us seemed quite unperturbed by Lady Bladen's cool reception. She spoke in low, charming tones of the singer and her performance but Lady Bladen cut her short. Never before had I seen her behave with such discourtesy.

"We know, we know; *we* arrived when the performance began. She is loud and her high notes are shrill. I doubt that we shall stay until the end. In fact, we were getting ready to leave."

That our departure was closely allied to the countess's arrival was lost on no one. She seemed, however, quite unmoved by Lady Bladen's animosity, turning to greet Margaret and her husband before directing a questioning glance in my direction.

"And are you enjoying London?" she asked, for Darius, who performed the introduction, explained that it was my first visit. I don't know what I replied. All I could think about was how beautiful she was and how close she stood to Darius. This, then, was the woman of whom Lady Bladen had spoken, the woman on whom Darius was "frittering his time."

They left our box as the second act began, but the evening was spoiled. I wished wholeheartedly that either we or she had chosen another night to attend Covent Garden. Apart from my own feelings, to which I could give no name but which disturbed me beyond measure, Lady Bladen was obviously upset. I whispered to her that if she wished to leave immediately I should not mind, and before Madame Pasta had begun her main aria of the evening, she rose abruptly and we all followed her from the box.

As we were about to descend the staircase, Darius came up and took his mother's arm. "You are right, as usual, mother. Madame Pasta is quite overrated. I'll come back with you. We still have time for a game of piquet if I have any takers."

A look passed between them, questioning on the one side, reassuring on the other. His mother smiled.

"I would greatly enjoy a game of piquet with you, Darius."

Not a word was said then, or later within my hearing, of the fascinating countess, but I could not forget her. Had Darius fallen in love again, I wondered, though Margaret had said no one would ever replace Philomena. No one could deny that she was an exciting woman. She had, too, the additional attraction of being influential in political circles. A combination of beauty, wealth and influence must indeed be devastating for a rising politician.

*   *   *

Darius's star was indeed ascending on the political scene. He had become a regular habitué of Holland House in Kensington, the cradle of Whiggery as father called it, for it was there, under the auspices of Lord and Lady Holland, that the brightest luminaries of the Whig party gathered together to rub shoulders with the country's foremost painters, poets, scientists and writers. The brilliance of an evening in such company I had not expected to be mine. I was thrilled beyond measure, therefore, to discover I had been included in an invitation to Lady Bladen to accompany Darius there. Yet it was Darius who posed an objection.

"Your father, I fear, would not approve, though I wish that you could go, for I believe you would enjoy it and learn a great deal. You have such a keen mind."

"But Darius, please, must father be told of it?"

"He was quite firm when he spoke to me of social engagements, and I fear an evening at Holland House is very definitely that, with the added detriment of being an evening in Whig company."

My face fell.

"I would really want you to go, Alexandra. I think you know that. But your father spoke to me most particularly on this matter—for, I suspect, this very reason."

It was Lady Bladen, convinced that I had seen nothing of London society during my stay, who put an end to all discussion.

"I shall personally take the responsibility of explaining to Mr. Cox-Neville, should he raise some objection, that I insisted that Alex go with us. It is not, after all, a ball or a rout but simply an evening of good food and good conversation, from both of which she will benefit. There is unlikely to be a published guest list in the newspaper—something I can understand he would not want. It has been for that reason that I have refused so many other invitations for Alex, refusals I did not wish to give. No, Darius, Alexandra must certainly accompany us, and I wish to buy her a new dress for the occasion."

On the matter of the dress, however, I remained obdurate; a new dress in my wardrobe when I returned to Wiltshire would surely give rise to comment. I had refused all previous offers of Lady Bladen to replenish my outdated wardrobe; this one too I refused, politely but firmly. Instead I retrimmed the green taffeta I had worn to the Linbury election ball with Mechlin lace purchased from Basnetts in the Strand, and fashioned and embroidered a pelerine to wear around my shoulders from silk from Spitalfields. The result, while by no means spectacular, was passably pleasing. It would have to suffice.

Despite my anxiety to visit Holland House, when the evening of our visit arrived, I was distinctly apprehensive. I dressed my hair four times, taking it down and brushing it out, completely unsatisfied until Lady Bladen's maid came and, undoing my latest attempt, plaited my hair at the back in a nine-strand Polish braid, coiled this in a crown around my head and pulled numerous *tire-bouchons,* loose curls, down at the side. The result was far too sophisticated and made me feel very uncomfortable, though she was obviously pleased with it and I dared not disappoint her by suggesting a change. Her glance at my dress convinced me she saw through all my refurbishment, but I consoled myself with the thought of it being far more difficult to impress a lady's maid than her mistress and, if Lady Bladen noticed anything it was the dressing of my hair, which, I believe, pleased her as little as it did me.

Apart from dubiousness over my appearance, my apprehension was caused in part by the reputation of Lady Holland, which long preceded my introduction to her—irritable, quick-tempered, a woman of fierce hatreds and equally fierce affections, she was renowned for ruling both household and visitors with a tyrannical hand. I wished with all my heart to make a good impression upon her, for Holland House was the centre to which Darius had gravitated and into which he had been accepted. For that reason if for no other, I wanted acceptance in that world of politics and literature, wit and beauty; yet I had never felt less comfortable.

They were all there: Lords Grey and Russell; poets Samuel Rogers and Henry Luttrell and Thomas Moore; Sir Samuel Romilly with Lord and Lady Landsdowne; Sydney Smith, clergyman and inimitable wit; and the perennial John Allen, who had come as physician to Lord Holland and stayed to become a constant, indeed an indispensable member of the household.

The evening began well, for Lady Holland, far from ignoring me as I had expected, insisted on personally conducting me on a tour of her rather odd collection of relics. As I followed her to examine the Byzantine candlesticks of Mary of Scotland, the gold-enamel snuffbox of Governor Howell, who had survived the horrors of the Black Hole of Calcutta, the ring containing his portrait which Charles II had given to his mistress the Duchess of Portsmouth, I tried to concentrate on her courtesy to me and forget that it was said she saved her most acrid humour for pretty, fashionable women. Her Buonapartist sympathies were proclaimed; she proudly displayed Napoleon's Legion of Honour, yet more peculiar was the lock of his hair and a sock "that poor dear man," as she called him, had been wearing on the day he died. Remembering the repugnance I had felt when Paul had forced me to take the part of Napoleon in our childhood games, these sympathies were alien to me, yet they were held by many. With an end to our wars with France and the rise of domestic difficulties, I had heard more than one Englishman express admiration for the French emperor, a strange turn of events for one such as myself, who preferred a clear delineation between good and evil. Yet here was England's archenemy enshrined in Holland House!

It was quite evident that Sydney Smith was a favourite with Lady Holland. She ordered him about imperiously.

"Ring the bell for the footman, Sydney," she commanded.

"Yes, indeed," he responded blandly. "And then would you like me to sweep the floor?"

But she was already bidding Rogers to hush. "Your poetry is bad enough—do I beg you, be sparing of your prose," a rebuke he received with a vinegary smile.

I was sure that Sydney Smith observed my discomfort, for he came over to me and began to talk of his own first days at Holland House, of how awe inspiring he had found everything. Yet to see him so completely at his ease made it difficult to believe. He inspired my confidence, though, for I found myself telling him all about Paul, of his going into the church and how much he detested the idea, how he would prefer law but father would not allow it. Mr. Smith understood perfectly, for he himself had wanted a career in law but his father had given him the choice of being a college tutor or a parson or going as supercargo to China and never darkening his doorstep again.

"I took the church as the lesser of evils, and all in all I do not dislike it, though it is no place for a young man of ambition such as I was then. Now, however, I see it offers a chance to make changes where they are most needed. I can well understand your brother. I wish you would ask him to come to see me if he ever gets to the wilds of Foston in Yorkshire, where I have my parish. It is, I regret to say, two hundred miles from that Great Parallelogram of Piccadilly, Regent Street, Hyde Park and Oxford Street that encloses more intellect and human ability, to say nothing of wealth and beauty, than the world has ever collected in such a space before.''

"You are a kind and understanding gentleman, sir. I shall most certainly tell Paul of our talk."

"And you, Miss Cox-Neville, are a very nice young lady."

"Nice?"

"Nice. You don't care to be nice?" he questioned.

" 'Nice' conjures up visions of prudishness."

"Far from it. Let me describe a nice person—one who inspires confidence, makes you talk and talk without fear of malicious misrepresentation, makes you feel you are reposing upon a nature which God has made kind and created for the benefit and happiness of society. A nice person has the effect upon the mind which soft air and fine climate has upon the body.

"A nice person, Miss Cox-Neville, never knocks over the wine or melted butter, does not tread upon the dog's foot or molest the cat, eats soup without noise, laughs in the right place and has a watchful, attentive and very pretty eye. Do you still object to being called nice?"

His eyes twinkled in his large, pleasant countenance.

"If you so see me, then how could I possibly object." I smiled back at him and knew we were friends.

At that point the evening showed every sign of passing well had not the announcement of dinner been preceded by the arrival of the Countess of Brentwood. If she noticed the coldness of Lady Bladen or the critical scrutiny of Lady Holland, she gave no more sign of it than she had before. Perhaps she had no need of those ladies' approval, for it was quite plain that she was a particular favourite of every gentleman present; it was equally plain that of those gentlemen, Darius was her particular favourite. One glimpse of her gown of black crepe over a black sarsenet slip, ornamented with deep pleats around the border of black velvet, the sleeves and low neckline lined with pearls, made me reexamine my own futile efforts at renovating my green taffeta. I knew once again that I was gauche and outmoded, that my hair was dressed in quite the worst way to show me to any advantage, and that the Countess of Brentwood was without a doubt the most beautiful woman present. As we were introduced, she gave no sign of remembering having met me before; indeed there was no reason I should have stayed in her memory.

We dined from Sèvres porcelain in a room hung with Genoese silk, velvet brocade and Boucher tapestries representing Greek gods. The panelled ceiling was ornamented with gold and white pendants, the Earl's coronet on the cornice alternating the famous *H* of the Earls of Holland. Venetian mirrors in gilt frames and marble busts of English men of history and literature surrounded the room. In my uneasy frame of mind, I found it rather intimidating, nor did I draw great comfort from my dinner companions, Thomas Moore and Samuel Rogers, both of whom, after an initial glance and indistinguishable murmur, talked over my head to one another. Moore, a dapper Irishman much given to toadying, was telling of a visit from Jackson, the eminent boxer, who had called on him that morning to ascertain the source of the line, "Men are but children of a larger growth."

"Dr. Johnson, undoubtedly Dr. Johnson," Rogers stated.

"No, no, I am quite sure it is not. In fact I told him I was sure it was Shakespeare, but though I've searched all day I've not yet found it."

"I believe if you will examine Dryden's *All for Love* you will find it."

Moore glanced at me with as much annoyance as surprise. "I dislike to disagree with such a charming young lady, but . . ."

"But I read it there only recently. It occurs in the third or the fourth act."

"Ah, dear Miss—Miss—"

"Cox-Neville."

"Yes, to be sure, Miss Cobb-Nevitt, how pleasing to be so young and so sure of oneself."

There was an appreciative titter at his wit, and I resolved to say no more. I might perhaps have passed through the remainder of the meal without creating any further notice had I not reached for my wineglass at the very moment the footman was about to serve my turtle soup. My hand brushed against the bowl, sending a few drops in the direction of the sleeve of Rogers's immaculate blue velvet evening coat.

"Don't worry, please think nothing of it, Miss—Miss Cod-Levitt," he insisted, rising immediately and causing immense consternation by making wild stabs at his sleeve with his serviette, bringing forth two servants armed with cloths to undo the damage.

Lady Brentwood smiled across at Rogers. "If you are trying to signal to me, Samuel, I wish you would be a tiny bit more discreet."

Rogers glanced furiously at me before replying, "I'm a plain man, madam. I should never dare to do such a thing, particularly finding myself in such a dishevelled condition.''

"God bless my soul, Rogers, I can't for the life of me think what your appearance has to do with it," Smith said blandly.

"To return the compliment, sir, may I say you're the most profligate person of my acquaintance," Rogers growled, his attention distracted from his coat.

"It does not surprise me to hear your opinion, for the whole of my life has been passed like a razor—in hot water or in a scrape.''

In the general diversion that followed, I smiled gratefully at Mr. Smith, and he very slowly and very solemnly winked at me while going on to describe *Granby,* a novel by Lister that he had reviewed for the *Edinburgh Review.*

"Excellent in every respect, except for the fact that one of the characters struck the hero. Nobody should ever suffer his hero to have a black eye or to be pulled by the nose. The *Iliad* would never have come down to these times if Agamemnon had given Achilles a box on the ear. Don't you agree, Miss Cox-Neville?''

"Indeed, to be a hero is to be greater than other men. To fall prey to a lesser character does ungild a lily.''

"My sentiments exactly.''

"I understood you to tell me you made a practice of never reading a book before reviewing it," Moore accused. "You said it prejudiced you so.''

"Ah, Tom, your memory is too good.''

Discussion turned to publishers. Moore had had some dissension with Longmans, and Smith mentioned a new house that had recently opened near St. Paul's churchyard.

"Hillaby, Alistair Hillaby is the name, and a very amiable gentleman he seems to be, too," he concluded.

I made silent note of Hillaby's name, for I had taken with me to London the manuscript of *Sum of Glory,* deciding that a novel unread is a sorry thing; let it be published, if that was possible, let it be criticized—even adverse criticism would allow of its existence—but let it not die in the box at the back of my wardrobe. If opportunity presented itself, I would seek Mr. Hillaby out.

After dinner Moore favoured the company with two of his songs, "Oft i' the stilly night" and "Believe me if all those endearing young charms," dedicating his performance to Lady Brentwood, who smiled graciously in response. Though I had not taken a liking to him, I found he had a melodious voice and an unassuming style. Throughout the evening I had made an effort not to look for Darius, for wherever he was, there, too, was the Countess, though possibly the reverse was true. Involuntarily my eyes sought him out as Moore sang,

"No, the heart that has truly lov'd never forgets,
But as truly loves on to the close,
As the sunflower turns on her god, when he sets,
The same look which she turn'd when he rose."

I was that sunflower, I thought, turning always towards him, yet would he never notice me as he noticed her? If not, would I remain that sunflower, never to bloom except in his presence?

"You are too pensive. I demand to see once again that smile which would force a gooseberry bush into flower," a voice cajoled at my elbow.

"Mr. Smith, you make it impossible not to smile when you ask it so nicely. But I fear you may no longer consider me a nice person."

"And what gives you that idea, Miss Cox-Neville?"

"You told me that a nice person does not spill his soup at dinner yet I contrived to spill mine and you were witness to the consternation it caused."

"Rogers is a fussy old fool, and Moore's not much better. But I said that a nice person never knocks over wine or melted butter. Those were both in perfect order at your place, and as far as I was aware you made not the slightest noise as you consumed your soup. Though you may wish it otherwise, to me you are quite the nicest person here."

"I do thank you for that, Mr. Smith, most earnestly I do, for I fear I have not been at my best this evening."

"If only you could see yourself as I see you now. But I realize it is not an old clergyman like me you wish to impress." His eyes drifted lazily towards Darius as he spoke. Am I becoming so obvious, I wondered, and went on quickly.

"I return to Wiltshire very soon, with Lady Bladen."

"Nevertheless, I trust that our paths cross again. Do remember to tell that young brother of yours to look me up."

XI

TIME PASSED MUCH more rapidly in London than it had ever done in Linbury, and, just when I was beginning to feel at home in the metropolis, Lady Bladen began to talk of leaving. Margaret invited me to stay with her in Hertfordshire, but I knew that father had allowed me a month away from home, and that month was long since past.

There was one matter, though, still unresolved. *Sum of Glory* rested, untouched, in my portmanteau. To carry it home after bringing it to London for the express purpose of finding a publisher was to admit failure. I remembered the publisher Mr. Smith had mentioned, Alistair Hillaby. He seemed a likely choice, but how to convey it to his establishment in Cheapside?

Luck favoured me with a visit from Augustus Fanshawe, who had followed in his brother's path to study law at Lincoln's Inn. He had heard from his mother of my visit to London and called at Great Stanhope Street to invite me to tour the Inns of Court, an invitation I eagerly accepted.

Augustus had changed little. He was still pedantic and plodding, but it was pleasant to see his familiar face and to hear of his life in London. Serving under a difficult and cantankerous barrister, his seemed an onerous existence with little money to show for it and little pleasure. Nevertheless, as we toured the handsome stone buildings, passing through the old gatehouse in Chancery Lane carved with the arms of Henry VIII, the most ancient part of the Inn, which led into the Old Square and the timeworn buildings with their small, uneven windows and great twisted chimneys, calm and serene in the midst of the bustle which surrounded them, I thought how Paul would have enjoyed the life that Augustus detested.

After we viewed the chapel, designed, like Charteris, by Inigo Jones, and examined the curious open crypt, which had once been used by barristers as a meeting place with their clients, we wandered in a desultory manner through the quiet gardens.

"It's wonderful to see you again, Alex. Do you think you will come back to London, for it will be months before I have the chance to get home?"

"I really don't know. I don't expect so. Since this is my last day, would you mind if we take a detour home so that I can deliver a packet to Cheapside?"

Augustus readily agreed. I was grateful that he asked no questions. He seemed only too glad that the journey back to Great Stanhope Street was to be prolonged.

The establishment of Alistair Hillaby, when we reached it, was dark and forbidding. Augustus made to accompany me, but before he could question me, I jumped down and assured him I would only be a moment.

Inside I found a clerk of advancing years bent over a heavy ledger. In response to my request to see Mr. Hillaby, he replied, without raising his eyes from his task, that he was not in.

"I have a manuscript for him." I set the packet on his desk without further ado.

"Who's it from?" he asked, looking up, taking in my plain attire. "Was he expecting it? If not, you'd better take it back, young lady. I'll not take responsibility for it."

His tone was sharp and insolent. I drew myself up to my fullest height and, adopting Lady Holland's sepulchral tones, announced, "My good man, see that this manuscript reaches Mr. Hillaby without any unnecessary delay, Otherwise I can assure you that you will be held directly responsible for what, to a new publisher, must make the difference between success and failure."

It was a vainglorious statement. I knew that as I made it, and I left him no opportunity to refute it, for without another word I swept from the room, uncomfortably aware of his beady eyes following my fast-retreating figure. Mr. Hillaby could but refuse it, I reasoned, and then I realized that I had left no address for its return. Nevertheless, I was glad to have taken it, and I chatted flippantly to Augustus all the way back. He lingered so long on our return that he was asked to dine, an invitation he readily accepted, so that our last night in London was spent with the constraint of a guest in our midst, one whom I felt Darius took to be a particular friend of mine, nor could I find a way to rid him of that idea.

As we journeyed back to Wiltshire the following day, Lady Bladen turned to me and said, "I am glad we went, but truly London was a sad place for me without my dear Septimus. I doubt I'll go back. Charteris is my home from now on."

I pressed her hand in sympathy for her loneliness, ignoring my own crushed hopes of ever seeing London again.

XII

LIFE WAS SOLITARY indeed on my return to Linbury. Even Charteris was unable to exercise its usual enchantment over me. Darius had returned to London immediately after accompanying us back, returned to the arms, I now direly supposed, of the enchanting countess. He had been, as usual, cheerful and brotherly toward me, even going so far as to tease me lightly about Augustus. There had been no return to that moment at Drury Lane. Sometimes I wondered whether I had only imagined the earnest tone of his voice, the pressure of his hand on mine, imagined that he had at that moment thought of me as I had for so long thought of him. Whether it had been imagination or not, I relived those moments and thought over all the other times we had been together. I loved him more than ever.

I missed Lord Bladen a great deal. I saw him in all the rooms where I had grown to know him so well—they were now empty indeed. Lady Bladen must have felt much the same, for she resumed her solitary ways, staying much to her own apartment upstairs. Thus the visit to London had not accomplished its desired end. She had, after all, missed her husband almost as much there as in Wiltshire. I saw her daily, and though we talked, there was little that I or anyone else could do for her. Mr. Linnell called, but she confided in me that his presence and his unctious comments irked rather than comforted her. I only wished that Mr. Smith had had his parish in Linbury.

Crumpet remained the one bright spot in our lives.

I had no questions from father to answer, for he was in Oxford when I returned. Paul had written to him evidencing open rebellion against taking the orders, and father had set out immediately to discipline him. That he had chosen to take Cassy with him confounded me; he usually had little desire for her company, and she would certainly be of no use in exerting force over Paul to pursue a course he deplored. Perhaps father had begun to realize Cassy's worth; their time together might serve to reveal her good qualities to him. I hoped he might return admiring and respecting her as I did.

Seton Place seemed strangely quiet, for Thomas was also away in Derbyshire with a college friend, and Netty had discovered she was pretty and was forever primping and no longer rushing around, for fear of disarranging her blond curls. Mother fussed over James, her baby, fearing, perhaps, that he too might grow up overnight and leave her with an empty nest.

My days again fell into a pattern; Charteris, Crumpet and writing.

Since talking to Augustus Fanshawe of his reading for the bar and perusing Blackstone's commentaries in Darius's library at Great Stanhope Street, I had become intrigued with the study of law. Why could a woman not follow it? Yet no woman had done so. I had discovered from Blackstone that women were, as far as the law was concerned, no different from children and morons; that a man could not legally grant anything to his wife, for to do so would suppose her to be a separate entity. Did marriage really mean complete submersion of the self? I thought over the women I knew—married or unmarried—yet the only one who seemed a person in her own right was the Countess of Brentwood, or perhaps Lady Holland, neither of whom I wanted for a heroine.

I was occupied in trying to formulate my ideas one afternoon when I heard sounds of an arrival. I jumped up, thinking it to be Darius, and ran to the library door. It opened to admit Geoffrey Poindexter.

"Oh, it's you." My voice must have dropped.

"You're disappointed," he challenged, throwing aside his travelling cape. "And here all the way from London I have anticipated meeting you again. Who was it you expected, some local swain—or Bladen, perhaps? Is he your idol?"

"I worship no idols," I replied, a trifle too quickly.

"A good God-fearing woman; there are so few of your kind to be found in town. It's delightful to rusticate for a while and rediscover the simple virtues. And where is that little fellow who made such a mess of my boots?"

"Oh, Geoffrey—I mean Mr. Poindexter, how kind of you to remember Crumpet."

"Do call me Geoffrey, I absolutely insist on it, for if you do not, I shall be forced to call you by that awful mothful of a name of yours, when Alexandra is quite my favourite name. And on the subject of names, I think Crumpet is quite perfect for that little chap."

I had never liked him better.

"I'm so very glad you came," I said impulsively.

"It is I who am delighted to see you. I've thought of you a great deal."

His intensity suddenly embarrassed me. "Let me tell Lady Bladen you are here. And Crumpet should be finished with his nap. I'll bring him down."

Lady Bladen, when she heard of Geoffrey's arrival, insisted that I stay to dine with him.

"You young people go on out and work up appetites worthy of the dinner cook is going to prepare," she commanded.

Geoffrey hoisted Crumpet onto his shoulders and we set off, across the sloping expanse of the lawn, down to the willows bordering the stream. In the oak woods beyond we occasionally caught a glimpse of wild deer, while the rabbit and hare scattered at our approach. Crumpet was attracted by the bright but deadly poison berries of the woody nightshade, and we had difficulty keeping his fingers from them until we played a game of hunting for the abandoned nests of the nightingales and blackbirds.

The sun was casting long shadows across the lawn by the time we returned, but still we were in no hurry to go inside, for the walk had been exhilarating. Geoffrey flung himself down on the grass and I sat beside him, while Crumpet, at our feet, pulled at the dandelion leaves that persisted despite the gardener's ongoing war against them.

"This is a lovely place," Geoffrey said at last. "Darius is a lucky devil. He's always been lucky, though. Ever since I was a boy I've wondered why everything always came so easily to him."

"Do you mean because of Charteris? You have inherited your father's property, though."

"Yes, Maplethorpe's mine, and a pack of his debts with it. Mother was the one with money—she's a Wentworth, like Darius. The money was hers, and she continues to keep a healthy hold on the purse strings."

"But eventually it will be yours."

"Yes," he reflected. "But it wasn't just Charteris I was thinking of. It just seems that everything that cousin of mine touches turns to gold, whereas adversely I turn things into stone . . . or sand . . ."

"Or salt?" I supplied.

"Or lead . . . or plasticine." He laughed as he said it, taking up the game.

"Or tin, or flint," I went on.

"Or lava."

I looked down at him, impatiently plucking at the grass with his slender, pale fingers. The last gleams of the sun caught in his long, fair hair as it hung across his face. Did he not realize how fortunate he really was?

"Some of the substances we mentioned can be even more valuable than gold," I said slowly. "King Cophetua, after all, wasn't all that glad when everything that he touched turned to gold."

"Darius is well aware of his own worth."

"Aren't you?"

He stared up at me, raising his eyebrows at the intensity in my voice. "Don't get that maternal look in your eye," he warned. "I hate that. Why I bring out the maternal quality in your sex I'll never know. It's a great mistake, which they discover only too late."

He pouted, seeming more like a little boy than ever.

"That sounds ominous, Geoffrey," I laughed. "Really, I don't feel maternal."

Yet even as I denied it, I knew that somehow he was right. There was a vulnerable quality about him, perhaps because he was unaware of his own good fortune.

"I couldn't feel maternal to you, anyway. You're older than I am. I was just thinking that you have so many fine qualities."

"Such as?" He looked up at me speculatively.

"You have a fine manner and appearance. You are a good conversationalist and have a ready wit. You are kind and compassionate."

"Kind and compassionate!" he snorted. "I wish Darius could hear you say that."

"Perhaps he can," I replied slowly. I had just caught sight of a tall figure striding in our direction from the house. Geoffrey followed my glance.

"Oh, God, that's torn it. My precious coz."

It was indeed Darius, and his arrival was as unexpected as had been that of Geoffrey earlier in the day. Their conjoint arrival was not predetermined, however, for Darius, with the briefest of nods at me, turned to his cousin to enquire most ungraciously, "And just what do you think you are doing here?"

"I'm on my way to see good old Wilmott." Geoffrey had regained his composure. After rising unhurriedly, he began brushing the grass from his bright yellow buckskins. "I decided to stop and see auntie. She didn't tell me you were expected."

"I trust your stay is not a long one." It was difficult to believe that Darius could be so uncivil, particularly to his own cousin.

"Now that you're here, coz, I don't expect it will be," Geoffrey drawled, "though I've had a perfect day. Alexandra saw to that. As a matter of fact, she was just telling me how kind and compassionate I am."

My cheeks flushed as Darius looked over at me angrily. His cousin's use of my Christian name seemed to annoy him, as though it implied more than existed between us.

"It is late in the afternoon. I expect that Miss Cox-Neville must return to Seton Place."

My already flushed cheeks darkened. I had never been dismissed by Darius in such a fashion. I turned on my heels, angry and hurt, and then remembered Lady Bladen's dinner invitation. I regretted having accepted it, but I had nevertheless. I turned back to say tersely, "Your mother has asked me to dine at Charteris this evening."

"Very well, then let us all go back to the house, shall we." His eyes fell on Crumpet, clinging to Goeffrey's boot, and he snapped, "Isn't it far too late for this child to be out? Must you drag him everywhere, Alexandra?"

Without a word I picked up Crumpet and made for the house, half-walking, half-running. As I went I heard Geoffrey remark, "He's a charming boy, Darius."

I glanced back to see how Darius received the compliment and caught the look of animosity he threw at his cousin. As I drew away from them, I could hear his voice, words indistinct but clearly harsh and bitter, and I wondered why Geoffrey should deserve such a tongue-lashing. We had had such a pleasant afternoon, and apart from the fact that I had enjoyed talking to him, he had been so very kind to Crumpet.

I wished I could have gone directly home, but Lady Bladen met me as I entered, full of Darius's arrival. Though no one could ever replace her husband, with his death, Darius had assumed the central role in her affections. One look at my dress, dusty from the walk, and she suggested I change into one from the wardrobe in the room adjacent to hers; she was sure I would find there something to fit me. She seemed so much her old self, I could not spoil the evening. I went upstairs without a word.

The opulence of the gowns I found there took me aback. I had expected to find clothes left behind by Patience or Margaret, but neither of them could have owned these silks and satins with their trims of Brussels lace, exquisite embroidery, appliqué and pearls. There was even one with soft white fur around the hem. I had never seen such dresses before, and I could not resist trying them up against me, though I knew they were far too elegant for our informal dinner. Nevertheless I fixed on the least decorative amongst them, a plain chemise of parchment silk with a pleated panel at the back. Though lacking decoration, it was quite clearly the work of a master designer. I brushed my hair and stood back to survey myself in the long glass. I must confess to being charmed at the image that stared back at me: tall, slim and unusually sophisticated. A glance at the clock on the mantel showed that I had spent far longer than usual on my toilet. I hurried from the room.

As I entered the drawing room, all conversation ceased. Lady Bladen glanced over at me in obvious appreciation. Geoffrey, too, looked at me appraisingly. It was Darius, however, who reacted with displeasure to my changed appearance. I saw that he had changed into black evening coat and knee breeches, and I hoped with the shedding of his travelling clothes he had shed, also, his ill humour. Such was not the case. He looked at me coldly, his lips compressed as though afraid to speak.

I could not understand him. Lady Bladen noticed nothing, though Geoffrey, always observant of Darius, apparently understood and appreciated his cousin's displeasure.

"Really, Darius, I don't know what is the matter with you," his mother complained at last after she and Geoffrey had carried the dinner conversation between them almost in entirety. "Are you feeling quite well?"

"Quite," he replied without looking up.

"And here is Alexandra looking so pretty, and you've said not a word about it."

"Indeed, we are boors, aren't we, cousin," Geoffrey riposted. "Though I must confess to sitting here all evening and thinking how delightful she was looking. That dress is positively the last word in *chic*. I doubt there can be two the same, though I seem to have seen one very similar to it before." Geoffrey smiled in a friendly fashion across to Darius. "Don't you like it, coz?"

"I rarely comment on women's clothes," Darius replied coldly.

Lady Bladen's face wore a look of sudden recognition. "So *that's* it! That is what has made you out of sorts all evening. Really, Darius, when are you ever going to recover from your loss? I realize only too well the suffering in losing someone you love, but unlike me, you are still young. Your life is still before you. You cannot spend it mourning a dead wife or refusing to see anything connected with her. Why, even your son . . ."

"That is quite enough, mother. I refuse to discuss this matter."

Geoffrey continued to cut his meat with decided relish, yet he was even more obviously entertained by the scene at the table.

"I'm afraid I don't understand." I looked over at Lady Bladen for explanation.

"It is the dress," she said briefly.

"The dress?" Still I was mystified.

"The dress you are wearing. It was Philomena's."

"Oh no!" I stood up abruptly. "Had I known, I should never have worn it. I shall change immediately."

"Do sit down, Alexandra. You can't leave in the middle of dinner," Darius snapped.

"I can and I shall."

Lady Bladen followed me upstairs as I was changing into my own dress.

"I am so sorry, dear. I had no idea Darius would react in such a fashion just because you wore one of these dresses."

I might have guessed it was Philomena's, for no one else had such discriminating taste.

"I didn't know. I wish you had told me."

"I'm sorry. Had I thought for a moment . . . but it's done now. You see, when Darius moved back to Great Stanhope Street, he had all Philomena's things packed up—the jewellery that had been her own he gave back to her parents, but her clothes were sent here to be given away. These I put away, for they were too extravagant to be generally useful. When I saw your soiled dress earlier, I remembered them and thought to make use of them. I wish now I had not, for it has upset him, as does everything connected with her. But please, Alexandra, don't fret. You have been completely blameless. The fault is mine. Please come down."

We reentered the dining room as the cherry tarts and coffee were being served. Darius was quiet though clearly anxious to make amends, but I was cold and aloof. I felt a sense of relief when the meal was finally over and I was able to announce that it was time for me to leave.

"But I was counting on you to make up a table for quadrille, Alex." Darius spoke with a joviality I was sure he did not feel.

I shook my head. "My mother expects me. Father is away. I should probably not have stayed at all. I should have left, as you suggested earlier this afternoon."

He flushed at my inference.

"Will you allow me to accompany you . . ." Geoffrey began, when Darius cut him short.

"It is my duty to see that Alexandra arrives home safely."

"I don't need you, either of you. It is only a short distance and I know my way."

"I know you do, but I would like the walk, if you will allow me." Darius took my arm in his and so it remained until we left the house. Then I shook myself free.

"Alex, I was rude earlier. I apologize for my behaviour."

I made no reply, and we walked in silence through the apple orchard towards the lights of Seton Place. I said nothing because for the first time in my life, I had nothing I wished to say to Darius. I was angry and mortified and I kept a swift pace along the path, nor would I allow him to take my arm to guide me in the darkness.

When I stumbled on an exposed tree root, he grasped my elbow, forcing me to stop and face him.

"I'm sorry, truly I am. I've been wanting to apologize to you all evening for being such a bear. I should never have acted as I did; it showed a lamentable lack of civility. It was just that—you didn't look like yourself this evening. You looked so—so grown up. How old are you now?"

"Nineteen," I said tersely.

"Well, then, you are quite grown up. Seeing you dressed in—dressed as you were—well, it just didn't seem like you, that's all, it seemed like—like someone else. Will you forgive my churlishness?"

I could not see his expression in the darkness, but I knew I was beginning to succumb, as I always did, to the charm of his voice, to his persuasiveness. I was a fool. I shook myself angrily. Was I to spend my whole life worshipping someone who didn't care for me in the least? My voice as it lashed back at him seemed that of a stranger. I knew I would say things that I should not say, yet I could not stop myself.

"But it wasn't simply because I looked older, or different, was it, Darius? In fact your ill humour had nothing to do with me at all. You don't really know who I am, do you—no, don't interrupt—I mean, you don't know who the real me is or what I am thinking. You don't even care. Your annoyance this evening was not caused by me at all. I don't exist for you, not in any special way. It was the dress, wasn't it? It was *her* dress, that was what upset you, that anyone should be allowed to touch anything that was hers, that anyone should have the temerity to appear in her clothes. I assure you, had I known it to be hers I should never have put it on. I know I am not to mention her name; you have told me that already. Yet I will. You may have loved her, you may love her still, but when are you going to acknowledge that Philomena is dead? When are you going to forgive Cr—John for being alive?''

"Alex, Alex," he put his arms around me. "You are wrong when you say I care nothing for you. It is just that there are things that you don't understand, that possibly you will never understand. Indeed there are those things I hope you will never have to understand."

Angrily I pushed him aside. "I realize that I am—naive, perhaps—but there are certain qualities of humanity understandable to all of us. One of those is the bond between parent and child. Geoffrey treats your son with far more warmth and kindness than you evidence, yet you are as unfeeling to your cousin as you are to John, more so even . . ." My voice broke. I began to cry tears I had held back all evening. Those unmentionable things had been said. I felt him stiffen; when next he spoke, his voice was cool and terse.

"I suggest you not allow yourself to be carried away by Poindexter's charm. I should warn you that he is not quite as affable, or, to use your words, as kind and considerate, as he might at first appear. It would be well for you to remember that."

"Your mother does not appear to share your ill opinion of him," I retorted.

"She does not know him as I do, and I have no wish to enlighten her in the matter of his character. I have no reason to believe he would do her any harm. You, on the other hand, he might."

"You would make a monster of him!"

"He makes a monster of himself."

We faced one another in anger.

"You have come quite far enough," I averred. "I know my own way. I have no need, indeed no wish, for your company."

I turned and ran from him. He made no attempt to follow, yet neither did he turn back. I ran from him, wishing to ever widen the distance between us. I had never thought to feel such anger towards him, yet at that moment I never wished to see him again. It was some months before I did.

XIII

"AND ONLY THINK, Paul's perfect fuddy-duddy of a tutor insisted on calling on us daily to give papa accounts of Paul's progress and insisted that we dine with him in his fusty lodgings on Pitt Road, or when we did not dine with him, he dined with us at the Clarendon. There was no getting away from him. Poor Paul, I pity him with such a tutor. What a silly man! If only you had been there, we might have had fun together exploring his idiosyncrasies, but on my own I could only make mental note of them to relate them to you, which isn't nearly as much fun."

Cassy was curled up at the end of my bed. She and father had arrived back from Oxford the previous evening, father apparently well satisfied with his visit. Paul had been brought into line, for he announced, affably enough, that he would be coming home for Christmas and that he had invited his tutor, Mr. Pomeroy, to accompany him.

"Come Cassy, tell me now so that when he comes I shall have been informed what to look for. Does he have a tick like Mr. Tyson, or walk pigeon-toed like Mr. William's boy, or fall asleep while he is at table like old Mr. Cromer? Tell me all the funny parts now. I want you to cheer me up."

"Me cheer you up," Cassy accused. "It is you who went to London and indulged in the high life. Oxford is a handsome town, but I'm sure nothing I did compared with your activities in London."

As a matter of fact, my London visit seemed very far away. All I could think of was my quarrel with Darius and the harsh words we had exchanged. But Cassy was right; I had undoubtedly had the better time.

"I promise I'll tell you about London, but first tell me about Mr. Pomeroy. You know how I like odd characters, and you've aroused my curiosity. How old is he and what does he look like?"

"I don't really know how old he is," Cassy said pensively. "He could be forty or he could be four hundred. He is small in stature, balding and rather like a little bird; he hops about from subject to subject, devoting one sentence here, the next there, never dealing wholly with anything, just taking it up and setting it aside, going on to something else, then setting that aside and returning to his original thought at the very point he left off. It is as though he were talking to several people at the same time, all on different topics, or as though you were conversing with several people although the only one there is Mr. Pomeroy. Though he is a terrible bore, you cannot succumb to that boredom, for you must follow the conversation every minute in order to give the proper response, otherwise you become totally lost."

"But does not a nod now and again suffice?"

"No, indeed. I tried that, but he demands an answer, otherwise he becomes very irritable and accuses you of not listening, as he did me on one occasion. It made me very nervous, I can assure you, and papa gave me such a black look that I dared not let my attention drift for a minute after that. I think perhaps his mannerism comes from being a tutor."

"Poor Paul," I said. "No wonder he has done so badly at Oxford. And how like father! Instead of changing his tutor, he invites him down here for Christmas."

"Well, enough of Mr. Pomeroy. Enough, enough, more than enough. If I thought I would have to spend another day in his company, I would scream. I know he'll be here for the holidays, but you'll be here and I dare say that together we'll find him quite funny. Now tell me about London."

I did as I was bid, and her frequent observations and fervently repeated wishes that she could have been there with me made me ashamed of the pleasure I had enjoyed compared with her own dismal experience.

"I wish you had been there, Cassy," I finished lamely.

"I wish I had too," she agreed. "I think even Salisbury with Aunt Maud, bad as it was, was better than Oxford and Mr. Pomeroy. Paul has all my sympathies."

Mr. Linnell had donned the blue of Advent for three Sundays at St. Mary's before Paul came down from Oxford and I had an opportunity to see Mr. Pomeroy for myself. Cassy had not exaggerated; in fact, if anything, she had been kindness itself concerning the tutor.

I had imagined a small, meek man, funny in a doltish fashion. I discovered instead that there was nothing really funny at all about Mr. Pomeroy. Small he might be, but meek he certainly was not. He held a very high opinion of himself, an opinion he assumed was held by the world at large no matter what might be done or said to the contrary. His manner of speaking on two or three, sometimes more, subjects at the same time, frequently interspersing Greek or Latin phrases of obscure origin into his conversation, was taxing and required a great deal of concentration. It was not long, however, before I decided that not one, let alone three, of his topics was worth the effort; and with that decision, I made no further pretence of humouring him. With my obvious indifference to him, which he straightaway classed as insolence, he spoke to my father most directly on the ill manners of the younger generation, staring fixedly at me as he did so that there could be no doubt as to whom he referred, bringing down father's wrath upon my head. Yet the fact that he could speak so concisely on the issue convinced me that when he had a mind to, he was perfectly capable of communicating clearly. Thus his affected and confusing manner of speech was nothing more than a means of bewildering others and perhaps thereby persuading them that he was indeed a learned man, one to be listened to, one never to dispute.

It was odd, but father, who was never known for his patience, showed no irritation with the peculiarities of our guest. Indeed, he took pains to adjust to his idiosyncracies. I had thought that Mr. Pomeroy had been invited to Seton Place in the hope that he would coach Paul for his exams, but father made no attempt to prevent Paul from going off on long rambles on his own; nor, after Mr. Pomeroy had expressed displeasure at my behaviour, did he punish me; he berated me, to be sure, but after that he suggested I stay clear of our guest and spend my time with Paul, which, far from being a punishment, was a pleasure.

I enjoyed my walks with Paul too well to discuss either father or Mr. Pomeroy with him. We did, in fact, talk little, though I told Paul of my meeting with Sydney Smith and my great admiration for him.

"He is so intelligent, so witty, yet at the same time so kind. Everything interests him. He enjoys a rich life—rich in the sense that he has influential friends, a variety of activities, yet he ministers to the poor. He is never afraid to speak his mind. I have been reading his articles in the *Edinburgh Review* since I met him. I am convinced he could do anything, yet he is happy in the church."

"You mean that he has adapted to it," Paul responded bitterly.

"Perhaps," I hesitated. "Yet if it is to be, if you are indeed to take the orders, I do wish you would talk to him. He is so—so very sensible."

"Should the opportunity present itself, I shall. But I don't want to talk about it anymore; not when I'm on holiday. I'm going to walk over to Nethertōn. Is that too far for you?"

"Of course not. I love being out."

"Away from home and from father—I know what you mean."

But if Paul and I were allowed to wander at will, Cassy was trapped. Father demanded her presence daily as he sat with Mr. Pomeroy, she between them intent on her knitting, though she confided in me that she spent as much time attempting to unravel Mr. Pomeroy's conversation as later she spent unravelling her pattern, which became hopelessly confused in her distraction.

"I do so like to see a woman whose hands are usefully employed," I heard Mr. Pomeroy intoning to father one afternoon as I crept past the sitting-room door on my return. Then with no perceptible change of voice, he went on to his opposition to Catholic emancipation, and my sense of the ludicrous made me hesitate to hear father's response.

"Do you not feel that the Whig stand is playing squarely into the hands of the Irish Catholics? If only they had more responsible, reputable leaders, but one look at Grey and Russell, both from great families yet tearing down the very backbone of their own country . . ."

It was a subject dear to father's heart and I heard him attempt to interject a comment, but Mr. Pomeroy had proceeded full tilt into the subject of our weather seasonal for the Nativity, "Not so very dissimilar from the time in Jerusalem."

Father, though no authority on the Scriptures, apart from the most familiar passages, muttered, "Bethlehem," half beneath his breath, but Mr. Pomeroy droned on, back to Cassy's industry.

"Miss Cassandra is to be commended. Indeed, I know of few young ladies who devote themselves as assiduously to their work as does she. *Ceteris paribus cetera desunt.*"

Father permitted himself a clearly audible grunt of assent, though I doubt it was connected with Mr. Pomeroy's Latin reasoning. It did not matter, however, for Mr. Pomeroy had returned to the Whigs. "Now take Canning. There's a man whom I believe may have seen the light at last, for he's beginning to support the matter of . . ."

I began to move away, uninterested in Canning or the measures he might or might not support, but I stopped, for father actually interrupted Mr. Pomeroy, interrupted and changed the topic, from one of Whig irresponsibility—his very favourite—back to the subject of Cassy.

"Of my daughters, Mr. Pomeroy, Cassandra is by far the most capable, the most domestic, the best household manager, most careful with her personal expenses, a fine needlewoman, in fact I think most highly of her in every way. She is a dutiful daughter; she will make a dutiful wife."

"She is indeed pliable. It is an excellent quality for a woman who by her very nature must bend her ways to those of a man."

"She is indeed," father agreed keenly. "I shall be sorry to lose her. It will be a lucky man whom she consents to marry."

I had heard no more. I did not stay to listen, for I was devastated by what I had overheard. Father's behaviour was clear. Now I knew why he had taken Cassy to Oxford, why he had invited Mr. Pomeroy to Seton Place—not for Paul but for Cassy. Well, his object would never succeed, for I knew Cassy detested that pompous fool of a man. She would never have him.

Yet two days later I saw Cassy run from the small morning room in the back of the house. She had taken to sitting there in an attempt, I believe, to escape the man who had that very moment, she was later to confide in me, sought her out in her hiding place and made his request for her hand. I was tempted to ask whether, on a matter of such import, he had been able to confine his speech solely to a proposal of marriage, but one look at Cassy's overwrought expression made the jocularity die from my lips.

"Oh, Cassy, don't. That silly little man—he isn't worth it. Don't allow him to upset you. Now that you have refused him, he will be forced to leave Seton Place, and I, for one, will not be sorry to see him go."

"But—I did not refuse him."

"You jest, Cassy. What do you mean, you didn't refuse him. It's not like you to vacillate—or to play with the affections of even one so foolish as Mr. Pomeroy." I tried desperately to understand. "I suppose you didn't like to hurt him. I know you are kind, Cassy, but you must be firm. You must tell him unequivocally that there is no hope. A woman must be quite clear in matters such as this."

"But Alexandra, you must understand," Cassy cried out in great agitation. "I consented to be Mr. Pomeroy's wife."

I stared at her without comprehension. Only when Cassy began to sob did I try to make myself understand her predicament. Father had been right; she was soft and pliable, she would not willingly hurt anyone; but in this instance it must be done. I held her close and tried to soothe her.

"Don't worry, Cassy. You can explain in the morning to father, and he will tell Mr. Pomeroy that you have thought the matter over and have decided you are not for one another."

"But I can't, don't you see? It is papa's wish, and mama's also. They spoke to me only this afternoon. They said he is a good man and has a good income and wishes to purchase a house in Oxford and to have a . . . a wife and a family." Cassy had blurted this out in one breath and then she burst into tears again. I did also. The idea of Cassy, dear, gentle Cassy, married to that odious man. It could not be. It would not be.

"They can't make you marry him, Cassy. It is you who have to say the words at the altar. You can never say them to Mr. Pomeroy."

"But I have no choice," she said, pulling distractedly at an already-sopping handkerchief. "Papa says it is unlikely that anyone else will have me. I'm not pretty, and I have little to offer in the way of money."

"That does not signify, and it is no reason to take such a . . . such a popinjay as this incredible bore. It is far better not to marry, Cassy, than to be the wife of such a man."

"I know that, Alex, but papa has given me to understand that I don't have the choice of remaining unmarried."

"What do you mean? Of course you may choose not to marry."

"No. He says he can't have us at home after we have reached our majority, and he cannot be expected to support us forever. The boys will have to support themselves in their professions, and we girls must marry if husbands are found for us. He says it is all we can do, all we are fit for. And he says he sees no other opportunity for marriage for me. He . . . he was quite blunt about my appearance and my . . . my lack of spirit. He said . . ." Her voice heaved so she was barely able to continue. "He said that I was lucky to have such a fine man offer for me and that . . . that he was very fond of him and looked upon him as a son already."

"But this is ridiculous," I exploded. "I doubt he is five years younger than father—a son indeed. I've always thought father a hard man, Cassy, and at times devious, but I cannot believe him to be completely heartless. He must see that no woman in her senses would want that nincompoop. If he doesn't see it, he must be made to see it. If you won't speak to him, I shall."

"Don't, Alex, don't. It will be worse for you and it won't help me, I can assure you. I've told you before the world is made for men and for their desires. We have no option but to do their wishes.''

"That is not so. I cannot believe it to be so, otherwise I would . . . I would see no point in living. I cannot believe that we have no choice. If you do not want Mr. Pomeroy for a husband, then he must not be forced upon you.''

"I pray it will not be so," said Cassy fervently, "but I fear it will be.''

Prayers on the subject of matrimony, I knew from my own experience, rarely received first attention, and I felt a more forthright means must be adopted. Thus the following morning I sought out my father in his study.

He was seated at his desk examining the year-end accounts brought that day by the bailiff when I entered, but he greeted me quite affably and asked what he could do for me.

"It's about Cassy, father. She can't marry that . . . she can't marry Mr. Pomeroy," I blurted.

He stopped, pen in midair, his brown eyes widening in annoyance. "I can see no reason why you should speak to me of Cassandra's marriage plans, Alexandra. She has not indicated to me that marriage with Mr. Pomeroy is offensive to her in any way.''

"That is because she is afraid," I explained. "Afraid that she has no choice in the matter and that you will not listen to her. Surely you can see, father, that Mr. Pomeroy is not a man capable of making any woman happy, let alone one of your daughters.''

He put aside his pen with a deliberate motion and he rose from his chair, his face flushed. "I can see no such thing, my girl, and I will not have you insulting a guest under my roof. Mr. Pomeroy happens to be a very learned man, a man of integrity and now a man of substantial means.''

"And when did he acquire these means, father?''

"An uncle of his died early this year and left him quite a considerable sum. He spoke to me of it when I visited Paul in the spring.''

"So that is why you took Cassy to Oxford with you. You had thought him a good match for her. Can't you see him for the pedantic fool that he is, money or no money?''

Father's face reddened to such an extent and his eyes bulged in a fashion that made me think him about to have an apoplectic fit, but then he seemed visibly to control himself. When at last he spoke it was in slow and measured terms. "Your sister,

Alexandra, is not an attractive woman. If you do not know it, I can assure you that it is so. My sister Maud has confirmed my opinion. She told me that no one looked at Cassandra twice while she was with her in Salisbury and that she would be lucky to find a husband at all. We may know her as a pleasant creature, but the fact is that she does not show to advantage when she is with others. I observed this for myself in Oxford and was only glad that her shyness, which amounted almost to cold indifference, did not deter Mr. Pomeroy in his resolve to offer for her. He had mentioned to me that now he had the means, he was of a mind to marry and have a family. I considered that a commendable decision, and I consider it fortunate that Mr. Pomeroy finds Cassandra fit to be his wife. She will have a comfortable home and a good and, I am quite sure, a devoted husband, and, God willing, in the course of time there will be children to bless that union.''

I could not reply. My eyes welled with tears, whether from anger or sadness, I could not say. His description of Cassy rang in my head: a ''pleasant creature'' who did not ''show to advantage,'' barely fit to be the wife of that odious man. Our Cassy who was so sweet and gentle—was that really all he thought of her? Did he merely wish to rid himself of another child?

He must have taken my silence for acquiescence, for he continued in a gentler tone, ''I try to do the best for all my children, Alexandra, and I expect my children, in turn, to trust my judgement. For the boys, apart from Thomas who is my heir, there must be professions. Paul, I believe, now understands his role in life, though he has given me difficulties. Now that Mr. Pomeroy is to become a family member, he has promised to write to a relative of his in Northumberland in the hope of securing a living for him. And for you girls there must be marriage. I shall see that it is as advantageous as your settlements will allow. I do not wish my daughters to marry unsuitably. I wish to find steady, reliable husbands for each of them, men of my own persuasion; but it is not an easy matter. I assure you that it is not. I am not a rich man. I cannot settle a great deal of money on you. Therefore I must be reasonable when offers are made.

''As I said, it is not an easy matter.'' Father was warming to his subject now, pacing the floor with his hands clasped behind his back, ''but I consider that I have done well. Eugenia is happy with George Ramsey. The Ramseys are, perhaps, as a family not quite up to the touch of the Cox-Nevilles, but they are satisfactory in other respects and Eugenia is handsomely provided for. I have no doubt that Cassandra will be equally well settled with Mr. Pomeroy."

I thought of George Ramsey, who, it was already whispered, was seeking excitement or solace with certain girls of notorious reputation in the neighborhood and spending inordinate amounts of his time away from home. A fine husband he was turning out to be, but as father had said, the Ramseys were satisfactory in other respects; they were rich and they were Tories. Mr. Pomeroy undoubtedly qualified as a son-in-law on the same grounds, with the added advantage that he had not been demanding in the matter of the marriage settlement.

"What did he get, father, Mr. Pomeroy—what did he get?" I blinked back my tears and clasped my hands tightly so that he could not see that I was shaking with indignation.

"What do you mean, what did Mr. Pomeroy get? Do you mean in the way of a marriage settlement?"

I nodded.

"It is hardly a matter to be discussed with you, Alexandra," he reproved, "but, nevertheless," here he looked self-satisfied as he meticulously straightened the papers on his desk, "let us say that Mr. Pomeroy was quite understanding in that regard. He understood that while my estate is not extensive, I have a large family, all of whom must be provided for. He took into account that Cassandra comes from good stock, good Tory stock, that she is healthy and young, capable of becoming a good mother and a thrifty housewife. He realizes the benefits of the match, the importance of a connexion with the Cox-Nevilles—he was certainly not insensible to that."

As he spoke, I could see father outlining the advantages point by point to Mr. Pomeroy. He had sold Cassy, just as he might have sold a mare from his stables. But it had not happened yet, and if I knew anything about it, it never would. I suppose he planned to rid himself of me in the same manner. That would not happen, either.

I took a deep breath as he finished speaking. "I can assure you, father, that if there is anything that I can do to stop Cassy from making this terrible mistake, you may be certain I shall not hesitate to act. You have my word on it. I do not intend to stand silently by and see my sister given in marriage to just anyone who will meet your terms. The marriage vows say to love, honour and obey. How could these vows possibly be applied to Mr. Pomeroy? No, no, it is far better that Cassy remain single than marry him. I know it is what she would prefer."

Father must have been convinced that he had won my approval, for I could tell as I spoke that my obdurate stand surprised him as much as it angered him. He made no attempt to disguise his fury.

"You will do nothing in this matter, Alexandra, nothing at all. I will not stand for your interference. You have no idea of what it is for a woman to remain a spinster all her life. And as for you, my girl, when your turn comes you will marry the suitor I choose for you or you will not stay under my roof. I cannot be expected to provide for the female members of this family *ad infinitum*, nor should Thomas be saddled with a gaggle of unmarried sisters to support after I am gone. He will marry when a suitable connexion is found, and the Cox-Neville name and estate will be his to carry forward. It cannot be depleted by impecunious spinsters; I will not allow it. Nor have I any intention of making the same mistake as my own father by settling money on you as he did on Maud. Her money will, of course, revert to the estate eventually—as long as we do not upset her. Nevertheless, I consider my father set a very foolish precedent in allowing Maude an independent income. Had he not, she would have settled down as a woman should instead of—but that is another matter and does not concern us now.

"You may have some romantic notions of marriage in your head, but marriage is nothing but a civil contract. Only the weak marry for love. I was a fool to allow Bladen to put all this learning into you. It has made you impertinent and conceited. Your time would have been better spent in cooking and needlework than in philosophy and debate, and so it shall be from now on. You will go no more to Charteris but stay at home and do as your mother and I bid. You may go now. I want you neither to speak to Cassandra nor to any of your brothers and sisters. I will not allow you to cause disobedience and dissension. You will stay in your room. I shall apologize for your absence to our guest."

With that he took up his pen and returned to his accounts. To be forbidden Charteris! Not to see Crumpet again, or Lady Bladen . . . or Darius. To have lost my fight for Cassy and all that, too, was more than I could bear.

"Father, please . . ."

"The matter is closed. I have nothing more to say to you. Go to your room and shut the door quietly as you leave."

He spoke without looking up. I could gain nothing by staying. As I left, I found mother outside in the hall. She must have heard everything that had occurred by her expression—worried, shamefaced, too—yet I had no right to blame her. How could she do anything after all these years of obeying father's every whim? Probably he had been foisted upon her as Mr. Pomeroy was now being foisted on Cassy. She might not have liked it any more than Cassy did, but she had accepted it and no doubt she now expected Cassy to acquiesce in the same manner.

"Mother . . ." I appealed, but she shook her head and held a finger to her lips, begging my silence. I knew it was fruitless to pursue the matter. Despondently I climbed the stairs to my room.

It was, I discovered, a relief to be alone. I could not have faced Cassy after my failure. I had accomplished nothing except to confirm that she was right: there was no hope for a reasonable solution. Cassy had understood that all along. She understood everything better than I and, unlike me, she accepted the inevitable. She knew only an immoderate fool uses his tongue to cut his own throat.

I sat in the window seat looking out at the stark outlines of the trees silhouetted against the slate-grey sky, clean cut and strangely beautiful. My eyes swept the bare horizon until they rested on Charteris atop the hill. So I had sat once before years ago, the day I had first fallen in love with Darius.

I rose abruptly and went over to my table to gather together paper and pen. That was where my solace lay. Yet I could not continue the story I had begun, a story of a woman rising to triumph, to live happily ever after. It was a myth. If I were to write a myth, let it be a classical myth. Cassandra, daughter of Priam and Hecuba, beloved of Apollo who gave her the gift of prophesy and then cruelly ordained that none of her predictions should be believed. I would write Cassandra's story. Cassy had predicted the outcome of my interview with father, yet I had not believed her. She had also predicted that she would have to marry Mr. Pomeroy; that I still refused to believe. Something must prevent it.

It was from Paul, who slipped in to see me unbeknownst to anyone, that I learned the engagement had been announced and the wedding fixed for Boxing Day.

"But why so soon?" I gasped.

"Mr. Pomeroy wants to return to Oxford to find a house before the beginning of Hilary, and father decided it best that Cassy go with him. Father has paid for the special license, so there's no doubt of his wish to hasten to tie the knot. Perhaps he's afraid that you will upset his plans."

"I would if I could, Paul, but there is little I can do except feel for Cassy, and she does not even know of that."

"There you are wrong, Alex. Cassy knows of your talk with father, everything, in fact. She told me how much she appreciated your speaking on her behalf, how much she admired your courage, but she is quite resigned to the match now."

"Resigned to the match! What joy!"

"Don't fret so, Alex. It won't help. Believe me, Cassy would not want it."

I attended church with the family on Christmas Day, and father, in the spirit of the season, invited me to join them at dinner, but he saw to it that I did not talk to Cassy, who was pinioned at the side of her betrothed throughout the entire evening. I had hoped to gain a word with her when the gentlemen took their port after dinner, but father must have divined this, for he dispensed with his favourite part of the evening, an unheard-of sacrifice, in order to join the rest of us at coffee in the drawing room. It was scarcely a festive occasion. Even the prospective bridegroom was quieter than was his wont, which was a boon, while Cassy said not a word. Father, as though to fill the silences, spoke a great deal with a gaiety I was sure even he could not possibly feel. Mother's smiles were forced and indiscriminate. It was her way of making all appear normal and happy, a festive family Christmas.

Though we could not speak, my eyes met Cassy's from time to time. There I saw nothing except the resignation of which Paul had spoken. When she kissed me good night, she pressed my hand as though comforting me, yet she was the one who should have been comforted.

That night, long after everyone was asleep, I lay wide awake thinking of her when, suddenly, there she was.

"I came to tell you to stop being so sad on my account," she whispered. "It won't be so bad."

"Oh, Cassy, it will. Don't do it, please don't."

"But there is nothing else I can do."

I sat up in bed. "We could run away."

"Where could we run to—and on what? We have no money; we have no one who will shelter us. No, no, it is useless."

I sat with my head in my hands. There must be someone we could go to. Aunt Maud wouldn't take us in, that was sure. We didn't know any relatives on my mother's side; I think most of them were dead. But there must be someone who would take us.

"We could work as governesses," I said at last.

"Without training and without references? You might know enough to teach, but I certainly don't. And where could we stay until we found a situation? Be practical, Alex; we can't run away."

"I'd sooner lead a life of sin than marry against my will," I said fiercely.

Cassy sighed. "Some man might take you for a mistress, but I doubt anyone would want a dumpling like me."

"Oh, Cassy, if only you knew how beautiful you are to me, you wouldn't talk of yourself so."

"If you were a man and unrelated to me, my problems might be solved. But you are my sister, my dearest sister to be sure, but equally as helpless as I am." She came over and took me by the shoulders. "I've come to ask a favour of you. I want you to come to the church tomorrow. I know you don't wish to, but it is my wedding and I want you to be there. Will you come?"

"Of course I will, for you, but I shall have to hold my tongue when the priest asks for those knowing reasons you should not be joined. I know a hundred at least."

"No scenes, promise me! It won't help anything, and it can make matters very much worse for both of us. Remember you are of a marriageable age. Don't make things harder for yourself."

"Can I run away to you if father makes me marry against my will?" I asked.

"Of course you can, and I'll hide you in a cupboard or under the bed . . ." She flushed suddenly and then said softly, "I must go now. I'll see you in the morning." She kissed me quickly and was gone.

The next day they were married. I held my peace and did not speak; in fact I said not two words the whole day. I never wished to see another wedding at St. Mary's. I wondered why such a beautiful church existed to bear witness to such dismal ceremonies. No wonder women cried at weddings. They knew what they were about.

XIV

LIFE WAS BLEAK indeed after Cassy left. Twice I broached the subject to father of allowing me to see Crumpet, or to ask that he be brought to see me. On all counts he was adamant in his refusal. I expected protests from Lady Bladen, but I discovered that father had written to Darius informing him of his decision. Darius, in reply, had called on father. I was, of course, not allowed to see him, nor was I told what passed between them, but since I was still precluded from visiting Charteris, it was evident that Darius had not succeeded in changing father's mind. Had he come at his mother's urging, I wondered, unhappily all too sure it was so. I cursed myself for continuing to love him when he never looked on me as a woman. He had Althea Brentwood to comfort him, in a relationship of pleasure, perhaps, a brief and shallow thing compared with the gash Philomena had left in his soul, but, nevertheless, one all too real.

I missed Crumpet terribly, but though I was willing to defy father to see him, I had little opportunity to do so. Mother made me responsible for those household duties that had been Cassy's, and she followed me everywhere, whether to be sure I carried out my tasks properly or whether from loneliness I could not say, yet it was too late to attempt to close the gap between us. She had let Cassy go without a murmur. I could never confide in her.

That time before spring passed on feet as leaden as the skies above us. With Cassy gone and Paul back at Oxford, I had no one. Of course Thomas was there at father's side, as James was at mother's, while Netty preferred Eugenia's company—but then I had had little in common with any of them.

When I thought I could no longer bear my isolation, father showed me a note from Charteris, in Darius's hand. My initial reaction was joy until I read it, and then I discovered that Lady Bladen was ill, very ill it would seem, and wished to see me.

"I suppose you should go in this instance, but don't think I am relaxing my decision. I shall not allow you to be a habitué of that house again, you understand that?"

I nodded, but I barely heard him. My thoughts were all with

Lady Bladen and the fact that I would see Crumpet again, and Darius, whom I had not spoken to since parting from him in anger.

I found Darius in attendance at his mother's bedside and he greeted me with a mixture of happiness and relief.

"Alex, thank goodness you came. How good to see you. All of us have missed you."

"Had I had my choice, I would never have stayed away, but you must know that."

I scarcely recognized Lady Bladen. Her face was thin and gaunt, her eyes sunken, without life or lustre. I took her hand—it was weak and lifeless—and I was not at all sure she recognized me. When Darius left us alone, I talked to her softly, reassuringly, struggling to hold back my tears. It was only at the mention of Crumpet's name that I was sure I had her attention, for then, feebly but insistently, she returned the pressure of my hands clasping hers.

"Dear Alex. It's about Crumpet—I must speak to you of Crumpet. He's been on my mind so. He loves you dearly, and he has missed you so, the poor little chap. I shall not be here much longer—no, don't be sad, because I am not, except for those I leave behind, most particularly that child. I will not have him left to the vagaries of domestics. He needs care, for I fear he's a frail child, but more than that, he must have love, and we both know that Darius is not—is not yet able to show the love I know he must have for his son. But it will come, it must." She sighed heavily.

"Please, don't strain yourself to talk now."

"I must. I want you to promise me that you will stay near him, watch over him—at least until Darius provides him with a mother. Promise you will do this, for me."

Her hands gripped mine convulsively. I would have promised her anything; to promise to watch over Crumpet was a matter of joy, though how I would persuade father to allow it, I had no idea.

"Gladly, gladly—as long as it is within my power, I shall care for him," I promised. "But we shall do it together, as we have always."

"No. My time on this earth is rapidly passing. I am convinced it is so, and in truth it is a relief, for I have had very little wish to live since Septimus died."

I began to protest, but she shook her head, smiling weakly. "If I am not sorry, you should not be either. I've had a good life. I've enjoyed it, but I don't regret leaving it. You meant a great deal to Septimus, Alex, and you have been more than a daughter to me. I had hoped . . ." She looked intently into my face. "But I think you know what I hoped. I have learned by this time that it is impossible to plan the lives of others for them. Perhaps it is even wrong to wish to do so. Darius must make his own decisions—and yet this is one I wish I could make for him."

It was strange to learn that Lady Bladen had cherished the same hopes as I had myself. I wished she had had as few scruples as father in planning the lives of others, but that wish died aborning. If Darius were to offer for me, it must be for myself, not to fulfill a duty to his mother or to provide care for his child.

"I trust he will do nothing foolish, for I am convinced that his place in the history of our country is assured."

"Darius will never act foolishly, Lady Bladen, have no fear of that."

Two days later Lady Bladen was dead.

I found myself in a predicament. I wanted to carry out the promise I had made to her, yet I was forbidden to go to Charteris. Following the funeral I received father's permission to pay my respects.

I discovered that Lady Bladen had already communicated her wish to Darius and he was as much in a quandary on the matter as was I. "Your father is adamantly set against your coming here. He believes we have made a freethinker of you, and perhaps he is right. Was it your visit to Holland House that upset him?"

I shook my head, going on to explain, coldly and quite factually, the details of Cassy's marriage and my opposition to it. I did not think I could speak of it without obvious contempt for Mr. Pomeroy, though I tried. Darius heard me out without a word. When he did speak, it was with calm, infuriating male logic.

"Yet surely it is a father's duty to do what is in the best interest of his daughter."

To think Darius of all people should side with father! Or was it simply that all men thought alike?

"Best interests! To marry her to an addlepate simply because he has the means to support her and his demands for a settlement are to father's liking!"

"But what were your sister's views on the matter?"

"She despised him."

"If that is so, why did she give her consent to marry him?"

Darius would never understand a woman's lot, her lack of freedom to choose, I thought bitterly. But then I realized that his question to me was the very one I had put to Cassy, and my reply to him echoed hers.

"To understand," I concluded, "it is necessary to understand father. When he decides on something, that is the way it will be. That is the reason I fear he will never allow me to come to John."

"I am not convinced that it is impossible, but first I must know if you wish to spend your time with the boy. He is growing and quite rambunctious. To watch over his care is hardly exciting for a young lady of your tender years."

"Of course I wish it," I replied vehemently. "The happiest days of my life have been spent here with John, and father is well aware of that. That is why in denying me Charteris, he knows he takes from me my greatest pleasure. In asking this your mother did not seek to burden me. She knows I love the child as though he were—" I stopped short, suddenly, embarrassed, "as though he were a member of my own family," I finished lamely.

Darius scrutinized my face, and I felt my cheeks flush.

"Then you really want it?"

"I really do."

"In that case I shall speak to your father. It may be, however, apart from his other objections, that now my mother is . . . is no longer living, he may be more inclined than ever that you should stay away."

"But why?"

"I am alone here. For that reason he may feel it improper that you should come. I shall explain to him that I shall be living in London, though I suppose I shall visit Charteris from time to time."

My face fell, though he misunderstood the reason.

"I reminded you once before: you must not give up before the battle has been joined. I am beginning to understand your father more. I cannot promise to be successful, but I think the argument I have in mind may win the day."

I had little hope of his success, but I discovered that Darius did understand my father far better than I thought. It was much later, however, that I discovered that the permission I received

from father to carry out Lady Bladen's dying wish had literally
been bought. Darius put it to him in the form of a bequest made
by his mother on her deathbed but not entered in her will, the
bequest to be given only on the condition that I provide company
for his son from time to time. If father thought it odd, he did not
question it; the money, of which I saw nothing, must have
assuaged his doubts. For my part, I was satisfied. I was allowed
to return to the surroundings and to the child I loved.

Thus I was relieved of the tedium of Seton Place and my daily
tasks to resume that pattern of delight, caring for Crumpet and
writing. The great house was eerily quiet and lonely, but spring
came with all of its promises, allowing Crumpet and me to spend
most of our time outside and, while he napped in the afternoon, I
wrote of the new Cassandra, the wise woman whom nobody
would believe, or else long outpourings to my own Cassandra of
those things I would tell no one else, though even to my dearest
sister I could never mention my greatest secret.

Her responses, however, were dismally brief. They told me
nothing of her life, but I presumed that, being able to write so
little, she must be busy.

Darius had left orders that my every need was to be supplied.
Thus my letters were franked and dispatched without father's
censoring. It was a freedom I relished. I started many a note to
Darius, telling him little things that happened—Crumpet's progress, the bluebells in bloom, the sickness of Mrs. Stuckney, the
birth of Eugenia's second child—yet I put them in the desk
drawer, unsent. He in return sent no messages. None, that is,
until June, when the housekeeper received word that he would
come with a large party—she was to have the guest rooms in
readiness and to take in provisions for at least twelve.

Though the annual spring cleaning had only recently been
completed, another round began. I was curious to know who
might be coming, but nothing was said and I asked no questions.
They were expected daily, but the month was almost out before I
arrived one morning to find that the party from London had
come the previous evening.

I was encouraged to find that Darius had been in to see
Crumpet on his arrival, even though it was late. Now that only
the two of them remained, surely the bond between them must
strengthen.

As we returned from our walk, I saw Darius coming towards
us accompanied by a tall, fair lady whom I had no trouble
recognizing, even from so great a distance.

Darius, in presenting me, reminded Lady Brentwood that we had met before.

"Oh, to be sure. Delighted to see you again." She smiled very sweetly, clearly not remembering me, and directed her fixed smile to Crumpet. "So this is your son, Darius."

"This is John," Darius replied. "And how has the young man been treating you, Alex? Not running you ragged, I trust?"

"You are his governess, then." Lady Brentwood seemed relieved to have placed my role in Darius's household.

It was Darius who hastened to reply that I was a neighbour and close friend of the family.

"How sweet and unselfish of her to devote her time to someone else's child," Lady Brentwood purred, smiling complicitly at me, her eyes cold and calculating. At once I was sure that she, of all people, had guessed my secret. I cannot say how I knew it to be so—whether it was her shrewd scrutiny of me or the way she put her arm possessively through that of her companion as she spoke—but I was convinced that in those few minutes, she had grasped the fact that I loved Darius, that I had long loved him. I felt suddenly naked, vulnerable, exposed before her whom I liked least. I left them quickly without another word, nor did I reply to Darius's invitation to lunch with them.

I hated and feared her with the instinctive reaction of an antelope finding a lion in its thorn thicket. Like the antelope, I wanted to run. I stayed away from her, in fact away from all the gathered company while they were there. The fortnight of their stay was spent in a round of fishing, riding, dining, card playing and inevitable political discussions, which I gathered went on long into the night.

Repeatedly Darius sought me out to talk to me, but I was uncommunicative. I was concerned that she might have told him of my devotion. I could imagine how she would make light of it, how she might tease him about his conquest; perhaps they might even laugh together about it. My cold, aloof attitude caused him to ask whether I was finding John a burden; when I replied negatively to that, he went on to ask whether I was experiencing difficulties at home. Again I shook my head and he retreated, puzzled, leaving me to dwell on my provincialism and my utter frustration.

Their departure was planned, and I found myself glad when Darius bade me farewell. The house was quiet when I arrived the following morning to discover that all the carriages had left early except for that of the master of Charteris. He, I presumed, had chosen to ride beside Lady Brentwood's coach, or perhaps inside with her. I put the thought of them together from my mind, yet it persisted.

Though I had longed for them to leave, all day I felt oddly dispirited. I did nothing, I wrote nothing and, when the time came for me to return home, I did not want to give up my solitude. I took up the *Meditations* of Marcus Aurelius and settled in the high-backed sofa by the window at the end of the library, overlooking the sloping back lawn. I read,

> Time is a sort of river of passing events, and strong is its current, no sooner is a thing brought to sight than it is swept by and another takes its place, and this too will be swept away.

Was that how it would be, I wondered. Would this pass? Would the countess be swept away? I put my feet up and let my attention wander from the pages up to the clouds that floated by, silent as time, soft as a spirit's sigh. Drifting endlessly across the endless summer sky, they were without weight, without substance. How would it be, I wondered, to be there among them, floating, fluttering, soaring without a care. Gravity loosened its hold of my body, my cares, my depression left me as I became one with them—free.

The next time I looked out across the lawn I was aware, with a start, of the long evening shadows of the cedars and the darkening sky behind them. The afternoon had come and passed as I slept. I heard the crackle of a fire in the hearth and idly wondered why it had been lit.

Apart from the fire, as I awakened I realized there were other sounds, muffled voices, one soft, the other a male voice. Could that be Darius, those mellow, seductive tones? The other I knew could only belong to one person—Althea Brentwood.

"You're a sensual woman, Althea, a thoroughly wonderful, sensuous woman, and you revel in that sensuality, as you should. You know just how to use every charm, every curve, every breath to bewitch me—more than that, to drive me to distraction as you do now."

I was horrified at the words, but more so at my position as eavesdropper on such a scene. My whole body flushed at the predicament in which I found myself.

A soft sigh was followed by a rustle and then a muffled sound—bodies, lips pressed together, I did not know nor did I wish to speculate. I looked for a means of escape but could see none. I lay still, desperately hoping they would leave.

"Now who is being driven to distraction," I heard my pet aversion purr. "Let's not go upstairs, Darius, it is much more pleasant here in front of the fire, your bare skin against my bare skin on this bearskin."

He laughed. "Punning at such a time, Althea."

"Not anymore," she sighed.

I had to do something and I had to do it immediately before they—even in my own mind I couldn't elucidate that thought further, but I knew I must do something before anything else happened. There were indistinguishable sounds—I could not tell whether the panting breaths were theirs or mine. My face was hot, my hands clammy. I had to act; I could not be a silent party to their intimacy.

Abruptly I coughed and cleared my throat. Then I sat up.

The sight that met my eyes did nothing to alleviate my acute embarrassment and humiliation. Lady Brentwood was reclining on the bearskin rug before the fire. It was well that fire was lit, for her clothes were in complete disarray. The bodice of her gown was open and pulled back to reveal full, white breasts. The reflection of the firelight danced across her pale skin and her long, blond hair, which was loosened and hung softly down her back. She looked like Helen while beside her lay Paris, coatless, his frilled shirt open, in the act of stroking those soft, exposed breasts with their pink, upraised nipples.

Darius must not have heard me, nor was I in his line of vision, but his companion certainly had. I saw her eyes widen abruptly until, recognizing me, she laughed. Whether it was her laugh that made him look around or the fact that her body had stiffened in his grasp, I do not know, but he, too, caught sight of me and his face darkened in embarrassment.

"What the deuce are you doing here, Alex?" he demanded, rising hastily and straightening his clothing. Then, as Lady Brentwood made no effort to move, seeming to enjoy my all-too-obvious discomfort, he bent over to pull her dress across her still-exposed bosom.

My face was burning as I stood up. I wanted to run from the room, but my legs refused to obey my command, and I stood gazing stupidly from one to another.

"Excuse me, I'm sorry to intrude. I didn't mean to, really I didn't. I was reading and I fell asleep. I only just woke up," I added hastily, unsure of how long they had been there. "I had no intention of transgressing on your . . . your . . ."

"Lovemaking," Lady Brentwood supplied with a low laugh.

It was that laugh that at last gave me back the power of my legs. As I ran from the room I could hear it follow me down the hall, out into the twilight air. I continued to hear it long after I slammed the heavy front door shut. Down the path through the orchard it echoed. Accompanying it was the intimacy of their embrace.

I could not obliterate that scene from my mind. It would never leave me. I lay in bed long that night, unable to sleep, my hands crossed over my own firm breasts, thinking how it must be to lie with a man, to be kissed by a man, kissed in the way I had heard them kissing. I did not think of just any man. I thought only of the man I had seen that night, and he had been doing all those things to that—that—that vixen. How I hated her! My sense of shame at witnessing such an intimate scene gave way to a sense of hopeless jealousy. I felt I could never trust myself in the presence of that woman again for fear I might tear my nails across her beautiful, mocking face or grasp that white throat of hers to silence that low, tinsel laugh.

My vituperation horrified me. I must be a demon to be capable of such malevolence.

Two days passed before I could bring myself to return to Charteris. Even then I might not have done so had it not been for Crumpet. I could not bear to face either of them again, though Darius I must see at some time, for he would return. By then, though the memory would not be forgotten, I hoped that its sharply etched image would have faded.

As I entered the library, my heart pounded, sending the blood flooding to my face, for there on the long settle sat Darius, reading the newspaper.

Had it been possible, I would have left, but he had seen me enter. I was forced to greet him, my flushed cheeks betraying my embarrassment. His own, I noticed, reddened slightly on seeing me.

"Alex, I'm glad you came today. I've been waiting to talk to you before I returned to London." He folded the newspaper and made to set it down on the bearskin rug until, seeing my eyes follow its course, he seemed to read the thoughts that rug brought to my mind and he put it, instead, on the table beside him.

"The fact of the matter is that I want to apologize to you for the scene you witnessed the other evening. It was certainly not the sort of thing any young girl should have been a party to, let alone one such as you who has led such a sheltered life. Obviously I had no idea you were in the house, let alone in the room. It embarrassed you, as well it should. It embarrassed me—and the lady. For our part, I can only say that we—we know one another well, we are adults and are both free, and though it may appear conduct reprehensible to you, we are both of a passionate nature—we allowed those passions to get the better of us. I do not intend to apologize for the conduct itself. It was, or should have been, between that lady and myself. I do, however, hope that you can put it from your mind.''

I said nothing; I could think of nothing to say. I could not bear to look at him. Not the scene for a young girl to witness, he had said. How long before he could understand that I was no less a woman than Lady Brentwood, that I had all the passions of a woman even if I had yet to experience them. I could understand their conduct. If I could not condone it, it was not because I considered such conduct reprehensible in itself, but only that I considered it reprehensible because he to whom I had been for so long devoted should indulge in such passions with a woman other than myself.

My silence made him uncomfortable and he went on awkwardly, perhaps to change the subject, "The *Edinburgh Review* came yesterday. I set it aside for you. I know that you enjoy it.''

I walked over to the small Louis XV desk at which I usually worked, and, picking it up, I leafed through it, not thinking of the magazine but only of what to say. Suddenly my eye was caught by the words *Sum of Glory*, the title of my own book! Hillaby had actually published it and Sydney Smith was reviewing it—he liked it, or on closer scrutiny I should say that he did not dislike it, for he was a discriminating critic who rarely praised highly. He had found that the hero was perhaps too perfect; he preferred the character of the heroine with her human frailties, which, he felt, exhibited more sympathy and understanding. His comments were perceptive for I was at that moment finding the model for that hero, then standing behind me and looking over my shoulder at the part of the *Review* that had my attention, somewhat less than perfect for his passionate attachment to a woman I disliked.

"Ah, Sydney's review of *Sum of Glory*," he commented. "It is strange, but for some reason, I cannot imagine why, I was sent an advance copy by the publisher."

I knew well why. It had been one of the instructions I had attached to the manuscript left so hastily at Hillaby's. I wondered what Darius would say if he knew the book was mine but I was too unsure of myself to own to it; all I could say, as casually as my beating heart would allow, was "Then you have read it?"

"Yes, I have."

"And do you agree with Mr. Sydney Smith?"

"To some extent, yes, the hero was entirely too idealized. No man is such a paragon of virtue. The author, in my opinion, has much to learn of men, for by creating such a hero he is robbed of his humanity. It is the heroine, with her failings, who truly conveys love."

"Byron has said that love is of man's life only a part while it is a woman's whole existence. I take it, then, that you agree with him."

"I believe I understand his meaning. Men lead far more active, varied lives. Their minds are crammed full of a great many things, while women are usually confined to domesticity and social happenings, a life that allows for greater reflection on the emotions. But there my agreement with him terminates, for he leaves the impression that love is less important to men than it is to women. I believe that a man, should he love, may feel the emotion quite as deeply, with passion equal to that of a woman. Perhaps even greater." The last words were added slowly, thoughtfully.

"Perhaps it is the fact that a woman has written the book that gives it that bias," I commented.

"You are indeed astute, for I don't remember Sydney bringing that fact out in his review."

Quickly I turned back to the magazine. He had not.

"I suppose it is only women who think men—some men, that is—perfect. That, perhaps, is why I surmised it to be written by a woman."

"It does, in fact, on the title page indicate that it is written by a lady, an unnamed lady, so you are right in your supposition. I feel that since a copy was sent to me, it should be some lady of my acquaintance, yet I can think of none with the acumen or the patience to write it, for I enjoyed the book. If I had been critical about this one aspect of it, it is only because I feel lack of experience of the nature of men to have caused it. She has, perhaps, yet to love."

"Or to be loved," I said, half to myself.

Darius had returned to his seat, to his paper. Yet as I glanced over at him, his body relaxed in casual elegance, his cravat perfectly tied, his coat of blue superfine immaculately fitting his shoulders, I suddenly saw him as he had been that evening, coatless, in disarray, consumed by those passions my hero lacked, passions I myself had yet to taste.

"What does it feel like, Darius?" I ventured on an impulse.

He looked up. "What does *what* feel like?"

"Making love."

His face reddened. "Really, Alex, just because you caught me in a compromising situation the other day doesn't mean that I should or will discuss such things with you. I have already apologized." He flicked the paper he was holding impatiently, keeping his eyes upon it though I knew he had stopped reading. "If you want to know about such matters you must ask your sisters. You have two of them married now, don't you?"

"I am quite sure Cassy would never talk of it."

"Is Cassy the one who married the tutor?"

I nodded.

"But your older sister, the pretty one, she is married to Ramsey, isn't she? Why don't you talk to her?"

"I would never talk to Eugenia on such a subject because I have never been able to talk to her about anything. She knows a great deal, at least she is always pr—always with child, though it seems that her husband spreads his passions quite liberally in the neighbourhood. And don't suggest my talking to mother, for I never would." How was it, I wondered, that I had the courage to speak of it to Darius? I had had no intention of doing so, yet I had been unable to prevent myself from putting the question to him. Was it, perhaps, because I yearned to learn from him and from him alone about love?

"Don't allow Ramsey's exploits to disillusion you about marriage; not at your age." He paused, then went on uneasily. "If it is the intimate aspect of marriage that worries you, I can assure you that it is not unpleasant."

"I didn't ever suppose it was."

Our eyes met and his embarrassment increased. He got up and walked over to the bookshelves.

"Turn to poetry if you really wish to know how it feels. A poet can put into words things a politican can never explain. Read the sonnets of Donne or Spenser, or even Shakespeare. All the poets who have written so inspiringly of the passions are men. Unfortunately no woman has yet done the same for her sex. It is a grave omission. A favourite poet of mine is an

Indian, a Brahman, who wrote this marvellous liturgy of love before his execution.''

He handed me a slim volume entitled *Black Marigolds*, by a man called Chauras. I remembered having seen it on his bookshelf when, as a child, I had explored his room.

"Why was he executed?" I asked.

"He fell in love with his king's daughter."

"Was that so bad?"

"It was if you were a poet."

I opened the book at random and read:

> Even now
> I remember that you made answer very softly,
> We being one soul, your hand on my hair,
> The burning memory rounding your near lips.

"I wonder if he would have been executed had he been a politician instead of a poet," I mused.

"Chauras wrote in the first century, but I suspect there were political factions even then. He might, perhaps, have been allowed to marry the princess instead of dying for his offence had he belonged to the right one."

Our eyes met again and we both laughed.

"She could have run away with him."

"Princesses don't run away with either poets or politicians."

I wondered. I thought of his remark about women poets.

"Perhaps the writer of *Sum of Glory* will turn to poetry and write of love from the woman's viewpoint," I suggested.

"Perhaps she will. She would probably meet with success, but I would hope when next she puts pen to paper, she will allow entirely human passions to members of both sexes."

"Undoubtedly she will correct that failing as her own experience increases," I assured him.

XV

IT WAS HOT that summer. I felt as lonely as the sun, which daily followed its appointed, solitary course across our cloudless Wiltshire skies. That Darius was always in my thoughts added to my sense of solitude, for I never saw him alone but always as I had seen him that night with his devastatingly attractive countess. How I loathed her as her image rose before me time and again, ruining my daydreams, even as she seemed to be ruining my life. I had assured Lady Bladen that Darius would never make a fool of himself, but might he not over a woman, over that woman?

Paul had taken the orders and had been requested by Mr. Pomeroy's relative to assist at a church in a remote village in Northumberland. He was unhappy at the prospect but resigned to the inevitable. I reminded him of my talk with Sydney Smith, and he promised, though without great enthusiasm, to see him when he went north. Other than that he said little to me or to anyone else.

Arthur Harrington, who had been with Paul at Oxford, was staying at Ramsey Manor. He came frequently to Seton Place, sometimes in the company of Eugenia, but more often alone. I presumed it was to see Paul, though Paul cared as little for his company as he did for anyone else's. Harrington had not changed. He was still the maladroit youth of the election ball. It was hard to believe he was older than Paul. His stutter had become more pronounced, perhaps because his father was insisting that he enter politics, something for which he was little fitted and had even less inclination. I felt for his predicament; it was one with which I was familiar, and I tried, as I had with Paul, to help him adjust to the inevitable.

I had become positively addicted to poetry, reading almost nothing else since that last talk with Darius, and I enjoyed reading aloud, though I felt affected if I did so alone. Arthur provided a splendid audience, for he listened without interrupting, in fact he said very little at all, though his fatuous expression, which I sometimes caught as I finished, was disconcerting. It was when I became aware of father watching us, that look of assessment in his eye, that I discontinued these readings. Nevertheless, Arthur Harrington remained a constant guest at our dinner table, and though I did not dislike him, I had no intention of being cast into Cassy's predicament and saddled with that lamentably awkward young gentleman. I therefore adopted a cool, even callous attitude toward him, hoping he would refuse to come as often, but though cowed and hurt by my indifference and changed manner, he was faithful in attendance.

I heard little from Cassy. Paul had seen her in Oxford. She was well, he said, as well as could be expected though perhaps even quieter than usual, which must have been quiet indeed. He had had little chance to be alone with her so he was unsure of the true state of her feelings. I knew her to be unhappy, for after those few dry notes she had sent in reply to my voluminous epistles, she had sent a letter delivered to me by Paul, a letter she had smuggled to him when her husband was not about, requesting that, though she loved to read all I had written, I write in future bearing in mind that hers were not the only eyes that perused her correspondence, both the letters she wrote and those she received. She loved me too much to have my fervent hopes and wishes become public knowledge, something she knew I did not wish any more than did she. I thought of her situation with pain and pity in my heart, which served to strengthen my resolve never to fall into a like situation and be forced to marry against my will. This resolve made me keep a safe distance from Harrington.

Eugenia came often. Now the mother of a boy and a girl, she was pregnant again and she complained bitterly and constantly of the fact to mother. I had never been close to her when she was at home. Now she was a pouting though still-beautiful matron, and I felt further removed from her than ever; she, in turn, showed the same indifference and contempt she had ever felt for me. There were times when I had the impression she resented my freedom and lack of entanglement, which was ironic after all the pains she had taken to entrap her husband.

My youngest sister, Netty, had inherited Eugenia's classic beauty and with it had earned Eugenia's place in father's affections. Though we were the last two girls at home, no intimacy developed between us, my fault as much as Netty's, for all my interests had been at Charteris while she was growing up. She was seventeen, and in my opinion an empty-headed flirt. She, I knew, thought of me in equally unflattering terms—I once overheard her describe me to Eugenia as a stuck-up bluestocking.

James—"my baby," as mother continued to call him—to her profound regret was bound for Oxford at Michaelmas, designated by father for a career in law. I wondered how father made his decisions on our destiny—was it with a toss of the die, or did he open the Bible at a random page, seeking divine guidance. To me, it seemed quite obvious that Paul would have better served as an attorney in London with the Fanshawes than he ever would on parish business in the wilds of Northumberland, yet, against all his remonstrances, he had been forced to take orders. James was still malleable, so perhaps he would adapt to his chosen profession with greater ease. In the meantime I was concerned for my own interests and was determined to avoid Seton Place, Harrington and father's scheming.

I spent as much time as I could with Crumpet. He was growing and enjoying the stories I spun for him, stories with characters who became almost real as they moved daily from one adventure to another. Sir Crumpet Carruthers was the hero who won out against all odds; his archenemy being the dreaded Lord Boris Blackguard, who was always in the wrong and who, though it seemed that he might triumph, always in the end failed to gain the day.

I finished my *New Cassandra* and, heartened by the publication of my first novel, I packed it up and forwarded it to Mr. Hillaby with an unsigned note, of which I kept a copy, expressing my hope that he would think as well of it as *Sum of Glory*.

In addition to reading poetry, I was writing it also, poetry of love, yet it was, I feared, without inspiration. Was it impossible for women to write of the passions? Darius had said none had ever done so. I read Keats and Shelley and knew my poetry lacked their fire, perhaps I was incapable of conveying my emotions, or was it simply that I lacked experience?

In August the heat became excessive, and I took Crumpet wading in the stream where Paul and I used to play as children. We found a pet frog and named him Sylvester and tried to train him to come when called by name, but he was a frog with a mind of his own, and I often thought that when we felt we had succeeded it was only because he himself had decided to move at that moment rather than respond to our calls. Our clothes were often wet and muddy, yet that seemed of no importance until Crumpet developed a cold, which rapidly developed into a bad chill. Mr. Wilson was called in, he prescribed his usual tonic and advised light meals, broths and avoidance of draughts.

I stayed with him; caring for him; giving him his medication; making sure he was warm, and that he ate his meals. Yet the chill persisted. It did, in fact, grow worse. Crumpet became wan and listless and developed a fever which would not abate. Alarmed, I wrote to Darius asking his advice. In reply he sent a London doctor to examine Crumpet, but apart from changing all Mr. Wilson's medications for his own, he gave little satisfaction and Crumpet was no better. Again I wrote to Darius, voicing my concern and insisting that he come without further delay.

He came, accompanied by yet another physician, who examined Crumpet with greater thoroughness. The gravity of his expression when he finished frightened me. I was filled with guilt for not having taken better care of him, for allowing him to wade, for not changing his clothes immediately. I had so often worn wet clothes myself, as had Paul, that I found it difficult to believe they could cause such grievous harm. Indeed, Crumpet had shown no ill effects from such play, which had ceased at the first sign of a cold. Still, I confided my fears to the physician who assured me wet clothes were not the cause of the malady. The boy, he said, was succumbing to a congenital lung condition, an inherited disease the cold might have aggravated but certainly not caused.

There had been no consumption among the Bladens, I was sure of it. I presumed then that he must have inherited it from his mother, though the physician, who had also attended Philomena, told me that he had noted no sign of it in her. Yet wherever the consumption had sprung from, it now held Crumpet in its grasp. His condition worsened. He became listless and then delirious. Despite all the cooling sponge baths, his temperature refused to drop nor could the persistent cough that racked his body be alleviated.

I was with him each day; Darius stayed with him each night. He came in often during the day while I was there to look at his son, to feel his burning forehead, to hold his hand. He was getting scarcely any rest; his face was haggard and drawn.

"You must sleep or you will become ill also. That will help nothing," I warned. "Please lie down. I promise to call you if there is a change."

"I can't sleep. Sometimes I wonder whether I shall ever sleep again."

That afternoon I was loath to leave, yet at four the nurse came, assuring me she would not leave him, and with one last kiss I left the room. As I descended the stairs, Darius passed me on his way to Crumpet's side. We exchanged greetings, yet he seemed dazed.

That evening I could scarcely endure father's heavy-handed conversation as he attempted to draw out Harrington for my benefit. I would have none of it, and father was left to handle the burden of conversation with the young man on his own. He cast many a malignant glance in my direction, which went unheeded, for my thoughts were elsewhere. I was more worried than ever.

I returned to Charteris earlier than usual the next day to find that Crumpet's breathing had grown so laboured in the night that Mr. Linnell had been called upon to offer up prayers on his behalf, a grim omen that Darius felt his son would not survive.

I rushed upstairs, barely glancing at Darius, who made no move to leave, as was his wont, when I arrived at the bedside, and I knew he feared the worst.

Crumpet lay still and quiet as though he acknowledged that his struggle was over and that he, like his onlookers, was marking the minutes as they slipped by until the end.

When at last he opened his eyes and called to me—"Ala"— just as he always had, I could not stop from taking him into my arms and holding him close.

"I'm here, Crumpet, I'll always be here."

Rocking his wasted body to and fro, I would have breathed for him if it had been possible.

Was it an hour, or only minutes, before Darius leaned over to stroke his hair gently and then, very softly but very finally, close his eyelids. Even when he took him from me and laid the tiny form out on the bed, I refused to accept that it was over.

Though I was asked to leave, I would not, indeed, I could not.

I helped wash the lifeless body, and dressed it in the white satin suit with the blue sash Crumpet had worn on most important occasions. I remembered how he had been cautioned to keep clean when he wore that particular suit. There was little danger of it being soiled again. It would be amply protected from the earth by the sterile coffin being prepared for it. Those hands I had held, chubby and warm, lay still and stiff. The horror of death at its most virulent, at its most poignant, in robbing life from a child was more than I could bear, yet I could not bear to leave. Why had God chosen to take him before his life had begun? There was little enough of justice in life; it seemed there was none in death.

All day I sat, watching, waiting for I knew not what. Nothing would ever bring him back, yet still I sat without moving, in the end almost without thinking. That face was beautiful, grave yet strangely peaceful in death. Was that how it would be? I stayed on with all sense of time lost to me so that when the nurse came, telling me it was past four, that I should go home, that I could do nothing more, still I made no motion to leave.

She put her arm around me and almost forcibly helped me from my chair. "Please, Miss Alexandra, please go home. Try to rest, try to eat, for you've had nothing. You did everything for the little boy in life. Now, God rest his soul, there is nothing anyone can do, excepting Him."

As though in a trance I left the room and descended the stairs, my heart still refusing to believe that to which my eyes had all day borne witness.

I had seen nothing of Darius since that morning. Even then I had paid him no heed, but as I crossed the hall and saw the closed door of the library, I knew he must be there. Anger arose, bringing feeling back to my benumbed body and brain. Well, perhaps he was satisfied—since death had taken Crumpet, he could no longer blame him for ending Philomena's life. He had never treated Crumpet with affection; not, at least, until the end, when I knew he had been greatly affected by the bravery with which his son had battled for life. Still, it is our actions in life for which we are accountable. He had been cold and unfeeling as a father.

The anger I felt welled up so that I could not resist the desire to confront him with it, yet when I went into the library, I thought that the great room was empty; in the dimming light I saw no one until, just as I was about to leave, I caught sight of a slumped figure in an armchair before the terrace window. He wore no coat or neck cloth. His shirt was rumpled, his hair unkempt, his cheeks unshaven. When he raised his head at my approach, I was shocked to see his dull, lifeless eyes, which appeared not to recognize me. At the sight of his dejection, all anger drained from me. I went to him, filled with anguish.

"I grieve with you, Darius. I feel his loss as you do. I know what you are suffering."

"Do you?"

He held out his hands to me and I took them. They were cold, icy cold, yet his face was flushed and feverish.

"You must take care of yourself. You have had no rest, you have not eaten. Making yourself ill will not bring back your son. Let me call the doctor to see you."

"No." He held fast to my hands. "No, Alex, no. Don't leave me, please."

To see the strong grow suddenly weak and vulnerable was almost as terrifying to me as the death I had witnessed upstairs. His eyes were haunted. Never had I heard such a tone of pleading. I responded to its urgency.

"Come." I drew him over to the sofa and he followed meekly, just as Crumpet might have done, and just as I might have done with Crumpet I pulled him down beside me and took him in my arms.

"Now cry," I ordered, as I had so often insisted Crumpet do when he had stubbed his toe yet was trying desperately to be brave. "Cry, please cry, cry as much and as long as you want to. But please do cry."

I took his face between my hands and smoothed back his tousled hair. Then I leaned back against the cushions and gently pulled his head down to my breast, stroking it, murmuring softly, "Let go, Darius, let go. Grief that never speaks will break your heart. Let go, please."

Slowly, very slowly at first, like clouds when there is no wind, the tears came. He was ashamed to succumb. His upbringing, his education, his entire heredity proscribed it, yet I insisted, murmuring softly I know now what, smooth sounds, soothing sounds, sounds a mother uses to comfort a child, sounds used from time immemorial to ease pain and sorrow, sounds without words, soft, assuasive, simple sounds, until at last his body convulsed and the tears flowed freely.

How long he cried I cannot say. It seemed an eternity before that sobbing ceased and his body grew lax and heavy upon mine. His breathing continued disturbed and laboured although I was sure that he slept, yet it was a torpor rather than sleep from which he periodically started with a sigh that became almost a wail as it broke from his lips. I held him closer, stroking, comforting him until he fell back to his troubled sleep. As I lay there, nursing him like a child, I reflected on the singularity of circumstance that had allowed him to bury with no outward show of emotion both parents whom he dearly loved, yet on the death of a son for whom he had evidenced so little affection, he was utterly broken.

Eventually the warmth of his body upon mine, the comforting of holding close to me one whom I had always loved, the down of the sofa cushions beneath me and my own lack of rest all overcame me. I closed my eyes and fell into a deep sleep.

I dreamed; I must have dreamed. There were strange and wonderful sensations in my dream, sensations I had never before known, sensations of life in the midst of death. It was as though my body were wildly alive, even afire, yet at the same time completely languorous; my body seemed an entity in and of itself, separated quite from my mind, which looked down upon its fluid state. My breasts were drawing, pulsing, throbbing, their centres hard and tingling with a strange new life. I heard my name repeated over and over again until the lips that whispered it were fixed upon mine and I was lost within a mass of sensations assaulting every part of me, breasts, thighs and then those dark, warm, moist, virgin recesses beyond until my entire body became apulse with a motion all its own, ungenerated by my brain. There was within me something not mine yet belonging as surely as though it were, for it brought with it a completeness long sought, a wholeness nature must have always intended. The pulsating rhythm of this joining continued, quickening, deepening, lasting how long I could not tell for I was completely lost in time, in space, in circumstance until my body convulsed violently in tingling tremors that threatened to send me reeling into a million fragments, coiling, dispersing ceaselessly in the firmament. That, too, at last, ceased and all was silent, still.

Then, only then, did I begin to think clearly. Then, only then, did I know that I was not dreaming, that I was not asleep in my bed at home, that I was very much awake. Then, only then, did I know what Vergil had known when he wrote in his *Eclogues,* "Now I know what love is." I knew it, too; it was a wondrous and an awesome thing.

Our bodies clung to one another, still moist and heated from their task, suffused by its sweet, clinging, musky odor. Darius, beside me, had fallen into a deep sleep, no longer flinching and disturbed, at last at peace. His head, resting on the cushion beside mine, was still. I lay listening to his regular, free breathing, holding him close to me. Once, twice I leaned over to kiss him. He stirred but did not waken.

My thoughts went to that small, lifeless body upstairs, with the accompanying dread of never seeing Crumpet alive again, and I was glad of the comfort of Darius's arms around me. There was a mysterious proximity of the death I had watched over all day and the wonder of life revealed for the first time.

I lay holding Darius close to me, turning over all that had happened, until the long case clock in the hall broke through my thoughts and I counted the hour. Eleven! I could not remain at

Charteris all night. Already there must be consternation at home. If father had any inkling of what had occurred, he would either force Darius to marry me or forbid me ever to see him again. I had no wish for either decreee. Darius and I would be together from then on, of that I was sure. I would tolerate no interference from father in the matter. But I knew I must return home and I knew I must not allow him to know where I had been.

Gently I extricated myself from Darius's arms and stood up. He stirred but did not waken. I felt his head and found that it was feverish. The air was chill, and I looked around for something with which to cover him. My eye fell on the bearskin rug, but no longer was I offended by its memories. While the countess and her captivating charms were not forgotten, after all that had happened to me that day, they were quite unimportant. I covered him with the rug but still I could not bear to leave him. I needed him at that moment more than ever I had. I smoothed his damp, unkempt hair and ran my fingers across the stubble on his chin, strangely delighted at being a party to such intimate disorder. Then, with one last kiss to my lover who stirred but did not waken, I straightened the disarray of my own attire and slipped out through the french windows on the terrace.

Light shone from almost every window of my home when I came within sight of it. As I drew nearer I heard voices outside, and I turned back. I must not appear to be returning from the direction of Charteris. Cutting through our pear orchard, I came out on the other side of the house, where I was accosted by Thomas.

"My God, Alex, where have you been? You have everyone in an uproar. Mother has fainted twice, and father is threatening to get out the militia. Where have you been all this time? We've looked for you everywhere. I myself went over to Charteris but they told me you left there soon after four. Where have you been?"

I heard father's heavy step on the gravel behind Thomas.

"Alexandra, is that you? My God, girl, where in the name of heaven have you been? Are you all right? What happened—tell me what happened?"

I was in a daze. My mind was so full of everything that had happened that I had given no thought to what I would tell my family, but I was determined they would never learn of it from me.

"Let me go in, father, please, I beg you. I've been walking, I don't know where, I just walked. John died today."

I burst into tears at the finality of those words and went inside. Under the bright candlelight of the sitting room, father eyed me critically. He waited until my sobs subsided before demanding, "Now tell me, where have you been and what have you been doing? As your father I have a right to know everything."

"I told you, I've been walking."

"And just where have you been walking until this hour?"

"I don't know—just wandering aimlessly. It has been a terrible, wonderful day."

The last adjective slipped out unintentionally, and father's eyebrows rose immediately on hearing it.

"A wonderful day, you say? And what, may I ask, has made it so wonderful?"

"Father, I'm quite exhausted. I don't know what I'm saying."

"I can see that quite plainly. What I want to know—and I want the truth—is have you been doing this wandering of yours on your own?"

I nodded.

"Are you sure—quite sure?" he questioned again, in sharper tone.

"Please, father, please leave me alone. I told you, John is dead. I'm upset and confused."

"Not until I get to the bottom of this. You can't expect me to accept it as quite normal that a daughter of mine should wander home close to midnight with no logical explanation for her absence." He scrutinized me closely. "You haven't been alone, my girl, of that I'm convinced."

My face flushed in betrayal.

"Out with it—you haven't been alone?"

I said nothing, but every line of my body must have bespoken my guilt.

"It was young Harrington you were with, wasn't it? He was here earlier, waiting for you, and I told him you were with the sick boy and at last he left. He rode over there to see you. Tell me the truth. I'll have it out of you one way or another." He was triumphant in his accusation, which appalled me, yet before I remonstrated against it I was seized by the dual opportunity of ridding myself of Harrington forever and escaping from father's interrogation. I could not bring myself to actually incriminate the innocent young man, yet I did so just as surely by hanging my head without reply to father's repeated accusations until at last he uttered an oath.

"My God, if he thinks he can play fast and loose with a

daughter of mine, he's mistaken. I shall let his father know in no uncertain terms that I will not have him calling here again. The father's a fool for letting that rascal of a Whig rob him of his seat. The son's a fool, for I'm convinced nobody is going to send him up to Parliament no matter what pressure is brought to bear. You're a foolish girl, Alexandra, and even more foolish to shield that young nincompoop for his wrongdoing. I consider you as much to blame in this as he—you should know by now that a lady's reputation cannot be too closely guarded. The insolent young puppy, thinks he can come here and conduct himself like a, . . ." A thought suddenly struck him and he seized me by the shoulders.

"Did he—did he take advantage of you in any way? You know what I mean—be honest now. If he did he'll marry you for sure, no matter what his prospects. I'll keep no despoiled daughter under my roof."

"No, father, no. I assure you he did nothing, nothing at all. I should never allow such conduct—from him," I cried out in anguish lest my schemes of ridding myself of an unwanted suitor should rebound on me so disastrously.

"Well, thank God for that at least. I've no wish to be saddled with a worthless son-in-law who like as not would lean on me for support. Let his own father take care of that. You can do better than Harrington."

"Yes, father, I'm quite sure I can," I replied fervently.

"And now the boy is dead you are relieved of any further obligation to the Bladens. I can see no further need for you to go over to Charteris. I never liked you being there at any time, but especially now Bladen is loosened from his ties, it could cause talk. Stay close to home in future. Now go to bed."

I left, fatigued yet relieved an unperturbed. Darius, I knew, would come for me.

XVI

BUT DARIUS DID not come, not the next day, nor the day after that. In fact I saw nothing of him until the funeral, which was delayed because he was ill. I longed to go to him, to seek comfort by sharing with him my abysmal sorrow, but I did not. I could not risk father's displeasure at a time when all depended on his acceptance of Darius, Whig though he be.

St. Mary's was filled, as it had been on the day Darius married, but the congregation differed from that fashionable throng, the gentry being outnumbered by tenants and villagers who had long known and served the family at Charteris. Tears fell on weathered, gorged and smooth red cheeks alike. The death of a child must inevitably cause greater pain than that of one who has lived threescore and ten, yet those tears were for that particular child and for that particular parent in sympathy with his grief.

Only his back, tall and gaunt, clad in deepest mourning as he sat alone in the family pew, was visible to me. I knelt firmly on the cushion beneath me, engrossed in the needlework design of intertwined grape leaves I had worked, to overcome my overwhelming urge to run to him.

Our eyes met for a moment as we followed the tiny white coffin to that solitary hollow awaiting it in the churchyard. His face was thin, wan and troubled as his grey eyes unsmilingly met mine. He nodded in recognition, nothing more, then turned to those villagers paying their respects and delivering condolences in simple, sincere and heartfelt phrases which I knew he would treasure a thousand times more than Mr. Linnell's loquacious eulogy.

"In the midst of life we are in death," the pastor intoned at the graveside. So it had been that night; in the midst of death we had been in life. Did he think of that also? I looked in his direction, but Netty moved in front of me and I was unable to see him without craning my neck.

"We therefore commit his body to the ground; earth to earth, ashes to ashes, dust to dust; in sure and certain hope of the Resurrection to eternal life.''

Though I had been with him when he died, it was only with the first sprinkling of earth, dark, stark, somehow obscene as it fell on the white coffin, that I frankly acknowledged to myself the permanence of Crumpet's death. I would never see him again. I would never hear him laugh, or say my name. He would never run to me for comfort or listen to my stories.

The lump, lodged in my throat throughout the service, quivered to allow a deep sob to escape from my lips. Darius turned in my direction—our eyes met and I knew that he, too, was at that moment facing that same devastating, irrevocable truth. He was pale, terribly pale, though perhaps his pallor was enhanced by the unmitigated black of his mourning coat, linen, handkerchief and crepe hatband.

I had to talk to him. The occasion must present itself. Father had raised the matter of my departure for Salisbury for my belated coming out. He was anxious that I leave as soon as possible because of my implied escapade with Arthur Harrington. Surely Darius must want to speak to me as desperately as I wished to speak to him.

The day was grey as we left St. Mary's. The bright sun had vanished behind a bank of clouds. Even the song of the birds seemed to echo a dirge. Father broke away to speak to Darius while the rest of us stood back like so many hovering crows. He must speak to me. He must. My ears strained to hear what passed between them; first father's dutiful expressions on his bereavement, followed by Darius's thanks and his murmured appreciation of the friendship and devotion I had shown to all his family, but most particularly to his son. It was an expression of gratitude, nothing more. It was certainly not what I wanted to hear.

"I'm glad Alexandra has made herself useful," I heard father say. "She is sad, very sad about the boy's death. I am arranging for her to go to Salisbury for a change of scene."

"I'm glad of that. I myself leave very soon. It may be some time before I return."

My heart sank at the words—no protest over my going, nothing. But surely he must say something. I hung back as father motioned us to leave and Darius came over to me and took me aside, out of earshot of the others.

"Alexandra, there is something I must ask you, something I

must know. It has been on my mind, yet I scarcely know how to put it into words . . .''

"Oh, Darius, you have been ill. I've wanted to talk to you so. It was hard for me to stay away.'' I wanted so much to hold him, to have him hold me, that it was almost unbearable.

"I know, Alex, how hard all of this has been for you. I could never bear to inflict pain upon you of all people, yet there is something I must ask, yet for the life of me I don't know how to do it.'' He twisted his beaver hat between his hands, making the long crepe band dance and sway at the motion. "The night that John died . . . did I . . . did anything happen?''

I looked at him in puzzlement. What did he mean? Surely he must know what had happened.

"I have been ill, quite ill; delirious, in fact. The doctor tells me it is not unusual at such times. When faced with those things we do not wish to accept, we block them from our minds, yet they persist to become intermingled with the unreal, making it impossible to tell one from another.''

His eyes were dark and so obviously troubled as he looked into mine, I could not bear it. He had made love to me, yet he did not wish to believe it, I thought bitterly. I dropped my eyes to the dancing motion of his hatband, unable to bear his gaze.

"Alex, you must be honest with me. I believe I may have wronged you, acted in some unforgiveable manner towards you— you of all people, whom I would never wish to harm. If it is not so, if what I think is merely a nightmare, please remove this further misery from my mind. Yet if I did—if I did hurt you in any way, I must make amends to you. Tell me if there is anything I must know.''

I could not reply. I knew not how to. The lump returned to my throat, making it impossible to speak even if I had wished to, but I did not. I had nothing to say.

I shook my head silently, wretchedly, hopelessly.

When at last I raised my eyes to his it was to see such unmitigated relief on his face that I believed he must have been in mortal dread of being forced to offer for me. That look of relief lowered my already abysmally low spirits.

"I cannot tell you how relieved I am to know it was a nightmare. You have taken such a load from my mind, Alex, for you are dearer to me than my sisters. I would never wish harm to come to you, least of all from me.''

I would say nothing. I could say nothing. My heart was cold

within. I longed to cry out to him, but of course I did not. When I spoke at last, my words were barely audible.

"You said you are leaving soon."

"Yes, I leave tomorrow."

"Where are you going?"

"To Italy."

"So far! How long will you be gone?"

"I don't know. I just don't know. At the moment I wish it would be forever."

He cared nothing for me if he wished never to come back. There was nothing more to be said. I held out my hand.

"I must go now. Father will wonder where I am. Good-bye, Darius. My thoughts go with you."

He took my hand between his. "I wish you everything that you wish yourself, Alex. I can wish you no more."

"Do you, I wonder." I saw Thomas beckoning to me, and before Darius could reply, I said again, "Good-bye," and was gone, past the newly covered grave, past the tombstones bearing the names of Cox-Nevilles who had preceded me. At that moment I longed desperately to be among them, in the quiet and peace of the tomb where I would feel nothing, care for no one. I belonged there, for my life seemed to be over.

XVII

I WAS LISTLESS. I went through my daily tasks as though in a trance, and then I sat doing nothing, nothing at all. There was nothing I wanted to do, nothing mattered anymore. I had nowhere to go. There was no one I wanted to see. Everyone in the world whom I loved was gone from me. I was bereft. Only one thought kept me alive in those days immediately after the funeral, one thought that persisted during those endlessly long days and nights. My body was benumbed, torpid, yet still it might hold life. Nothing could alter the irreversible truth that Crumpet was dead, but Darius might still have a child, his child and mine.

At night I lay in my narrow bed, my hands resting upon that region from which a child must come, wondering, wondering. I prayed that I carried his seed, yet if it were so, I had no idea what I would do. Go to Italy to find him, perhaps, to throw myself at his feet? Yet if he should not want me, what then? Or if he married me, would it be only from a sense of duty? I did not know, but I knew I wanted his child more than I had ever wanted anything. One night as I tossed and turned, it occurred to me that perhaps Darius had not gone away on his own; perhaps *she* was with him. Suppose he had turned to her for solace, suppose—suppose he had married her. I sat bolt upright, horrified at the thought. Quickly I rose and knelt by the side of the bed to pray that it might not be so, but then I remembered my other unanswered prayers. It was best that I not tell God what to do. What would be, would be.

What would be, was. Before the month was out I saw that with its usual monotonous regularity my little friend, to use mother's phrase, had come. No friend this. I cried at the first show and railed at fate as the show of blood gave evidence I was not with child; I sobbed at its continued flow left me empty, lifeless. Crumpet was gone; there would be no other on whom to lavish the love and affection I craved to give.

Mother had never before seen me so overcome by my monthly course. She did not, of course, mention it to father beyond hoping that the change of air in Salisbury would revive my spirits. Father, I suppose in an effort to hearten me, spoke repeatedly of my coming out. It seemed to me ridiculous at twenty, having already seen so much of life, to be introduced officially to society, yet when the time came I was glad to leave Linbury with all its associations.

Travelling to Salisbury from Linbury, though both were in Wiltshire, was in many ways like travelling to another county, for we of the northern part knew as little of the south as we did of Kent or Cornwall. We crossed the lonely, deserted plains close to Amesbury, and I remembered that Sydney Smith had told me he had been a curate there after ordination, a pretty feature in a plain face, he called it. At Amesbury, too, I was reminded again of the romance of Queen Guinevere, for it was there, in the abbey, that she had ended her days as a nun; there Sir Launcelot had sought her out to tell her of the death of her king and of his own decision to become a monk in Glastonbury. Perhaps I, too, should become a nun, I thought dismally, though the thought of being married to the church had little appeal to me. I was sure God wanted no unwilling brides. I would remain a spinster.

As we neared Salisbury, the hill of Old Sarum loomed on the

horizon. It was a notorious burgage borough. I had often heard Darius and his father speak of it as one of the prime examples of the inequities of our system of representation, for it was owned by the Earl of Caledon, who personally selected and sent up two members of Parliament at each general election.

In the distance I discerned the outline of Salisbury's great cathedral, with the sun reflecting on its narrow, gothic windows. It was imposing in proportion even from afar, and its grandeur grew with every passing mile, providing my eye with a harmony of grey stone, green foliage surrounding it, blue sky and golden sun beyond. Salisbury could not be without merit, I decided, centred as it was by such a magnificent edifice.

The quiet cathedral town was dominated by the society of the close that surrounded the cathedral, in which Aunt Maud's house was situated. It was a tall house, angular and imposing, very much like Aunt Maud herself, and it dominated the houses surrounding it very much in the way Aunt Maud dominated the blending of lay and clerical people around her. Under other circumstances I might have found the round of provincial social activities—a canter on the downs in the morning, croquet on the lawns in the afternoon, calls, tea parties and an occasional assembly or ball—pleasant, even relaxing, but from the beginning Aunt Maud, with the frankness Cassy had found so intimidating, let me know the intention of my visit was more than recreational.

She looked me over critically from head to toe on my arrival. "You'll do," she pronounced. "But not those clothes. Didn't my brother get you a new wardrobe?"

I showed her the two dresses I had had Mrs. Birdsock make for me. I had deliberately chosen them to show myself to least advantage. Even the Linbury seamstress had protested at my choice, and I had packed them away before mother could see them.

"Pink!" Aunt Maud sniffed. "You can't wear pink, at least not that pink, not with your hair. And they look like sacks, no fit to them at all. Here you are with a shape worth setting off and you've nothing to show it in, while Cassandra, on the other hand, had enough trouble trying to hide hers. She was lucky to find a husband. I told my brother so when he wrote to me of her marriage."

I held back the taunt which rose to my lips on the subject of Mr. Pomeroy, but I suppose she read it in my face.

"This Mr. Ponsonby—"

"Pomeroy."

"Pomeroy, Ponsonby, what difference does it make. The fact of it is that he has taken Cassandra, with very little charm and very little money, either, from what my brother tells me. She's a lucky young woman, and I want you to remember that. You may have an attractive face and a pleasing figure—though not in those things—but you've little enough else to offer, so don't get high and mighty about whom you'll have or not have."

She gave me implicit instructions on whom to encourage, what subjects I should discuss and matters I should avoid for fear of controversy.

"Nothing puts a man off more than a woman with views of her own."

She instructed me to be pleasing without being obtrusive, and she hoped I would behave more prettily than Cassy, who had been so painfully shy and retiring that people simply forgot she was there.

"I shall write to my brother immediately to send money so that we can purchase something more suitable for you. He can't expect to get his girls off looking like perfect dowds."

"You take this marriage market seriously," I commented.

"I do. And you had better also if you know what's good for you. You're not here for your health, you know. That's all there is in life for a girl—a good match. You might as well make the best one you can."

"But you didn't marry," I pointed out.

"You're a saucy one!" Her sharp eyes challenged me. "Well, it's all right for you to speak your mind to me, but mind you don't do it outside. No, I didn't marry. I was left well provided for. I saw to that, much to your father's displeasure. But you, my girl, have no such resource and don't forget it."

I smiled. We had taken each other's measure, and while I had not won, neither had I lost.

I didn't mind the croquet with earnest curates, nor the teas with worthy dowagers, but the balls and assemblies were dreary. My attention constantly wandered from my partners' polite conversations of sermons and canticles to the warm climes of the country of orange blossom and bougainvillea. I haunted the circulating library and revelled in Byron's poems written in exile in Italy. It was there that, for the first time I saw my own *Sum of Glory* in print between boards. On an impulse I took it down for Aunt Maud to read, and, as I laid down my coins for the loan I longed to announce that the book was mine, that I was the author, but my aunt was well known there—she would have learned of it and told father. No, my triumph, must, of necessity, be a personal, a lonely affair. Aunt Maud read my book without putting it aside to comment as was her usual practice. Occasionally she sniffed, whether in disgust or dismay I could not tell, while I paged through Susan Ferrier's fashionable novel, *Marriage*, and waited for her to speak. At last, curiosity forced to me to ask her what she thought of it.

"Not bad—quite convincing in fact. It's nice to find a spirited heroine for a change instead of these insipid creatures one finds so often in Maria Edgeworth or Hannah More. When you return it find out whether this—" she turned to the title page for a name— "this *lady* has written anything else."

I was absurdly pleased as much by her manner of reading as by her words. I could have told her that the author's second work was even then in the publisher's hands. That she very much hoped it would see print. But I didn't; I merely replied with civility that I would enquire when next at the library.

The only time I was on my own was in the early afternoon, just after luncheon, when Aunt Maud took her nap. It was then I began writing again, poetry to soothe my troubled breast, sonnets and odes, ambitious undertakings requiring all my powers of creation. I was filled with grief and emptiness at the death of the child I had held most dear; with wonder at a night of love; with bitterness at my state; bereft of child and lover; and it was through words and ideas which flowed into my mind and from my pen, in simile and metaphor, in octaves and sestets, in pentameter and hexameter that I began to live again.

I took care to conceal my work, for some of the poems were so intimate, so passionate, I knew they could be shown to no one, least of all left to the eyes of Aunt Maud or one of the servants. Yet its concealment strengthened my pleasure in it. It was mine and mine alone. Through it I kept alive private moments, moments gone, never, perhaps, to return. Yet it was through these poems that I could make them live for me forever.

Unlike Cassy, I never lacked partners at the assemblies. I was considered pleasing, even charming, delightful, by many of Aunt Maud's friends, most of whom at one time or another put forward the perfect choice of a husband for me. Aunt Maud had great hopes, but I disappointed them all. She was at a loss to understand why no gentleman attached himself to me despite all promptings, why no offers of marriage were forthcoming. She was, of course, unaware that I made sure none would be made. Whenever I saw a glint of interest that promised to develop into something more, I dashed it with icy silence or drowned it in tedious outpourings or terrified it with enthusiastic entrapment until it fled in fright, its owner relieved at his narrow escape.

Thus I parted from Aunt Maud at Christmas, still a maiden though not untouched, in fact in no changed condition from that in which I had arrived. Despite her dashed hopes our parting was friendly. She presented me with a five-guinea gold piece as a present and invited me to return in the spring.

I was spared father's catechism on my Salisbury matrimonial prospects, whom I had met there, what was their income, to whom were they connected, the catechism Cassy had so dreaded, by the presence in the neighbourhood of Howard Ramsey. He had returned home on company leave for the holidays and had been anxiously awaiting my arrival.

Initially I found his company quite pleasing. He talked a great deal of India. To be sure, much of it was disappointingly businesslike—the country's economic prospects, native labour and methods of getting the greatest return from the least effort (he had, it appeared, done his part and had returned as he had promised to do, a veritable nabob). I learned little of the scenery or the social customs of the people but nevertheless he provided a worldly touch at our Christmas gathering, which was not the happiest for me with memories of Crumpet, Darius away and Charteris closed and with no plans for either Cassy or Paul joining us. Howard paid great attention to me but I saw no harm in it. I knew he was soon to return to India; there could be little danger in being entrapped by a man who showed no indication of settling down.

I should have been forewarned by the manner in which father openly favoured Howard that his intentions were perhaps more than passing. I can only excuse my lack of prudence by the fact that I had kept such a close guard in fencing likely suitors while in Salisbury that when I returned home, I was unprepared to continue to defend my free state. It was not until I noticed how often Howard and I were left to our own devices that I suspected father of planning another match. By that time Howard, assured father offered no objection, openly flaunted his attentions. Too late I began a campaign of discouragement.

Howard began to talk of purchasing a property in the neighbourhood, and I heard him discuss with father the condition and desirability of houses that were available. I believe they even went so far as to examine some of them. Father outrageously encouraged Howard in grandiose plans for expansion of buildings, entering into long and detailed provisions for acquiring additional acreage. Though I was often turned to for an opinion or a word of encouragement, I said nothing, a silent, reluctant observer.

I had hoped to thwart father's now-unconcealed plans for my future by outstaying all onslaughts, for I knew that Howard was to return to Calcutta in the spring, but as his attentions became increasingly difficult to ignore, I was hard pressed to avoid his asking the question I least wished to hear.

Despite all my precautions against it, the subject arose after dinner one night. I had fled to the sitting room at the rear of the house, the very one Cassy had used for a refuge. I should have known it for an unlucky retreat, for no sooner had I flung myself into an armchair and opened my book than I realized Howard had guessed my intentions and had preceded me. He was esconced in a high wingback chair—with its back to the door. I had been unable to see him on entering.

"I thought you would come here." He smiled in self-satisfaction.

I got up, intent on leaving, but he rose too and thus stood between me and my means of retreat.

"Don't leave, Alexandra. I came here expressly because I want to talk to you on your own."

"No!" I said in great agitation. "No. No. I won't listen."

He must have taken my refusal for timidity, for he hastened to assure me he had father's permission to address me.

"But I do not wish to be addressed. In fact I refuse to be addressed."

Howard was perplexed. "But your father assures me that you are quite free," he asserted, as though that made his suit not only perfectly permissible but also highly desirable.

I began to protest, then decided against it. I would have to hear him out at some time; this was as good as any. There would be father's wrath to face, but that was inevitable since I had been unable to avoid the confrontation.

I sat stiffly in my chair. Howard stood beside me and grasped my limp hand.

"I've liked you for a long time, Alex. Even when we used to play together and you were such a tomboy, even then you attracted me. You weren't like other girls—you were full of daring. I was sure you'd grow into a dashed desirable woman and I was right. The day that George married your sister, the day I kissed you, I decided then and there that you were the one for me. I've thought about you all along while I've been away, I've thought about this moment, imagining your white skin under my hands instead of dark, coarse . . ." He stopped short, his already florid complexion taking on a darker hue. "I hadn't meant to say that, but I won't pretend to have been an angel. Experience in a man, unlike that in a woman, is an advantage. I won't try to hide the fact that I desire you. Why should I? It should please you to know that I intend to be attentive and to make you happy in that way as in every other."

I wished desperately that he would finish so that I could refuse him and thus put an end to this distasteful conversation. He may have sensed my impatience, though without understanding its cause, for he concluded abruptly. "The fact of the matter is, as I suppose you've already guessed, that I want you to be my wife. I'm well off now, your father knows that, and I'll be even better off when next I return from India, but I see no reason why we should wait to get married. I intend to buy a handsome house and see you settled in it before I leave. And feeling as I do, I see no reason why you'll not be left with a swelling belly—that should keep you busy and out of trouble while I'm gone."

He could not have phrased his proposal in a manner less certain to please me. As he paused, I drew breath for a firm, concise refusal, but I had not counted on being pulled from my chair and enfolded against his chest, his hot mouth covering mine, precluding any verbal protest, his hands kneading my body in a manner that absurdly reminded me of cook working over a bowl of bread dough—had my mouth been free I might have been hard put not to laugh outright. His hands were fervent and damp in their appointed round; my skin in contrast grew cool and unresponsive beneath them. Had he kept them on my back I might have allowed him to finish his embrace, but when I felt him fumbling at my breast it was too much. I pushed him roughly aside, obviously catching him off guard, for he staggered and released me. I could see from his expression that my action had surprised him. Perhaps my passivity had led him to believe I enjoyed his embrace, but though taken aback, he was undaunted.

"That is quite enough, sir. You had no right to thrust yourself upon me before allowing me the civility of replying to your offer."

If he was at all abashed, he was in no way out of countenance. He reached into his pocket for a small box, which I suspected must contain a ring, and I hastened to continue before he might attempt to place it on my finger.

"I thank you for your offer but I do not wish to marry you."

My reply could not have been plainer, yet Howard stood staring at me as though he had not understood a word I said. Either he thought not to have heard me correctly, or perhaps to tempt me, he opened the box to reveal a gold ring set with a large opal. He removed the ring from the box and made to place it on my hand, but I pushed it aside.

"Perhaps I have not been plain enough. I have no intention of marrying you now or at any other time. Do you quite understand?"

He stared in obvious disbelief, his mouth slightly ajar as though about to speak without knowing precisely what to say. Then his expression grew ugly and his voice, when at last he spoke, was hard and determined.

"Your father expects you to marry me. I expect you to marry me. Since I can conceive of no reason for your refusal except a false sense of modesty or a certain coyness which is not entirely unbecoming, though I trust you will soon overcome it, I shall ignore your response. I may perhaps have been a little hasty in my caresses. I was possibly overeager. I can only say I have waited for you for a long time and I want you." There was an unrelenting quality about him that was more frightening than open anger. His eyes, fixed at first on mine before they moved to my mouth, were hot and compulsive. "No matter what you say, Alex, I have no intention of giving up, I can assure you of that."

"You may do as you please, sir, but a wedding needs the consent of two people. You will not have mine."

I pushed past him and pulled open the door. At the end of the hallway, looking expectantly in my direction, was father. Ignoring him, I ran upstairs, leaving Howard to report on the outcome of his offer. There would be the devil to pay, I knew that, but I was prepared to fight and I would not fail. I would never accept Howard Ramsey.

It was not long before I heard father's heavy footsteps outside my door. He entered without knocking.

"Well, my fine young lady, whom are you waiting for, pray tell me—a prince of the realm, is it? Or do you perhaps consider yourself fit only for an emperor? Pray enlighten me, which is it?"

His heavy sarcasm was laced with anger. I faced him squarely, aware of the futility of attempting to reason with him yet attempting it anyway.

"Father, try to understand. All I want is a man I can love and respect. I can never hold either sentiment for Howard Ramsey. I don't even like him, let alone love him. I must respect the man I marry—if I do not I prefer to remain in my single state."

"It seems to me we've discussed this matter once before when Cassy married. You were set against that, too, I remember, but it's a happy union."

"A happy union! How would you know? You've never seen her; she never comes home. How can it be happy with a man who reads her letters, who tells her what she may and may not write and read."

"It's a sensible man who has control of his own household, and that's what you need, my girl, a man to control you. You've been getting your own way far too long. I've been negligent in allowing it. Now I'm bearing the fruits of my indulgence. Well, in this matter you will listen to me and you will obey. Young Ramsey is not a man to be trifled with. You'll marry him because there's no earthly reason why you should refuse him. He's young, healthy, rich and a fine-looking fellow to boot. Why he wants you when there's many a fair woman would be glad to throw her cap at him I can't imagine, but want you he does and he'll have you, mark my words. You reach your majority soon, and I won't keep you under my roof as an old maid when you've had a perfectly good, I may even say a superior marriage offer." Father's voice was slow and firm as he spoke, his manner as unforgiving as I knew only he could be. He couldn't force me to the altar but he could make life unlivable.

I needed time to think. I had no intention of giving in, but I had to think.

"Give me a week to think it over, father. Allow me to consider it, please," I persuaded.

"I'll give you till tomorrow night to accept Ramsey, not a minute more. You'll accept him then and you'll accept him prettily. You will stay in your room until you do."

I turned away from him, ignoring his good night. He left, slamming the door behind him. I had not gained much, I thought as I gazed around at my four familiar walls. I was glad that I possessed an active imagination. I would need it, for it seemed that those four walls would be all I would be seeing for a long time to come. I thought of Cassy's, "You'll be next," just like the first Cassandra in her predictions, but this one I refused to allow to come true. I would not be next, not with Howard Ramsey at least. If only Darius were home.

XVIII

IT WAS AS though my prayers had been answered.

Alice brought my breakfast the next morning, sniffing as she laid down the tray. "In disgrace again, I see, Miss Alex. At your age, too. When will you learn to mind your father?"

I ignored her remark, and knowing of her friendship with Miller at Charteris, I asked how things were going up on the hill, asking in perhaps too casual a tone to conceal my interest whether anything had been heard from Lord Bladen in Italy.

"Don't know nothing about Italy, Miss Alex, but Miller said he was out with the hounds this morning."

"Out with the hounds, here, with the Bedwyn pack?" There was no disguising the excitement in my voice.

"I don't know of no other," Alice replied drily, eyeing me suspiciously, so that I turned my attention to the tray and commented that being indoors wasn't much of a hardship on such a blustery day.

When she left, I bounded out of bed. It was too good to be true—he was back! My problems were solved. I would go to Charteris and throw myself at his mercy. Now was no time to consider niceties like propriety. I would declare myself, declare my love for him. He had loved me once. I would tell him of it, tell him all that had happened that night. I knew he had loved me then. He had called my name and no other. He had loved me passionately. I remembered his face as I had kissed it. I knew he had been happy then; there was no reason we could not be happy together always. I would make him happy, I vowed I would. I would make him forget Philomena.

All my years of waiting were at an end. I felt deliriously exultant. All my dreams would at last come true. I began to hum as I pulled open my wardrobe to decide what to wear. I would go to Charteris and wait. If he was hunting he probably would not return until the afternoon, but I would be there when he came. I hummed Tom Moore's air "Those Endearing Young Charms" as I chose a soft blue-green kerseymere with a pelisse of matching tone, for I could see the cold wind whipping at the trees.

No, the heart that has truly lov'd never forgets,
    But as truly loves on to the close,
As the sunflower turns on her god, when he sets,
    The same look which she turn'd when he rose.

Tom Moore's words were far more fitting to me than to the Countess to whom he had sang them. I wouldn't be afraid of her anymore, I decided.

Mother came in and I hastily pushed the dress back into the wardrobe.

"Good morning, dear," she kissed me perfunctorily. "You are sounding happier than I had expected."

She stood awkwardly looking around, not knowing where to begin. "You have a charming aspect from this room, Alex."

"Yes," I replied noncommitally, and she went on even more awkwardly.

"Father asked me to talk to you, Alex." She looked at me for help, but I knew what father had asked her to talk about and I had no help to give. She began again in a hesitant voice. "We all have to do things in life that at the time may not appear to be exactly as we would wish, but they have a way, Alex, of turning out quite satisfactorily once we adapt ourselves to them."

I watched, not without pity, as she spoke. Would I resemble her twenty years hence, colourless, no light in the eye, no lilt to the voice—would that happen to me? Would I try to persuade my child to adopt a course of action decided by my husband? She was a model of submission: submission to father over countless years of marriage, submission to her father over countless years before that. I totally rejected her way of life: I would not pattern my own on it. Yet even so I felt a deep tenderness, for suppose she had not always been so—suppose she had once felt as I did at that moment, suppose she had once fought for her own life—and lost. I found myself crying. I flung myself in her arms and held her close to me.

"Oh, mother, mother. I really do love you."

"Alex, Alex! My dear Alex! You are so impulsive. Of all my children you have worried me most. I was so afraid you would do something . . . something rash. At first I thought the education you received, so far superior to that of your sisters, might make you more understanding of the realities of life, but I can see the reverse has happened. You are more dissatisfied now than ever. Perhaps that is why women should not be educated."

"But education is more important to us, mother. We are the ones who hold the lives of future generations in our hands."

"It is not education we need to mould those lives, Alex. We need to learn the art of pleasing, we need to learn to use our wiles. That is how women survive, by using their wiles, and that is what you must learn, Alex, if you too wish to survive. You are too blunt, too straightforward."

"Then tell me, mother, how I can use my wiles to keep from marrying Howard Ramsey?" I asked.

She took my face in her hands and wiped a tear from my cheek. "I don't believe you can, Alex. Your father is set on it and Mr. Ramsey is set on it. I think you must resign yourself to the marriage, but if you do as I advise you will survive it."

"But I don't want to survive marriage, mother, I want to live it. Once I take those vows I shall be married for the rest of my life. I don't want to survive my life, I want to live it. I want to live with someone I love, or if I ask too much in that, at least someone I respect."

"I know, dear, I know. I was young once. But you will see, it will work. You will have children and then you'll find your time is occupied with their welfare, not merely centred around your husband. Your life will be full. I think Howard Ramsey is a very presentable gentleman. He is quite handsome, wealthy, and his family is known to us. There would be no surprises. Eugenia is nearby—you could perhaps become close to her, though I know you always preferred Cassy." She paused, as though unsure whether to continue, then bravely plunged on, "I don't know whether Howard has frightened you by being too . . . too demanding . . . but if so you'll find that will wear off."

"When he follows his brother down to the village girls, you mean."

"Alex, how do you know anything about that!" She was horrified.

"Almost everyone does, mother, except Eugenia, and she may, too, for all I know. Perhaps she even encourages it. No matter. Despite his wanderings he manages to keep her constantly pregnant."

Mother's expression indicated that the conversation was distasteful to her and she said in a reproving tone, "It is the role of a woman to bear children, Alex."

"I know," I said wearily. "But why were we given brains as well as wombs?"

Mother eyed me doubtfully. Perhaps she was unsure whether

"womb" was a nice word. I was about to point out to her that it occurred often in the Bible, but instead I kissed her.

"Thank you for coming, mother. I'll think over what you have said. I told father I would give him my answer tonight."

"That answer must be yes, Alex," she whispered as she hugged me. "Otherwise he'll make life unbearable for you."

Her tone of voice indicated that she knew whereof she spoke. I clung to her again for a moment before she left.

When Alice brought my lunch tray, I took the food from it and stuffed it in a drawer. I was too excited to eat. Then I dressed and combed my hair. It was useless to attempt to do much with it with such a wind outside. I listened to make sure the family were in the dining room at lunch before quietly making my way down the staircase, across the empty hall and out into the clear, crisp air.

The wind whipped at my hair and cheeks, and for the first time in months I felt happy. I was free. I wanted to dance. If I could have sprouted wings, I would have flown to Charteris, but I doubt I could have arrived there much quicker than my scurrying feet carried me. My face was glowing from the cold air and my hair in complete disarray when I arrived at the great front portico, but I had never felt so radiantly alive.

Fate favoured me for Darius had already returned. I found him in the grand saloon, still in his red hunting coat, standing before a crackling fire, sipping sherry. His face was bronze from the warm Italian sun, his cheeks pink from the cool English wind, the colour of his complexion making his slate grey eyes quite blue. My heart beat faster at the sight of his smile, at the sound of his voice. I had so long imagined being alone with him just as we were. Yet when the moment arrived, I wondered how to begin. I suddenly wished for the gaunt, unshaven man who had been my lover rather than the handsome, self-assured Adonis who greeted me, warm though his greeting was.

"Alex, Alex, how good of you to come. You must have known I was thinking of you." He laughed and held out both hands to me and held me at arm's length. "You look absolutely wonderful. What have you been doing with yourself?"

"Nothing in comparison with you. You look marvellous . . . Italy must have agreed with you."

"It did. It always does. Come, let me take your pelisse. And let me pour you a glass of sherry. I hear you are out now, so I suppose that is in order."

I nodded. "How long have you been back?" I asked.

"I got back from Italy last month. I've been busy in London and thought I'd come here for a few days. It was probably a mistake, though. There are too many memories here." He turned away but could not disguise the catch in his voice, and I knew we were both remembering Crumpet.

"When did you get here?" I asked after an interminable pause.

"Yesterday."

Yesterday, I thought. Fate had really been kind to me.

"Yes, and damned cold I'm finding it after Italy."

I sat on a straight-back mahogany Chippendale chair sipping the sherry he handed me while he reclined opposite me on the sofa, twirling the golden liquid in its stemmed glass. If only he weren't quite so handsome, so confident, so friendly; if only my heart wouldn't pound so; if only I knew where to begin, perhaps I would be able to do so.

"Now tell me about yourself. What have you been doing?"

"I just got back from Aunt Maud's in Salisbury. She presented me to two bishops and various clerics, a baronet or two, their wives, their daughters, their—their sons—the usual Salisbury social scene—but I expect you are acquainted with it."

"No, tell me about it."

I did, rattling on about the depressing parties I'd attended as though they'd been gala affairs, highlighting some of the more memorable characters I'd met while painfully aware that the conversation was nowhere near where I wanted it to be, when suddenly Darius turned it in the desired direction.

"And did no eligible suitors present themselves?"

It was the moment. I would pour out my story of Howard Ramsey, of my predicament. Then I would declare my love for him. For courage I swallowed the rest of my sherry in one gulp, but as I took breath to begin he interrupted me.

"No, wait a moment, Alex, before you begin that list, for I know it must be a long one. I have something for you."

"For me—a present?"

"Yes. So you can't accuse me of not thinking of you while I was gone."

Everything was going to be all right. He took a small box from the Chinese cabinet by the window. My heart beat faster—was it possible—could it be a ring? How acceptable it would be in comparson with the one I had spurned last night. Had his intent and mine been the same all along?

"What is it?" I asked eagerly.

He handed me the box. "Open it and you'll see."

He smiled at my fumbling fingers, yet his smile faded at my disappointed "Oh," for the box contained not a ring but a cameo. True, it was the most beautiful cameo I had ever seen, an oval carving of the three graces surrounded by square-cut diamonds that caught the rays of the winter sun as I lifted it from the box. It was the most beautiful piece of jewellery that I had ever been given—yet it was not a ring.

"You don't like it. I can see you don't, and here all along I thought you would."

"No, how can you think that. I was—I was surprised, that's all." I ran my fingers over the carving. It wasn't a ring but it was beautiful, and he had chosen it for me. "It's exquisite, really exquisite. I didn't expect anything at all."

"You never do expect anything, do you, Alex. You're not like other women."

"I think, perhaps, that I am not." I took a deep breath. "That is why I refuse to marry against my will. Father is trying to force me to—just as he did Cassy."

"So!" His response was sharp, and he raised his eyebrows in question.

I waited for some protest but when he next spoke, his voice, like his face, was expressionless. "And who is the chosen gentleman?"

"Howard Ramsey."

"Ah, young Ramsey—just back from India, I hear, and quite the nabob."

"Yes, I think that is why father thinks so highly of him. That—and he's a Tory."

He laughed. "You're probably right."

"It isn't funny, Darius, it's deadly serious. They're trying to force me to have him, but I won't."

"Then tell him so."

"I did, but he won't take no for an answer."

"Why?" He got up and refilled my sherry glass. "Is he in love with you?"

"I don't think I would describe it that way. He just—he just wants to possess me."

"And you don't want to be possessed?"

"No; at least not by him."

"Is there someone else you want to possess you?"

He looked at me steadily, so steadily my gaze faltered beneath his. Yet I must speak.

"Yes, there is."

"So Alex has fallen in love—I wondered when that would happen. I seem to remember once you foreswore all men, and I told you then it would not always be so. And who is it that has stolen your heart—though perhaps you'd rather not tell me."

If only he wouldn't tease me, just as though I were his sister. But there was no going back. I must tell him.

"I have been in love for a very long time, Darius. I was in love even when I told you that. I did not foreswear *all* men, I foreswore all men but one and that one I've loved since I was in short petticoats. I've never thought of any other man. I don't suppose I ever will."

I answered the question I saw on his lips. "It's you, Darius. I've loved you for as long as I can remember."

He said nothing. The only sounds came from the clock on the mantelpiece and the crackle of the fire. His silence frightened me, and then I realized why he said nothing—he was thinking of Philomena. It was her shadow that lay between us. He had said he would never remarry, but I didn't care.

"Marriage isn't important to me, Darius. I know how you feel about that and I don't mind. I don't even mind that you will always care for Philomena. I just want to be with you, to be near you. These past months without ever seeing you have been bleak and empty. You are the only thing in life I care about. Please take me back to London so that I can see you sometimes, so that I can hold you, comfort you when you are sad, laugh with you when you are happy. I'm not asking you to marry me . . ."

"Alex! Alex! My dearest Alex! What are you saying?"

"I'm saying I love you, Darius, that you are the only man I care for, the only one I shall ever care for."

"Alex! My dearest Alex!" he repeated, his voice filled with emotion. He stood staring at me, as though seeing me for the first time, saying nothing so that I was forced to ask.

"But you, do you care for me, tell me, I must know."

"I do, Alex, but . . ."

"But what?" I prompted. "How do you care—is it the way Chauras felt for the Indian princess in *Black Marigolds?*"

And when he still hesitated I hastened to add, "I love you enough for both of us, Darius, even if you don't feel that way now, I don't care, I shall be satisfied with anything, anything."

"Alex," he said abruptly, "there is much to be said, but this is not the time, we can't talk now."

"But why not now, I don't understand. We must talk now.

Darius, I love you, let me stay with you, please, I never want to go home again, I only want to be with you.''

And then I did the only thing that all my instincts had told me to do ever since I had arrived, though I doubt my brain had any part in that decision. I ran to him and threw my arms about his neck, drawing his lips down to mine.

It was satisfying and exciting to be in his arms again, to smell the fresh country air on his red jacket, to feel the crispness of his hair beneath my fingers, the warmth of his cheek against mine. Most of all to know again his lips taking possession of mine, for while I had begun by kissing him, it was he who was kissing me. Softly at first, then demandingly, urgently.

''Alex!'' he murmured at last. ''Alex, my sweet, impulsive Alex! There is much to be said, but not now.''

''Why not now?'' I queried once again.

''Because the moment is inopportune,'' he paused before finishing uneasily. ''You see, I am not alone.''

''Not alone?'' I questioned, a coldness gripping my heart and the reply came, not from Darius, but from a low laugh behind me. A laugh I knew only too well.

''So the little student has learned well, has she not. She must have been a great comfort to you in your trials, Darius.'' Lady Brentwood, as elegant, as lovely as ever, entered the room—all grace, all charm.

''Your tone is unpleasant, your criticism and implications totally unjust, Althea.''

''I meant nothing by it, Darius, except had I known you were being comforted by your sweet little neighbour I could have saved myself a long and tedious journey. Might I enquire how long this liaison has been going on?''

''There has been nothing going on, as you put it, nothing.''

''Nothing?'' Lady Brentwood raised her eyebrows in mock surprise. ''I find you in a most amorous embrace and you say there is nothing, dear me, I find that very difficult to understand.''

''Alexandra came to talk something over with me. She is, as you know . . .''

''Yes, I know, you told me she is a friend and neighbour, though she's always had designs to be much more than that.''

Darius ran his hand through his hair in exasperation.

''Really, Althea, there are times you make me wish Adam had gone to his grave with his ribs intact.''

''You'll never convince me of that, Darius, not you of all

men." She laughed again, that low, soft laugh. It rankled like poison in my soul.

Darius turned to me, "Alex, I'm sorry, but you can see this is neither the time nor the place to talk . . ."

"Darling, it didn't appear that you were doing very much talking when I arrived, though I know the dear girl is noted for her erudition. But I'm afraid I interrupted something."

"No," I said decisively, picking up my pelisse, "you interrupted nothing."

"Let us say it wasn't quite as intimate as the last time we met, but of course then it was you who did the intruding," she reminded me.

"I shall intrude no longer."

Darius was plainly out of countenance.

"Alex, please! It is impossible to discuss anything at the moment. Go home, at least for now. I shall come to you tomorrow, I promise."

"Tomorrow you may go to the devil." I pulled the cameo he had given me from my dress and put it on the table. "Give it to her; it is she who deserves your gifts—she's your mistress, I should have remembered that. You have no need of another."

He called to me, but I did not turn back. I left the front door ajar as I ran from the house, racing down the path between the stark trees. I ran fast, faster than I had in going, yet it was with a heavy step and a heavier heart. I ran until I could run no more, then I slowed to a walk, continuing deliberately but apathetically towards Seton Place.

Always I had believed that once Darius knew that I loved him, his eyes would be opened and he would return that love. It had not been so. Not only was there the ghost of Philomena to contend with but the warm and only too real Althea Brentwood. I might have overcome one but not both. I had thrown myself at his feet and he had refused me—my lifelong love had been spurned. It was over.

I was shattered. As I moved inexorably in the direction of home, of father, of Howard Ramsey, I considered what must be done. I could see no alternative but to run away, but where? As rationally as the turmoil within would allow, I turned over in my mind the places where I might seek refuge.

Northumberland—Paul's stipend barely covered his own expenses; while he would give me anything that was his, to go to him at this time, just when he was beginning to settle down, could only mean unhappiness and upheaval for him. Besides, it was the first place father would look for me.

Oxford—I couldn't go to Cassy, not with that wretched man at her side. He would see to it that I was returned home without fail.

Salisbury—Aunt Maud had been kind to me after her fashion. We had parted amicably. But she was father's sister; her first allegiance would always be to him. She would probably think that Howard was a worthy suitor. No, there could be no shelter in Salisbury.

I didn't even consider Eugenia as a possible refuge. Being married to Howard's brother automatically put her in the enemy camp, though I didn't doubt that she would have been there no matter whom she had married.

I thought of my scanty resources. All I had was the five guineas Aunt Maud had given me when I left Salisbury. It would be enough to get me away from Linbury, but even with my limited financial acumen I knew I could not live on it for long.

Suddenly I remembered the *Sum of Glory*. It must have brought in something. I didn't know how many copies, but some had been sold, for I had seen it in several circulating libraries, and Sydney Smith had reviewed it in the *Edinburgh Review*. Unless Mr. Hillaby was a completely unprincipled rogue, some of the proceeds from its sale must belong to me. Of course! I would go to him and demand whatever monies were mine by right. I would throw myself on his mercy, ask him to help me find somewhere to stay until I could obtain some kind of situation. I was resolved on a course of action. I would put Darius and his countess from my thoughts. Why should he take me when he had such obvious delights so readily available from a woman of his own world. I had been naive to expect it. I had made a fool of myself over him, a complete fool, but it would never happen again, not over him, not over any other man. I was quite decided on that. I would rely on no one, only myself.

With my plan decided upon I walked boldly in the front door, caring not whether my father saw me.

He came out of his study as I slammed the door shut, his face like a thundercloud. "I thought I told you to stay in your room, Alexandra. I shall teach you not to disobey me anymore."

I looked at him dispassionately, wondering what punishment he had in mind now. Running away would be worthwhile if for no other reason than to be out of reach of his heavy-handed rule, let alone Howard's lecherous leers, but I had no intention of showing my hand too soon and thereby risking the success of my escape.

"I've been for a walk, father, to think over our talk last night, and I've decided to accept Howard Ramsey's offer."

Father's eyes widened in surprise before his face became wreathed in smiles. "I knew you would see it in the end, Alex," he said. "I only want what is best for you, and you're a clever girl, in fact you are probably the brightest of my children. I knew that the advantages of the match could not escape you. Howard has been looking at the Belden mansion on the Savernake road today. Some renovation will be necessary, of course, but he says it will do very well, and you'll be near enough to Seton Place to see us. He thinks . . ."

I didn't want to know what Howard thought, I was only astonished that my cool reception of Howard's proposal had not deterred him in his estate hunting. I cut father short. "There's plenty of time for that, father. I must go up and change for dinner now."

"At least let me be the first to congratulate you."

I reached up and kissed him on the cheek, the kiss of Judas, but I felt no remorse, only a terrible weariness.

Upstairs in my room I suddenly remembered Paul's clothes, the ones I had worn to the political rally at the Red Lion. I had put them in a box at the back of the wardrobe. I searched for it feverishly and found it under a pile of worn garments set aside to be used in quilting. Escape as a boy would be much easier, and since my hair was long and heavy and might not stay tucked under my cap I would cut it off, but that didn't matter. I only wished that I had had a topcoat of Paul's, for it would be cold, but there was none. I would just have to put warm things underneath. I found some plain scarves that might pass for a boy's, and tied the five-guinea piece in the corner of one of them. In going through my drawers, I found the lunch I had not eaten and I stuffed what I could of that into the pockets of Paul's jacket. I would probably be hungry later. Then I put everything back in the box and hid it in the wardrobe and got ready for dinner.

The evening passed without great incident. Howard was elated with his victory. He talked copiously of the future, with father sitting back and listening, satisfied that he had brought his reluctant sheep back into the fold. Mother said little, which was normal, while Netty hung on Howard's words and kept whispering to me how lucky I was. I think Thomas and James were impressed with their new brother-in-law-to-be, or their presumed new brother-in-law-to-be, thinking perhaps to follow eastwards in his footsteps. I said nothing, my silence probably being taken by Howard to be the silence of a newly affianced maid overcome at the thought of the joys and mysteries that awaited her, and by my family as the silence of submission. Howard insisted that I accompany him to the front door as he waited for his horse to be brought round, and father handed me a wrap and with it his tacit permission to bid my fiancé good night in private.

Outside Howard pulled me to him.

"You won't regret your decision," he said heavily, breathing father's best port in my face. "I'll make you the smartest lady in this part of Wiltshire. Perhaps I'll get a title for you. How would you like to be Lady Ramsey?"

Being anything Ramsey was repugnant to me, and when he pressed his lips on mine, I turned my head slightly so that his kiss fell on my cheek. His hand came up like iron and gripped my jaw unmercifully.

"No, no, my dear Alex, that won't do. I won't have that. You have obeyed your father in the past, but from now on you will learn to obey me."

He brought his lips down on mine, and with his fingers clenched on my cheeks, forced open my jaws so that his tongue could pass between my teeth and probe the recesses of my mouth. I felt violated, but when he finished I said nothing except to wish him a good night.

"That's better," he said. "I warrant you'll soon warm to my ways."

I went in and up to my room without a word to anyone, though I knew father and mother were waiting for me to return to the drawing room. I suppose I should have bid them a good night that would have been good-bye, but I could not bring myself to do so. I might cry, and that would ruin everything. I thought perhaps I should write them a note, but when I sat down in front of a blank sheet of paper I found I had nothing to say to them. I removed the ring Howard had ceremoniosly placed on my finger earlier in the evening and laid it on my dressing table. It would, I hoped, be returned to him.

When I was sure that everyone was asleep, I got up and put on Paul's clothes, and in the dark I hacked off my long curls and

then crammed Paul's cap over the shorn tresses. I put the hair
into my pocket. I would throw it into the hedgerows on my way
for the birds to discover and use in their nest building. I did not
wish to leave any evidence of the guise in which I had left. They
would enquire for a young woman, not a scurvy boy. With good
luck my escape was assured.

XIX

I REACHED THE Castle in Marlborough just as the morning light
was breaking over the downs. I hadn't thought to take so long. I
knew the road and six miles was no great distance for I walked
quickly, but I had not taken into account the bitterly cold wind or
the darkness of the night, which made even the most familiar cross-
roads difficult to negotiate.

I was soaking, for it rained, and I had no change of clothing.
All I carried was a package containing some of my stories and
poems, my journal, and the copy of the letter I had sent to Mr.
Hillaby with *The New Cassandra*. The walk had been difficult,
and it was with great relief I saw the tower of St. Peter's loom
through the grey morning mist as I made my way down the High
Street to the Castle.

Once there I was, however, at a loss. Never having travelled
by stage, I knew nothing of how or where to purchase tickets for
the journey. I asked advice of a young lad leaning against the
wall in the courtyard; he directed me inside, but with such a
curious scrutiny I wondered whether my disguise was the cause
or whether it was my voice that made him stare. In any event I
decided to say as little as possible. I only hope the sight of my
five guineas would eliminate questions, and in the taproom I
duly presented my gold piece to a thin, agitated man who
appeared to be taking care of the stagecoach passengers.

"I should like a seat on the London Mail—inside, if you
please."

I thought at first I had given myself away or at least said
something terribly wrong, for he looked me up and down indig-
nantly before saying to the world at large, "Look at this young
chap, gents, look at 'im. Wants to ride inside, if you please,

inside with the women and the toffs. I'd never 'ave thought of such a thing in my young day, spending a fortune to ride inside when he could go out in the fresh air for 'alf the price. And I don't doubt that this is all the money 'e 'as to 'is name.'' He held up my miserable gold piece, which he had rightly assessed to be my entire fortune, for examination by all and sundry. "But that's what we find today, boys molley-coddled from the cradle, want nothing but luxury. What was good enough for you and me's not good enough for them, oh no.''

There were a few guffaws from the still-sleepy passengers. I felt every eye in the room fixed upon me, probably the only one there who craved anonymity. I longed to run from the room, never to return, but it was more imperative than ever that I gain a seat on the coach after the scene he was causing, for if asked, people would surely remember me.

"Anywhere'll do," I said gruffly, aware of my face reddening beyond the scarlet already wrought by my walk through the bitter night.

"Just as well, my lad, for there's only one seat left and that's outside," he said, taking my money and giving me change, which I stuffed into my pocket. It was on the tip of my tongue to demand why he hadn't told me that in the first place, but I held my peace.

"Where's your things—they're due to pull out any minute."

I pointed to the small packet I carried.

"That all you got." I ignored his sarcasm and nodded.

"Better take it up with you then, but mind it don't get in the way of the other passengers."

I took off outside to board the coach, and as I climbed up to my perch, I remembered that I had not had the hot toddy I had promised myself. Still, I was aboard; that was what counted. I would get it at the next stop.

By the time we reached the Black Bear at Hungerford, I was almost frozen. I climbed down with the rest of the passengers, who were now becoming friendly with one another, though they had ignored my presence. As I purchased the toddy, which did indeed warm my insides, my heart became heavy in paying the reckoning, for I discovered that the obnoxious man at the Castle had sadly shortchanged me. I had barely enough money left to cover my food along the way. It meant I would arrive in London quite penniless. Nevertheless I was away, and cold, tired and hungry as I was, I was free, for the moment at least.

I climbed up into my perch with renewed energy, with a

determination to last out the journey and not allow myself to be cheated again. My fellow passengers had, apparently, well partaken of liquid refreshments at the stop, and they were soon passing a jug from one to the other, not forgetting the coachman, who became so jolly as a result that he almost overturned us into a ditch. Luckily we were not upended. The wheels, however, were quite stuck and we had to wait several hours before being pulled out.

I had refused to take any of the grog, shaking my head whenever the jug was passed to me, but as my fellow passengers became more mellow they began to have sport at my expense and soon I was obliged to drink the raw, fiery liquid, which burned my throat and made me cough and splutter, to their immense amusement and my indignation, though it may well have kept me from freezing.

Talk became coarse, and the coachman began singing lewd ditties and, ignoring his accident, taking curves and traversing villages at a frantic pace. I clung onto my seat and jammed my hat firmly down on my head, fearing that to lose it would expose my face and my ragged haircut, so hastily undertaken before I left, and surely reveal that I was no boy.

Thanks to the coachman's negligence we did not arrive in London that evening but were forced to continue through the night. At Reading a large, heavy-jowled man got up beside me. He grew loquacious as the night hours wore on, asking questions and telling me of his trade. He was, he told me, a draper who could make good use of a youth like me if I moved fast and didn't mind working long hours. I hardly found his offer tempting, empty though my pockets were, for he greatly troubled me with his pinching, mauling hands, which he refused to keep to himself. I could not tell whether he had a penchant for young boys or whether he had seen through my disguise, but I was obliged to stay awake and keep as far away from him as our crowded conditions would allow.

I was thus in a very poor state when we pulled in to the Swan with Two Necks in Lad Lane early the next morning: bruised, my clothing wet from the sporadic showers and my fingers and face chilled and chapped. My box companion asked cheerfully whether he could take me anywhere, but despite having only two copper pennies left after giving the coachman the tip he demanded, I shook my head. I would have to walk to Cheapside, and I was none too sure of the way. It was, however, the safer means of transportation, and holding my parcel under my arm, I ran from the seething activity of the yard into the London streets, anxious to become lost in the populace so that neither my fellow traveller nor anyone searching for me would find me.

Had I felt more alive than dead, and had I known in which direction to walk, I would have found much to interest me in my surroundings. The streets were teeming with vendors of every imaginable food and ware—meats and sausages, shawls and dresses, tin pots and pans, potatoes, apples and breads that smelled so sweet I was forced to stop and buy a roll and a cup of saloop, a sweet, hot drink, lavishly spending three ha'pence of my twopence. It was a luxury, yet I had to keep from chattering.

I was jostled by clerks rushing to their shops and offices, raffish bucks who had obviously not seen a bed, at least of their own, that night, poorly clad chimney sweeps pushing their way through the crowds with their long brushes, prostitutes, cripples and drunken wretches of both sexes. It was the tumult of the streets, I believe, rather than the directions I received that made me turn towards Shoreditch rather than the river, for later I was to discover that Lad Lane gave egress onto Gresham Street, which ran parallel to Cheapside. It was a walk I could have undertaken in a quarter of an hour, instead of which two hours later I was hopelessly lost in the midst of the Spitalfields district, which had so upset me on my earlier visit to London. In the year since I had seen it, it had not improved. In fact the poverty, seen at street level rather than from a coach, was even more distressing.

Again I stopped to ask directions, this time of an old woman selling roasted chestnuts from a charcoal brazier. As I warmed my hands on her fire, the chestnuts smelled so appetizing that I could not resist spending my last ha'penny on a bag, which I swallowed while trying to follow her mumbled instructions. Then I was off again, only to be even more hopelessly lost half an hour later.

In the course of the morning I had had several frightening experiences. One young lad had attempted to steal my packet and another had tried to entice me into a house, for what purpose I did not stay to find out. I was frightened, hungry and wet and I felt I had not the strength to find Mr. Hillaby's office even had I known the way. As I sat by the side of the road to rest, trying to think what I might do, a small urchin of indistinguishable age came and sat beside me.

"Wotcher guvner!" he said cheerily.

I didn't reply, too weary even to talk. Then I pulled the address from my pocket and showed it to him.

He grinned. "Can't read. I'm no tosh."

I read it to him and an instant look of recognition crossed his face.

"That where you want to go? I'll show you. Me dad's not far from there," and off he ran with a hop and a jump, myself following as well as I could. It was an effort to keep up with him, and I had no idea whether he was taking me where I wanted to go or leading me into some trap, but I felt I had little choice. I had to trust someone. We went through stinking alleys filled with such filth and stench they made me want to vomit, but whenever I paused, the dark little figure ahead of me would turn round and wave his arm, giving an infectious grin, so that I found myself stumbling along after him, nauseated or not. I must have recrossed streets I had earlier passed through, but I was dazed and recognized nothing. At last we came out on a busy thoroughfare and he pointed to a dark building.

" 'Ere we are," he said triumphantly.

My eyes focussed on a brass plate bearing the name of Alistair Hillaby, Publisher and Printer.

I felt dizzy and afraid I could not stand up without trembling, for my legs were weak, my head ached and I had a raging fever. I was in no condition to confront a publisher for the first time, and realizing that I might have difficulty in convincing him that I was really the author of the books he had published, I was glad I had brought with me the copy of the note I had written to him on submitting *The New Cassandra*. I pulled this from my packet before signalling for the boy to wait for me for I was most anxious to reward him for his pains. Then I went inside.

The surly clerk, the same one who had received my manuscript when first I visited that office, again barely looked up as I asked for Mr. Hillaby, muttering only that he was at home. I was in despair. Did he never spend time at his business establishment?

"But I must see him. It's a matter of life and death. Please help me. Where does he live?"

The clerk looked me over curiously, prepared, I was sure, to make a curt reply, but his expression changed as he took in my dismal appearance. Without another word he turned and wrote something on a piece of paper.

"Just don't tell him I gave it to you," he growled.

I tried to thank him, but already he had turned back to his accounts, so, without further comment I hurried back to my companion who awaited me in the street and told him the address I had been given.

"Cor lumme! 'Ans Place, that's Chelsea. Well, come on then, but we'd best move quicker than we done up till now."

The idea of moving at a faster rate was grotesque, but my young companion was off at a jog trot with me behind him, summoning up strength I was sure a moment earlier I had not possessed. I cannot think where we went, except the streets became wider and somewhat cleaner and the people we passed were better dressed and of an elevated station in life from which they regarded my companion and myself with acute disfavour and suspicion. They stared in disapproval, first at my ragamuffin companion, then at my ragamuffin self, drawing their cloaks closer around them as though they expected we might steal the very clothes from their backs. When I thought I could go no further, my companion showed me how to catch rides on passing carts by waiting at corners and, as they slowed down, grabbing for the bars behind the rear wheels. It worked quite well for a while, till one driver spotted me and gave me a fierce lashing across the back with his whip. My companion picked me out of the gutter.

"You'll soon get used to that. It don't 'urt after a while. But you gotter make yerself small when you get on. Don't stand up there like you bought a ticket."

"I'd sooner walk," I said through clenched teeth. I thought the pain would never go away.

"Awright, come on then!"

It was quite dark by the time we reached the steps of the Hillaby residence on Hans Place. Groggily I signalled for my companion to wait as I mounted them. If Mr. Hillaby refused to see me, I believed I would die there on the spot.

The door was answered by a manservant who took one look at me and told me to be off in no uncertain terms. I had the presence of mind to wedge my body across the threshold before he could make good his threat to close the door on me.

I pulled the cap from my head and shook out my ragged but, nevertheless, decidedly feminine curls, saying in my normal voice and my very best diction, "I will see Mr. Hillaby without delay. If you know what is good for you, my man, you will get him immediately or else, I can assure you, you will regret it."

It was said with all the bravado I could muster. The manservant's jaw dropped but he did nothing to stop me from walking into the neatly polished, tiled hall, where I sank into a chair to await my publisher.

A grey-haired man, stern-faced, with small spectacles perched on an overly long nose, dressed in tweeds of good cut though certainly not in the height of fashion, came into the hall, bent, I was sure, on ridding his house of my presence.

I stood up, swaying slightly, and pulling the now very crumpled copy of my letter from my pocket I extended it to him in an extremely grubby hand.

"Mr. Hillaby, I am the author of *Sum of Glory* and *The New Cassandra*. I've come to London to discuss my account with your house and future publications."

He was completely nonplussed. The manservant stood by, itching, I suspected, to throw me out under his master's approving eye. I closed my eyes for an instant, praying that he would receive me. Divine aid must have been at hand, for when I reopened them it was to see Mr. Hillaby glance briefly at the letter before gripping my still extended hand in welcome.

"My dear young lady, what a pleasure. Do come in. Mrs. Hillaby will be delighted to meet you. I'm sure you have had a long and trying journey. You must want some tea." He spoke as though my visit were expected, my odd garb an everyday occurrence. I could have hugged him.

I wanted to tell him about the boy outside, but as I began to speak the world grew dim. The last thing I saw was the black and white tiles of the hall floor coming up to meet and enclose me, strangely soft and welcoming.

From a canopied bed, under a soft eiderdown, I looked out on a plethora of pink and white rosebuds. They were everywhere—on the walls, on the jug and washbowl, on the eiderdown, even on the nightgown I was wearing.

I wondered if I could be in heaven. My body seemed oddly formless, weightless. I looked down at my hands lying idly on the bedcover. There was a strangely white, translucent quality about them. I must be dead, but was this heaven or hell? It was warm, which indicated the latter, but none of the sermons I had heard had ever led me to believe there could be pink and white rosebuds in *that* place. Though my life had not been without blemish, St. Peter must have taken pity on me and allowed me into heaven. But if I were dead, why did I think in the same manner as when I was alive? Why did I start to reason as I had always done? And heaven or hell, surely I couldn't be alone. Where was everybody?

I tried to raise myself onto my elbows to look out of a nearby window, but I had no strength. I fell back and lay still for some moments before attempting to move again. By raising my head slightly from the pillow, I could see rooftops, many rooftops. Where were they? I closed my eyes and tried to think, but I could remember nothing.

A door creaked and I opened my eyes to see a plump, rosy-cheeked lady, somewhat past her prime, dressed in a pink-and-white-striped morning dress.

"Oh, dear, you're awake at last. Alistair and I have been so worried. I must admit we were afraid you would die, and we had no idea who you were or where you came from. It would have been awful to put you into an unmarked grave."

I nodded in agreement. The idea of being in any grave, now that I had discovered I was alive, was most unpleasant.

"Well, don't tire yourself trying to talk now. We must get some nourishment into you first."

I shook my head. I had no hunger.

"Oh, but you must," the lady insisted. "We'll never get you out of that bed and find out who you are unless you eat something and get some strength. Just a thin gruel, that's all. I think you can manage that. I'll send it up with the maid and I won't trouble you until you've eaten it."

With difficulty I did manage to swallow the gruel, but then I immediately fell back into the pillows and went back to sleep.

I don't know how long I slept, but when next I awoke I was ravenously hungry. The lady I had seen previously came back, and soon a meal was brought to me on a tray; eggs, bread and warm chocolate, all of which I devoured under the lady's watchful eyes as she sat by the window with some handwork in her lap, to which she applied herself from time to time. I could see questions in her eyes and was determined to answer them as well as I could once she had explained to me where I was.

When the tray was removed, she began.

"Now, my dear, if you'll forgive my curiosity, Alistair and I are most anxious to know your name and where you are from. We've been harbouring you for almost two weeks now, and we fear someone may be looking for you, someone who is concerned about your whereabouts."

"But could you please first tell me who you are and where I am?" I asked in bewilderment.

"Of course. I'm sorry, but I thought you knew. I am Mrs. Alistair Hillaby. My husband is the publisher of *Sum of Glory* and *The New Cassandra*, novels you authored. The manuscripts were sent to him anonymously, so we had no way of knowing who had written them. It was quite a predicament for us, I can assure you.''

It was the mention of my books that brought back everything to me—Linbury, father, Howard Ramsey, Darius. So I was in London at my publisher's house, exactly where I wanted to be. I felt greatly relieved. I knew, though, that no matter how kind the Hillabys had been to me, I could not reveal to them my true identity. I had no desire for father to be informed of my whereabouts.

''You must have thought my arrival odd,'' I said at last. ''I travelled to London from a . . . a small village in Northumberland.'' This was Paul's county but it seemed sufficiently remote. ''And I felt it wiser to adopt male attire for the journey. One hears such terrible tales of young women being accosted in London. My luggage was stolen and I was cheated out of most of my ready money,'' that was true, for I had suddenly remembered the odious little man at the Castle in Marlborough, ''and I found myself penniless, with nothing to show for myself except a small package that contained some of my work, mostly poems.''

''Yes, I know, my husband has those. He read them and with great interest. You must not think him inquisitive. It was merely that he had hoped they might divulge your identity, but they gave little clue except . . .''

I looked at her sharply. I could not remember writing my name on them. I tried to think. ''Except what?'' I asked at last.

''Except—well, the stories are good, but from the poems we think you may have had an affair of the heart—and an unhappy one.''

I leaned back into the pillows and closed my eyes. I tried not to think of Darius. I preferred not to. I refused to. Instead I concentrated on a name, a name I knew I must soon supply to this pink-and-white lady in this pink-and-white room. Could I, I wondered, keep my first name—I liked it—and invent another family name? But I was afraid that an association might be made in future. No, unfortunately Alexandra would have to go. If I were a character in my own book, I wondered, what would I call myself? Verity—truth—I liked that. But I was not telling the truth. Besides, I felt the signet ring on my left hand, the ring Darius had given to me with its engraved initial *A*. No, Verity would not do at all. Althea! I shuddered as the name came to my mind. Why did it upset me so? Then I remembered the Countess of Brentwood; it was her name. I certainly would never adopt a name of hers. Arabella! That was it, but Arabella what? Arabella Black, Brown, Grey . . . no, they were so common they sounded fictitious. I thought of authors and poets I liked and suddenly a line by Christopher Marlowe ran through my head, "Come live with me and be my love and we will all the pleasures prove . . ." It contained the very sentiments I had hoped to hear pour from Darius's lips that last time. Instead—but that was all past now. I was being reborn.

"Arabella Marlowe," I said with a note of finality, opening my eyes.

Mrs. Hillaby, who had returned to her needlework, perhaps thinking I had gone back to sleep, gave a slight start. "I beg your pardon, dear."

"Arabella Marlowe—that is my name."

"Oh, I see, Arabella Marlowe of Northumberland. And where in Northumberland would that be?" she enquired with genuine interest.

"Arabella Marlowe of Willowbrook, Northumberland," I replied firmly. I had no idea whether such a place as Willowbrook existed in Northumberland, but I gave it rather than Paul's parish, in the event enquiries might be sent.

"Well, Miss Arabella Marlowe—it is *Miss* Marlowe, I take it?"

"It is, indeed," and always will be, I added to myself.

"Well, Miss Marlowe of Willowbrook, Northumberland, welcome to London."

PART TWO

London Sunflower

But one, the lofty follower of the sun,
Sad when he sets, shuts up her yellow leaves,
Drooping all night; and, when he warm returns,
Points her enamour'd bosom to his ray.
—JAMES THOMSON,
The Seasons: Summer

XX

IT WAS THE London of the literary world to which the Hillabys now introduced me, the world of Scott and Southey, Landor and Crabbe and Lamb and myriad others of whom I had read but never thought to meet. It was a world I adopted with delight and zest.

Many was the time I thanked Sydney Smith in my heart for directing my footsteps to Mr. Hillaby as a publisher, for he had been scrupulously honest on my account. From the *Sum of Glory* I found I had amassed over one thousand pounds, a veritable fortune. With *The New Cassandra* on the stands, Mr. Hillaby assured me of even better prospects. For one who had thought herself penniless, it was a miracle.

If I regarded Mr. Hillaby as the source of my newfound fortune, he was no less delighted with me. Neither he nor his wife could do enough for me. Indeed, Mrs. Hillaby mothered me beyond any mothering I had ever received.

There had been great speculation on the identity of the lady who had written my anonymously published novels, they being variously attributed to Mary Shelley, Lady Caroline Lamb, Susan Ferrier and others. When I was sufficiently recovered, Mr. Hillaby, who had been pestered for the author's name, was anxious to present me so I might acknowledge my work and lay all rumours to rest.

I demurred, for I was loath to be the source of any publicity. My family might not hear of it, but Darius, whom I heartily hoped never to see again, was in London, and the figures of the literary world moved in the Holland House set of which he was very much a part. I did agree, however, to join the informal gatherings that met regularly on Thursday afternoon at Hans Place, when poets and writers, known and unknown, met to discuss and dispute whether Sir Walter Scott was a genius or a passing fad, whether Byron was an opportunist or genuinely interested in the Greek cause, whether Cowper's was the poetry of a madman or written during his lucid moments. To be treated as an equal by these men—for apart from Mrs. Hillaby, who fussily arranged for everybody's comfort, I was the only woman present—to have my ideas sought, my opinions solicited, was wondrous indeed for one who not three weeks thence had thought herself friendless. There were times I feared it might all be a dream, that I might awaken in my room at Seton Place, confined there for some misdemeanour, unloved, unwanted.

Apart from the stimulation of my new life, Chelsea in itself was an exhilaration after Linbury. I took long walks each morning, past the Ranelagh Gardens, once so renowned but fallen into disfavour with the rise of Vauxhall on the other side of the river, a solitude filled with ghosts of the past, along Cheyne Walk, sometimes stopping to purchase a Chelsea bun from the celebrated Bun House on Fivefields Row.

More by coincidence than by design, I usually set out as a crocodile of girls issued forth from the school four doors away from the Hillabys' house on Hans Place. I would follow their progress as they stepped smartly along under the aegis of a dragonlike lady who followed them in short, waddling stride not altogether unlike that of a penguin. One morning I was to discover that I was not the only one to derive amusement from this scene, for behind the gorgon I observed an urchin waddling in imitation of her gait. As he strutted past me he winked. It was the wink that brought instant recognition.

"Hello! Hello!" I cried out to him. His stride faltered, and he looked puzzled. The schoolmistress whose ire he had clearly aroused glanced back with hostility and surprise on seeing the source of her irritation being kindly acknowledged by one whom she had previously greeted agreeably. As she urged her girls on, her stride in its haste became even more penguinlike.

"I thought I should never find you again. Don't you remember me?"

The boy eyed me cautiously.

"You helped me, don't you remember—the day I came to London, you helped me find Mr. Hillaby's house here on Hans Place. Without you I could never have got here, I know I couldn't. Ever since I've wanted to thank you, to repay you for all the trouble you took."

Still the boy looked doubtful. I reached into my reticule to pull out a guinea, which I gave him. He stared at the gold piece in his hand perhaps not believing in his luck and for an instant I thought he would run off. Then he turned back and looked closely at my face.

"Cor!" he ejaculated. "Yer never that shallow pate I brought 'ere. Naw, yer not that rum squeaker, yer can't be!"

I nodded, laughing. "I am that rum squeaker."

His jaw dropped in amazement.

"Come on! I'm going to buy you a Chelsea bun."

As we walked towards the Bun House, I explained to him some of the circumstances that had led to our meeting. Though I didn't reveal to him my true identity, I told him more about myself than I had previously told anyone else in London. There was an instantaneous bond between us. His name, he told me, was Tim Felder, and he lived in Spitalfields but curiosity had driven him back to Chelsea more than once in an attempt to discover what had happened to the young rustic he had left there.

After our meeting he came often, never asking for me, simply waiting outside until I took my walk and then accompanying me. Though I gave him money to buy new clothes, his ragamuffin appearance never changed. He said his father took it from him as soon as he discovered it to buy more gin. Even when I bought clothes myself to give to him, these, too, disappeared to be replaced by his rags, gone, I supposed, to the pawnbrokers or sold to the barrow merchants. He looked shamefaced when he appeared without them but offered no explanation, nor did I ask. All I could do was see that he was well fed while he was with me.

We made an ill-assorted pair, my threadbare friend and me with my stylish short haircut, which had been necessary to overcome the ragged cropping I had given it, but falling as it did in soft curls around my face, I had to admit it was attractive. And for the first time in my life, I had been able to purchase a completely new wardrobe, all of my own choosing. I chose canary yellow silks, emerald green taffetas, even a daring bright geranium-striped walking dress with flowing pelerine and a saucy straw bonnet lined with that same geranium-colour silk, against which my chestnut curls gathered in complementary shading. As we walked we drew many a curious glance, but we were too busy to pay heed. I enjoyed his company and he mine. It was always a disappointment for me when I looked out for his thin, elfin figure and it wasn't there.

With *The New Cassandra* already in its third printing, Mr. Hillaby again broached the subject of the reception he wished to give in my honour. He entreated me to set a date in order that Mrs. Hillaby might send out the invitations. It would, he assured me, not be a formal gathering but more an enlargement of our

Thursday at-homes. Most of those invited I would already have met, though there would be others, friends and supporters of London's literary world. He begged me to consider it, not to be intimidated by the thought but to allow the reception to take place. Without divulging my misgivings, I could find no valid reason to refuse him.

Each day with my new wardrobe, my new hairstyle, my new friends, my new interests, I became more completely Arabella Marlowe, a flower who turned to London's sun, and less and less that Wiltshire moonraker who had turned only to a sun who had never perceived her. When Mrs. Hillaby insisted I must have a special gown for the reception, though I demurred that I had more clothes than I needed, I gave in to the luxury of ordering that gown from Madame Fanchon's exclusive establishment on Bruton Street.

Thus one clear, bright afternoon in early March we set off for London's fashionable West End. It was the first time since my arrival that I had left Chelsea, and I felt some qualms that I might meet some acquaintance from that previous London visit. Yet I was sure that if that should happen, with my changed appearance no one would recognize the gauche provincial who had attracted so little comment.

But there was one encounter on which I had not reckoned. At Madame Fanchon's, proud that I could afford it, I had chosen a nile green brocade, terribly expensive, terribly extravagant, with its twisted gold thread. As soon as my eye had fallen on it, I knew it had to be exorbitant and I wanted it, perhaps for that reason, yet I hesitated.

"An excellent selection, Mademoiselle Marlowe," Madame Fanchon had purred. "The Countess of Brentwood was examining this very piece only yesterday. Her taste, I can assure you, is unequalled. I told her that if she did not decide upon it then, it would be gone. She will be disappointed, but ladies must make their choice."

"They must, indeed," I had concurred, determined then to have it, feeling an absurd and childlike satisfaction in robbing that lady of something she desired.

Following Madame Fanchon's advice, a very plain design for the exquisite brocade was selected, after which Mrs. Hillaby and I quit her establishment to go over to Gunter's to order cakes and sweetmeats. Because it was so fine we decided to go on foot to Berkeley Square, and the carriage was ordered to await our return.

I was on the point of following Mrs. Hillaby inside Gunter's when I heard my name called. I say my name, yet it was the name I had set aside—Alexandra, a name no longer mine, which I heard. I had no need to turn my head to know who called.

Darius pulled his phaeton alongside me. I saw him throw the reins to his groom and make to jump down. In that instant my anger at our last meeting overcame me, the humiliation, the rejection I had suffered. Again I heard that soft laugh that had followed me. He had his Lady Brentwood; for my part I wished never to see him again—never. Without a word of greeting, in fact without any recognition of his presence, I turned away from him, passing quickly into a narrow street that ran alongside Gunter's, determined to make my way on my own back to where the Hillabys' carriage stood.

"Alex! Alexandra! Stop!"

People turned in curiosity as I raced to lose myself in the crowds on Bond Street. A gang of young blades, taking me, I suppose, for a demimondaine, caught hold of me and held me in their midst. It shielded me from Darius as he passed by searching for me, yet afterwards I had difficulty releasing myself from their clutches. It was only when with my clenched fist I bruised the cheek of the most obnoxious among them, who tried to force a kiss upon me, informing him in my sharpest tones that my uncle, Lord Holland, would seek redress for the grievance, that with muttered apologies they allowed me to proceed. By a circuitous route, making sure Darius was nowhere in sight, I made my way back to Bruton Street and the Hillaby carriage. Mrs. Hillaby, already there, was flustered and tearful.

Flushed and out of breath, I attempted to explain that I had felt dizzy and had chosen to walk back to the carriage rather than go inside Gunter's, but I had lost my way.

"I do hope that this event will not be too much for you," Mrs. Hillaby worried. "If that is the case, the plan must be cancelled, for though I know Alistair is excited over it, as I am myself, yet your health comes first with both of us."

It was a tempting offer, one I would readily have taken, yet the Hillabys had planned it with such great care. It was to be the most sumptuous entertainment they had ever given, and they put much store by it. I could not disappoint them.

"No, no. It was a passing thing, nothing more. I have rid myself of my malady. I am quite cured of him—of it."

Yet I was not entirely cured, for even as I had run from him there had been an absurd wish deep within me, a wish to turn back, to throw myself in his arms, to hold him. It was nothing but nostalgia, I told myself. Never would I allow myself to submit to such madness again; I had overcome it. That was all past. I had a new life, one in which he played no part. Yet I was glad that Chelsea was a safe distance from Great Stanhope Street, and I resolved not to venture into Mayfair again.

By the following week the Hillabys' usually quiet and decorous home was in an uproar, with a flurry of caterers and merchants scurrying hither and yon. Mrs. Hillaby was in trepidation. She confided in me that she had never before entertained quite so grandly; she only hoped that their rooms would not prove too incommodious for the numbers expected, and she worried about every little detail. It was too late to cancel it, but I did protest the trouble they were going to and the expense, for they were not wealthy. Mr. Hillaby would not listen.

"It's not every day that I have the chance to introduce a talent such as yours to this land of shopkeepers, as Napoleon would have it. All of this gives me pleasure, and Mrs. Hillaby also; she frets, but that is her way. There is, however, one concession I would ask of you. It is perhaps not the time—I had meant to talk to you of it later—yet I would like to make announcement of it on that occasion. It concerns the work you brought with you when you arrived. I have gone through it; there are many items that have merit. I would like to announce publication of another work, or I should say, of a selection of your short works."

"But those were fragments I brought with me, of uneven quality. I don't believe—"

He cut me off. "Would you allow me to be the judge of its merit?"

I hesitated. "There were some pieces that should not be published."

And again he insisted, "Will you not trust to my judgement? I promise that I would publish nothing unworthy of you, nothing better left unwritten, nothing from the private pages of your journal that I can assure you, I have not read. I only ask for those pieces that intrigue and interest. It would be the perfect occasion to announce this new work, with the literary world under our roof and yourself the guest of honour."

It was a persuasive argument, for it was a world to which I very much wanted to belong. I gave him my consent, though I again cautioned him against publication of any personal material.

"Let me be the judge," he again assured me. He had judged

so well in the past, I could not doubt him. "I shall choose nothing to your detriment."

By evening the uproar had calmed to a steady hum, which was broken intermittently by the discordant strides of the chamber musicians as they tuned their instruments. The drawing room, never large, now overflowed with flowers and potted plants of every description. Footmen fell over one another in the hallway as they scurried back and forth with punch bowls and champagne buckets. Mrs. Hillaby hovered over the groaning buffet table with its sumptuous spread of meats, cheeses, cakes and petits fours, exotic fruits and that pâté de foie gras which Sydney Smith, in all solemnity, had assured me that had he heard trumpets as he ate it, he would be convinced he was in heaven.

I donned Madame Franchon's dress, duly delivered that afternoon—how different from those I had taken with me to Salisbury, but then, how different my situation. Now I wanted to be admired, and as soon as I saw the Fanchon creation I knew that I would be. The skirt flared at exactly the right point, from a waist that seemed smaller than usual; the design was a masterpiece of understatement except for the elegance of the brocade itself. I had no jewellery, yet I needed none. I still wore the signet ring, which had been on my finger since the day Darius had given it to me. I had tried to remove it after that last abortive meeting, but it refused to come off. My short curls brushed loosely around my face, the merest dab of powder on my nose, a splash of Arquebusade, Mrs. Hillaby's greatest extravagance, and I was ready to receive the guests, a surprising number of whom arrived on time.

I had not wanted any of it, yet as the evening began I found I was thoroughly enjoying myself, feeling relaxed and quite at home among London's literati. I was at ease, that is, until I caught sight of the short, dapper figure of Tom Moore. Would he, I wondered, recognize in Arabella Marlowe his young dinner companion from Holland House?

There was no sign of recognition on first sight, only a fawning that previously he had reserved for Lady Brentwood. As I replied to his greeting, however, a look of puzzlement crossed his face. "Have we not met before, Miss Marlowe? Perhaps you have been a guest of Lord Lansdowne at Bowood?"

I assured him I had not, yet his puzzlement continued. "Do help this poor Irishman's memory," he pleaded.

"Had I met you before, Mr. Moore, how could I possibly forget it?" I smiled enigmatically, and he accepted the compliment.

"You speak as one from Ireland yourself. It is, perhaps, from that enchanted emerald isle that you hail?"

"No, I regret I am unable to make that claim. I am from Northumberland."

I breathed a sigh of relief as he replied, "Northumberland. I have yet to have acquaintance in that county, but if you are any indication of the beauty of their ladies, I shall journey north without further delay. Still, with your colouring I would have taken you for Irish. Were both of your parents from Northumberland?"

I preferred not to dwell upon Northumberland or upon my parentage, and abruptly I changed the subject. "I am told you have an admirable singing voice, Mr. Moore. I hope that later we may persuade you to favour us with one or two of your songs."

"Only on the condition that I be allowed to dedicate them to you."

"I shall take that as a great compliment."

"I cannot enough compliment such a combination of talent and beauty, rare Miss Marlowe. London welcomes such a sunflower in its midst."

He bowed low, and I breathed freely. The moment had passed. He had not recognized in me the girl with the madeover dress and the unbecoming hairstyle of that evening at Holland House.

My relief, however, was short-lived, for a far worse trial faced me. Mr. Hillaby was bearing down upon me, accompanied by a figure far more familiar to me than that of Moore.

"Miss Marlowe, allow me to present Lord Bladen. He is, as you may know, a leading Whig spokesman and, even more commendable, a great patron of the arts, like his father before him. Your family is from Wiltshire, my lord, is it not?"

Darius, his eyes fixed on mine, made no attempt to reply, and Mr. Hillaby continued awkwardly, "Lord Bladen was telling me as we met how much he has enjoyed both of your books and with what pleasure he has looked forward to meeting you."

For the first time that evening I found myself unable to command my tongue to speak. As Darius took my hand and bowed low over it, I could clearly see the tension in his still-suntanned face. As neither of us spoke, Mr. Hillaby looked expectantly from one to the other of us, yet all I could think of as Darius studied me was how had he been able to find me?

"Now that I see Miss Marlowe, I realize that we have met before. It was stupid of me to overlook it," Darius said at last, to answer Mr. Hillaby's curiosity. "Yet I cannot tell you what pleasure it gives me to become reacquainted with her."

Still I made no response to the greeting or to the scrutiny that accompanied it, and Darius went on, "But it seems I must refresh your memory, Miss Marlowe. It was in the country, and not so very long ago."

"Yes," I replied at last. "I do remember it."

Mr. Hillaby, I knew, was intrigued by this meeting, and I was relieved to hear his name called repeatedly before he could put the questions that I could see were on his lips.

"You must excuse me," he said with reluctance, "but my wife beckons. I am quite sure she has become bogged down in an argument with Crabbe and wishes my support. It always places me in an awful predicament, for my usual sympathy is with Crabbe, yet to preserve conjugal serenity I shall probably have to side with Mrs. H."

He paused, smiling, waiting for a response to his dilemma, but with none forthcoming, he left, though without great alacrity, to join his wife and her companion.

Darius continued to hold my hand firmly between both of his. "Alex! Alex!" he said softly, "you can't possibly know how I feel at this moment—to find you in London—here—after I've searched for you everywhere. I had given up hope of finding you until I saw you the other day, but then you ran from me. I'm at a complete loss."

Mr. Hillaby had evidently mentioned the oddity of my meeting with Darius to his wife, for she looked over at me anxiously and I smiled at her reassuringly as I replied coldly to my companion, "I had no idea that my whereabouts could be of any great interest to you." Yet curiosity compelled me to ask, "But how did you find me here?"

"I was invited to come—but surely you must have invited me yourself? And to think I almost didn't come, thinking it another lionizing event on an evening when I least felt in the mood for it. I might never have come; I might never have discovered that it was you all along, Alex, who was the author of the books Hillaby had sent me. Now I know why I received them."

And now I knew why he had been invited. I myself had been unknowingly instrumental in his name being on the invitation list. How stupid of me!

"But since you were in London, why no note, no message, nothing? You knew where to reach me," he demanded. "That was cruel, Alex. And the first indication that I have that you are still alive and you run from me, without a word of explanation. Why?''

''I wasn't aware from our last meeting that my well-being was of particular concern to you.''

''How can you say that, Alex, after all . . .''

He broke off as he saw Tom Moore bearing down upon us.

''Alex, I must talk to you,'' he said quickly.

''Not here, not tonight.''

''Then when—torrow. May I call tomorrow?''

''Very well, tomorrow,'' I agreed reluctantly.

''At eleven?''

I nodded silently as Moore joined us.

''Lord Bladen. Aha! Seeing you both together reminds me of where I have seen this delightful young lady. It has been puzzling me ever since I arrived, and she would deny that we had met before. Yet now I am sure of it—it was with your dear mother at Holland House. Though I thought that Miss Marlowe had one of those hyphenated names, Smith-Jones, Crump-Hesketh or the like, was that not so?''

Darius, sensing my discomfort, intervened. ''You're right, Tom, but when have I known you to be wrong? Surely, however, you of all people must know the efficacy of adopting a nom de plume, particularly important for a lady. It allows Miss Marlowe to express herself freely. I am sure that neither of us could wish to inhibit her freedom.''

His look was so implicit that I barely heard Moore's, ''Yes, of course, but Miss Marlowe, what was your—''

''Come, Tom,'' Darius intervened again, ''you let your curiosity get the best of you. There is a matter I have been wanting to take up with you—how is your book on Sheridan progressing? I thought of it, for I met someone at the House the other day who had known him well. He was telling me of the time he and Sheridan were in mortal conflict over a Treasury bill. Sheridan accused him of being indebted to his imagination for the facts and his memory for his wit—caused quite a fracas, he was still furious over the remark, though, I must confess, I heartily concur with Sheridan.'' Darius had slipped his arm through that of the poet, and with one last complicit glance at me, he drew him away.

He would not, then, give me away. I tried not to think of our interview the following morning and the difficulties that must arise as I turned to greet Sir Walter Scott, who asked most kindly if I would tell him all about my new book, of which Mr. Hillaby was madly boasting.

Though we did not exchange more than a dozen words during the course of the evening, I was constantly conscious of Darius's eyes upon me. Occasionally he would smile at me as I was in earnest conversation with a guest, and despite all my resolves, I felt again all those emotions I was determined to deny.

After supper Tom Moore dedicated to me "Those Endearing Young Charms," the song he had sung for Lady Brentwood at Holland House.

"As the sunflower turns on her god when he sets,
The same look which she turn'd when he rose."

It would never be so again. I was determined that when I saw him the next morning, no matter what he said, I would not allow myself to fall under his spell. My life had been spent adoring him, but that life was over.

XXI

THE HILLABY HOUSE was in an even greater uproar the day following the grand event than it had been before, though it was not for want of help, for servants were everywhere, tripping over one another, Mrs. Hillaby in their midst, all in utter confusion. I knew that I should have offered my assistance, but if my surroundings were in confusion so, too, was I.

I chose to receive Darius in Mr. Hillaby's study, it being the quietest room, though on that morning it more resembled a greenhouse than a study, for the potted plants and bowls of flowers had been set there temporarily while the drawing room was being cleaned, awaiting removal again I knew not whence. As they had stood in floral tribute the previous evening, now they stood, a little dejected, but yet resolved to serve an event which I dreaded far more.

My sleep had been fitful; I had resolved now to say one thing, now another, to Darius when he came, I would be polite but distant and very, very firm. Nothing he said or did would cause me to waver from following any course in life but my own, and never, never again would I fall victim to that lifelong infatuation I had held for him; he had rejected me and my abject, childish confession of love, and he had done so in the presence of a woman I most despised.

Yet I was forced to remind myself of my stand when he arrived, for the sight of his familiar figure in those unfamiliar surroundings brought forth feelings I had foresworn. I showed him to a leather armchair amidst an assortment of ferns, choosing for myself Mr. Hillaby's desk chair and thus placing the expanse of manuscript-cluttered mahogany between us—to little avail, for no sooner had I sat down than he took another chair, moving it close beside me.

"Alex! Alex! If only you could imagine how I feel at this moment, to find you unharmed, the same dear girl and yet suddenly grown—your appearance, everything about you makes you so—I was going to say beautiful, but that you have always been—you have grown to womanhood and I had not realized it. I watched you last night, so very worldly, such grace, such finesse, and I could scarcely believe it was Alexandra Cox-Neville of Seton Place."

"But you are wrong, Darius. It was not Alexandra Cox-Neville of Seton Place but Arabella Marlowe. I am glad you asked to call this morning, for it is that very point I wish to emphasize, particularly to you, for you are the one person in London who could ruin everything for me. Have you sent word to father of my whereabouts?"

"No. I have done nothing yet, nor would I do so without your consent." His face had grown grave, but almost immediately he returned to his previous jubilance. "I just can't tell you what a relief it is to find you—safe, well—no, more than well, radiant. These past weeks I have searched for your face in a thousand faces. I would have welcomed the sight of you no matter how I had found you, yet when I did see you that afternoon near Gunter's, looking so very devastating, I must confess I felt a pang. I thought you must be under the protection of some influential lover."

"Would it have been so wrong if I were?"

Darius shook his head. "Alex, you know very well it would. You are from a respectable family, until now you have led a cloistered existence—such a life is precarious, difficult at best, and certainly nothing you could or should ever consider."

"I seem to remember you said so once before."

"That was a ridiculous suggestion you made to me, and certainly no solution to your problem. Yet it was that which made me fear the worst when I saw you that afternoon. When you made that—that . . ."

"Proposition."

"Call it what you will. It was obscene. Yet that day at Chateris I could not tell you how I felt, for we were interrupted."

"Ah, yes, by your dear friend Lady Brentwood. Such an arrangement with her does not seem obscene."

"Really, Alex, you cannot compare yourself to Lady Brentwood."

"And why not?"

"I have no intention of denigrating that lady—she is, as you quite rightly point out, my good friend—but you and she have led totally different lives and because of that you are totally different women. I did not come this morning to discuss Lady Brentwood. I mention her only because her presence precluded the discussion on which we are now embarked."

"She laughed at me."

He flushed slightly. "She felt jealous. She is older than you . . ."

"And wiser."

"I doubt that. Again, I only speak of her because her presence at Charteris, unexpected as it was, prevented me from being able to talk to you until the following morning, when I went to Seton Place to find all in an uproar. Young Ramsey was there, pacing the floor, with your father attempting to placate him and to stem your mother's hysterics at the same time. I am sure they thought me the villain of the piece, that you had flown with me, until I asked for you. I said nothing of your visit but set out on my own search of you. By all I had gathered, I thought you must then have been on the other side of Hungerford. Even so I might have caught up with the stage, but all my enquiries for you at the Castle were futile. No one of your description had boarded it that morning. I decided on Salisbury, for I knew you were acquainted with that town. There I met your aunt. I must say I rather took a liking to her outspoken manner, but of course it was a fruitless trail. It was while I was returning to London, racking my brain for where you might have gone—I knew it would not be Oxford, though I did not rule out your brother in the north—that I remembered the night you came to that political rally at the Red Lion dressed in your brother's clothes. I turned back to the Castle, and instead of asking for a young lady, I gave your general description but as that of a boy. Then I found you were remembered quite distinctly in Marlborough.''

''I don't doubt that,'' I commented drily, remembering the occasion.

''Dearest Alex!'' Darius smiled ruefully. ''What you must have been through. It need not, indeed it *should* not have happened. I followed your trail to London, but once there it was lost completely. You left the Swan in a hurry; no hackney driver that I could find had carried you anywhere. All my enquiries on stagecoach runs going north were without avail. Yet even so I went to Northumberland to see Paul. I did not ask for you when I discovered you were not there and that he had not heard of your disappearance. I knew of your closeness to one another and how he would worry, as I was worrying. I told him that I was on my way to see Francis Jeffrey in Edinburgh and had broken my journey. On my way back I stopped to see Sydney at Foston. I knew that he had taken to you and you to him that time at Holland House. Knowing of his empathy and understanding, I thought you might have gone there. I talked to him. He has a daughter much your age and was filled with sympathy. But his advice to me was to go home, to wait. He was convinced that you were sensible—that though you are impetuous, you would do nothing foolish, nothing unworthy. In that brief meeting how much he had learned—more, I realize, than I in all the years I've known you. Sydney was right, for it was not long after I had returned to London I caught that glimpse of you. And now, here you are.''

I could not help but be affected by his concern, yet he would have done as much for his sisters, and that was how he thought of me, while to me he had never been a brother.

''Now that you know where I am, what my name is, will you tell father?''

''Not if you do not wish him to know, though I think it hard that he should not know you are well, moreso for your mother. That, however, must be your decision.''

He was right, of course. I had long pondered how I could ease mother's mind without alerting father of my whereabouts, yet I knew her to be so thoroughly dominated by him that she would be unable to keep any intelligence I might send to herself.

''Your father once told me that the harebell stands for submission. My mother is like that harebell; she submits to my father, she submitted to her father before him, she has never known a life of her own. But now, for the first time, I have, and it is dear to me. I am my own mistress. I support myself on money I earn, money honestly earned. I can go or stay as I please. I can make my own decisions; I can stand by those decisions knowing them to be ones I myself have chosen to make.

"No, Darius, I cannot tell my mother where I am. I would it were possible to relieve her anxiety, but if mother knows, then father must know. If father knows he will force me to return, to marry Howard Ramsey or, if my exploit has discouraged him, it will be some other man of father's choosing."

Yet your father could not force you to marry if you were already married," Darius said slowly.

"But you know I am not, nor under the protection of one who would stand up to father."

"You are not married, Alexandra, not yet. Yet it is possible that before you inform your father of your whereabouts, you could be married."

"To whom?" I asked sharply.

"To me. That is, if you would wish it."

I felt the colour drain from my cheeks at the words—the very words I had so long awaited, words I had always wanted to hear, words of which I had dreamed. Yet on hearing them, rather than elation my response was anger: anger and resentment that those words came so late. My silence clearly perturbed him.

"I'm sorry, but I do not, perhaps, express myself well."

"On the contrary, you express yourself admirably on the floor of the House. It was my wont in times past to extract your speeches from the newspaper and keep them in my diary."

"I meant that I do not express myself easily with members of your sex. As I have told you before, I am a politician. At times such as this I would wish to be a poet or to have your command of words."

"You seemed at no loss for words with a certain lady one night in the library. I believe I recall some very pretty statements, thoroughly worthy of a poet, even a play on words—bare skin on bearskin or something of the sort."

"The play, as I remember it, was the lady's," he replied tersely.

"The play, it seemed to me, was being enjoyed equally between gentleman and lady."

Darius flushed. "It is thoroughly unfair of you, Alex, to bring up that incident at this moment, but since you have, I can only repeat what I have said before: the lady is my good friend and has been for a long time. To deny there has been intimacy in that friendship would be a falsehood, one of which you would be only too well aware . . .''

"And if I were not, would you deny it?" I countered.

"Quite honestly, Alex, I really don't know. To boast of it is to malign the lady. We are both adults; we have both been free and have not harmed others by seeking solace in each other, but it has been little more than that, on my part at least. I have had no thought to remarry, until now.''

"And now, why do you ask me now?" I demanded.

"Because I wish to marry you. Ever since John died your place in my affections has changed, I cannot exactly say how or why. You have always been dear to me, but you grew dear in quite another way. While I was in Italy so often my thoughts turned to you, wondering what you were doing. When I searched for you I remembered every line of your face, every expression— and then I found the letters you had written to me, the ones you put away in the desk, I knew then that you needed me, and I need you.''

Had it not been for his mention of Crumpet I believe I would have succumbed completely, but remembering his coldness to his child hardened my heart.

"I meant to burn those letters. In truth they were not so much written to you as for background material for a novel I thought to write.'' It was a cold, callous lie and I saw him flush as I spoke it.

"They were addressed to me," he said quietly.

"They were addressed to you by the same foolish girl who threw herself at your feet in besotted admiration, in the absurd infatuation she had held for you since childhood. She came to you in desperation, thinking you her saviour, and you turned from her. Had you come to her for anything, anything at all, she would have moved heaven and earth to get it for you—but not so you. You sent her home, to the place she had run from, back to the suitor she found so objectionable, while you dallied with— with your good friend.''

"I had no idea that Althea—that Lady Brentwood was coming to Charteris, but since she did I could scarcely discuss your predicament in her presence. I went to Seton Place as soon as I possibly could.''

"But it was not to propose marriage, was it?''

"In all honesty, I must admit it was not. I came to help you. It was when I knew you were gone, when I searched for you, especially when I read your letters, which told me, more than your spoken words, of your love . . .''

"You don't know what love is, Darius. Your attitude to Crumpet shows you are incapable of love, unless it is for some-one who no longer exists—you can love a memory but not a person with human foibles. You had no time for Alexandra Cox-Neville, and now you are proposing to someone who does not exist either, to the very chic, talented, sought-after Arabella Marlowe. Such an imaginary woman is to your liking apparent-ly, but Arabella Marlowe refuses you. She does not choose to marry."

His face had turned pale as I spoke. "I seem to remember Alexandra Cox-Neville foreswore marriage also."

"She did and she does. You said earlier that you thought I was under the protection of some powerful lover; and later that I needed you. You believe, just as father does, that without a man's protection, a woman is helpless. That is not so. I have proved it is not so. Father, even if he should find me, will never make me go back. And I don't need you, Darius, I shall never ask for your help again."

Even as we faced one another in open adversity, watching his eyes grow dark, his grave expression, his hands clenched, I knew I could not put from me in so short a time one who had so long been the centre of my existence. But if I lied when I said I did not need him, the time would come when that would be so. I was determined to be free. My brain had decided it; my heart must follow.

"I trust . . ."

"Please, Alex—Miss Marlowe, say nothing more. You have made your position perfectly plain. It is well that you did so, for it puts an end to the matter. I assure you I shall never reopen it."

The finality of his words momentarily overwhelmed me, so that though he rose from his chair, I made no move to follow.

"If I may make one last comment . . ." he said.

"Yes, yes, of course."

"This microcosm of London that has embraced you I know well. I am a part of it. It is fickle. I must warn you that what it loves today, it may either ignore or, worse yet, detest or deni-grate tomorrow. Your host, your publisher, Mr. Hillaby, is a provincial. He may know the world of publishing; he does not, however, know the world of London society, the world into which you will be thrust, whether you want it or not, after last night. Be on your guard. You are a woman of great sense—more than that, of great common sense, that least common of senses. I am sure that you will use it well."

"Society's acclaim will never go to my head."

"You are quite unlike others of your sex. But so I have said before, I believe."

The tension between us softened, and I felt unaccountably glad. I saw he was about to leave and I would have made to detain him but the door opened and a maid entered.

"Oh, I'm sorry, ma'am. I didn't know you was here. I've come for the plants."

"Later, Mary," I said quickly, but before she closed the door Mrs. Hillaby appeared.

"Dear me, Arabella, I didn't know you had a visitor. Go along, Mary, I've told you so many times you must not interrupt."

"Yes ma'am." But while Mary left, Mrs. Hillaby made no motion to do so.

"You remember Lord Bladen, Mrs. Hillaby," I said reluctantly.

"I called to tell you how much I enjoyed your reception of last evening."

"It was nothing, nothing at all." Mrs. Hillaby's dismissal of the event belied the commotion in the hall beyond as something quite large and heavy fell with a thud. "Oh dear, oh dear. I'm afraid I must leave you. I think I am needed."

"I was on the point of departure myself, Mrs. Hillaby. Miss Marlowe and I had quite finished our discussion." He turned and bowed to me. "I shall remain an admirer of your work, Miss Marlowe, though I must reiterate an earlier-voiced criticism: you should not underestimate the passions—the sensitivity of men, which are equally as profound as those of the fairer sex."

Then he was gone.

I ran to the window to watch his tall figure descend the steps to his waiting chaise. Tim was there, and I saw Darius stop for an instant and say something to him. He reached into his pocket and handed Tim a coin before taking the reins from his groom. A flick of the whip and the horses sprang to. He left without a backward glance.

XXII

As DARIUS HAD predicted, following the Hillabys' reception and the attribution of *Sum of Glory* and *The New Cassandra* to my authorship, Arabella Marlowe became the darling of fashionable London, the highly sought-after prize of all those hostesses who made it their life's work to provide their guests with the latest and the very best of everything. The echelon of society into which we were thrust was previously unknown to the Hillabys, and they found it difficult to hide their awe of it. I felt much like Lord Byron when he wrote, after the publication of *Childe Harold,* "I awoke one morning to find myself famous." Unlike Byron, however, the excitement caused by that fame soon grew thin, for I saw, perhaps heeding Darius's warning, the emptiness of a society that must feed itself continuously on the rage of the moment, the unusual, the bizarre. It was not me they toasted; they scarcely made any attempt to know me, nor were they impressed by any literary talent I might have possessed. It was primarily because Lady Olway boasted that I had charmed her guests that I immediately became the pearl of Lady Amhurst's drawing room, followed by being guest of honour at the Countess of Dene's ball. The Hillabys revelled in the new scene, but though I accepted the invitations it was more for their pleasure than my own, for I hated the scandal and I eschewed the gossip that surrounded me in those fashionable halls. I longed for the stimulating exchange of ideas of those Thursdays at Hans Place, but none was to be found. I could scarcely utter three words together before a positive tide of aimless comments from my admirers washed them away. Even those Thursdays at Hans Place were spoiled for me, though not for the Hillabys, by the invasion of the smart set who now claimed them as their own.

There were within the drawing rooms I frequented groups less vapid than those that surrounded me, groups engaged in discussion far more to my taste, but Darius was usually in their midst, and though we met amicably enough, there was a constraint between us. He never sought me out; I could not seek him out. All too often the Countess of Brentwood was at his side.

When first she had met me as Arabella Marlowe, I had been wearing the nile green brocade she had admired at Madame Fanchon's. She had eyed me scrupulously from my short chestnut curls to my cream satin slippers.

"Miss Marlowe," she purred sweetly. "It is Miss Marlowe, is it not? Darius instructed me not to use your other name, though for the life of me I can't remember it."

"Such a pleasure to see you again, Lady Brentford."

"Brentwood," she corrected sharply.

"Do please excuse my stupid mistake, Lady Brentwood. I always think that it evidences a certain lack of civility not to make some effort to remember names correctly. I should hate you to think me uncivil."

She scrutinized me again, recognizing in me perhaps for the first time a worthy adversary.

"Allow me to compliment you on the cut of your gown, Miss Marlowe—exquisite, though the brocade is possibly a tiny bit *outré*."

"Yet Madame Franchon informed me *after* I had selected it that you had it in mind for yourself. I am glad that you rejected it, however, for the colour needs a more vibrant setting. With your pale skin and pale hair, it would not show to advantage."

"How clever you are with words, dear Miss Marlowe. It is impossible to move today without hearing your praises. But you must excuse me. Darius becomes bored when I am away too long." She crossed the room to where Darius was in deep conversation with Lord Grey and took his arm in a deliberate, possessive manner knowing full well it would infuriate me.

Though I turned my back on them to join in a discussion of Lord Braverton's wager on his new greys, caring not one whit whether he won or lost, my thoughts were all with two members of the group to whom I assiduously kept my back, and I was sure that the Countess of Brentwood knew it. She better than anyone else, I suspected, could fathom my secrets. For that, if for no other reason, I kept myself as far removed from her as possible.

Darius was scrupulously polite to me whenever we met. Often I wished him less polite, less restrained, yet we could never regain our old footing; not after all that had passed between us. Often I felt his eyes on me, but when mine challenged his, he turned from me. Not that he was hostile—his open and avid praise of my work was often mentioned—yet the relationship between us was distinctly formal. It lacked its former ease and intimacy.

The only time I caught a glimpse of the Darius I had known of old was when I was accosted by a dowager duchess who took me for the author of *Moral Tales*.

"I do so enjoy your books," she gushed. "They all contain a lesson and a fine one. I insist on my grandchildren reading them. They're as good as a sermon."

"But, Your Grace, I think you mistake me for . . ." but I was interrupted.

"I know exactly who you are. I came here tonight expressly to tell you of my pleasure at your work. I have read *Ormond* and I liked it exceedingly well."

"*Ormond* is a fine book, Your Grace, but it is by Maria Edgeworth," I insisted.

"But you are not Maria Edgeworth?" She frowned.

"No, ma'am, I am Arabella Marlowe."

"Arabella Marlowe! Never heard of you. Why do you go around saying that you wrote the *Moral Tales* and pretending to be an author?"

"I'm sorry, ma'am, I'm afraid you are mistaken," I began but she cut me off.

"I am *never* mistaken, Miss . . . whatever your name is. I shall tell everyone in the room that you are an imposter and not at all who you claim to be."

She flounced off in high dudgeon, the long plume in her turban quivering in time with the indignation of her quivering chins, and I found myself looking directly at Darius, who, leaning against a pillar, arms folded, had been following the conversation with some relish.

"An imposter, Miss Marlowe? And the duchess threatening to expose you?" he teased.

"She took me for Maria Edgeworth," I explained lamely. "I can't imagine why," I added.

"Neither can I, for you don't resemble a writer of moral tales, though since I have reread your books I find they do have a moral."

"Ah!" I could not disguise my pleasure. "And what is that?"

"They are a cry for women's independence. They emphasize inequities that exist between the sexes, inequities which I have never seriously considered. I suppose I have always taken it for granted, as you pointed out to me once, that women should depend on men for their well-being. I never considered that because of that their lives must always remain circumscribed, narrow. I thought it was what women wished. I realize, though, that it is often by necessity rather than choice."

"That is exactly what I wished the reader to consider, but you are the first to speak of it. Others speak only of the story, but you . . ."

"Hello, coz, I might have known you would have ensnared the charming guest of honour. But you cannot keep her to youself. I insist that you present me."

Before I turned I knew that another precious moment had been snatched from me by the one who had so robbed me one evening at Drury Lane.

"Alexandra!" Geoffrey gasped as I turned. "But you were pointed out to me as Arabella Marlowe, the lady whose name is on everybody's lips."

Darius made a stiff bow. "I shall leave you to your explanations, Miss Marlowe."

As he withdrew, I wondered, quite unkindly, whether some unseen hand guided Geoffrey to prevent any possible intimacy between myself and his cousin. It was an unfair thought, for as I drew him aside to explain my new identity and the reasons therefor, he was so completely understanding, so thrilled at being part of my secret, promising not to divulge a word, swearing to it, crossing his heart, and hoping to die, just as Paul was wont to do, that I felt a great rising of affection for him.

This affection, however, did not extend to the friend who accompanied him, Sir Clarence Wilmott, just arrived in London from his estate in Hampshire: a tall, sparse men, older than Geoffrey, with lazy, heavy-lidded eyes that, despite their outward lassitude, followed women, pretty women, in a predatory fashion. The way in which his glance raked me as he was introduced made me feel that he saw right through my elegant brocade, that I was quite bare.

Geoffrey caught me as I glanced beyond to where Darius stood with the hostess and Lady Brentwood.

"He won't be back."

"Who won't be back?" I parried.

"You're looking for Darius and you know it, Alex; don't try subterfuge with me. He won't come back while I'm around."

"I'm sure you're mistaken. He wouldn't come back anyway."

He shrugged. "Perhaps."

It was a waltz, and Sir Clarence asked me to join him, but once on the floor I regretted my acceptance. He held me far too close, and his speech was laced with innuendoes that no amount of innocence could pretend were innocuous. I disliked him intensely, and it surprised me that he should be a friend of Geoffrey's. I couldn't help but mention it.

Geoffrey laughed. "Don't pay any mind to Wilmott. He takes himself for a ladies' man, that's all, and nothing will convince him to the contrary. Actually he's a very considerate fellow—to me, anyway—doesn't mind ponying up for a fellow when things are tight, something no one else will do. But I grant you he doesn't show to advantage in mixed company."

"Well, if he's a good friend of yours, I shall have to bear with him, though I wish he would behave in a more civilized fashion."

Thereafter I was polite but I refused all efforts on Wilmott's part to persuade me to dance with him again. Geoffrey, however, I delighted in. He was a link with my old life, but with those parts of it I had most enjoyed—with Lady Bladen, with Crumpet, with Charteris . . . with Darius.

The next day I drove with Geoffrey in the park. He talked of his last visit to Charteris, of his sorrow at the death of his aunt.

"I didn't come to the funeral. Darius wouldn't have wanted it."

"Surely not."

"I know him; he would not. I wanted to, though, for she was more like a mother to me in many ways than my own, who, I'm sorry to say, is Wentworth through and through, like her brother, or Darius himself, for that matter. She's tight-fisted, doesn't realize that a fellow needs money to live. She makes all kinds of conditions. I'm sick of hearing her say I should follow the example of my dear coz—she thinks he's a paragon of virtue, while I think it a pity he didn't inherit more from his mother than her looks."

I demurred, yet though I could find in Geoffrey's complaint a reason, misconstrued though it might be, for his dislike of Darius, yet it did nothing to explain why Darius reciprocated that dislike so heartily.

"You at least have the sense not to fall in love with him, as so many silly young things do—or have you?"

His quizzical look forced a quick denial from me. "Perhaps there was a time when I had the sort of crush you're talking about, but that was ages ago. Like you, I'm fancy free."

"We're alike in many ways. Who knows what the future may hold."

If I managed to hide from Geoffrey my feelings for his cousin, I could not hide from him my dislike of his friend, whom I found so completely insensitive that, although I ignored him in an attempt to avoid his cloying attentions, he seemed to enjoy rather than be rebuffed by my attitude. I requested Geoffrey never to bring him when he called at Hans Place, to which he agreed, though not without demur; he plainly wished to accommodate his friend's wishes, in repayment, I suppose, for Wilmott's generosity.

In my flurry of activities my morning walks with Tim were not forgotten. In fact, I found my conversations with him vastly superior to many I listened to in Mayfair. He had a common sense combined with a quick intuitiveness truly rare in one so young. I thought it sinful that he could neither read nor write.

"Cor! Wot would I want that fer," he blustered when I insisted I should teach him.

"It could be very useful to you, and it certainly couldn't harm you. You would understand a great deal more of what is going on around you. You could read the banners on the newspapers, for instance."

"All that's nuffin to do wiv me."

"And if you could read it would make it much more difficult for others to take advantage of you. As it is now, you have to take another's word for what is written. If you could read you would know for yourself."

"P'raps. I dunno though. 'Spect it's boring."

Yet I knew he was wavering. The next time I met him I had with me a book I had requested Mr. Hillaby to get for me, a book from which I had first learned to read: Daniel Defoe's *Robinson Crusoe*. It was not an easy book, but Tim became so involved in the tale, as I thought he would, and since I refused to read it to him, he was forced to make it out for himself. More than anything I enjoyed watching him as he puzzled over a word, sounding out the syllables until suddenly it fell into place, and with recognition, relief and jubilance he formed the word.

"P'raps there is something in this reading stuff after all," he agreed finally.

XXIII

I HAD RETURNED to Hans Place one morning, filled with delight at Tim's progress, to be met by voices raised in anger. They came from Mr. Hillaby's study, and stopping for an instant, I heard my name and recognized immediately the voice of Mr. Hillaby's visitor. Without pausing to knock, I entered.

"I trust I do not intrude, but since I appear to be the subject of your discussion, it seems only just that I should be allowed to join you."

Darius rose at my entrance and bowed stiffly. He held in his hand a slim volume that seemed to be the matter of contention between them.

Mr. Hillaby's face was flushed; his upper lip glistened with perspiration, making it appear to me that the argument between them had been of some magnitude.

"Miss Marlowe, I am glad that you are here, though I had hoped this matter to be resolved before your return. Lord Bladen has taken exception to the publication of your latest work, which I have readied for distribution to the booksellers."

I looked from one to the other in puzzlement, and Mr. Hillaby came to my rescue, reminding me, "Your new book—the miscellany of short pieces—you must have seen the copy I had sent to you along with the volume of *Robinson Crusoe* that you asked for."

I remembered there had been another volume in the packet. I had taken it for another reader and had not looked at it. I wondered, since it was my book, that Mr. Hillaby had not commented on it or asked my reaction, but I had left the matter in his hands. I trusted his judgement.

"Yes, to be sure. And does Lord Bladen consider it unworthy?"

"It is not a question of being unworthy, Miss Marlowe; I believe you are quite aware of that. I find much of it superior, even exciting. I wish it were not so, for its quality will ensure that it be read, yet from all I know of the world, it will not be for its quality that it will be remembered but for its content."

My heart quickened. "Its content?" I glanced quickly at Mr.

Hillaby. Surely, surely he had selected with care. He had assured me that I could trust his judgement. He flushed slightly under my scrutiny, which did not reassure me. "You find its content distasteful?"

"No, not distasteful. It is simply that there are—" he broke off and ran his hand through his hair, "Al . . . Miss Marlowe, I am of the opinion it would be better—for you—if some of the poetry had not been included."

So it was the poetry he spoke of. My suspicions of what I might find there increased, yet outwardly I remained calm. "Because the content does not please you."

"Because the content—of some—is too . . . too personal."

He confirmed my worst suspicions. But surely Mr. Hillaby could not have included the love poems, at least not those I wrote in Salisbury. My cheeks grew hot at the thought, but I refused to let Darius know my concern.

"I know you have no great opinion of women writing poetry. You have mentioned something of that before."

"It is not a question of my having no great opinion of it. That is not the matter of dispute. It is the question of how its publication will affect you; that is what concerns me."

"While I know that a woman, like a child, is expected to be seen and not heard, my other publications have caused me no regret."

"But your other publications have not covered such material."

"I suppose other gentlemen may feel as you, out of sorts with the romantic content, but after all, most of the poems were written when I was much younger and subject to—to girlish infatuation I have outgrown. They are to be forgiven rather than denigrated."

He thrust before me the book he had been holding, opened midway. "And this, madam, does this concern a girlish infatuation, as you put it?"

My heart sank as I recognized the first words.

> My breast 'gainst yours, we breathe, our arms entwined
> The breath of love, of life dearer by far
> After love has revealed what youth divined
> Love's glory and love's force spectacular.

It was indeed the sonnet written in Salisbury to recall that night of love. I had never thought it would reach any eyes but mine, though at one time I had wanted Darius to read it, but not now and certainly not under these circumstances. Yet—yet now he had read it he must know that what he had spoken to me of in St. Mary's churchyard was, in fact, no dream but a reality. He must know what had happened between us on the day Crumpet died.

I waited for him to speak, my eyes fixed on the page, not reading, for I knew every word by heart. But when at last it came, his voice was colder, harsher than before.

"And who was this lover of yours? Ramsey? Or that gangly youth with the stutter? Or one of these fancy swains who's been dogging your footsteps in London?"

"But you must know," I said in bewilderment.

"Don't tell me it was Poindexter!" He visibly pulled himself up after this last burst of anger. "You must excuse me, Miss Marlowe, it is not my business, as I can see you are about to point out to me, nor is it my concern. Nevertheless, for your sake, for the sake of our long and close connexion, I must intercede in the publication of this book. It cannot, indeed it must not be openly sold."

His imperious tone, his assumption that he had any obligation, any right to make my decisions, more than anything stiffened my resolve. I snapped the volume shut and threw it down on the mahogany expanse of Mr. Hillaby's desk.

"You have absolutely no right to interfere in my life. This is my work. Mr. Hillaby is my publisher. If he considers it of sufficient merit to warrant publication, then I have no objection to it."

"Of course it is of sufficient merit," Darius retorted. "Mr. Hillaby is well aware of its merit, but he is even more aware of its value on the marketplace. I have already offered to make good his loss, to buy all the copies he has so far printed—to no avail, and why? Because he knows it will sell; it will sell in great numbers. But as much as you and as much as he gains by it, the cost will be to you and to you alone. And that cost will be enormous. It is you who will suffer by its publication, not Hillaby. I have told you before: I know London. Those who now adore you will vilify you if this book appears. Even if your name were not emblazoned on the title page—that might be preferable, though with your close association to Hillaby it would probably be placed at your doorstep. You might, however, then deny it."

"I have no intention of denying it. The book is mine and mine alone. If Mr. Hillaby chooses to publish it, I shall do nothing to stop it," I replied heatedly.

Mr. Hillaby was clearly upset by Darius's remarks.

"My dear, I wish only your good. If it is as Lord Bladen fears, that publication of this book will in any way make you an object of notoriety, then I shall certainly withdraw it and destroy the plates. I would never wish you harm. I must say, though, that I selected the material with care. I included the love poetry because I considered that its place was there. Some of it perhaps less veiled—a shade too intimate, perhaps—but I cannot believe that it warrants Lord Bladen's violent objection. If, however, you are in any way of the same mind, I shall certainly not distribute it."

"You have my permission. By all means distribute the book as you had planned, Mr. Hillaby. Lord Bladen has commented in the past that it was a great shame that no woman had written of the experience of love. I have tried to correct that omission. If he finds it not to his liking, so be it. Evidently he is of the opinion that it is only men who may express themselves adequately on the subject; women must submissively read and admire their words."

"You avoid the issue," Darius interjected in exasperation. "If you insist on this book being published, you are asking to have every roué and rake in London at your heels. I know these men; I was educated with them, I have played with them, I know how their minds work. I know this . . ." He took the volume from Mr. Hillaby's desk and it fell open at the offending sonnet so readily that I felt it must have been opened there innumerable times before. "This will not be read by them as a work of literary merit, I can assure you of that, for they have little interest in such matters. It will, however, be taken by them as an indication that you are a woman of experience, experienced in the arts of love, and by publication of that fact you make yourself open to their advances. They know that you are without the protection of any man of rank. You will be completely vulnerable."

"But Miss Marlowe is under the care of my self and my wife, my lord. We would allow no harm to come to her."

"I'm sorry, sir, but you must realize that you have no rights over Miss Marlowe or obligations to her. You are not her father or her husband, or in any way related to her. You can make no claims against anyone who wrongs her. She will be forced to suffer brazen advances from quarters she will least desire them from, to suffer insults from women who best know how to denigrate their own sex. If this book is published, I warrant Miss Marlowe will either become a hermit in your house or will end by running home again, something I am sure she has no desire for."

"That I shall never do," I asserted. "Nor, Lord Bladen, do I believe in the grim picture you paint. Byron has written much that ranks, in subject at least, with this. If society ostracized him it was not because of the merit of his poetry but because of his personal life. Mine is above reproach."

Darius was plainly exasperated. "Miss Marlowe, you may consider it so, but after this book comes out, no one will believe it to be the case no matter how much your conduct indicates the contrary. Nor can you expect any forgiveness such as Byron received. He is a man—can you not understand the difference that must make?"

"You mean that the double standard of morality applies also to the arts."

"There is unquestionably a double standard that applies to the arts—to poetry—as it does to everything else. It may perhaps one day be broken, but that day is not today, nor will it be this year, nor next, nor in the next decade; I doubt we shall see it in this century. Those who try to break it, unless they have wealth and position to protect themselves from society's castigations— as well as a hard exterior—will suffer. You have more wit, more intelligence, more creativity, even more courage than most men I know, but you cannot do it. To believe that you can is foolhardy and can only lead to suffering. When I mentioned to you some time ago that no poets of your sex had written of love, I had not considered the consequences they would face by so doing. Had I realized that you might take it upon yourself to correct that inequity, I should not have spoken of it. I wish to God I had said nothing if my words prompted you, or if it is that thought that makes you refuse to withdraw it now. If you allow its publication you ask to be ostracized by those you would choose to receive you, pursued by the most raffish elements within society and generally vilified. I beg you to reconsider, Miss Marlowe. Think carefully on what I have said, please."

I was shaken by his vehemence and unable to prevent myself from being swayed by his arguments.

"How came you to know of it?" I asked at last.

"But I sent an advance copy to Lord Bladen. I had done so with your other books at your instruction; I thought you would wish it." Mr. Hillaby glanced from Darius's entreating face to my own flushed cheeks. "You must excuse me, but I take it that you know one another well and have done for some time. If Lord

Bladen has some position in your life of which I am unaware but to which I should accede, I must heed his warning.''

"Lord Bladen has no position in my life, Mr. Hillaby, none whatsoever. In this instance I wish you had not sent the volume to him, for he has not the right to intercede. This is my work and I must stand by it. If there are, as he suggests, certain scurrilous elements who will read into it some interpretation of their own, there is little I can do about it. I can only point out that the poem to which Lord Bladen so strongly objects occupies only one page of the volume. If he considers it too—too sensual, I can only say that I have seen sensuality far more openly expressed than in this volume. Perhaps it should make others reflect on their own morals rather than mine.''

"I suspect your criticism is directed at me, to which in reply I would quote a possible ancestor of yours, Miss Marlowe: 'that was long ago and in another place.' I would willingly defend my own conduct if that were the matter at dispute. But it is precisely because society's morals as a whole are dissolute that they will be most severe upon you for what they must consider a break in your moral standard, as though their censure of you denies or corrects any wrongdoing on their part.''

He argued so earnestly that again I was swayed, but he saw my weakening and made to take my hand in his. Abruptly I pulled away from him and took the offending volume from Mr. Hillaby's desk.

"I have no intention of changing my course of action, Lord Bladen, nor do I wish you to instruct me in what I should or should not do. I and I alone choose to allow the publication of this work, and nothing you can say will prevent it. I shall ask that a copy be sent to Lady Brentwood for her comment, as I take it you must consider her an authority on the subject.''

"I would it were Althea who would face what must await you after that work appears.''

"She has experience,'' I remarked caustically.

"She has knowledge of that world and those people. She can handle rebuffs in a way you, I suspect, may not be able to—but your choice is made, and from all you say I take it that your decision is final.''

"It is.''

I felt uncomfortably close to tears and made to leave, but Darius laid his hand on my arm and added in a softer tone, "Remember, though, freedom is a heady thing. It should be used wisely. You have made your decision; nothing I can say, apparently, will change it. Nevertheless I ask that you take care. You will accept neither my advice nor my protection, so there is little I can do except to assure you that I am ready to help, should you ever need me.''

"I thank you, Lord Bladen, but I asked for your help once and it was not forthcoming. I shall never ask for it again.''

I left the room without bidding him farewell.

XXIV

Love's Breath was on the tables of London's booksellers the next week. Though the work was entitled *Selected Short Pieces by the author of Sum of Glory and The New Cassandra,* the love sonnet occupying only a very small part, nevertheless it was never referred to by any other name. The literary critics were for the most part kind, some even generous, though questions were raised on the salubrity of portions of the work and one critic even went so far as to label it salacious. It sold wildly. Within two weeks it was in its third printing.

Mr. Hillaby was elated at its success. Though I had less reason to be satisfied, I consoled myself with the thought that my personal gain would make it possible for me to set up a residence of my own. The Hillabys had been kind, but since Darius's visit our relationship had grown strained. Mr. Hillaby may have feared blame would fall on him should Darius's dire warning prove justified. That, perhaps, was the reason he deliberately ignored changes in attitude that began with subtlety but that became increasingly blatant as time passed.

There was no abatement in the flow of invitations received at Hans Place; indeed, if anything they increased in number, for nothing was talked of but *Love's Breath.* If I had been welcomed before as an author, now I was perceived and received as a curiosity, one that warranted cultivating, yet hardly in a friendly fashion. Matrons would press me to attend their soirees yet often shun me after arrival, whispering behind their fans, their eyes turning quickly away whenever I glanced in their direction. Their husbands they guarded closely, their watch being not entirely without justification, for many a gentleman who had previously

treated me with courtesy and respect now approached with
innuendoed comments that became increasingly difficult to treat
as the subject of jest. The more bold among them went further
yet, leaving no doubt of their aspirations in terms that could not
be ignored. And the more callous, although possibly the more
honest of them, made outright requests for assignations. I found
the behaviour of all these gentlemen, perhaps because they were
gentlemen and because that behaviour occurred within most
impeccable drawing rooms, far coarser than had been the coachman's lewd ditties on that ride from Marlborough.

I kept my head high, determined not to give in to the pressures
I faced. Mr. Hillaby assiduously turned away from any unpleas-
antness, yet I could not blame him—the decision to publish the
book had ultimately been mine, though I had known even as I
made it that it stemmed, in part at least, from bravado. I did not
want men to make my decisions for me—first father, then Darius—
but as a result, I had to bear the consequences. Thus I continued
to grace social functions that became increasingly intolerable,
spurred on by the fact that wherever I was, there, too, was
Darius. He would know the very moment I succumbed to the
hostility he had predicted and by which I was surrounded. I
refused to give in.

Whereas before he had rarely joined me, now he was always
at my side. He never mentioned that scene in Mr. Hillaby's
study, nor did he say a word on the accuracy of his predictions.
How much he was aware of I could not tell, for whenever he was
at hand I was spared insult. He kept up a steady flow of
conversation, from conducting wagers on the exact height of
Lady Jersey's turban to the very tip of its single ostrich feather,
to considerations on the slow progress of parliamentary reform.
He was not to be put off by sly allusions to *Love's Breath* but
used them to comment on Brougham's idea of rewarding literary
merit by bestowing the Guelphic Order on deserving poets and
writers and suggesting that my name should be among them. I
never ceased to marvel at his ability to control and direct a
conversation without ever appearing to dominate it. At times I
thought of his remark about having difficulty expressing himself
on the morning he had proposed marriage to me—how long ago
that seemed—yet no man was more at ease with the spoken
word, at least in the social setting.

There was never any private conversation between us, one
reason being that wherever Darius was, there, too, was the
elegant Lady Brentwood. She would take his arm in her casual

yet all-too-possessive manner, her fingers managing to linger upon his whenever he handed her a glass of sherry or champagne, and her eyes fixed upon his face whenever he spoke. All of this was calculated to annoy me, yet I cannot say that she did it for my benefit, for whereas her previous attitude to me had been critical, even hostile, by contrast it became far kinder than those I thought had befriended me. Yet I was unsure whether her friendliness to me stemmed from a desire to please me or to please Darius.

I was quite sure that Darius was behind the invitation I received to Holland House. If Lady Holland received me coolly, it was also with the same moderation she reserved for Lady Brentwood and those other ladies of fashion and beauty who were her guests rather than because of any reputation that had preceded me, of that I was sure, for she herself had faced much the same censure when her marriage to Sir Godfrey Webster had been dissolved because of her adultery with Lord Holland. If society had ostracized her for her sins, she had imperiously refused to recognize it and went on to make Holland House the centre of all brilliance and wit, so that those who had refused her admittance were soon begging for an invitation to join her circle. Her humour was acid, her rule over the household absolute, yet she had warmth and a keen interest in everything. I admired her.

I was unsure whether Lady Holland recognized in Arabella Marlowe the ill-dressed, ill-at-ease provincial girl who had graced her table once before, but Sydney Smith, who was present, most certainly did. His lips twitched in the compulsive good humour that was his style as he greeted me.

"Miss Marlowe, how very nice to meet London's latest literary lioness. I understand society has put their stewing pan over the greatest fire they can build to fry away and get everything they can out of you."

I acknowledged this with a wry smile.

"You might be interested, Miss Marlowe, in knowing that I have had the pleasure of becoming acquainted with such a nice young man—a curate but I refuse to hold that against him—Cox-Neville by name."

"Oh, Paul!" I gasped before I could help it. "How is he, Mr. Smith?"

"Quite well, quite well. At least so he was the last time I saw him not three weeks ago, though I must say he was disturbed over the disappearance of a sister of his, quite a favourite, I gather."

"Would you—would you mind conveying to him that I—that she is well and unharmed?"

"Unharmed in body if not in spirit, Miss Marlowe, for I hear there is much unkindness directed towards you."

"Nothing I cannot bear, Mr. Smith. It is of no consequence."

"You are a gifted young lady, never forget that, and a sensible one, too, not to allow those wagging, idle tongues to inflict wounds."

"Am I still that nice young person, as you once designated me?" I asked, half-shyly.

"You are the very nicest young lady of my acquaintance, Miss Marlowe. I hope that you will remember that. I shall be delighted if you will allow me to take you in to tea. You know when I am in the country I always fear that Creation will expire before teatime. Thank God for tea! What would the world do without tea? How did it ever exist before—I am very glad I was not born before tea!"

Not only tea but comfort and compassion he bestowed on me.

Along with the support of Sydney Smith and Darius, there was also that of Geoffrey. Yet all too often he was accompanied by Sir Clarence Wilmott, whom I detested. If I had considered that gentleman outrageously familiar before, he was now intolerable. Even though I kept myself aloof from him, he watched me intently wherever I went, like a panther waiting for its prey, smiling knowingly whenever, by some mischance, my eyes met his.

"He's horrid," I told Geoffrey one morning at Hans Place.

"But what has he done?" Geoffrey demanded.

"Nothing. He just—he just looks at me, that's all."

"A cat can look at a queen—not too original, I know, but nevertheless it's true."

"Yes, but it's the way he looks, as though he would eat me for breakfast."

"Hmmm," Geoffrey mused. "Perhaps you're right. You know, I once heard that a bunch of the Wilmotts got lost on Dartmoor, and by the time they were found only one of them was left."

"What happened to the others?"

"The surviving Wilmott had eaten them!"

"Oh, Geoffrey, do be serious."

"I won't. You're making far too much of this, Alex. That cousin of mine is far too serious; he's frightened you half to death. He had no right to do that. You need a little levity. You've written some jolly good verse—not left much to the imagination, to be sure, so you've aroused some of the old biddies' ire and the gentlemen's feelings. You have mine. Like Wilmott, I'm afraid I took you for a bit of a prude.''

"You're nothing like Wilmott, Geoffrey. I'll never understand your attachment to him. You are gentle and considerate. Quite frankly, I don't know what I'd do without your friendship.''

Unexpectedly he leaned over and stared intently into my face. "Alex, it would be much more than friendship if you'd allow it.''

"Oh, Geoffrey, don't spoil everything. I really need you, now more than ever, as a friend. I don't want anything more, not just from you but from any other man. I want an independent life, you know that.''

"And you are able to have it now with this book of yours selling like hot buns. You're becoming so rich you'd probably never consider a poor suitor like me.''

"Don't be ridiculous, Geoffrey. If I were to consider any suitor at all, it would be you.''

He paused, his light blue eyes catching mine in piercing hold. "Is that really true, Alex? Don't tease me, because I've always liked you but I thought you preferred Darius. Most women do; they always have. And I think he likes you, especially now. I'm not the first to remark on the way he's been hanging around you. Is there something between you two—or has there been? I know you were always at Charteris.''

"There's nothing, I already told you that,'' I snapped, a trifle too quickly.

"And you do prefer me to Darius,'' he insisted.

"Didn't I just say that if I were to consider any suitor it would be you? Need I say more? But since I'm not, all of this is ponderously heavy.''

"And I wish you wouldn't be so hard on old Wilmott.''

An uncharitable retort rose to my lips, which I squelched with an invitation to Geoffrey to accompany me on my morning walk.

Tim was waiting on the steps as we came out, and I greeted him warmly. His was a friendly face in a city in which I no longer felt comfortable. Even in Chelsea I had fears of being accosted, and I appreciated Tim more than ever.

I made to introduce Tim to Geoffrey until I caught sight of the look of disdain as he took in the boy's unkempt appearance. Before I could intercede, Geoffrey ordered. "Be off with you— the likes of you don't belong in this part of town.''

"Geoffrey!'' I protested. "Tim is my friend. He helped me

when first I came to London and he's been faithful to me ever since. We always walk together."

"I don't give a farthing for that, Alex. I wouldn't be seen on the street with such a ragbone."

Tim ran his eyes over Geoffrey's dandified figure and very slowly, very ostentatiously he wiped his runny nose on his sleeve.

"S'oright, miss. I'll come back when the toff's not 'ere." He eyed the myriad silver buttons on Geoffrey's dark red morning coat. "Can't fer the life of me see why anyone'd want all them buttons that don't do nuffin."

"Insolent little tramp!" Geoffrey glowered at Tim's thin, retreating figure.

"Geoffrey, he's just a boy."

"A nasty boy! A dirty boy . . ."

"An unfortunate boy, Geoffrey. And a friend I would not be without."

"Oh, come on, Alex, don't let's talk about the boy. Let's talk about you."

But we ended up, as we usually did, talking about Geoffrey. He was an unending source of interest to himself, yet as he prattled on, he was so thoroughly engaging that at times he hardly seemed older than Tim and certainly not as wise. His attitude to Tim, though it distressed me, stemmed, I was sure, from the fact that he was comfortable only with his own social peers.

Though Geoffrey was my friend, it was Tim I came to rely on more and more, especially after an unnerving incident that occurred a few days later.

Since the publication of *Love's Breath*, I had had a suspicion that I was being followed, yet not being of a hysterical bent, I was sure that my imagination must be playing tricks with me. My follower, or suspected follower, was a decidedly ill-favoured man of such strange aspect, having the body of a pugilist with nose and ears showing signs of having been pummelled far too often for their good, that when I remarked him several days in succession walking behind me at a discreet distance, I decided it must be more than imagination or mere coincidence. I resolved to accost him, yet whenever I tried to do so, he vanished.

One morning as I sat by the river with Tim, listening to his reading, I caught sight of the little man. Whispering my suspicions to Tim while pretending to be correcting his pronunciation, together we hatched a plan to find out who he was. Tim bade me good-bye and left while I stayed where I was, acutely aware that the man stood some distance from me engaged in studious contemplation of the water. As soon as I caught sight of Tim creeping up on the man from behind, I approached him directly; when he attempted his usual disappearing trick, Tim caught hold of one of his legs and held onto it like a terrier.

"Gotcher, yer cove!" he yelled in exultation.

"All right, my man," I grasped his arm while Tim tightened his hold on the struggling man's leg. "You have been following me for a long time. Everywhere I go, there you are behind me. It's no coincidence. What is it you want? Whom do you work for? Tell me, because one way or another I intend to find out."

"Orl right, miss." He grinned foolishly, showing a mouth almost completely devoid of teeth. "You got me, you 'ave an all, but honest I ain't done nuffin. You can't accuse me of 'aving put a finger on you, not a finger, now can you?"

"I'm not accusing you of that, but don't deny you've been following me. Why?"

"They tole me you was a poet. I just 'appen to like a bit of poetry, that's all." He grinned again.

"You like a bit of poetry," I repeated stupidly.

"Yes, miss, I'm a bit of a poet meself, you see."

"Repeat to me some of your poetry," I demanded.

"Oo, I don't remember it by 'eart."

"How odd." I opened Tim's book and pointed at the page. "Read this."

His face flushed. "I can't, miss."

"There's no shame in it if you can't, but if you don't know your poetry by heart and you can't read, then you can't write, so how can you be a poet. What do you want of me? I want the truth, and I intend to have it or I'll inform the authorities you're a common thief."

"But I ain't robbed you of nowt, now 'ave I?"

"You've robbed me of my peace of mind."

"I didn't mean no 'arm to you, so don't make trouble for me. It would go bad fer me. See, the party I work fer wouldn't like it, wouldn't like it at all. I might lose me position, me livelihood. You wouldn't want that, would yer, miss?"

"For whom do you work?" I demanded, a suspicion dawning on me.

The man fidgeted, stomping his free foot.

"Out with it or I'll have your job anyway," I admonished.

"I ain't saying."

"Is it Sir Clarence Wilmott?"

He looked down without answering, yet I had caught his start of recognition.

"You don't deny it. Just what were his orders to you?"

"I ain't sayin' nuffin. I ain't done nuffin. I'm a poor man wot's done nuffin."

It was useless. Tim and I didn't have the strength between us to drag any information from him. I dug into my reticule and found a shilling.

"Here, take this. I don't ever want to see your face again, and that goes for your master also. You may tell him that from me. I am forewarned. Should I ever catch sight of you again, I shall inform the authorities whether you've done any harm or no, do you understand?"

He took the shilling and stuffed it in his pocket, nodding at his luck. I signalled to Tim to let go of his leg, and he was off as quickly as a darted beam of light.

"You didn't ought to 'ave given 'im a shillin'," Tim objected.

"I'd give a lot more to be rid of him, and his master, and all this notoriety. Fame is the breath of fools, Tim, remember that."

XXV

I SAW NO further sign of the pugilistic man after that. Everything seemed to be settling well. The first tension had passed, and though *Love's Breath* continued to be a topic of discussion, it was no longer *the* topic. I felt the heat of victory after a crisis has been surmounted. Darius had predicted that society would force me to flee. I had, however, stood my ground, and though I could not claim that the matter had been laid to rest, nevertheless there was quiescence after the storm. I refused to consider that that quiescence might be nothing more than the eye of the hurricane.

Darius had never raised the matter to me, yet on the evening of Lady Framingham's ball I was of a mind to remind him of it. I felt especially pleased, for the new evening dress I wore, of white crepe over a jonquil satin slip, the sleeves piquantly cut in sharp pleats edged with jonquil satin in the Chinese mode, which was all the rage, had been favourably commented upon by my hostess as I entered. This in itself was a victory, for Lady Framingham had been among those who had taken to cutting me dead whenever the opportunity presented itself.

My pleasure increased when Darius asked me to stand up with him for the "Boulanger." It was the first time I had danced with him since that waltz at the election ball in Linbury, though unlike the waltz, the "Boulanger" did not allow for any private discussion, otherwise I might have reminded him that his dire warnings had been for naught.

Lady Brentwood, dancing with our host, threw an intimate smile at Darius from across the floor, and because she ired me, I deliberately moved to block her view, yet I was determined not even she would put me out of sorts that evening.

Nor was I overly dismayed at Sir Clarence grasping my hand too tightly as we met in the set, though the next time I encountered him I clasped my fist in such a manner as to make that impossible, ignoring his lazy smile as he recognized my action.

I sat at supper with a large group, of which Darius was a part with, of course, the ubiquitous Countess of Brentwood, and Lord Grey, Tom Moore and other members of the Holland House set. Lady Framingham was noted for the elegance of her table; she had that night quite outdone herself by serving fresh crab canapes, foie gras en chausson, terrine of oysters, each table being decorated with an enormous savarin saturated with strawberries and madeira.

The vintage champagne that continually refilled the glasses became the source of a number of toasts—to the sovereign; to Wellington, our national hero; to the remembrance of Nelson; to our hosts and their fine entertainment; on and on until the wine itself, in all its excellence, became a subject to salute. The guests were merry, tongues were loosened but in good fellowship rather than backbiting. A sense of relaxation, of ease, pervaded, so that I felt no qualms even when Wilmott arose to lift his glass.

"To the ladies, without whom our lives would indeed be barren!"

His toast was greeted with a murmur of assent. "The ladies! The ladies!" and glasses were about to be raised when Sir Clarence lifted his hand to signify that he had not finished.

"And to one very special lady known to us all. There is, I believe, not a gentleman amongst us, if truth will prevail, who would not willingly choose to offer himself to that lady, to be held by her in the manner that she has so clearly and so publicly described."

He paused, and I felt every eye upon me. Though I wished they would not, I knew that my cheeks flushed horribly.

"I, for one, so offer myself most willingly. To Miss Marlowe!"

Sir Clarence raised his glass to me from across the room. There was stunned silence as the assembled guests, glasses partially raised, looked to one another as though for guidance.

I held my head high and replied in a deliberately crisp and cool manner. "I thank you, sir. I take your toast in the manner I am sure you intended—in all courtesy."

But Wilmott would allow no alleviation of a situation that was rapidly growing more tense.

"I hoped, Miss Marlowe, that you would take the toast in exactly the manner in which it was given."

He made the insult impossible to ignore. Apart from scurrilous rumour and unscrupulous newspaper accounts, it was the first time I had ever been attacked publicly and by name. Before I could decide whether discreet silence or immediate withdrawal was preferable, Darius was on his feet, his face white with rage, crossing the room to forcibly remove the glass of champagne from Wilmott's hand, slamming it down so hard that its golden, bubbling content spewed across the table.

"Miss Marlowe, as a poet, has the right to express herself as her heart and her pen dictate, without the fear of insult and injury from scum like you, Wilmott. You will retract your statement, sir. You will apologize to this lady immediately for your unhappy and unwise suggestions, and then you will leave and we shall try to forget that you and your despicable tongue exist."

Like lions engaged in mortal combat, they eyed one another. Geoffrey, at Wilmott's elbow, was the only one who seemed to derive any amusement from the situation, for a smile hovered at the corners of his lips. I could only put it down to the amount of champagne he had consumed, for there was nothing even vaguely amusing about the scene.

Wilmott was silent. He had not, I was sure, foreseen this turn of events, but then none of us had.

"Well, sir, I hear nothing. You saw fit to wrong a lady who had done harm to none of us, yourself included, though many have chosen to malign her. You will apologize or you will answer to me."

"It was never my intention to harm the lady. I simply wished to succumb to her. To succumb can hardly be considered an insult." There was more bravado than mockery in Wilmott's reply.

"To use the name of a lady in such a context demands either immediate apology or satisfaction; you have your choice."

"Oh, no!" The cry was wrested involuntarily from my lips, the only sound in the sickening silence. Wilmott seemed to struggle with himself. I resolved that however brief his apology might be, however inadequate Darius might consider it, I would insist on accepting it so that he could no longer pursue the matter. I would return to Hans Place to decide, once in that place of refuge, whether I ever wanted to leave it again.

But before Wilmott could speak—and I was sure he intended to—Geoffrey interrupted softly, "I know you'll not allow your actions to be dictated by Bladen, so although he is my cousin, I agree to act as your second."

And whatever words had been on Wilmott's lips died unspoken.

"If your silence indicates that you refuse to withdraw the malicious remarks you have directed at Miss Marlowe, you leave me no alternative. My seconds will call upon you to arrange time and place so that this matter may be settled between us. The choice of weapons is yours."

With a whispered aside to Lord Grey, who had risen and stood behind him, Darius left the room.

Whereas before there had been silence, after Darius's departure a steady hum broke out that rapidly became a roar.

In the glance that was exchanged between Lord Grey and Lord Russell, I saw the all-too-evident political implications of Darius's action. The custom of duelling to settle arguments, ever since the duel between Prime Minister Pitt and Tierney, who led the Whig opposition, had been a matter of much disfavour. It had been completely suppressed in the army and the navy, and though it occurred from time to time, it never did so without an outcry. No matter what happened, Darius could only suffer. Lady Bladen's last words reverberated through my head: "I trust he will do nothing foolish, for I am convinced that his place in the history of our country is assured."

"Darius will never act foolishly," I had asserted.

To think that he had acted so unwisely—and to think that I had been the cause of it. It didn't bear considering. I made no protest as Lord Grey led me from the room.

XXVI

"IT MUST BE stopped—it must be stopped!"

I could see only the outline of Lord Grey's face in the dimness of the carriage. He had been asked by Darius to see that I got home safely, and not wishing to entrust me to Mr. Hillaby, who was busy attending his hysterical wife, he had insisted on taking me himself. Once outside, however, I had demanded to be taken to Great Stanhope Street rather than Chelsea, so that I might try to reason with Darius.

The footman, on my arrival, immediately recognized me and addressed me as Miss Cox-Neville, to Lord Grey's consternation. I insisted on seeing Darius and seeing him alone. Nor would I take the footman's word that he would receive no one. I hurried down the hall to the study. There I found him at his desk earnestly engaged in writing. He looked up in astonishment at my abrupt entrance and in askance at the footman who trailed close on my heels.

"It's not his fault—I insisted on seeing you, Darius. I refuse to leave until I talk to you."

"Very well." He signalled to the footman to leave, and when the door closed behind him, he went on. "There is nothing to be said, Alex; nothing will change my mind, if that is your intent."

"But what on earth possessed you? How could you do such a thing!" I stormed. "It is a foolish act. It must be stopped. Wilmott's words meant nothing to me, but your response will ruin you whatever the outcome. I cannot allow it."

"The choice is not for you to make, to either allow or disallow it. You have told me that you make your own decisions. So, too, I make mine, based on my own judgements. I judged Wilmott this evening to have gone far beyond the pale of propriety. Since he chose not to respond by civilized means to make amends, then less-than-civilized methods must be employed to make him guard his tongue. Those methods are possibly the only ones he understands."

"But Wilmott is not worth it, Darius. Do, please, consider—I beg of you. Settling the matter in this fashion cannot possibly have the consequences for him that it will for you. Your career is at stake, and win or lose on the field of honour, that career will be at an end. You have credited me with common sense in the past—do, now, use some of it yourself. Think of your country if not of yourself. What good can you do for England if you are dead—or alive, for that matter, for you will be forced abroad if you kill him. He is not worth the sacrifice. What he did does not demand it.''

''Wilmott is a scurrilous, insulting blackguard. He will go on being a scurrilous, insulting blackguard until someone teaches him a lesson in his own terms.''

''He is above all foolish, and I am beginning to think you equally foolish if you don't extricate yourself from this quagmire. I am sure he does not want it. I could see in his face that you caught him off guard. Everything happened so quickly; you didn't give him time to back down. I am convinced that he does not wish to fight. I am sure that he can be made to apologize if he is approached in the right manner.''

''The choice was his. I asked him to apologize publicly if he did not wish to meet me.''

''Publicly, privately—what does it matter? Men and their foolish honour. Can honour set a leg or mend a wound? Falstaff was right: honour's nothing but a scutcheon—I want none of it.''

''Then it is well that I fight Wilmott and not you, Alex. For goodness sake, don't cry.''

''I'm not going to cry,'' I said, tears falling down my cheeks.

''Here, take this.'' He held out his handkerchief to me and I took it distractedly without making any attempt to stem my tears' flow.

''I'm only crying because you make me angry, that's all,'' I sobbed, pulling compulsively at the handkerchief in my hands. ''Go and waste your life, it means nothing to me. Go and kill or be killed—death must have his day, I suppose.''

''I promise I shall not entrust my elegy to anyone but you, Alex, but it won't be required yet—not yet.''

He took the crumpled handkerchief from my hands and gently wiped my cheeks. ''Do please go home and get some rest.''

At that moment the door behind him burst open to reveal Lady Brentwood, closely followed by the embarrassed footman, who hastened to excuse the intrusion. ''I'm sorry, my lord, I couldn't . . .

But Darius waved him away as Lady Brentwood began. ''I had to see you Darius, but . . .'' she suddenly caught sight of me, "but *you* I had not expected to find here. Have you not made enough trouble for one night?"

"Althea, no recriminations, I beg of you. That was why I proscribed visitors this evening, though my proscription seems to have acted as an open sesame to my door."

"But you cannot refuse to listen to your friends at such a time. Lord Grey is waiting patiently to see you, and Lord Russell has gone to fetch Lord Holland."

"Good lord! Can't a man settle matters after his own inclination!"

"You are not just any man, Darius, and what you propose to do may forever ruin you. Your friends are, of course, affected out of consideration for you personally. But apart from that, many people are relying on you to take over the reins of leadership for which they have groomed you. How often have you been mentioned as the party's brightest hope, the man other men will follow. And what have you done with all the trust that was placed in you this evening? You have tossed it away, not over some monumental matter but over . . ." the look she threw me was filled with contempt, "over a trifle."

"Althea, I shall tell you as I've just told Alexandra. I run my affairs as I see fit . . ."

The door opened again. This time it was Lord Holland, closely followed by Lord Russell and a thoroughly anxious, thoroughly distraught footman.

"It's all right, Hill. I know it's not your fault, though we might as well post a sign and invite the world inside, for it seems everyone is determined to be here to tell me what to do."

"Everyone wishes to tell you what not to do, Bladen. Russell here, and Grey who is outside consuming your best brandy, we all refuse to leave until we have thoroughly been over this whole thing with you and outlined the consequences. I won't be dragged all the way over from Kensington in the middle of the night to be told you'll see no visitors."

"I am well aware of the consequences, sir, nor would I have had you dragged here on such a fruitless mission had I been forewarned of it. However, since you have come, I shall talk with you," Darius consented. "Alex, you must go. I shall arrange for a carriage to take you back to Chelsea."

"She may have the use of mine," Lady Brentwood interposed.

"But is that quite safe?"

"My groom is always armed, nor can I remember you ever having exercised yourself over my safety in riding abroad."

"Althea, you know what I mean, after all this business," he entreated.

"Of course I do, Darius. Now do go along and don't keep these gentlemen waiting any longer. I shall see you afterwards."

She smiled brilliantly until the door closed behind them, and then she turned on me. "I hope you are quite satisfied, Miss Marlowe, or is it as Miss Cox-Neville you will go down in infamy as having ruined one of England's most gifted and aspiring statesmen."

"I don't give a tin farthing for my name," I retorted. "*His* is the only name that concerns me, just as it does the rest of you."

"Then why did you not think of that before, when he pleaded with you not to allow your precious poetry to be published? He knew something like this must result. It is for that reason he has insisted on accepting every invitation to which he supposed you would be a party, for that reason he has stayed close to you at this time, for that reason he has prevailed upon me to side with you. Yet how have you repaid his consideration—you never thought of him, only of yourself and your own glory or fame or whatever it is you sought for yourself."

"It wasn't that. My own glory, as you choose to put it, was not the reason I opposed his intervention in my life. Certainly I never believed any disaster such as this would be a consequence."

"It would seem that he is unlikely to intervene in your or anyone else's life again. I hope that satisfies you. He will be labelled a harum-scarum hothead who throws everything over for some lightskirt. His chances of rising to cabinet rank, even to that of first minister, must be forever dimmed. Thank God Wilmott is not noted for his marksmanship, though whatever happens Darius will be forced out of England in all likelihood. But he will not go alone, that I vow."

"Lady Brentwood, my concern is every bit as great as yours. I have tried to reason with him without avail. Why do you not speak to him? He will listen to you."

"If he listened to me, do you suppose I should still be Lady Brentwood? No," she sighed, "he will not listen to me."

For the first time I saw her not simply as a rival but as another woman, albeit one who shared my caring for the same man, and that her caring, though I might wish to deny it, was also deep and sincere. Yet I had no time to waste on such reflections. Something must be done, but what? Darius insisted on challenging Wilmott. He would not be dissuaded from it, nor would he seek conciliation. But what if Wilmott could be made to apologize publicly. For one moment he had seemed on the point of doing so, if only Geoffrey had not most unfortunately intervened. Geoffrey . . . that was it!

I picked up my wrap.

"Wait, I must call my carriage."

"That's all right, Lady Brentwood. I won't be needing it."

"But where are you going?"

"Out of Darius's life—forever."

XXVII

"WHY DARIUS CHOSE to make all that fuss is simply beyond me. True, the toast might not have been in the best of taste, but it is Wilmott's humour. He is not necessarily a paragon of propriety, everyone knows that. Darius himself might have expected it. No reason for him to go off like a rattlepate and then act so sanctimoniously and cause all this fracas."

"I know, Geoffrey, it was foolish. I suppose there are some who cannot quite understand or appreciate Wilmott's humour, but that matters little at this point. What does matter is the challenge. This duel must not take place tomorrow, and you can see that it does not. You will help, won't you Geoffrey—please!"

From Great Stanhope Street I had gone to Geoffrey's lodging in the area of St. James's to await him there. I had ignored his landlady's disapproving stare when I had demanded admittance. My already tarnished reputation was of little importance.

Geoffrey swung the jewelled fob from his waistcoat back and forth, idly watching its progress.

"You will do something, won't you?" I pleaded once again.

"Not much I can do, Alex. Darius makes his own decisions, always has. It's his lookout. If he's made a ramshackle business of it, I can't be blamed nor can I stop him. To be quite frank with you, I'm not at all sure I would, even if I could."

"But he's your cousin. The same blood runs in your veins."

"I reminded him of that once. It didn't seem to impress him, as I remember—infuriated him, more like it."

"But he would do as much for you, Geoffrey, I know he would."

"Would he?" He regarded me quizzically. "I doubt it. But he won't have to anyway, for I'm not so doltish as to go around challenging people to duels over nothing. Wilmott may be considered a bit of a roué, but he's not that bad a shot."

"Oh, Geoffrey!" I wailed. I pulled at the edge of Darius's handkerchief, which I still clutched in my hand. "Something must be done to stop it, and done tonight."

"You conducted yourself sensibly, Alex. No blame can be placed on you. Why do you come to me to plead for a cousin who has shown no regard for me?"

His eyes were fixed intently on mine. I somehow knew that on my reply depended the outcome of the whole terrible affair.

"Because—because I cannot live with the life of a man on my conscience."

"A man?" He raised his eyebrows. "The life of which man is it that inflicts your conscience?"

"Either of them; it makes no difference. If either of them should die, or—or if either should be wounded—maimed—either Sir Clarence or Darius, it makes little difference—it would be on my conscience. Can't you see that?"

It was a lie, yet only partly a lie. I could in no way suffer as much for Wilmott as I would if harm were to befall Darius, and yet it was not wholly a lie. Duelling was man's foolish way of settling arguments for which women chose subtle and far less drastic measures. I wanted no one to come to grief because of my actions.

"If we can't stop Darius, couldn't we prevent Wilmott from showing?"

"And be called a coward? Hardly his touch, Alex."

"But Geoffrey, he's your friend. You could talk to him. If he were to write an apology to Darius, he could put it down to his humour, to the fact that he'd partaken too freely of the champagne, that he had meant no harm by his remarks, that he was sorry if they had been misconstrued, that he was heartily sorry for the whole business—as I am sure he is. Then Darius could hardly insist on fighting him."

"But why should he say any of that?"

"Because you ask him to."

"And why should I ask him to do any such thing?"

"Because I ask it of you."

"I see."

In the long, tense silence that ensued, Geoffrey's eyes were peculiarly alert and assessing as they held mine.

"I see," he repeated at last. "Perhaps something can be arranged. Perhaps I can reason with Wilmott."

"Oh, Geoffrey, I knew that if anyone could do anything it was you." I breathed freely for the first time since that chilling scene at Lady Framingham's.

"But if I am willing to do this for you, there is something you should be willing to do for me in return, something I've long wanted—ever since I first met you, in fact."

"Anything, Geoffrey, anything."

"I want you to marry me."

The silence that followed these words was painful in its intensity. I was bewildered. I could not understand why my marrying Geoffrey should be a condition in preventing a duel between his friend and his cousin. I could not understand why he wanted it, for though he might have hinted at some serious inclination, I had never believed it. I did understand, however, that on my answer depended Darius's future.

"I shall, of course, marry you, Geoffrey, if that is what you wish."

"In that case I shall speak to Wilmott."

"Tonight?"

"Tonight."

He got up and took my hands. Very slowly and very deliberately he bent down and kissed me on the lips. Perhaps because I was tired and dazed, I could feel nothing when he kissed me, neither pleasure nor revulsion; nothing.

"I'll go and speak to Wilmott now. And tomorrow we'll leave for Maplethorpe so that mother can meet you."

Geoffrey had been as good as his word. There had been no duel.

I had sent word to Tim to go to Great Stanhope Street and let me know what happened. He had followed in his usual surreptitious pillion fashion as Darius and his seconds had made their way in the cold morning light to Hampstead Heath. There they had waited what Tim said was an eternity before a coach drew up to deliver a letter, a letter that seemed to annoy Darius as much as it relieved his seconds.

As they went to climb back into the coach, Darius had spied Tim clambering up behind the coach.

"You're a ubiquitous fellow. Come along and have some breakfast with us," he had said.

"Did he ask who sent you?" I demanded of Tim.

"No, but 'e asked a lot 'bout wot I wanted to do."

":What did you tell him?"

"Now I learned a bit of this reading stuff I sort of like it. I mean, I wouldn't mind knowing a bit of sums and things."

"You shall, Tim, you shall."

My parting from Tim was more difficult than from the Hillabys, who, still recovering from the previous evening, were, I felt, almost anxious to see me go.

I was too relieved since the catastrophe had been averted to care. I could now recall Lady Bladen's last words without flinching, for at least I had not been the cause of Darius ruining his life. I preferred not to consider how much I had been spurred to action by Lady Brentwood's vow that she would accompany him if he were to be forced abroad. No, my long-lasting passion for Darius was over—finished perhaps before it ever began. It had never been a mutual passion. It never could be with the ever-present ghost of Philomena and the all-too-earthly presence of Lady Brentwood. The whole thing was finally at an end. I would be married. I had no idea why Geoffrey wanted to marry me—it was not love that prompted it, of that I was sure, yet it didn't matter. It would be a suitable match, for I never wanted to love again.

Marriage would free me completely from father. I suppose it was that knowledge that prompted me to write asking my parents to join us at Maplethorpe without the slightest trepidation. Geoffrey had insisted that the engagement be formally entered into before the announcement was published, and I appreciated his compunction in wanting father's approval first. There could, however, be little doubt of his receiving it—a baronet who, despite his complaints of his mother's tight hold on the purse strings, was not exactly impoverished, and though he was not a Tory, neither was he a Whig; he was completely apolitical. Besides, if it came to father's ears that I had published novels, worse yet, poems he would certainly conclude unbefitting for a daughter of his to have written, he would be only too grateful that I had found a gentleman who would have me.

XXVIII

LADY POINDEXTER WAS large where Geoffrey was slender; she was forthright where Geoffrey used charm; she was plain, even careless in dress where Geoffrey was never to be found, even in the morning, in anything less than immaculate attire; she was more at ease with her dogs and horses than she ever was with her son. Her qualities, however, endeared her to me: her frankness and, too, the fact that in feature she so resembled her brother, who had been my dearest friend. That liking increased especially when father arrived, blustering and bellowing at my conduct—not that father did not have reason to complain, for if I did not consider that I had been wrong in fleeing from home, I had been at fault in never letting them know my whereabouts—Darius had reminded me of that. On that account Lady Poindexter did not oppose father, but she was quite firm in pointing out that what was past was past, that it was useless to dwell upon it, that we were joined together for a happy occasion, that she was delighted in me as a daughter, that she hoped father would become acquainted and similarly delighted in Geoffrey as a son. If she said this last with the merest sniff, it was a sniff to be audibly repeated by father as he became acquainted with Geoffrey, for Geoffrey had summoned from London his solicitor, and after father's arrival they were closeted together to discuss the matter of a marriage settlement.

Though I had no wish to support father, I felt forced to speak to Geoffrey about his persistence over financial matters.

"You know that I have money of my own, money from my writing. It will be yours as well as mine when we marry. We need nothing from father."

"Indeed we do. I have found out to the penny what he gave with your eldest sister. Why should he do one jot less for you?"

"But why does it matter now? I thought you wanted to marry me for myself. I am not nor have I ever purported to be an heiress."

"Alexandra, of course I want you for yourself, you know that. But don't you see that now is the only time to get anything from your father? Nothing will be forthcoming later, perhaps when we really need it. It is only what is due to you that I demand. It is yours by right, and I shall insist upon it."

Insist he did, and his insistence won the day.

"A very pretty young man you've chosen, Alexandra; pretty astute," father raged. "He'll make a pauper of me. I suppose that's what you want."

"You did not have to agree to his demands," I replied.

"Did I not! Did I not indeed! He showed me this. I'm lucky to have you married at all after this."

Father thrust at me a copy of *Love's Breath*, and I could not prevent a gasp. He had to know of my writing eventually, something I knew would bring out his direst rebukes on scribbling women, but I would have wished he had not learned of it with that particular work.

"That a daughter of mine should stoop to scribbling at all, but that she should produce such—such disgusting verse—I should never be able to live it down if my friends learned of it. I can only hope they will never make any connexion between you and this—this," contemptuously he turned to the title page, "this Arabella Marlowe. Nothing short of blackmail, designed to impoverish me."

"I hardly expected you to understand or appreciate my writing, father."

"Trouble is that I—and everyone else I expect—understand a damned sight too well, my girl. When you left home I thought perhaps it was because Ramsey had—had pressed you too hard, that that was why you ran away. Reading this, I doubt it. It was simply your willfulness, for Netty had nothing to complain of in him. I even suspect that Ramsey wasn't forceful enough with you. That'll not be the case with this pretty young man you have chosen for yourself. Only good thing to be said for him is that, unlike the rest of his family, he's not a Whig."

"Netty? Father, what has Netty to do with Howard Ramsey?"

"Why, she married him not a month after you left him in the lurch, didn't your mother tell you? Fortunate thing, for it embarrassed all of us to be left with a jilted suitor. And a very good match it is, too, already about to bear fruit."

Mother had not mentioned it in the tearfulness of our meeting. She had held me at arm's length to examine me before pulling me to her and hugging me so hard I thought all the breath must be forced from my body.

"My dear daughter—Alex! How often I have lain awake

thinking I might never see you again, and here you are, so well, so elegant. What a relief it is, truly!''

"Mother! Mother!" Tears poured down my face. "I am so sorry I did not send word to you, truly I am, but I thought I should be forced back, forced to marry against my will."

"And here you are, marrying a gentleman of your own choosing. You are fortunate."

I hesitated for an imperceptible moment before agreeing, "Yes, indeed."

"I am glad for your sake, Alex, for now I am convinced you could never accommodate to a situation not of your choosing, as has Cassy."

"How is Cassy, mother?"

"Very well. Her match with Mr. Pomeroy is most satisfactory. They have adjusted well to one another. Cassy is a neat, careful housekeeper, and he . . . he is much improved. She has almost cured him of that rather curious tendency he had of moving rather rapidly from one subject to another in conversation—I don't know whether you noticed it."

"I did, mother," I replied rather drily. "And Paul, how is Paul?"

"He is quite settled into the parish. He doesn't write often but when he does his letters are full of schemes he wishes to carry out to improve the lot of impoverished parishioners. There are times when I fear he may be a little too innovative for his rector, yet they seem to be getting along well now that Paul is engaged to his daughter, Dolores."

"Paul—engaged!"

"Yes. Dolores is such a pleasant-sounding name; one doesn't hear it too often."

"It means sorrow," I said, half to myself.

"Well, dear, it may, but I'm quite sure she is not at all sorrowful from what Paul tells us. But we shall see for ourselves soon, for he is to bring her to us before they marry. Your father insisted on it."

As matters stood, there were times when I felt it was my name that should have been Dolores, for though it could be said that a successful conclusion had been reached—for with the announcement despatched to the *Times* and the *Morning Post*, Geoffrey and I were officially engaged—in the midst of plans for the engagement dinner and the wedding to be held at St. Mary's in Linbury, I felt oddly detached, strangely emptied of emotion.

Geoffrey was attentive, filled with jubilance at having had his way, and I annoyed at the way in which he had won it.

"But Alex, your father was bound to discover it anyway," he replied to my complaint of his disclosure. And of course it was true. Yet it was his mother with whom I felt most at ease. When I offered to help her in planning the engagement dinner party, she gladly gave into my care the task of addressing the invitations. My hand faltered as I came to Darius's name.

"I believe he is away," I lied.

"Oh, I do hope not, for I see so little of him as it is. I am sure he would set aside other plans to come, for this is a family matter and Darius is a man who thinks always of the importance of the family. We must send him a card. I shall address a letter to him myself."

I was glad his aunt knew nothing of his challenge to Wilmott, though with her obvious preference for Darius she would very likely have found alleviating reasons for his act.

"If only Geoffrey were more like Darius rather than his father." She looked up from the guest list she had been studying and sighed. "I know, I should not speak ill of the dead and particularly as my husband was never a well man, suffering as he did with that lung condition that killed so many in his family—I always felt it was because of that that he was so . . . so promiscuous, so profligate. I was relieved that Geoffey escaped inheriting it, but I am glad I had no other children, for that risk haunted me.

"I would be less than honest if I implied we were happy together, for he led a rather dissolute life, something I kept from my brother. I sometimes wonder whether it was that or the disease itself that caused his early demise, for I had withdrawn from him completely. He was a thoroughly selfish man, and in his willfulness I fear Geoffrey resembles him too closely. I was delighted, however, to see the good judgement Geoffrey used in choosing a wife. I had not thought he would bring to me a young lady of your good sense. If anyone can manage him, I think it is you. I believe you may succeed where I failed with his father."

"There is nothing bad in Geoffrey, Lady Poindexter," I assured her. I thought of him as he had been with Crumpet. "He is really kind at heart. I believe he is often misunderstood."

She kissed me. "My dear, how lucky Geoffrey is to have you for an advocate."

Yet Geoffrey's kindness to children did not extend to Tim Felder, for whom I had set aside a sum of money to provide for his education. In fact, he had been adamant in his opposition to it.

"We have no money to waste on young ruffians like that. There will be children of our own to educate."

"I promised this to him, Geoffrey. Our children will have all the advantages that Tim never had."

"Let's not discuss that little ragamuffin now, when we have things of much greater importance. We will talk of it later, but not now, please."

He had made to take me in his arms, but the door opened to admit father and the conversation became general. Yet I longed to resolve the issue, for I had discovered that under the terms of the marriage settlement, all the money I had earned would come completely under Geoffrey's control. When I had objected, it had been father who had overruled me.

"That is entirely as it should be, Alexandra. A woman's fortune should always be administered by her husband. Your mother had no complaints on that score."

"Don't you trust me, Alex?" Geoffrey had asked me.

"Of course I do." My reply was a trifle too swift. "I just feel that I should retain some independence, that is all."

"But marriage is a dual state, not an independent one," he had argued.

"Exactly," father interposed.

"Yet your mother retained her fortune, Geoffrey."

"It is because of that, Alex, that I insisted upon that clause. It was always a point of dispute between them. I don't want that ever to happen to us."

Remembering his mother's disclosure to me of the unhappiness of her marriage, I thought perhaps Geoffrey did believe that to be the reason, though that was not his mother's opinion. Reluctantly I allowed myself to be convinced, though if Tim were to receive the education I had promised him, then Geoffrey must be persuaded. And he would be persuaded—on that I was adamant.

We were at tea on the day the announcement of our engagement appeared in the newspapers, when an unexpected visitor was announced. It was Darius. His eyes were fixed upon me as soon as he entered, though I could scarcely return his greeting. I had not seen him since that night after the incident at the Framinghams', yet he appeared that afternoon far sterner, far paler than he had on that dreadful night.

I busied myself with a piece of fruitcake, which had seemed

quite delicious the moment before he arrived but which suddenly had all the allure of sawdust and stuck in my throat in much the same manner.

I had never seen Lady Poindexter greet her son with quite the same degree of warmth with which she greeted her nephew.

"My dear Darius. This *is* an occasion. But I had not expected you so soon. We only just despatched your invitation to Thursday's engagement party, did we not, Alexandra? But of course you must know Geoffrey's affianced bride, for the Cox-Nevilles live close to Charteris."

Darius greeted father and mother, but before he could speak, Geoffrey, who had been closely watching his mother's all-too-obvious pleasure on seeing her nephew, interrupted, "But are you not going to congratulate Alex and me, Darius?"

"I read of your engagement in this morning's *Times*."

"And you came all this way to congratulate us in person. We are honoured, are we not, Alexandra?"

I seemed to have lost control of my tongue; I nodded, glad to be relieved of speaking by Lady Poindexter.

"Now, Darius, come and sit beside me and tell me all of that latest happenings in the House. How is Liverpool reacting to Huskisson's latest budget—I've always thought him quite an incompetent prime minister. I'm sure you must agree."

Father's face flushed with annoyance, and Darius hastened to intervene. "Mr. Cox-Neville, I am quite sure, does not share that opinion, aunt, and as a Tory he is as much entitled to his convictions and his party loyalty as you or I."

"Oh, I had not realized that you were a Tory," Lady Poindexter exclaimed as if knowing that fact about father made everything else about him understandable.

"I am indeed, ma'am. Your son tells me he has no political leanings, however."

"That is true," Lady Poindexter mourned. "Geoffrey is totally oblivious on that score."

"And my cousin is not here to discuss politics, are you, Darius? You came on the matter of my engagement, yet I have yet to hear you say two words together on the subject. You must allow him to do so, mother, for it is so seldom I hear Darius congratulate me on anything."

When he did not reply immediately, Geoffrey prompted, "But you did come to congratulate me, and Alex, too, of course, didn't you, Darius?"

Again he was slow in replying, until all eyes were upon him.

"It was very sudden, was it not? You said nothing of it when last I saw you, Alexandra. When was it decided?"

"Ages ago, really," Geoffrey interceded. "But we could say nothing until mama had been consulted, and Alex's papa, too. At the risk of appearing bold—though I think it may now be known by all—Alexandra confessed that I was behind her coming to London in the first place."

"I see." Darius's voice was cool and distant.

My shock at Geoffrey's outright lie must have been apparent because he added quickly, "You don't have to worry, Alex. I divulge no secrets that I have not already disclosed to your papa. Now that our engagement is known, I felt no longer compelled to remain silent."

Darius looked directly at me. "Then this was not a matter suddenly decided upon?"

I was again rescued from replying by Lady Poindexter.

"This poor man has been here almost a quarter of an hour without an offer of tea. As Sydney always says, what is life without tea! Alexandra, dear, would you pour it?"

Darius followed me over to the tea table and murmured as I lifted the heavy silver teapot, "I must talk to you, Alex—alone."

I looked around at the assembled company. "It's impossible."

"When I leave I am going to wait in the copse near the gate. I shall wait there until you come. I must see you."

He left, over his aunt's protests, some half-hour later. Geoffrey saw him out and was oddly pensive when he returned. I wondered whether he could have overheard Darius asking me to meet him, and I waited before announcing that I was going to get some air before dinner.

For a moment I thought that Geoffrey would join me; then he stretched his legs before the fire and yawned. "A nap is more to my liking."

His eyes were closed before I left the room.

XXIX

I COULD SEE his tall figure waiting long before I reached the copse of elders near the main gate, and my heart beat faster at the sight. I had been foolish to come, I told myself, yet when he gripped my hands and led me over to the stone bench, I could recognize only joy at being able to talk to him away from the others.

"Alexandra, I simply couldn't believe it when I read of your engagement in this morning's paper. I had to come to see whether it was really so. I knew of your friendship with Geoffrey. I was aware that you liked him, but the idea had never occurred to me that your liking went beyond friendship, that you would ever contemplate marrying him. He said earlier this afternoon that it was a decision of some long standing, yet you never spoke of it."

Rather than comment on Geoffrey's untruth, I replied, "We have spoken together little of late, Darius, certainly of nothing near to the heart of either one of us."

"I suppose not, and yet it saddens me that you would not mention to a friend of many years—more than a friend—a matter of such import."

"It did not seem so once before. Then you did not show as much concern."

"You will always consider that I let you down over Ramsey, won't you, no matter what I may say of my intentions to the contrary."

"It's past, Darius, it's all past. Ramsey is married to Netty, I hear, and is very happy, so it would seem that all is for the best."

"And you," he demanded. "Are you happy?"

"I am sure that I shall be," I answered quietly.

"Yet I am not sure of that, not at all sure. That is the reason that I asked to talk to you—alone. It was impossible to say anything inside. Had I known how things stood between you and my cousin, I should have spoken earlier."

He stopped and then stood up, his arms crossed, his fists clenched, and was silent for a moment before continuing.

"What I have to say is not easy for me to say, nor will it be easy for you to hear, yet say it I must. I owe it to you.

"I have tried to warn you before of my cousin. You have called him kind and considerate—if that were so I would not fear, as I now do, for your future happiness. Geoffrey is—how shall I say it—he is a man to whom nature has been kind, yet he has consistently refused to recognize that kindness. In reality he wants for nothing—aspect, health, money, estate—yet always he wants something more, something he thinks he lacks without knowing exactly what it is. He has always had a completely absurd and utterly unwarranted jealousy of me and anything that was mine or—or anything that he thought I desired. Whatever it was, he sought to make it his and then destroy it.

"I recognized this tendency of his quite early in life. I used to come often to Maplethorpe until I saw how much my aunt's kindness to me embittered him. I tried to befriend him, to show him that there was no reason to be envious of me, that I wished him well, yet I believe he took my offer of friendship for patronage; anyway he rejected it. More than that, at every turn he carried on a campaign of slurs, spite and resentment against I know not what. My friends paid little heed to him. I cared even less, for his malice harmed him far more than it ever harmed me, until—Philomena."

"Philomena?" I questioned. "But what harm did he do to Philomena?"

"After my marriage, Geoffrey seemed to change. He came often to the house we occupied on Grosvenor Square. Philomena found him amusing. She was young, she wanted to be entertained, they shared many of the same tastes. At that time my interest in politics was awakened, and Philomena found many of my companions stuffy and boring, whereas Geoffrey moved in those circles that amused her."

"But there was nothing wrong with that, surely. After all, he was your cousin. You say they shared similar tastes. Was it wrong that they should be friends?"

His face was tense, his mouth set in a tight, straight line. When he spoke the words came slowly, with difficulty.

"Philomena died in giving birth to Geoffrey's son."

I gasped. "You mean that—that—"

"I mean that John was not my son, but Geoffrey's."

"No, Darius! No! You could be mistaken."

"I am not mistaken. I wish I were. John was Geoffrey's son, not mine. He made sure that I knew it."

If I was not convinced of the truth of what he told me by his voice, his set face, I remembered Lady Poindexter's story of her husband's death of lung congestion—a hereditary disease Geoffrey had escaped. But Crumpet had died of lung congestion!

"So that was why you were so—so . . ."

"So lacking in feeling toward the child. I'm afraid so. I had no right to treat him as I did, whatever the circumstances of his birth. I have thought of that so often since he died—though it does little good now, I suppose. I have prayed for forgiveness, just as I asked him forgiveness at the end, when it was too late to make amends. You were right, Alexandra, so very right in criticizing my harshness. You have been instrumental in making me see so many things in a new light. I used to be so sure of myself, so sure I was right. It is you who have made me stop to examine my words, my motives."

"But I did not know . . ."

"You could not know, nor would you now know, for I was resolved that no one should ever know of it. The only reason I tell you now is because you plan to marry. Before you take that step you must know the kind of man that Geoffrey is."

"What you have told me is a terrible thing, Darius, and yet . . ."

"You are going to say that such things happen and you are right, such things do happen. Had it been a case of love, even of wild infatuation, I might not have forgiven perhaps, but I could have understood. I know, however, it was not love, nothing like that, not on his part; it was cold and deliberate." His voice quivered slightly as he finished, "It was certainly not love on Philomena's part either."

He would always worship her and be convinced of her innocence whatever she had done, I thought angrily. I remembered how he had reacted the time I had worn her dress. It had reminded him too deeply of her loss. What must it have cost him to confess to me that she, that paragon of all that was perfect, had been unfaithful. He would never have it that she could love anyone but him.

"I don't believe that Geoffrey loved Philomena. It was from spite that he acted—just as I believe spite is behind his marriage proposal to you. I don't believe he loves you only because I believe Geoffrey is incapable of love for anyone except himself, if that self-indulgent feeling is deserving of being called love. He thinks to harm me by marrying you."

"But how could our marriage possibly harm you?"

"Perhaps he thinks that I—that I want you. As I told you before, he pursues anything he thinks I desire."

There was a rustling in the leaves behind me, a breeze wafting through the stillness of the afternoon air. Did he desire me? He had not said he loved me, but then that was a passion he had held only for Philomena. Was it possible that Geoffrey had seduced Philomena maliciously because she was his cousin's wife? And his proposal to me: that had surprised me. Was it possible that he thought Darius wanted me? Did Darius really want me?

His face was expressionless as he continued. "I think I can understand what prompted Geoffrey's proposal, but what I cannot understand is why you accepted him. You told me once you wanted independence. You had the means to be independent. It mystifies me. Why did you accept him, Alex? All the way from London I've asked myself that. Was it really a matter of long standing between you?"

"That last night I saw you—"

"The night of the Framinghams' ball, the night Wilmott insulted you?"

"Yes, I—"

I turned abruptly. The rustle of the leaves was not caused by the breeze after all.

"So this is where you are, Alex. I've been searching for you this past half hour. And you still here, coz—I thought you well on your way back to town by now. Such serious faces—what can you two have been discussing? For a young statesman who has just triumphed in a situation that could well have spelled his doom, and for a young lady on the brink of entering the ardent arms of matrimony, I find such doleful looks hard to understand. Won't one of you, pray, enlighten me?"

I flushed in guilt for being found in what must appear a clandestine meeting, for all I had just been told. It was Darius who replied.

"Alex and I know one another possibly better than do you and I, Geoffrey, although we are cousins. For many years she has been a part of my life, indeed almost a member of my family. For that reason I asked her to come here to talk to me. I wanted to be sure of her feelings, to know that there was no reason other than her own choice prompting her decision to marry."

"You think no woman can want me freely, by her own choice, don't you, Darius?" Geoffrey's eyes glinted angrily.

"Women may dog your heels and vie for your favours, but not mine. Well, it is not so. I thought I had already convinced you of that."

Rooks cawed in the branches of the elders above, their raucous cries exacerbating the tension below. I thought only of ameliorating that tension by suggesting we all return to the house.

"No, I am going back to town, but before I do so only tell me, Alex, that this match is your choice, your desire."

From Darius's earnest entreaty I turned to Geoffrey's flushed young face. Darius had offered me no alternate choice, only the opportunity to break an engagement so abruptly entered into. I had given Geoffrey my promise, yet the rest of my life lay in the balance. Was it not independence I had desired?

Geoffrey, perhaps aware that I was wavering, took my hands in his. "I need you, Alex, really I do."

It was more than Darius did.

"I promised to marry you, Geoffrey, and I shall."

"I should never underestimate you, cousin. No woman can ever resist being needed."

"I never bear malice," Geoffrey said, putting his arm around my shoulders. "We shall look forward to seeing you at our wedding, shan't we, Alex?"

"Of course."

Our eyes met for a moment before he strode away without another word, yet I was left with the feeling that there was more he wanted to say.

Geoffrey was cheerful as we walked back to the house. "Love is really in the air." He took several deep breaths, smiling in satisfaction. "Anyone'd think it was still spring. I even seem to hear bells—wedding bells."

"Our wedding will not be for a month yet."

"Oh, I realize that, and Darius's I suppose may even be after ours. Isn't it funny how one wedding spawns another."

"Darius's wedding!"

"Why yes, I thought that was what you two were talking about."

"No, he said nothing of that."

"That's odd, I thought he would have done. After all, he said you were like a member of the family."

"But who is it—who is he to marry?"

Of course, I knew before Geoffrey said the name that it was

Althea Brentwood. So at last she had what she had always
wanted.

Geoffrey beamed. "We should have a double wedding—what
do you say, Alex? Don't you think that would be fun, the four of
us together before the altar at St. Mary's—Darius and Althea,
you and me—quite an event—keep that rector on his toes making sure that he united the right pairs. It wouldn't do to join you
and Darius by mistake, would it?" He laughed heartily at his
jest. "Don't you think it a good idea, Alex?"

The idea made me feel as I had felt when I had been forced to
act as bridesmaid at Darius's wedding to Philomena: utterly sick.

"Well, what do you say, Alex?" Geoffrey persisted.

In his jovial mood he seemed only very young, not in the least
spiteful or malicious. And whether Darius had been right in his
assessment of his cousin's character or whether mistaken, was it
of any significance now that Darius was to marry? My marriage
to Geoffrey would be satisfactory, for expecting so little from
him, I would not be disillusioned.

"Weddings are private affairs, Geoffrey. I am quite sure that
Darius and Lady Brentwood will wish theirs to be as intimate
and private as we wish ours to be."

"Ah, but you're wrong there, Alex. I wish the whole world to
know of our wedding, and as many as possible to be there to
witness it."

XXX

THERE WAS AN exquisite blue-and-white Worcester tea service
from Lady Poindexter, and my parents presented us with a silver
tray engraved with our linked initials, a generous gift after all
father's complaints of the expense of the wedding. A covered
Wedgwood bowl from Aunt Maud was displayed alongside a
Staffordshire porcelain platter decorated with a raised-leaf-design
border from the Ramseys. Sir Clarence Wilmott sent crystal
champagne glasses with his acceptance of the wedding invitation
Geoffrey had insisted on extending to him; Darius sent a chiming
mantel clock in a red-and-gold lacquer case with his refusal. I
felt much relieved that he would not be at the ceremony.

The whole family assembled to celebrate the event. All of my sisters were in varying stages of pregnancy. Eugenia, possibly as befitted the oldest, was closest to term; though normally in confinement at that time, she had insisted on coming to Seton Place more for the chance of amusement than to see me. She spent most of the time complaining but that, too, had always been, for Eugenia, a form of amusement.

Netty's term was not quite as advanced, and, this being her first child, she was not as thoroughly disgusted with woman's role in the reproductive process as was Eugenia. Since Howard had purchased the Belden mansion, not far from the George Ramseys' property, Fern Hall, scarcely a day passed that they were not in one another's company. They were, as she constantly informed me, best of friends. This did not prevent them from running to me with little tales of one another, but that was, I suppose, part of friendship as they understood that relationship. No doubt they talked about me together behind my back, for I was sure that the amount of attention being bestowed upon a black sheep irked both of them.

Cassy, my dear Cassy, was also with child. She, however, mentioned it little, yet there was a gentle serenity about her that said more than words ever could how happy she was with her state, how right she felt it to be, how motherhood was for her the most important, the most wonderful thing that had ever happened to her.

She bore with equanimity Mr. Pomeroy's fussing over her becoming overly fatigued, over real or imagined draughts, over the amount she ate or did not eat and his long and endless speculations over a suitable name—he was quite decided it was to be a boy.

Whenever he drifted back into his old habit of conversing on more than one topic at a time, Cassy would say quietly but very firmly, "Mr. Pomeroy, you were speaking of the abnormally warm days we are experiencing (or the corn laws or the disgraceful conduct of Oxford undergraduates or whatever else it might be). Do, please, finish that thought, for we are all interested in your observations on that particular subject."

And quite meekly, he would agree, "Yes, my dear, to be sure, you are right, quite right, as you always are."

I might detect a gleam of amusement in Cassy's eye as she glanced at me before going back to the baby clothes she was knitting, but that was all. She never mentioned the matter to me when we were alone. In fact, she rarely spoke of her husband at all, though it was clear that they were indeed happy together.

So it was with Paul, who arrived on the stage at Marlborough with his beloved Dolores and his rector and soon-to-be father-in-law, Mr. Tyson. No one could have been more threadbare, more impoverished in appearance than was Paul with his black broad-cloth coat and breeches, which had an oddly green cast to them, his crumpled white stock and, atop all, a lacklustre shovel hat. Yet no one could have been in better spirits, with a deep good humour that refused to be doused by anything, even father's frugality towards him and his fiancée. Knowing the extortionate settlement Geoffrey had forced from father when we needed so little compared with Paul, I suffered, but Paul it affected not one whit.

"Don't concern yourself on our behalf, Alex. Dolores and I know how it must be. We are prepared for a life lacking many of the comforts enjoyed by others, but we have one another and that is all that matters. Truly, I expected nothing from father, and that is what I received, but I have far greater reward than money could give. I am only glad that you are happy—you *are* happy, aren't you, Alex?"

I turned away, not wishing to face that question.

I marvelled at the changes in Paul—his patience, his tact, his understanding. Not Geoffrey's splendid velvet coats, silken breeches and embroidered waistcoats, contrasting as they did with Paul's worn garments, could cause envy, nor Thomas's boasts about the estate's increased yield due to his foresight, not even James's endless detailing of the case law he was studying at Lincoln's Inn, once Paul's greatest aspiration. On the contrary, he complimented Geoffrey on his sartorial elegance, he agreed with Thomas that his methods were an improvement and he asked advice of James on legal problems within the parish.

Could it be that father had been right all along, I wondered. He had, after all, insisted that Cassy marry Mr. Pomeroy and that Paul enter the church, courses in life both had resisted, yet both were perfectly happy. I, on the other hand, had chosen my own path. I had chosen my husband or at least I had accepted him without coercion—father had had no part in it—and I had to admit that I was not happy. It gave me cause for consideration.

I had not looked forward to seeing Howard Ramsey again, yet it had happened naturally enough after Sunday mattins the first week following my return to Linbury. Mr. Linnell had pounded the pulpit until the dust rose from the velvet cushion on the subject of the return of the prodigal son, of the goodness of the father who took him back. It was difficult to believe that his choice of subject for his sermon was coincidental but I made every effort to ignore the connexion.

"Welcome home, Alexandra," Howard had greeted me in a friendly fashion as I left the church at Geoffrey's side; he was quite plainly impressed with Geoffrey's appearance and his title and he drew me aside to comment, "That's a pleasant young nobleman you have found. So that was what you were after. I thought perhaps I had pressed my attentions upon you too hard until George showed me the published poems that are laid at your door—thank God, I thought, that things turned out as they did, for I'd want no wife of mine writing such things—it is a relief that Netty has no literary aspirations. I can plainly see that far from going too far, the trouble probably was that I did not go as far as you would have wished." He sighed. "That's what comes of being a gentleman, but I suppose it all works out for the best. Netty and I are well suited, and you and Sir Geoffrey, by your own admission, are also. Allow me to congratulate you, and I must convey these same wishes to your chosen gentleman."

Aunt Maud also had learned of my writing, I know not from what source. Father, I was sure, had said not a word on the subject, yet she accosted me with, "You were a sly one bringing me that book in Salisbury and enquiring for me after the author when all the time it was you." She turned to father, "Do you not think, brother, that her talent comes from our side of the family? You must have read grandmama's diary. It reads quite like a novel and includes some verse."

Father flicked the pages of his newspaper impatiently without looking up. "Grandmama never wrote that sort of verse—never."

"I think Alexandra's poetry is beautiful. I especially enjoyed that one, let me see, how was it—'My breast to yours . . .' "

"That's quite enough, Maud. You only like it because you are a maiden lady and you don't understand it."

"I may be unmarried, brother, but I understand perfectly what occurs between a man and a woman."

"Maud! You are almost as bad as Alexandra. Whatever you do I trust you won't wield your pen on that thoroughly—thoroughly immoral subject. I want no further discussion of this—this scribbling."

"My, my! Austin is touchy!" Aunt Maud observed after father had noisily folded his newspaper and stalked from the room, firmly closing the door behind him. "Tell me," she leaned confidentially towards me, "is he quite satisfied with this suitor of yours?"

"I believe so."

"And you—are you quite satisfied?"

"Yes, of course." I wished I could have kept the defensiveness from my reply.

"I don't believe you are, though. He's quite a good catch, of course—a baronet, not without fortune, though Austin has complained bitterly to me that he's bled him dry. He isn't hard up, is he?"

"I don't believe he is."

"You're not, either, for that matter. You needn't have married if you hadn't wanted to."

There was reason in what Aunt Maud said. Now that the danger of the duel was averted, I suppose I might have reneged on my promise. That had occurred to me more than once as the days moved inexorably towards that day of days, my wedding day. Why did I not simply admit to Geoffrey my mistake? Why did I not put a stop to all the preparations? But I did nothing, and deep within I knew why I did nothing, for Darius was to marry again. If he was to marry, then so would I. The motive was not a sensible one, yet nothing had ever been sensible in my feelings towards him.

"He's a very pretty young man, this suitor of yours," Aunt Maud commented one evening, watching Geoffrey enthrall the assembled company with an account of a play he had witnessed at Drury Lane—a thoroughly inept production, he described it, yet he remembered with accuracy every mistake on the part of the actors, the playwright, the director, telling all so lightly, so wittily that under other circumstances I might have been as caught up in his recital as was everyone else.

"A man of Attic salt, but I don't like him as well as that other gentleman of yours."

"You mean Howard Ramsey?"

"Netty's husband? Dear me, no, stodgy fellow—I'd quite forgotten you were once to marry him. No, the other one, the one who came searching for you when you ran away."

"Darius Wentworth—Lord Bladen, you mean."

"That's the one, Lord Bladen. Quite beside himself, he was, at your disappearance. Blamed himself for some reason. He was all for setting out again immediately when he found you weren't in Salisbury, but it was late and I insisted he stay the night. We talked all evening, a lot on politics—his are not mine, of course, but he has some good arguments and he can make them seem so thoroughly reasonable. I was sorry when he left the next day. I had hoped you would have him. Why didn't you? I was sure he intended to offer for you."

And when I made no answer she pressed me, "Well, didn't he?"

"Yes, as a matter of fact, he did."

"And you refused him—for this one?"

"You might say, though it didn't happen quite in that way."

"I credited you with more sense, Alex. Where is he now?"

"In London, I think. He's marrying again, I understand."

"Undoubtedly," Aunt Maud sniffed with an air of finality. "Well, you've made your bed, now you must lie in it."

If her choice of words seemed unfortunate, there was no doubt that she fully intended it should be.

Though I should never be able to forget that it had been Geoffrey, not Darius, who had fathered the child who lay in St. Mary's churchyard under the stone engraved with the name Darius had given him, yet that was in the past, and for the present Geoffrey and I were adjusting to one another. Would I, perhaps, one day be happy with Geoffrey as Cassy was with her Mr. Pomeroy? It was possible, for my attitude towards him had changed when I discovered that I had won out in the matter of Tim's schooling. A letter from Tim was forwarded to me by the Hillabys. It was ill-written, to be sure, full of spelling errors, yet it contained such excitement, such exhilaration in describing his first days in school—not easy ones by any means—and showed that he was responding to learning very much as I had in those days when Lord Bladen had undertaken my education. Again and again Tim thanked me for giving him such an opportunity in life, and I, in turn, hurried to show the letter to Geoffrey and to thank him for not countermanding my instructions.

He glanced briefly at Tim's scrawl. "As long as you're happy, that's all that matters," was all he said. His modest acceptance of my thanks made me think that Darius's dire assessment of his character had been occasioned more by the wrong Geoffrey had done him than by the cool judgement that was usually his; it made me believe, also, that I had misjudged him.

I was more than chagrined, therefore by a reply from the school to a letter I had written outlining certain courses I considered essential in Tim's course of study, informing me that the suggestions would be forwarded to Lord Bladen for his approval, a necessary adjunct since he was supplying the boy's board and tuition fees.

"How could you allow me to believe that it was *my* money that was paying for Tim's education?" I stormed.

"I said no such thing, Alexandra," Geoffrey reminded me. "I only said as long as you were happy, that was all that counted. And really, when you look at it, isn't everyone getting what he or she wants? The ragamuffin has some rudiments of learning stuffed into him, which is apparently what you and he want, and all at Darius's expense, who no more notices it than a sheepdog notices one more flea. Yet for acting the benefactor he'll earn your undying gratitude, which, I'm quite sure, is his only reason for doing it."

"You're incorrigible, Geoffrey," I fumed.

"I'm not incorrigible at all. I just see things as they are."

"It's ridiculous that I should have to consult you, anyhow, on how I may spend my own money."

"Alexandra, we've been all though that matter. I don't want to discuss it again." For all the world the words might have come from father rather than Geoffrey, and for the first time my unspoken fear that I might be changing one oppressive master for another seemed real.

"Why did you want to marry me, Geoffrey?" I asked suddenly.

He came and took me in his arms. "My darling Alexandra, you don't believe, still, that I love you, but I do. You will know that to be so very soon. You may not always understand me, but life with me will never be dull, that I promise you."

"No, I doubt that it will." I thought of Darius, of Philomena, of Crumpet; no, I feared it would not be dull. "Why do you dislike your cousin so?"

"What makes you say I dislike him? He may not be my most favourite cousin, however."

"But he is your only cousin."

"Patience and Margaret are my cousins also."

"Geoffrey, you know what I mean—he's your only male cousin."

"Let's say, then, that I dislike him because you've made him the hero of your novels, in fact of everything you've written, for *Love's Breath* is to Darius, isn't it?"

He caught me off guard, and before I could think how to reply he went on triumphantly, "I knew it! You've no need to say anything. I knew, of course, you were not untouched, and I guessed it must be Darius who had broken the seal of Hymen. Indeed, it was obvious after you'd portrayed him with such girlish adoration in your novels—I suspect Darius may be the only one who hasn't recognized himself—but then he's too busy posturing as England's great young statesman to observe the obvious, while in reality he's nothing but a scurvy politician who would circumvent God if that were possible."

"You've hated Darius long before me, though. You had no compunction in seducing his wife." I hadn't meant to say it but it was said, and it was Geoffrey's turn to be taken by surprise.

"Well, well, well," he murmured at last, "so he told you about that, did he? What did he say?"

"That you were marrying me from spite, that you had seduced Philomena for the same reason."

"He still can't believe she could love anybody except him because he was so besotted with her. It's the same with you. He didn't expect you to marry me; that caught him unawares."

"But Darius himself is to marry, you told me so at Maplethorpe, so your marrying me can make no difference to him. He cares nothing for me."

"I think otherwise. I want you to promise never to see him again. Promise!"

"But how is that possible not to see him again? He is your cousin, after all."

"You know very well what I mean—you're never to see him again alone. I'm not talking about social occasions. It is not an unusual demand for a husband to make."

"You're not my husband yet."

"But I shall be the day after tomorrow, and it is better that things are clearly understood before that ceremony takes place. Or have you changed your mind now that your precious Darius is safe from Wilmott's retribution? You have changed your mind before, I know that."

I knew that I didn't love Geoffrey, and despite his assertions to the contrary, I doubted that he loved me. But I thought of the house, indeed the entire village, filled with guests and confusion for the celebration, of the dress upstairs in my room of white silk overlaid with Honiton lace with its long train of matching lace, of the wedding cake now being iced in the kitchen below, of the table set up in the hall, groaning under the weight of the wedding gifts. Yet all of that was not the reason for answering as I did—it

was the thought of Darius married to his Althea Brentwood. If
anyone were to make him forget Philomena it would be she.

"I shan't change my mind."

"Then you promise you won't see him again?"

"I promise."

He smiled, a sudden, boyish child. "From now on I shall be
the only hero you'll write about, the only one you'll want to
write about, you'll see."

He kissed me forcefully, his lips clinging to mine, yet for all
its vigour it was a kiss strangely passionless. But possibly the
fault was mine, for at that moment I was devoid of all emotion.

XXXI

THE BRIDE ABOUT whom the celebration centred was clearly in-
consequential the day before it was to take place. Apart from an
afternoon rehearsal at St. Mary's, I had nothing to do. Since I
had promised not to see Darius again, I decided to write a note
thanking him for all he was doing for Tim and begging that he
tell him to whom he owed his gratitude. Then I went in search of
Alice to deliver it; she was always delighted to have a reason to
visit Charteris and Miller, her friend there. But when I found her
in the living room, she was in the midst of turmoil of furniture
being moved to accommodate the guests expected for the wedding breakfast. "How is everything going between you and
Miller?" I asked her.

Her face became a trifle redder as she replied, "He's asked
me and I've agreed, Miss Alex. We're to tie the knot at
Michaelmas."

"Alice! I'm so happy for you." Impulsively I hugged her,
setting her cap askew.

"No more happy than I am about you, Miss Alex. Downstairs
we all thought you was destined to be an old maid after that last
business, but you found yourself a real beau and no mistake.
Miller told me when he stayed at Charteris last it took him all of
two hours to get dressed, and I never seen anything like those
waistcoats he wears, fit for a bird of paradise, I told cook after
that valet of his showed me some of them. He's a beau all right,

your Sir Geoffrey, and I hope you won't do none of your rampaging around when you're Lady Poindexter. Now get along with you. I've no time to talk for I don't know how I'll ever get everything finished.''

I wandered outside, the note still in my pocket. In the orchard there was a fine crop of apples ripening, and I picked one and munched on it as I walked. Ahead was the boundary between my home and Charteris. I had a sudden desire to see it once more. Why should I not deliver my note? There was no chance of running into Darius, for having refused to come to the wedding, he was hardly likely to be found in residence. It would have been unbearable if he had come to witness it.

I followed the path through the woods where I used to walk with Lord Bladen and crossed the sloping lawn where I used to play with Crumpet; approaching the house from the back, where I saw that one of the terrace doors to the library was ajar. I could leave my note without disturbing anyone.

An aura of peace enveloped me as I stepped into the great room with its vaulted, painted ceilings and encircling bookcases. There by the terrace door was the sofa where I had comforted Darius the night Crumpet had died. Gently I ran my hand across its padded cushions as I passed. I averted my eyes from the bearskin in front of the fireplace as though the disarrayed countess still lay there, laughing at me.

Crossing to the small Louis XV desk where I used to write, I took the note from my pocket and was about to lay it there when I started abruptly on hearing my name.

"Darius!" For it was he, sitting in the high-backed settle where he had been hidden from my view as I entered. "What are you doing here?"

He rose and came over to where I stood. "I might say that I live here and make the same enquiry of you."

"I came to leave this note—here, it is for you."

"From you?"

"Yes. It concerns Tim. I wanted to thank you for all you are doing for him. He continues to believe I am the one who is helping him even though I told him it is not so. You must let him know that you are his benefactor."

"He is quite right in thanking you, for without you I should never have known of him, never have done anything for him."

"That is as may be. Nevertheless it leaves a false impression, one I wish you would correct."

"I shall if you wish it.''

He stood before me, the note unopened in his hand. "How are you?"

"Quite well. And you?"

"Well enough."

"What brought you . . ." "I've thought over . . ." we began simultaneously and then laughed.

"You first," Darius said.

"I was going to ask what brought you to Charteris."

"I decided it was churlish of me not to attend your wedding, for you've been so close to—to all of us. I just sent a note to your father telling him I would attend the ceremony, though I shall have to return to London immediately after and cannot be at the breakfast. I'm sure you understand."

"Oh! I thought you were not coming," I blurted.

"Would you rather I had not? I thought I had behaved badly in refusing to be there. I wanted to make amends."

"No, no. Of course not. Father—everyone will be pleased to see you. Aunt Maud has spoken most highly of you."

He laughed. "Did she tell you of our political arguments?"

"From what she said she thoroughly enjoyed them."

"So did I. She's a very determined woman. You take after her."

I found his fixed gaze disconcerting. "What was it you were about to say just now?"

"Oh—yes—I've thought about our last talk. I should not have spoken to you of Geoffrey as I did. He is my cousin; he is to be your husband—I was wrong in telling you of the child. That is all in the past now. At the time I thought to intervene for your protection, not believing there might be genuine regard between you. Now I think I was wrong and I apologize for speaking as I did, saying those things that might poison your mind against him. I had no right to do so. It is one reason that prompted me to attend your wedding. Geoffrey is my cousin, part of the family. You, too, will soon be part of that same family. There should be no ill feeling between members of a family—at least I want none on my account."

"Yes, I see." So at last I would be, if not the sister Darius had always thought me, at least some sort of cousin, a family member. It was a light in which he had always seen me. And yet—yet he had loved me once, there, in that room.

Half to myself, I whispered,

"Even now
I know that I have savoured the hot desire of life
Lifting green cups and gold at the great feast
Just for a small and a forgotten time,"

and Darius took it up and finished,

"I have had full in my eyes from off my love
The whitest pouring of eternal light
The heavy knife—as to a gala day."

"*Black Marigolds*—Chauras—I didn't realize you knew him."

"It was you who recommended that poem to me—in order to find out what love is."

"And you did."

"Yes, I did. As a matter of fact, I came to discover love here—in this room," I stopped, afraid I had said too much. "I must go, Darius; there is a rehearsal this afternoon."

"A rehearsal?"

"A wedding rehearsal."

"I didn't realize one rehearsed for a wedding."

"Geoffrey thought it might be a good idea."

"Perhaps he's right—a perfectly orchestrated event with no surprises."

"There can hardly be any surprises for the bride on the wedding day or on the wedding night, thanks to you, cousin."

We both spun around to see Geoffrey, arms crossed, leaning against the open terrace door.

"So this is how you keep your promises to me, is it, Alex?"

And I flushed. I had forgotten all about that promise.

"I did not break it intentionally. I came to leave a letter, not realizing that Darius was here."

"Letters are simply another way of refusing to part." Geoffrey was smiling as he walked into the room, yet it was a smile totally devoid of warmth.

"May I ask what this promise is?"

"Alexandra promised she would no longer see you."

"For God's sake, Geoffrey, you imply more than exists. The letter concerns Tim's schooling, nothing more. There is nothing between us."

"But it was not always so, was it?"

"I don't understand what you mean, nor can I understand your insinuation of no surprises hurled at me earlier."

"You know very well what I mean." Geoffrey had lost his smile. "I suppose, though, that it evens the score over Philomena."

Darius's voice was tense and hard as he snapped, "What are you saying?"

"Geoffrey, we must go—the rehearsal . . ."

"No," Darius interrupted, "not until Geoffrey has told me exactly what is the meaning of all his implications."

"One might expect such coyness from a woman." Geoffrey's lip had curled in contempt until Darius reached over to grasp the high rolled collar of his purple velvet coat.

"I have asked you a question. I expect an answer." Each word was uttered slowly, deliberately, and he sook Geoffrey as he spoke.

"All right, all right, Darius, but leave go of me first—I'll play along with your game, just as though you didn't know already."

Once released, Geoffrey stood carefully smoothing down the collar of his coat. "You, Darius, are the lover of Alexandra's poem. I guessed it to be you and she confirmed it to me only yesterday—isn't that so, Alexandra."

"Yes," I whispered.

"Surely, Darius, you are too much of a gentleman to deny the word of a lady." Geoffrey eyed Darius's clearly bewildered face. "It is hardly flattering, Alexandra, but perhaps you should remind the gentleman of the time and place—unless it occurred too often in too many places."

"No, Geoffrey," I retorted without thinking, "it happened only once and then it was quite by chance."

Ignoring Geoffrey's mocking "By chance!" Darius put his hands on my shoulders. "Look at me, Alex! Look at me," he commanded.

Slowly I raised my eyes to meet his.

"Now tell me when, where this happened between us."

"Here, in this room," and seeing that he was still bewildered, wishing to avoid more questions, I added, "It was the night Cr—John died."

"So—so, that was not a dream after all." His hands dropped to his sides. "Why did you deny it when I asked you?"

"You were ill and—I thought you did not want it to be so. You seemed so relieved after my denial."

He walked across to the window, silent for a moment, before turning back to me. "Then you cannot marry Geoffrey. It is not right that you should."

"Share and share alike—it's all in the family, old boy. I reminded you of that with Philomena."

It all happened so fast—the sudden approach, the even more unexpected blow which I didn't see coming, nor did Geoffrey, for he staggered under the force of the stinging slap of Darius's open hand across his cheek.

"That was utterly boorish! Come along, Alex, we're to be at St. Mary's at three."

"Are you going with him or staying with me?" Darius put the question coldly, even sternly.

To stay with him—how could it be possible? There was his engagement to Lady Brentwood, and even if that were not so, there would always be Philomena between us—his anger was because Geoffrey had reminded him of her—I would never wish to share him.

"Come along, Alex, do hurry. We're late as it is," Geoffrey called from the door.

"Well? Are you going with him?" Darius asked roughly.

I hesitated. If only he had taken my hand, if only he had smiled or said that he wished I would stay . . . but his face was impassive. I had been right that day in the churchyard after Crumpet had been laid to rest when I thought that if he knew what had occurred he would feel bound by duty to right what he considered a wrong. I sought no amends.

"I must go."

"That is your choice, then."

I crossed to where Geoffrey awaited me outside on the terrace, but once there I could not prevent myself from turning to look back at him as he stood alone in the vastness of that room with all of its memories.

"Good-bye, Darius."

But he made no reply.

XXXII

"YOU'RE TERRIBLY PALE, Alex. Are you sure you feel all right?"

As she spoke Cassy adjusted the Honiton lace overlay where it had become caught on the hem of my white silk dress.

"I think I'm scared, Cassy. Did you feel so when you married?"

"You could not possibly feel as I did on that day. Do you remember how sad we were? It all seems so silly now—at least it does to me—even impossible that I could have been sad to marry Mr. Pomeroy. I know that to you he may not seem the answer to a maiden's prayer, and I'll not deny that those first months together were difficult. He, I think, felt obliged to act the role of the heavy-handed husband, I that of the submissive wife, for those were the roles we both had seen enacted in marriage. But gradually we became our own selves with one another, the selves we had kept hidden from the outside world. We became more honest and much closer to one another than I had ever dreamed possible."

"How wonderful that you are happy—I knew it as soon as I saw you."

"I'm very lucky."

"Mr. Pomeroy is very lucky."

Cassy smiled. "We're both very lucky."

"I wrote a book once—how long ago it seems now—about Cassandra, *The New Cassandra*—you, of course, but based on the Cassandra of mythology, who was given the gift of predicting the future though no one would believe her. What do you think lies ahead for me, Cassy?"

Cassy bent over to adjust the folds of my train and I could not see her face as she replied, "That's hardly a fair question, Alex. None of us knows what the future may bring."

"You could simply have told me that I should live happily ever after, just as princesses do in fairy stories."

Cassy straightened up. "Do *you* think you'll live happily ever after, Alex?"

"No—I'm not sure—I mean, I don't know."

"Well, I don't know, either. If anyone had told me on that

252

Boxing Day two years ago that I would be standing here on your wedding day prating about my own happiness, I should have accused them of being mad. It is good that we don't know what the future holds—that was no gift Cassandra received. Rather it was a curse."

"I suppose you're right, Cassy. You're usually right. I suppose that is why I asked you. I wanted reassurance."

"I'm sure everything will be well with you, Alex." She hesitated. "It's just that . . ." but she stopped midway without completing her sentence.

"It's just that what?"

"I probably shouldn't say this, but for a long time, ever since you were quite little, in fact, I've been convinced—or perhaps I've convinced myself—that you were madly in love with Darius Wentworth. He was quite the handsomest man around, and I've always been awfully romantic. When you were sick in church on his wedding day, I was sure that was the reason, and then you spent so much time at Charteris. When you turned from Howard Ramsey while I had that silly infatuation for him—which was every bit as silly as you told me it was—I thought it was because you loved Darius Wentworth. Now I hope you are going to tell me how silly all of my speculations were." But with one look into my troubled eyes, Cassy sighed, "But I was afraid you would not."

I was saved from reply by the arrival of Eugenia and Netty, who had stopped to see my dress before going to St. Mary's.

"Quite lovely, quite, quite," Eugenia murmured, "though I do think I prefer the Cluny lace of my own wedding dress. I had considered Honiton but a fine Cluny is not to be outdone, intricate and more delicate by half than Honiton, though this suits you, Alex, for you were always the more robust in appearance of all of us. I must say, though, you don't look very robust this morning—your face is peaked, very peaked. Pallor in a bride is as it should be, but a little colour in your cheeks would not be amiss. Pinch them if need be, unless you have any alkanet salve at hand."

"There was no time for a wedding dress for me," Netty mourned, "with everything coming about so suddenly after Alex . . . oh, well, I'm a fortunate woman, and Howard never ceases to tell me how lucky he is that things turned out as they did."

I kissed both of them and they left, deep in controversy over the length of the train of my dress, one thinking it too long, the other not long enough.

Mother hurried in. "Do go downstairs, Cassy. I shall see to anything else that needs to be done. Mr. Pomeroy is pacing the floor, sure that you will be late. I've told him the wedding can't take place without the bride, though quite honestly I believe he can't bear you to be away from him for so long."

Cassy squeezed my hands; as she kissed me, she whispered, "You're strong, Alex. You'll be all right no matter what," and she hurried from the room, turning from me in an attempt to hide the tears in her eyes.

"You're so pale, Alex," mother worried. "Did you sleep well?"

Though I had not slept at all, I nodded.

Mother took my hands in hers. "You're very cold. I do hope you're not going to be ill. Do you remember that awful time when you were a bridesmaid at Darius Wentworth's wedding? Your skin felt like this then, cold and clammy. Let me get you some of my sal volatile."

"No, mother, that won't be necessary. I'll be all right, really."

"I do hope so, dear." She hugged me close. "I do love you, Alexandra, more I think than you realize."

"I know you do, mother, and I love you."

We were both crying when father came in.

"Really, this won't do, it won't do at all. Mr. Pomeroy is growing impatient, and the carriage is waiting to take Alexandra and me. Come along now or we'll all be late."

Mother kissed me. "I'll send in Alice with a wet cloth for your eyes. You can't go to the altar with them all red."

It was quiet in the carriage. I stared out at the hedgerows. Occasionally we passed a cottage where the family was gathered outside to wave us on our way. Rather than a triumphant journey, it felt to me like a tumbril headed for the guillotine.

The silence was at last broken by father. "I know that we have not always got along as well as we might, Alexandra. Of my children you have been the most difficult, the most rebellious. You never hesitated to hide the fact that you found me overly stern and repressive, yet so my father was with me. It is, after all, the role of the father to lead his children as he sees fit. I hope you will agree that not all of my decisions have been wrong."

"No, father, my brothers and sisters are all quite content."

"And you have chosen your own way. You can blame me for nothing in this match of yours."

I turned back to watch the hedgerows again, which were now positively racing past, propelling us ever onward towards St. Mary's, where everything and everyone—Darius, too—awaited our arrival. Father knows that this marriage is wrong, I thought dully, he knows, and there is no one to blame except myself.

Before the carriage drew up before the church porch where Mr. Linnell awaited us, father spoke again, clearing his throat as though embarrassed. "I want you to know, whatever you may have thought in the past, that I love you. I have often thought that of my children I love you most, because you were never afraid to speak and to act on your decisions. You know that I have not always agreed with you, but I have admired your courage."

"Oh, father."

As he helped me down from the carriage, he squeezed my hand. "Good-bye, Alexandra Cox-Neville. You will be Lady Poindexter when next I address you."

I waited in the vestry for the ceremony to begin. Perhaps it would be more appropriate to say that I hid in the vestry, away from father in deep discussion with Mr. Linnell, away from the gaggle of giggling bridesmaids Eugenia had selected for me. My body was cold, icy cold, while my face was oddly hot. My stomach churned as it had on the day Darius married. The heavy perfume of the tea roses that decorated the altar assaulted my nostrils. I couldn't breathe—I had to have air. I bundled the train of my dress under my arm and slipped silently through the door, not looking right or left, afraid I might catch a glimpse of Darius being shown to the Bladen pew.

Outside on the south porch I felt a little better until my eye fell upon that white tombstone with its kneeling cherubims marking Crumpet's grave. Though I could not read it from where I stood, I knew its inscription only too well:

John Frederick Wentworth
Beloved son of Philomena and
Darius Wentworth
Born 6 April 1820
Died 17 August 1823
Though brief his Time on Earth
He Brightened the World by his Presence.

At the sight of it I knew beyond any possible doubt that I was going to be sick. Quickly, to get out of sight, I ran to the back of the church, only to meet with the curious stares of a group of waiting coachmen. I ran on, through the church gate, along the path which led from the village until, freed from the sight of everyone except God and the birds chirping gaily in the trees above me, I stopped to wretch, throwing up a horrible green-yellow phlegm, after which I felt relieved, though I could not rid myself of the evil-smelling substance, which had splashed the front of my dress and positively doused its hem. Desperately I wiped at it with the train I still carried in my arms, which, instead of improving the dress, completely ruined the train.

I had to return to the church, to explain. Perhaps another dress could be found, something from my trousseau at home. The wedding would have to be delayed. It was already delayed, for I could hear the strains of "O Perfect Love" being repeated again. Above me, in seeming competition, the free song of the birds rang out.

I knew I had to go back and yet I did not move. I stood listening, waiting for I know not what before gathering my soiled skirts and crumpled train and starting out at a steady walk, which became a jog and then a run. Faster and faster I ran, away from St. Mary's and the strains of "O Perfect Love," away from the gathered throng, away from my home and everyone I knew.

I ran until, out of breath, I could run no more. Then I slowed to a walk. A stray dog of indeterminate origin had joined me in my flight. He bounced along at my side in great enjoyment at the adventure.

The sun rose higher and higher in the sparkling clear sky, yet there was no responding clarity in my heart as I walked on, my hand on the dog's head for comfort, afraid to think of the mad act I had just committed. I could never be forgiven—never, never.

I gave a sudden scream, momentarily frightening the dog, as the heel of one of my thin satin slippers caught in a hole in the path, throwing me forward into a patch of stinging nettles.

I cried out, my hands, arms and face badly stung by the leaves, but worse yet was the pain in my foot, which I had badly wrenched in the fall.

Strange though it was, I felt glad of the pain. It seemed justified because of the wrong I had committed against my parents, against Geoffrey and his family. The pain also made me realize that I was still alive, for until that moment I had been in a daze. At that moment, too, I realized how utterly exhausted I was. Standing was painful, and I threw myself down into the thick, green grass, dotted with marjoram and wild pansies, which grew along the hedgerows. The cool greenness was balm to my throbbing skin. I closed my eyes and attempted to overcome the guilt I felt at the scene I had left behind. Sleep came to my rescue, the sleep that had eluded me throughout the night; it came over me as a blessed mantle of peace. The dog snuggled down at my side, providing warmth and comfort as I slept.

Twilight was approaching by the time I awoke. I lay still, the memory of what had happened slowly coming back to me, but I tried desperately to put it from my mind as I took stock of my circumstances. The stinging from the nettles had subsided, but my foot was painfully sore and swollen. I could not walk far. There were no nearby cottages, but sitting up, I could see what had to be the road to Marlborough, across the meadow. I would make for that and wait for some passing conveyance to take me—where I did not know except I could do nothing until my foot was attended to.

Dragging it behind me, relying on my good foot and steadying myself first with the dog who had stayed with me and then with the aid of a stout stick he found for me, I limped and struggled across the meadow. What an odd sight I must have made in my now-filthy wedding dress, the dog at my side. I could hear Alice sniff, "Made a mess of yourself again, Miss Alex." I had indeed made a mess of myself—of everything.

It was slow progress for the pain was excruciating. Several times I stumbled and fell. A farm cart passed, then a carriage before I reached the road, but neither heard my cries for help.

By the time I got there, dusk had fallen. Few people would pass once night fell. Disconsolately I sat down by the roadside, glad of the company of the dog.

"My Bucephalus!" I named him after Alexander's charger, wishing he might carry me away. He was hardly large enough for that, but I don't know how I could have survived without his friendly, good-natured presence.

It was only when I had given up hope of finding help and had started to make a bed for the night beside the hedge that I heard the clatter of horses' hooves on the roadway. I heard them long before a light from the front of the carriage rounded the bend in the road.

Gathering all my strength, I stood up and limped to the centre of the road. The horses came towards me at a frightening rate. I was terrified they would run over me. Wildly I waved what was left of my tattered train, no longer white but still it stood out in the gathering dust. That and my furious cries must have reached the horses, for they became alarmed and skittish. I heard the coachman swearing at them. I could not move to get out of their path, and when I was sure that the carriage must pass over me, the horses reared wildly to a stop not a foot away.

The coachman, still swearing madly, took up the lamp as he clambered from his seat. He held it high above his head so that I could see him as clearly as he could see me. Looking into his face, I gave a cry of terror. "No, oh no! Not you!"

The last thing I saw as my surroundings faded into oblivion was the grinning, misshapen face of the little man who had followed me all over London, the servant of Sir Clarence Wilmott.

XXXIII

IN THE DARK, rhythmic rumbling of the coach as it sped through the night, I regained consciousness. I was held close against the chest of a man. I felt the wool of his coat beneath my cheek. His arms around me supported my bruised and battered body, shielding it from the worst of the jolts as the horses raced along the rutted road. I was no longer cold, for over me had been placed a great coat or cloak, while close to me was the warmth and comfort of the one holding me. It was only when I realized who the one must be who held me in such close embrace that involuntarily I stiffened, at which he stroked my hair.

"Don't move; you're quite safe. We'll soon have a doctor to care for that foot of yours. Just lie still."

"Darius! Is it really you?"

"Of course it's me. Who did you think it was?"

"But that man—the coachman—I know him. He followed me in London—he is in the employ of Wilmott. Or did I just imagine I saw his face? It's all been such a nightmare."

"Ritchie, I must admit, is not the handsomest of men, but he is reliable and very resourceful, as a rule, though he admitted to me that you and Tim bested him."

"You mean he worked for you all along?"

"I know he didn't admit it to you because I had instructed him not to. My only reason for having him follow you was that I feared for your safety, yet I knew you would resent what you would only construe as interference."

"Oh, Darius, I was awfully stubborn over that whole matter. I've wanted to thank you, to tell you I was sorry for my refusal to believe you. You warned me of what would happen if that book appeared."

Impulsively I hugged him and he held me close. From the floor of the carriage came a growl and a short bark.

"Bucephalus! I'd almost forgotten him, but he has practically saved my life today. Thank you for bringing him, too."

"It wasn't so much a case of bringing him; he wasn't to be left behind."

"I feel so safe with both of you."

But the mood of satisfaction dispelled as the remembrance of that morning came back to me.

"I did a mad thing, Darius; but of course you must know."

"I gather that everything at St. Mary's may not have gone exactly as rehearsed."

"But you know it did not—you were there."

"No—no, I wasn't. I didn't attend," he replied shortly.

"But I thought you told me—"

"I know. I said that I would, but I didn't."

"Something prevented you from going?"

"Yes, something prevented me. And you—don't tell me just cause was found that the marriage should not take place."

"The truth of the matter is that something prevented me from attending also. Oh, I got to the church with father all right, but before the ceremony was to begin, I felt terribly sick."

"Just as you did when you were a bridesmaid."

"Yes, exactly so. I had to leave the church. I didn't go back."

"Weddings must not agree with you."

"I fear not."

There was a long pause before he asked thoughtfully, "Tell me, why did you agree to marry Geoffrey? It didn't make any sense. You are so very different from him in every way. And, too, you have told me more than once that you never wish to marry."

"In turn I might ask why you challenged Wilmott to a duel. There was no sense to that, either."

"Perhaps not, though I fail to see the connexion."

"That duel could have ruined you, and for what? I went to

Geoffrey when you refused to listen to reason. Wilmott was his friend. I thought he could persuade him to apologize. Geoffrey asked me to marry him, and I agreed."

"It was a condition."

"It wasn't exactly put in that way."

"Nevertheless, it was. So you agreed to marry him for my sake."

"I didn't keep my promise. I broke it in the most awful way imaginable, in front of everyone we knew. And father and mother—for the first time I came to believe they loved me; now I've hurt and embarrassed them and I'll never be able to make amends. Wisdom, for me at least, does not appear to come with age."

"Alex, Alex! There are times when your wisdom astounds me. I've told you how much I've learned from you. You are loyal and true and very wise, yet at the same time you are the same girl who used to play with her brother in the stream that divides my home from yours. Do you remember those days?"

"I never forget them—and poor Sylvester."

"But I meant your brother, Paul."

"Sylvester was his frog."

"Now that I had forgotten."

"You called me a saviour of frogs and infuriated Thomas by telling him to take me for an example."

"I see I haven't your memory for life's more memorable moments."

My laugh turned into a cry as the carriage lurched at a particularly rough part of the road, jolting my injured foot.

"Go easy, Ritchie!" Darius called out. "Let us reach the doctor with no more injuries than have already been suffered."

"Yes, me lud," Ritchie replied, and we continued at a fast but steadier pace.

Darius held me close, and I curled up against him, safe and secure. I began to relax and feel sleepy until I thought of the scene that must be taking place at home at that moment.

"They'll never forgive me, Darius, never."

"You don't know that to be so; for myself I doubt it. You said yourself that you've only just realized they care for you. I suspected that for a long time, though I know there were many things on which you did not agree. But rest now; it will all work out, and for the best, you'll see. For now, rest."

And I did, in my tattered and soiled wedding dress, wrapped in his arms, gladness in my heart that the arms that enclosed me that night were his.

My foot, the doctor found, was sprained, not broken. With the supportive bandage he applied, it felt much easier. His wife was applied to for a change of clothing. I don't know what she must have thought of the state of my dress or, more particularly, of the kind of dress that it was, but nothing was said and we parted on the best of terms after refreshments, which I set upon with the greatest relish.

Everything was going to be all right, just as Darius had said it would, just as it was meant to be. I was sorry for the harm I had done to Geoffrey and the hurt I might have caused his family and mine, but my present happiness far outweighed that sorrow.

"Where are we going?" I asked as we started out again.

"I have been turning over in my mind what is for the best, and with your approval, I shall take you to Althea Brentwood. She is an understanding lady. There you can decide what it is you want to do—that is, if you agree?"

"Yes, yes. Of course."

I had forgotten all about Althea Brentwood. But how could I—she and Darius were to marry. How stupid that I had not thought of it. Abruptly my newfound contentment deserted me. Fitfully I dozed throughout the remainder of the journey; though Darius continued to hold me, no longer did I feel the satisfaction nor the right to that place in his arms.

Lady Brentwood received me kindly—more kindly than I expected or, perhaps, deserved. She had a room prepared for me; she even arranged to accommodate Bucephalus in her elegant Orchard Street home. If there had been animosity between us in the past, she said nothing of it. She was all graciousness, but then she could afford to be, for she had what she had always wanted—Darius.

A wardrobe of clothes appeared so readily that one might have thought she had anticipated my arrival, and her physician called to examine my foot and announce that I was healing rapidly. I was, in fact, treated by her with such generosity that I hated myself for the resentment that rose in my heart whenever I thought of her marriage.

Tim came immediately, informed of my whereabouts by Darius, strangely unlike the boy I knew in smart broadcloth coat, crisp white cravat, shining leather boots. "I'll never be able to thank you enough for wot you—for all you done for me."

"It's Lord Bladen who deserves your thanks, Tim."

"Yes, but you see, none of it would've 'appened—happened—without you. 'E—he keeps telling me that, and it is so. I do thank you, Miss Cox-Neville."

"Beautifully put, Tim, but I hope you won't worry so much about your manners that you allow that natural warmth of yours to become hidden behind them."

"Not on yer life!" He winked, and then I knew it was my Tim.

"I'm so very proud of you, of the way you've adapted to your schooling—everything. You'll always be very special to me."

"And you to me; Lord Bladen, too. Is 'e—he here today?"

"No. I haven't seen him since—since my arrival."

"Spect 'e's—he's busy. He's a busy gentleman, though 'e always takes time to talk to me and explain things."

"I expect he is busy."

I saw nothing more of Darius, a fact that both distressed and relieved me. I wanted to talk to him, but not there, not under Lady Brentwood's roof where I felt constrained, for they were, after all, betrothed.

Sydney Smith, who was in London, called the next day. "Miss Cox-Neville still, unless you have adopted some other enticing name." His lips twitched in that roguish manner so peculiarly his own whenever he was teasing, and he constantly teased.

"I shall keep this name forever, though I shall write as Arabella Marlowe."

"So you have foresworn the married state—a pity. And where shall you live?"

He had touched on a matter of concern to me. Kind as she was, I could not stay with Lady Brentwood, indeed, though she spoke little of Darius, the knowledge that they were soon to be man and wife daunted me.

"Will you return to Wiltshire?" Sydney asked.

"No, I cannot do that."

"Perhaps a change of air in the north is what you require. Mrs. Smith and I would be delighted to see you at Foston."

"You extend an enticing invitation, Mr. Smith." Foston in Yorkshire was not far from Northumberland. I would be close to Paul. I could deliver in person the bank draft I had had prepared as a present for him and Dolores, my money being my own once more. I was quite decided on the visit by the time Lady Brentwood came in, followed by the maid and the silver tea tray.

Sydney Smith greeted her with, "I am told by that proverbial little bird from whom one hears everything but who is so rarely seen that you, dear lady, are to marry."

"You, Sydney, hear everything before anyone else."

"I must admit I used to think that England had only two amusements—vice and religion—but I must amend that to three, for where should we be without gossip? And when is that happy event to take place?"

"Quite soon, I think. We have both been married before, and, indeed, we have known one another for so long that there is scarcely any point to delay the ceremony now that we are quite decided upon our course."

"I wish you happy, Lady Brentwood. My usual advice is never to gamble in the game of life—be content to play for sixpences. Miss Cox-Neville has decided that she considers marriage too high a stake for her to risk. I must commend her decision, particularly in view of the young man with whom she intended to embark on the choppy sea of matrimony; but in your case it is different; the gentleman is worthy of the play."

"Please, Sydney, I beg you, neither sing his praises nor preach me a sermon."

"My dear madam, there is not the least use in preaching to anyone unless I chance to catch them ill, and your countenance says everything to the contrary. You're positively bursting with health and happiness. I am going to take Miss Cox-Neville back to Foston with me and instruct Mrs. Smith to feed her until she glows in just the same manner."

"You're going to Yorkshire?" Lady Brentwood questioned.

"Yes, I am decided on it."

"I had hoped you would stay for my wedding."

"No, that I cannot, for you leave imminently, do you not, Mr. Smith?"

Sydney Smith would, I was sure, have arranged his plans to accede to Lady Brentwood's wishes, but some note of pleading in my voice or in my eyes made him reply.

"I leave London at nine o'clock in the morning, and I'm afraid I can never cure myself of punctuality."

"I shall be ready."

"I am sorry you leave so soon, for you are most welcome to remain here. It is true I have many arrangements to make, but you need not feel you intrude. In fact, I wish you would attend the ceremony.''

"I dislike weddings," I said abruptly, and immediately I was ashamed at my lack of magnanimity. "I do wish you happy, though, truly I do."

"All in all, life has been good to me. I trust it will be equally good to you."

I watched as she poured the tea with such grace, such charm. Life had been good to her; she had won what she had always wanted. I had no right to cast a pall on her happiness. I would be glad to leave London.

XXXIV

I WAITED FOR my humour to improve at Foston. Sydney was kindness itself, Mrs. Smith was a dear and I got along admirably with their daughter, Emily, but my thoughts returned constantly to Orchard Street. I wish I could say they did so because of my new friendship with Althea, but it was rather because now I knew *he* must be there, now they must be married, now on their way to Italy, for though nothing had been said of it, in my mind I had decided that was where they would go for their wedding trip. I even decided when they would return and the number and sex of their children, all such machinations increasing my despondency, while, since I could never speak of it, Sydney decided living in the country to be the cause.

"It is hard to survive twelve miles from a lemon. The charm of London is that you are never glad or sorry for ten minutes together, whereas in the country you are one or the other for at least a fortnight, and you, Alexandra, are very definitely the other."

"I'm an ungrateful wretch to be moping around this way after all you've done for me."

"There is a rule here at Combe Florey that everyone has the right to be what she wants to be. So mope away if you feel so inclined. Throw yourself into it, enjoy it!"

* * *

Paul arrived one day to see Sydney, not expecting to find me but relieved when he did.

"Was it so awful, Paul, that day at St. Mary's?" I asked after we settled down together on our own.

"Well, it wasn't exactly comfortable. I counted nine times that the organist played 'O Perfect Love' until either he or the organ or both gave out. Everyone tried not to look in the direction of Lady Poindexter. She was all alone in the Bladen pew. I don't know what happened to Darius, for he was supposed to be there. And then Eugenia said in that piercing whisper of hers, heard all over the church, 'Surely she hasn't done it again!' Father didn't appear. He was either still waiting or off searching for you with Mr. Linnell. Mother, of course, became hysterical, but luckily dear Dolores was next to her and able to comfort her—I can't imagine where we all would have been without her. Howard, at least, looked cheered. I suppose he rather liked having company in being jilted by you—no offence meant, Alex—and anyway he was awfully impressed by Geoffrey, so I bet he thought it was good company. Actually I was impressed by Geoffrey, though I hadn't been up until then. He stood by the altar all that time, his face quite expressionless but calm, and when the music stopped, he turned around to the congregation and said in the most normal voice imaginable, as though being left at the altar were an everyday occurrence, 'I'm famished, and even though it appears there's not going to be a wedding, I can't see any reason why all that good food should go to waste. May I suggest we indulge our appetites.' And he did just that—he ate like a hungry bear and had everyone in gales of laughter. Of course, I must admit we were all so tense that it was a relief to laugh, and we laughed at the merest trifles, but that doesn't detract from his admirable conduct. I took him for a petulant, spoilt boy but he seemed to grow up before my eyes."

"And father?" I asked hesitantly.

"Father is father. You know, whatever he says, he means well."

"Yes, I know. Well, at least I'm glad that Geoffrey is all right."

Yet I was not, and I knew why I was not. Writing had been my cure before and it should be again. I decided, and asked Sydney for paper and pens, which he willingly supplied, giving me, along with them, the use of his desk at his favourite bay window

"My only admonitions are to write immediately after breakfast, for no one is conceited before one o'clock, and be sure to put your pen through every other word you write. There's nothing like it for imparting vigour to style."

An hour later found me without a word on paper—no, that was hardly true, for I had written many, many words in that hour, but not merely content with striking out every *other* one as Sydney had instructed, I had become completely dissatisfied with every one of them. Each page had in turn been crumpled up and flung into the fireplace or, I should say, in the direction of the fireplace, for most of them surrounded the hearth like so many snowballs, which Bucephalus, as dejected as myself, refused to retrieve. I had just landed one dead centre in the middle of the grate and was feeling more elated about that than anything else I had done that morning when Sydney came in.

"I'm sorry to interrupt you, for I can see you have been performing most vigorously, but you have a visitor who will not wait even to please the muse."

Bucephalus was up, wagging his tail in sudden excitement, and was off down the hall, barking, but my eyes were fixed on the gentleman shown in by Sydney.

"Father!" My confusion caused me to flush and grow pale at he very same time. "Oh, father!"

I waited for his admonition, the berating I knew to be my due, but he said nothing; he only held out his arms to me and I threw myself into them.

"Father! Father! I'm sorry, really I am. I simply couldn't marry him, that's all. I've been so afraid you'd never forgive me, at least not again."

I could never remember father holding me to him as he did then. After hugging me, he pulled away, saying gruffly, "Well, that's enough of that. I'm glad to find you well, Alexandra."

"How's mother?"

"She's had her usual number of hysterical bouts—I rather think she enjoys them—but she's very well now she knows you're all right."

"But how did you know? I was too ashamed to write."

"Bladen told us."

"Darius?"

"Yes, he came down after the furor had subsided, and I went back to London with him. He introduced me to Lady Brentwood, a fine lady even though she is a Whig, and very hospitable she was though in the midst of preparations for her own wedding. She told me you had come north with Mr. Smith.''

"I'm very sorry, father, about—about everything. I don't deserve to be forgiven a second time, and I know it must have been worse than before because everyone was there waiting. I just couldn't face it, that's all.''

"I don't deny it was awkward, but the young man deported himself better on that occasion than on any other in my brief acquaintance with him. For a brief moment I *almost* regretted he would not be my son-in-law.''

"*Almost* regretted!'' I repeated, "But I thought you wanted me to marry him, that that was why you agreed to that outrageous settlement.''

"I don't deny I want you to marry—I still do—but I knew that marriage was not right for you. He's interesting, amusing, but he'd never have been able to handle you.''

I turned to him, dreading his response. "And you have another prospect for my hand?''

"I do, and I've come for that purpose. I want to see you settled, Alexandra, once and for all.''

My heart sank. Would things never change?

I heard Bucephalus scraping at the door and, letting him in, I vented my anger on his excitement. "Down, Bucephalus! Oh, get down, do!''

I took hold of his collar but he would not be still, pulling me, instead, across the room to the french windows. There I received my second and greater shock of the morning, for admiring Mrs. Smith's bed of petunias was—

"Darius!''

His name escaped from my lips with such force that, even though he was some distance from the window and deep in conversation with Sydney, he turned and started towards the house as I began running towards him.

"What are you doing here? I thought you must be in Italy by now.''

"Italy?'' He looked puzzled, and I realized that I alone had decided that that was where he and Althea would spend their honeymoon.

"Is Althea here?'' I asked.

"No, she should be in Paris by now.''

"In Paris? On her own?''

"Of course not. She has her husband with her.''

"Her husband! But I thought that you . . . that she . . .''

The puzzlement cleared from his face. "Surely you didn't think that Althea was marrying me! What on earth gave you that idea?"

"Geoffrey told me so—that day you came to Maplethorpe. He said it was all arranged."

"The machinations of that dear cousin of mine! Althea married Harry Caxton. She had known him for ages—he was a friend of Lord Brentwood. I'm sure you met him at Holland House. He's a fine man."

And Darius went on to desctibe Harry Caxton, and I nodded, even though I couldn't remember him at all but just because I was so relieved.

"I've seen Geoffrey a few days ago. We talked at some length," Darius went on thoughtfully. "He's changed, Alex, and I do believe that we understand each other better now than we ever have. Of course, being Geoffrey, he'll be dining out on his almost-wedding for months to come. He's terribly amusing about it, though I suspect some of his humour comes from an absurd and unwarranted feeling of inadequacy. He told me that he had had a lengthy discussion with his mother on the way back from Wiltshire, and at his request, she has made concessions— she has agreed to allow him more money, yet what is better, more responsibility in the handling of the estate. In return he is giving up his acquaintance with Wilmott, who had a terribly bad influence upon him. But what I think pleased him most was her admission that she had always wanted him to be like—to be someone he was not. She agreed that she had been wrong, that she would accept him as he is, remembering his fine qualities and not dwelling on his shortcomings. I think their relationship has changed. I think, too, that he is only just beginning to realize what a very fortunate and gifted fellow he is."

I bent down to pluck a dandelion and held it up against my palm. The yellow petals didn't shine the way those of the buttercup used to on Crumpet's chin, but I shouldn't mention him, not then at least. Instead I said, "I had a long talk with father, Darius, and he has forgiven me."

"I've had a long talk with him, too. In fact it's the first time I've spent any length of time with him, and strange as it may seem, both he and I were amazed to find the number of things we *do* agree on, Tory and Whig though we be."

"He's picked someone else out for me," I blurted out.

"Yes, I know."

"But I can't, Darius, I can't and I won't marry to please

father. I know I owe him a debt of gratitude for standing by me after all I've done, but to accede now—why, I might just as well have taken Howard Ramsey and have done with it.''

Darius grew thoughtful. ''But I understood, at the time that you preferred me to Howard Ramsey,'' he said slowly.

I turned in bewilderment. ''You!''

''Perhaps it was presumptuous of me to speak to your father— after all, you had already rejected my suit once before—yet I still think, as I did then, that we need one another.''

''You—you mean father meant you,'' I repeated.

''Yes. I went back to see him after I left you at Orchard Street. I asked for your hand and he agreed, but I had thought he would say nothing until I had spoken to you. I wanted to know your mind first. Had I known you were irrevocably fixed on your single state it was better left unsaid, though if you wish to continue to write—and I urge you to do so—in view of all that has happened, you could more freely do so as my wife.''

It was too good to be true, and yet, perversely, it was not put to me as I would have had it.

''That is sensible and kind, Darius, but both you and father overlook the need I have to love—and to be loved.'' Convulsively I turned the dandelion round and round in my hands as I spoke, watching the twirling of its petals. ''I love you, Darius, I always have and I expect I always shall, but I know you love Philomena, and though Althea might have been willing to share you with a ghost, I am not.''

''Do you mean that!'' He caught hold of my arm and then lifted my chin until I raised my eyes to his. ''Do you really mean that, about loving me that way?''

His eyes searched mine as he continued, ''It's not a sort of hero worship, is it, Alex? I must warn you I'm a very real, a very human man. And I'm no hero. It was one reason I liked Althea, because she knew that. Philomena never did. She saw me as something I never was, a sort of knight in shining armour—I think I was supposed to be off killing dragons or fighting tournaments for the privilege of wearing her ribbon or whatever it was knights did in the courts of love—worship from afar. I don't know which of us she placed higher on a pedestal, but there we were, together but separate, frozen in place. As far as she was capable of loving any man, she may have loved me, but I petrified her on our wedding night and she never wanted me to touch her again. I was bewildered—I tried patience, impatience, kindness, anger, all to no avail against her tears and recriminations, and at last I left her alone. She was, as I think you will agree, captivatingly beautiful, utterly charming, she was even affectionate until away from her social milieu, where more was desired than a smile or a tap of her fan. Then she became as cold as marble, horrified that her body might be touched, sullied—I believe the very thought of congress was defiling to her.

"She was drawn to Geoffrey, for they were very much alike—both young, charming, handsome, willful—but his will was the stronger of the two. He forced her to submit to him, and for that I hated him—it was an act of malice, not one of passion, and Philomena, with all her faults, was not deserving of such treatment. She was silly and shallow, yes, but primarily because she was a spoilt child who never grew up and who never wanted to grow up. I gave up hope of ever changing her, and the marriage I had entered into so blissfully became, for me at least, an unmitigated disaster of which I have detested any reminder. Philomena, once she was assured I would leave her alone, enjoyed it, for it afforded her the protection she needed to play her games without having to pay the piper, but she was to discover, to her distress, that Geoffrey didn't play the game by her rules.

"For my part I grew horribly bitter, and it was Althea who changed all that. I welcomed her warmth, her response, even though she knew I wasn't in love with her. She made me feel wanted, made me feel alive again. I threw myself into my career, swearing, after Philomena's death, never to marry again. When you offered yourself to me that day at Charteris, I was still of such a mind. Then you disappeared and I knew I loved you and it was too late."

"No, Darius, no, it isn't too late for us."

"Alex, you once accused me of not knowing what love is, but I believe now that I do—it's not that immature infatuation I felt for Philomena, nor the passion I had for Althea. It is deep and caring—caring for the well-being of another, respecting her, wanting to be with her, to hold her, to make love to her in all passion and to be content, satisfied, once that lovemaking is done. I know that I love you, Alex, and yet I am troubled by your love for me."

"But why?"

"Geoffrey said you had made me the hero of your novels, that is what troubles me. A long time ago I told you, though not then knowing you to be the author, that the hero of that first book was too perfect. I'm not perfect, Alex, not by a long shot; I'm only too human, and that is how I love you, not in a divine but in a human, imperfect way."

"Oh, Darius, I love you, I've always loved you, but never more than I do at this moment. Geoffrey was right when he recognized you as the hero of my novels, but if you find too much perfection there, I should remind you that you are also the hero of my poems—*Love's Breath* is about us."

I don't know how much later it was, after an interminable blending of kisses, one following another, each more insistent, more demanding, more satisfying than the last, each of which I never wished to end, each arousing in me the passion I had known on that night we had been together, arousing, I knew, that same passion in Darius, that I heard a snuffle, which multiplied to become, before we could bring ourselves to relinquish one another, a positive paroxysm of coughing.

"I often say that marriage resembles nothing so much as a pair of shears, so joined as not to be separated, devilishly punishing anyone who comes between, so I suppose I take my life in my hands by announcing to you that lunch is ready."

Darius tucked one arm through mine, the other through Sydney's, replying as we made our way back to the rectory, "We thank you, Sydney, as a man of the cloth, for overlooking that the intimacy of our embrace just now occurred before taking the vows of matrimony which sanction it, vows I was about to search you out to administer."

"Nothing gives me grater delight in my calling than performing that sacrament where I personally believe it most fitting, and have, I might add, ever since I first saw you two together. As for overlooking the intimacy I just interrupted, I would remind you that there are not, as so many people will have it, three sexes—men, women, and clergymen—but that parsonages are peopled with chubby children by exactly the same passions as are other households!"

So it was that almost a decade after I had fallen in love with him, in the village church in the parish of Foston, I was united in marriage by Reverend Sydney Smith, under the approving eyes of my father, attended by Dolores, Paul's betrothed, with Paul acting as best man, to Darius Wentworth, sixth baron of Bladen.

About the Author

British-born Diana Brown has lived and worked throughout Europe and the Far East. Ms. Brown, a librarian, now lives in San Jose, California, with her husband and her two daughters, Pamela and Clarissa, who are named after Samuel Richardson's heroines. Three other Regencies by Ms. Brown— *The Emerald Necklace, A Debt of Honour*, and *St. Martin's Summer*— are also available in Signet editions.